SURRENDER THE DEAD

Also by John Burley

The Absence of Mercy
The Forgetting Place
The Quiet Child

SURRENDER THE DEAD

A NOVEL

JOHN BURLEY

wm

WILLIAM MORROW

An Imprint of HarperCollins*Publishers*

SURRENDER THE DEAD. Copyright © 2021 by John Burley. All rights reserved. Printed in the United States of America. No part of this book may be used or reproduced in any manner whatsoever without written permission except in the case of brief quotations embodied in critical articles and reviews. For information, address HarperCollins Publishers, 195 Broadway, New York, NY 10007.

HarperCollins books may be purchased for educational, business, or sales promotional use. For information, please email the Special Markets Department at SPsales@harpercollins.com.

FIRST EDITION

Designed by Diahann Sturge

Library of Congress Cataloging-in-Publication Data has been applied for.

ISBN 978-0-06-243187-5

21 22 23 24 25   LSC   10 9 8 7 6 5 4 3 2

For my sister, Kristin,
and my father, Dennis

Hide and seek until the dawn
Billy, Sally, Jake, and John
They looked in places big and small
But never did they find them all

—Nursery rhyme

Hey! Where do you think <u>you're</u> going?
—Scrawled on the wall of the Amtrak
train station, Wolf Point, Montana

SURRENDER THE DEAD

1

IT WAS SOMETHING SMALL THAT BUILT TO A FURY.

The weather report out of KVCK predicted light snow—an accumulation of two to four inches—that would taper by midafternoon. By Northeast Montana standards, that was practically a summer day. Three years ago, it snowed in early June, two days shy of the end of the school year. Angela Finley was only eight then, but she remembered it, the way the morning sky had gone from light blue to a dense mat of gray while she stood there at the corner bus stop with her mother. She'd worn a yellow dress that day, something that was too small but worth holding on to. "That doesn't fit you anymore," her mother said when Angela appeared in the kitchen, but Angela had wanted to wear it anyway, knowing that the dress would soon be hanging in her sister Monica's closet instead of hers, just one more thing she'd be forced to surrender.

Combing her hair this morning in front of her bedroom window, Angela looked out at the February haze and thought about that dress, the color of lemonade and daffodils and afternoon sun. It hung in the dark now in the back of her sister's closet, just as she'd known it would. But on that day in early

June, she'd been running late and there had been no time to change. It was a small victory to leave the house in that dress, one dampened only by the dropping temperature. As Angela stood at the corner, her mother had turned back to fetch her daughter's jacket, but the bus had arrived while she was gone and Angela had climbed aboard. By the time the driver pulled into the school parking lot, the day had gone cold, and Angela's breath had made tiny plumes of smoke as she walked toward the building. It had not yet begun to snow, but she had felt it coming, like the distant roll of thunder before a summer storm.

She'd learned that day that winter was a wild thing that could visit whenever it wanted, and she thought about that now as she descended the flight of wooden stairs toward the kitchen.

"Wear your boots today," her mother told them as Angela and her sister sat at the table over breakfast. "It's cold outside. Radio says it might snow."

"Yes, ma'am," Angela responded. She glanced at Monica, who was dragging the back of her fork across a thin film of jelly on the surface of her toast.

Dan Finley stretched his right leg out beneath the table and tapped the seat of his younger daughter's chair with a steel-toed work boot. "Hey," he said, "you hear your mother?"

Monica looked up and nodded her head, her brown curls bouncing like a collection of miniature pogo sticks.

The room fell silent as their father studied the two of them, his gaze moving from one face to the other and back again. He curled his fingers around the handle of his coffee mug, lifted it to his lips, and took a sip.

Angela's mother dried the surface of the counter with a hand towel, folded it once, and draped it over a hook attached to the cabinet below the sink. "You girls get your books together," she told them. "Bus will be coming soon."

Monica slid out of her chair and left the kitchen, humming a song from one of her favorite TV shows.

Angela lingered at the table, her eyes on the crust-laden plate in front of her. "If we get snow, can I go sledding with my friends?"

Her father took one last sip of coffee and pushed his chair back from the table. "Shovel the driveway first," he said. "It gets dark early. Make sure you're home before then."

AT NORTHSIDE ELEMENTARY, the school was fifteen minutes into period two when Angela glanced toward the window and noticed the flurries: big wet flakes that peppered the glass but melted on contact. She sighed. At eleven years old, she figured she'd seen just about every type of snow there was to see. This was the wet and sloppy kind. It could fall all day and never amount to more than a few inches. It wasn't until much later, in period six, when Emily Soto leaned over and whispered from the chair to Angela's left.

"We're going sledding at Jacob's Field after school. You in?"

"Won't be any good," Angela whispered back. "Nothing but slop."

"Are you *kidding*? There's, like, *two feet* of snow on the ground and it's still dumping."

"*Really?*"

Mr. Turner looked up from his desk. "Something you'd like to share with us, Ms. Finley?"

"No, sir."

"Then let's keep it down, shall we? Unless you and Ms. Soto would like to stay after school to catch up on your reading."

The class was quiet after that. At the end of the period,

Principal Hastings announced over the intercom that afternoon homeroom was canceled and that students were to head straight to their buses.

Angela filed through the doors with the rest of them and boarded the number three bus that serviced the northeast section of town. She looked out at the streets as the bus made its way through the neighborhood. The school parking lot and primary roads had been plowed, but everywhere else the snow looked waist-deep or higher, the parked vehicles burrowed into the stuff like beetles.

Erin Reece popped her head above the seat back in front of her. "Jacob's Field, right? You going?"

"Yeah," Angela said. "Who else will be there?"

"Me, Deirdre, Robbie, Emily, Meghan." She shrugged. "I don't know who else."

"I have to shovel the driveway before I go. I'll meet you there."

Erin scowled. "That'll take forever. Can't you do it tomorrow?"

Angela shook her head. "No, I have to do it today. Otherwise it turns to ice and my dad gets mad."

The inside of the windows were fogging. Angela wiped hers with the palm of her hand and looked through the glass at the falling snow. It was 3:40 P.M. How long would it take to get the job done? she wondered. By the time she cleared the driveway and walked across town to the sledding hill, how much time would she have before sundown?

"You could help me," she suggested. "It would only take half as long if we did it together."

A small crease appeared in the center of Erin's forehead. "I don't know," she said. "Robbie and me, we're supposed to pick up the sleds and go straight from his house. The others will be waiting."

Angela nodded. "Yeah, okay." She wiped at the glass again and looked out at the neighborhood. "It was a stupid idea anyway. I'm not even sure if I have a second shovel."

Erin rested her chin on her forearm. "I mean, we could come by, but . . ."

"No," she said. "You'd be getting in my way. I'm really fast with the driveway. I've been doing it, like, forever."

The bus slowed and Angela stood up, grabbed the strap of her backpack, and slung it over her shoulder.

Erin tapped her friend's leg with the toe of her boot. "We'll meet you there, right?"

"Soon as I'm done," she said, and walked down the aisle toward the open doors.

Outside, the road was plowed but icy. Angela waded through the front-yard drifts. She stumbled once over a hidden root, but a minute later she was at her door, using her key and moving through the house to where her father kept two snow shovels—one red and one blue—that leaned against the interior wall of the garage.

Angela picked the one with the red blade, the one she always used. Outside, it was coming down harder than ever. Two feet of snow was more than she could lift with the shovel. She cleared it in layers, tossing each scoop on top of the growing mounds on either side. It was not a long driveway, but her progress was slow, and the parts she'd already shoveled were filling in with new precipitation. In an hour, she realized, it would be hard to tell that she'd done anything at all.

Angela wanted to call her father to ask if she could do this later, after the snow had stopped falling. He worked at the Columbia Grain processing plant. The phone number was posted on the refrigerator door, but Dan Finley had emphasized to his family that it was to be used for *emergencies only*.

"If you call that number," he'd told Angela when he first got the job a few years back, "my boss has to come get me. I have to stop working in order to come to the phone." He lifted her chin with his index finger until she was looking him in the eyes. "My boss doesn't like it when I have to stop working," he said. "If it happens too much, maybe he'll decide to give my job to someone else. We'd have to leave this town and the friends we've made here." He touched the side of her cheek with his thumb. "You understand?"

She'd nodded and had never used the number to call him. But now she stood in the driveway, wrestling with her indecision. Her friends were probably at Jacob's Field already, screaming and laughing as they careened down the steep slope that stretched more than a hundred yards—longer than the high school football field—before it flattened out near the bank of the Missouri River. The sun was low in the sky. If she hurried, she could have an hour of sledding, maybe more. She would come home for dinner, turn on the outside light, and shovel the rest of the driveway before she went to bed. Most likely it would have stopped snowing by then, and the driveway would *stay* cleared as she shoveled, instead of filling in around her.

It took only a few minutes for Angela to change into something dry, and she left her wet things in a basket in the mudroom. Her snow pants were hanging in the closet, and she put those on as well, then the same boots she'd been wearing throughout the day. She fetched her plastic sled from the garage but left the red shovel sticking out of the snow so that her father would see that she'd *at least tried* to clear the driveway before she left.

Trying is good, she thought. *Trying could mean the difference between getting a scolding or something worse.*

Jacob's Field was on the other side of town, about three-quarters of a mile from where she lived. Angela stuck to the roads that had been cleared. She jogged for most of the distance, moving off to the side to make way for the occasional car as it rolled slowly past, kernels of ice crackling beneath the tires. She crossed the open corridor of the railroad tracks that divided the town into its northern and southern sections. The rails themselves were hidden beneath the snow, and Angela stepped on one of them with the sole of her right boot before descending the small embankment to Sixth Avenue South and passing the quiet grounds of the high school on her right.

She was near Jacob's Field now, an expanse of land that stretched along the southern section of a parcel of farmland owned by Nathaniel Jacob. Angela had never met Mr. Jacob and knew of him only because of the sledding hill. She had seen him once, standing on his porch and looking south toward the river, although his view of the hill and the water below was obstructed by a line of pine trees that stood along the ridge where the land began to slope downward. It was not a secret thing, the kids sledding there. Mr. Jacob had no children of his own that Angela was aware of, and it was rumored that he lived alone, that his wife had died a long time ago, although no one seemed to know exactly how. Angela had asked her father about him last winter, curious after seeing the man standing on the porch in his olive baseball cap and flannel jacket.

"I don't know," her father said, his hands resting on the copper pipe he was working on in their basement. "Nathaniel Jacob keeps to himself mostly. Did he talk to you?"

"No, sir. I saw him from across the field."

"Well"—Dan Finley stood up and wiped his hands with a rag—"he prefers to be left alone, I imagine. Did he give you and your friends permission to use his field?"

"Yes, sir. Jeff Stutzman's brother asked him about it a few

years ago. He said it was fine, as long as we stayed away from his crops and none of us got hurt."

"Stay away from his crops, then," her father told her. "Go around the long way if you have to."

"Yes, sir," she said, and that's what she always did, taking the long way down the side road instead of cutting across the northern section of the property. Today the road was un-plowed, and it took her longer than usual, wading through the waist-high powder toward the tree line that marked the top of the hill. On the other side of those trees were her friends: Emily Soto and Erin Reece; Meghan Decker with her new braces and self-conscious smile; and Deirdre McKinney, whose father had run for town mayor twice but lost both times to a man named Zachary Brody.

"Hey. Hey, girl."

Angela turned to look. There was a man standing in the snow behind her, along the buried section of road she had just traveled. He was wearing a brown winter hat and a heavy dark green jacket. The clothes made him look bulky, but it was hard to tell much about the features beneath. His pants were caked with snow, and his neck and face were wrapped in a scarf a shade darker than the jacket. There was a white van parked along the main road behind him.

"No sledding today," he said. "Storm's getting worse."

Angela stood there, her plastic sled tucked under her right arm. She looked around. Her mitten made a soft zipping sound as it brushed against the side of her snow pants.

"Everyone's gone," the man said. "I can give you a ride home if you want." He took a few steps in her direction. "I'm sorry to make you leave. I'm sorry and that's the truth."

"Are you Mr. Jacob?" Angela asked. She'd been coming here for four years and had seen him just that once.

"I work for him. Take care of the farm a little and fix things around the house." He shifted his weight from one foot to the other, and brushed powder off the sleeves of his jacket. "It sure is coming down hard out here."

Angela heard it then, the shriek of one of her friends—*Deirdre,* she thought, *the one with the loudest voice*—coming from Jacob's Field on the other side of the tree line behind her. She turned her head at the sound.

"Come on now," he said, but his voice sounded funny—the pitch high and a little squeaky.

Angela took a step backward. It was difficult in the snow. "I thought you said everyone was gone."

"That's right," he said, and took a few more steps. He was standing in front of her now, close enough to reach out and touch her if he wanted. "I told them to leave, but maybe they came back. They'll get in big trouble if they did." He cupped a gloved hand around Angela's upper arm, the one that was not holding the sled. "Enough talking. It's time to go."

"I can get home by myself."

"No, no," he said. "Children don't listen."

He clamped down on her arm and pulled her toward the van. Angela tried to yank free, but his grip was strong as they plodded through the snow. She stumbled a bit, but didn't fall. Up ahead was the van, its side door open, letting in the weather.

"Let me go. I don't want to go with you."

He shook his head. "Too late for games, too late for fun. Tomorrow's big adventures are all but said and done."

They were moving fast through the snow, and Angela wondered what would happen if she stopped walking, made her legs go slack and fell to the ground. Would he wrap his other hand around her arm and drag her the rest of the way? She remembered the warnings her mother had given her when she was younger. "Don't take rides from strangers," she'd said. "If a stranger tells you to get into his car, you don't do it, do you hear me? You run away or call for help."

"Let *go* of me."

He stopped walking and looked back at her. "What's the matter?"

"I'm not supposed to take rides from strangers. My father would be *very angry* if he found out." She thought of the shovel, jutting out of the snow beside the abandoned driveway. "I'm already going to get in trouble."

The man seemed to think about this, his head cocked to one side. He reached up with his left hand and adjusted his hat, although the right hand remained clamped around Angela's arm. "Don't tell him," he said. "I'll drop you off a block away."

"No," she said. "I'm sorry, but I can't." She looked up at him, but the snow fell in her eyes and she looked down again, tried to blink it away.

"Okay," he said, letting go of her arm. He pulled at the fingers of his left glove. "I didn't mean to scare you."

"Thank you," Angela told him, and there was a perfect moment of silence between them, when all she could hear was the soft patter of snow falling around them.

She took a breath in, readied herself to say goodbye, and that was when he struck her, full force with a closed fist in the center of her face.

Angela fell backward into the snow without realizing she had fallen. Her vision blurred and there was a high-pitched drone in her head, as if someone was humming a steady note without pausing to take a breath. She could feel hands wrapped around her left ankle, dragging her through the snow.

The sleeves of her coat bunched as he pulled her. There was

snow against the skin of her right wrist, and something large and flat dragged along beside her, its plastic underbelly scraping like a spatula across the frozen surface.

She let go of the thing and dug her hands into the snow, but the powder was loose and there was nothing to hold on to. Angela kicked at the man's hands with her other foot and brought the heel of her boot down on his knuckles.

"Stop it," the man said, but his grip loosened.

Angela pulled hard, tried to wrench her ankle from his grasp. On the third yank, her left foot slid free of its boot. She scuttled backward a short distance, then turned and got to her feet.

He grabbed her by the collar of her coat, and she heard a sound—something between a sob and a moan—escape from her body. Angela ripped off a mitten, found the tab of her zipper, and yanked it downward. He grabbed her hair as she wriggled free of the coat. She lurched forward anyway and felt a searing pain as the roots separated from her scalp.

Even then, the man could've tackled her, but he stepped on the plastic sled and his right foot shot out from under him. He went down in the snow with a fistful of hair in his hand, and he clung to it as he scrambled to get up again.

Angela ran, or at least tried to. Moving through the drifts was like running in water, the powder clutching at her legs but allowing her to pass. She got a twenty-foot head start before the man was on his feet and coming after her. She could hear him breathing, a quick measured sound that scampered back and forth between them like a rabbit in the bush.

Don't take rides from strangers, her mother called out across the field, and although the voice was only in Angela's head, she could picture her standing there on Mr. Jacob's back porch, her hands wrapped around the wooden rail as she watched her daughter fleeing through the snow.

The sound of the man's breathing grew louder. Was he closer or just getting tired?

I'm faster than he is, Angela thought. *I can beat him.* But there was no boot covering her left foot, and already it was getting numb. How much longer could she go, she wondered, before it was nothing but a piece of wood beneath her?

Call for help, her mother said, but when Angela opened her mouth and tried to scream, the sound was small and full of terror.

She raced through the snow, her body moving as fast as her legs could carry her. "*Heellllp!*" she screamed. "*Heelllllllp!*" She listened for a response, but it was only the sound of the two of them breathing now. Her mother's voice had gone quiet in her head.

My friends are on the other side of those trees, she thought, but in her panic she had veered rightward, away from the ridgeline. If she changed course now, he would cut her off before she made it to the pines.

Angela ran for as long as she could. Twenty minutes later, the sun was on the horizon, an orange sphere with contours that appeared to shiver in the gathering dusk. By the time the man returned to his van, it had stopped snowing, and the sky above was laced with ribbons of lilac and violet. The muscles of his legs trembled with fatigue, but he stopped to gather the plastic sled, coat, and boot that had been left in the snow. He tossed them into the van, then turned to scan the empty field behind him. The land was dark and draped in shadows, but he could still see the path they had cut through the snow. He wondered how much of it would be left by morning.

The wind gusted from the north, and a thin tuft of powder slid across the frozen surface toward the distant pines. Everything else was quiet.

Gone by morning, he thought. Then he turned back toward the van and lowered the body off his shoulder.

2

ERIN REECE LEANED FORWARD AND SWITCHED OFF THE RADIO. THE truck slowed as she approached the unincorporated village of Vida, passed two churches and a post office, and just like that the village was behind her. She eased her foot back down on the accelerator and coaxed the Chevrolet pickup toward its optimum speed of sixty-five miles per hour, since anything faster made the steering wheel shudder. She'd gotten the truck ten years ago, during her second year of vet school. It was an old thing even then, the green exterior faded almost to the point of being white. There were a few functional limitations. The passenger door could be opened only from the inside—not a problem, really, since her only semi-regular passenger was a three-year-old Rhodesian ridgeback named Diesel. The dog had accompanied her on this trip, and he lay stretched out on the bench seat with his head on her lap.

"Getting close to home, boy," Erin said, although Diesel had never lived in Wolf Point, a community of some twelve hundred residents that was flanked by the Missouri River to the south and the two-million-acre expanse of the Fort Peck

Indian Reservation to the north. Like much of Montana, it was driven by an agricultural economy. Farming and the livestock trade were its primary sources of income, supplemented by all the other things—schools, grocery stores, a small hospital—that make a city run. There was a time, back when Erin was growing up, when the population of Wolf Point was more than twice its current number. But there were things that had happened there, things that could change a place, and by the time Erin left for college, a common sentiment among many of the locals was that Wolf Point's best days were already behind it.

Some of it was bad luck. A few years back, an early October snowstorm claimed the lives of thirty thousand cattle across Eastern Montana, decimating livestock and forcing many of the local farmers into bankruptcy. Her father had lost cattle as well, but enough survived that he hadn't lost the farm. *What would I have done if he had?* Erin wondered, because David Reece had decided long ago that he was never leaving Wolf Point, and for fifteen years Erin had sworn to herself that she was never coming back.

Up ahead, she could see the metal frame of the old Lewis and Clark Bridge. Before its time, there had only been a ferry to shuttle cars from one side to the other. In the dead of winter, though, when the river was frozen solid, people used to drive across, although not all of them made it.

Erin let up on the gas a bit as she neared the river. In February of 1926, two young men named James and Rolla Cusker hit an open spot in the ice on their return trip from a basketball game late at night. Their car punched through the surface, and the men were swept away in the fast-moving current. It was several days before their bodies were discovered. By then, the flesh would've been eaten away in places, like the body she and

Robbie had found in the river when they were children, the face bloated and purple, the eyes retracted into their sockets beneath a brackish membrane of river filth. Miles Griffin was sixteen years old, one of many casualties of Wolf Point she remembered from her childhood. In a way, she thought, he was one of the lucky ones, since most of the missing never surfaced. They just disappeared into the landscape and the dark belly of the town's collective memory.

The tragedy of 1926 led to the construction of the Lewis and Clark Bridge four years later—the only one to span the Missouri River for three hundred and fifty miles in either direction. It was obsolete now, a historic relic overgrown with grass but left to stand beside its inevitable but unremarkable replacement. Erin's stomach gave a small lurch as she passed the steel carcass of the three-span truss. She tried to think of the last time she had seen it, and then thought even further back to the days when she would sit on its girder and look westward across the plains toward the setting sun, her feet dangling two and a half stories above the surface. When she was ten years old, she had etched her initials, *E.R.,* on one of its beams. That was a long time ago, the year her father got out of prison but still three years before her mother went missing.

Erin glanced at the bridge once more in her rearview. Her father's farm was on the eastern outskirts of town, less than a mile from here, but she passed the access road without turning, heading instead for Wolf Point's more populated section. To the left of the highway sat the single runway of the L. M. Clayton Airport, a modest track of asphalt with no tower and only three cars in the dirt parking lot as she drove past.

To her right were the railroad tracks that paralleled the last three miles of highway before Wolf Point. Roy Shifflet had found Curt Hastings's Ford F-250 pickup nuzzled into a snowbank here—the driver's door open and the engine still running. It was the same night that Rose Perry had gone missing on her walk home from work. Two unrelated people traveling along different paths in the late evening. Both of them had grown up in Wolf Point, and neither one of them was ever seen again.

Erin slowed as she passed the Silver Wolf Casino, the highway curving to the left and then right before it became Main Street. To the right was D&J's pawnshop, followed by a hardware store and a series of bars advertising poker and keno. Erin rolled to a stop at Third Avenue South, waited for the light to change, then proceeded through the intersection. Prairie Cinemas was still standing, a single-screen theater she had frequented as a kid. She wondered if Connie Griffin still ran the place, leaning over the concession booth with her thick hands pressed against the glass countertop. Connie had lost a son to Wolf Point, and a few years later she lost another.

Eventually she got to Sixth Avenue. She stopped there and gazed across the street at the brick-walled structure of Wolf Point Junior Senior High School.

When Erin thought of her hometown, it was the high school and her father's farm that she pictured the most. Maybe it was because these were transitional places, where childhood had ended and the path toward adulthood began. There was part of her that wanted to return here, to be eight years old again and surrounded by her close-knit circle of friends. If she could go back, knowing what she knew now, maybe this time things would be different. She believed in that, in the possibility of second chances. It was why she'd left after high school, why she'd refused to come back until now. Fifteen years was a long time, but it wasn't long enough. She could feel the past pulling at her, all these years later, and the distance between then and now suddenly seemed like nothing at all.

Erin closed her eyes. She'd received the phone call from Dr. Houseman—Wolf Point's only family practice physician—four days ago. She hadn't answered it, and in Erin's defense, the message he'd left on her voicemail hadn't mentioned that her father was ill, only that the doctor needed to talk to her. She'd imagined that he might be calling about a high school reunion or just to catch up after all these years. It was strange how people felt the need to do that, to reach into their past and try to resuscitate it like it was something worth saving. When he left another message the following day, Erin hadn't listened to it, only recognized the number from the day before and decided she would get to it when she could. She hadn't been avoiding it, really, she'd just been . . .

"Busy," she said to herself in the quiet of the truck's cab, and Diesel lifted his head and gazed up at her.

When Dad recovers, I'll take him back to Colorado, she thought. But from what Mark had told her over the phone, her father's condition sounded serious, maybe even life-threatening. She tried not to think of it that way, but Mark had used words like "sepsis," "ventilator," and "pneumonia." That had scared her. And despite the things that had happened here, it had been enough to bring her back.

"How's he doing?" she asked over the phone, and Mark's answer had been careful, enough for her to know that the outcome was anything but certain.

"Things seem to have stabilized," he said. "His blood pressure has improved. I'm hopeful that pretty soon we can remove the breathing tube."

Breathing tube, Erin thought. It wasn't the first time she had pictured him that way. How many years had her father been struggling, hanging on to his little piece of survival in a town that had taken away everything else?

"That's good," she heard herself say, but on the other end of the line, Mark was quiet. "What is it?" she asked, gripping the phone a little harder. It was several seconds before the doctor responded.

"Erin, I have Jeff Stutzman sitting in the waiting room outside of my office. You remember Jeff?"

"Yes," she said. "Jeff." She had known him from school and the neighborhood, of course. Jeff had been on the wild side, prone to fighting and getting into trouble. But it was his older brother, Kenny, whose name still resonated in what was left of her family. Kenny Stutzman. A thin twist of a kid with red hair and freckles. Ten years old when her father hit him with the Bronco on that rainy night in April. The road Kenny died on was renamed in his memory, and three years of prison and a lifetime of guilt wasn't going to bring him back.

"Jeff is on the police force here in Wolf Point," Mark said. "He was promoted to lieutenant two years ago."

"Police," she said, and Erin felt a touch of panic, as if maybe they'd finally decided they wanted more from her father. The boy had been only ten. His head was crushed, but he kept right on breathing for an hour.

"I'm going to bring him in now," Mark told her.

"Who?" she had asked, glancing toward the front door in her home in Colorado.

"Jeff. Lieutenant Stutzman."

"Oh. Yes, of course," she said, and Erin waited on the other end of the phone while Mark went out to fetch him.

It's Jeff who's sitting in the other room, she reminded herself, *not*

Kenny. Kenny died that night in the emergency room. They buried him in a plot at Wolf Point Cemetery.

She held the receiver in her hand and listened to the distant sound of voices on the other end of the line. She cleared her throat and tried not to think about the many ways a person can be dead and keep right on breathing until the very end.

"Erin? Erin Reece?" a man asked.

"Yes."

"This is Jeff Stutzman. We knew each other back in school."

"Yes, Jeff. I remember."

"I think Dr. Houseman explained that I'm a lieutenant now with the Wolf Point Police Department."

"He did," she said. "Congratulations."

"Thank you," he replied, and his voice did not project the gruff, antagonistic presence she remembered from her child-hood. Instead, he sounded soft-spoken and remorseful, as if it pained him to bother her in the wake of the news she had just received from the doctor.

"I'm sorry about your father," he said.

"Thank you, I . . . I appreciate that."

"He's in good hands, you know. Mark takes care of pretty much all of us here in Wolf Point."

"Yes," she said, "we're lucky to have him." She paused. *We're* lucky, she'd said. She was still six hundred miles away, but already she could feel herself being pulled northward, the place wrapping itself around her. She glanced again at the door. "Mark said you wanted to talk to me about something."

"Yes," Jeff said. "I was wondering if we could arrange a time to meet when you get here. There are . . . some things I'd like to go over with you."

"Things," she said. "What things?"

"It's complicated. It would be easier to talk about in person."

Erin was silent for a moment, turning his words over in her mind.

"What is it?" she asked. "Something's happened."

"It can wait until you get here."

"It'll take two days to make the drive."

"That's fine," he said. "I'll see you in a few days, then. Your father needs you. I'm . . . I'm glad you're coming."

"Of course I'm coming," she'd said. "My father's in the hospital."

Only, it hadn't been that easy, had it? And the years since she left had been riddled with their own private struggles. She'd struggled in college with feelings of isolation and depression. Vet school at Colorado State had been better, the rigorous workload distracting her from the kind of inward reflection that led to nowhere good. After that, it had been private practice, first as a veterinarian for a small-animal clinic near Boulder, but eventually establishing her own practice in Fort Collins, about sixty miles north of Denver. There had been a steep learning curve, not just in the practice of medicine but in the art of running a business. She'd taken a loss during the first two years, but this year she was turning a corner. In another year or two, if things continued to go well, she could hire someone to cover Saturdays and maybe—

"I'm sorry," David said, and just like that she was ten again, standing in the kitchen of her childhood home. He was sitting in a chair at the table, looking lost and out of place on that first day home, like a bear in human clothing. His deep blue eyes studied her for a moment, taking in the many ways she'd changed while he was away.

"I'm sorry I had to go away these past three years," David said. "You know I've missed you."

"I missed you, too, Daddy."

He smiled. It was the kind of smile that made him look sad and happy at the same time.

"You've gotten taller," he said. "I noticed it a bit when you came to visit, but . . . I think you've grown even more since then."

She shrugged.

"You've been taking good care of your mother?"

"I help her with the dishes."

"That's a good girl. I'm sure she appreciates that."

Erin reached out with a child's hand and touched his arm. "What was it like in prison, Daddy?"

He turned his head for a second to look at the telephone that hung from the wall. She looked, too, and ran her eyes along the twisted cord that dangled from a silent receiver.

"It's lonely," he said. "Days pass and nothing happens."

She turned back to him. "It sounds boring."

"I think it's meant to be boring," he told her. "You can see the wasted part of your life right out in front of you."

Erin was silent for a moment, considering. "How can you *see* that? Is it real?"

"No," he said. "It's like a dream, but every day is the *same* dream. All you want to do is wake up and go home to the people you love."

She smiled. "Like me and Mommy."

"Yeah," he said, "like you and Mommy."

She leaned forward and lowered her voice to a whisper. "Mommy cried a lot while you were gone."

He nodded. "Your mother is very strong and very brave. So are you."

"I'm not that strong," she told him. "Jacob McCloskey can beat me in arm wrestling."

"No," he said. "I don't believe it."

"It's true."

"Let me see your muscle."

She flexed her arm for him, and he reached out and felt her bicep with fingers that were rough and calloused.

"Whoa," he said, "it's like a rock. No one can beat you in arm wrestling."

"Jacob McCloskey can."

"Is he a robot?"

Erin shook her head.

"Is he a gorilla?"

She giggled. "No, silly. He's a boy."

"Oh, I see. A boy robot gorilla named Jacob McCloskey."

Erin laughed. "A boy robot gorilla named Jacob McCloskey."

David stuck out his lower jaw and scratched the top of his head. He stood up from his chair and lurched around the kitchen.

"*Jacob McCloskey! Jacob McCloskey!*" she screeched, pointing.

Erin ran from the room, and David lumbered after her down the hall, snorting and chuffing as he went. Even when they were playing, it was a little scary being chased by her father, something frightening within a game.

Eight years later, she'd gone away herself and left him here in a town he might never escape. In the fifteen years since then, she'd found ways to keep herself busy, to put Wolf Point behind her in every way she could.

"We should go and see him," she said, and Diesel's tail went back and forth once and then lay still.

("You know I've missed you.")

("I missed you, too, Daddy.")

She leaned forward and clicked on the radio, an old 1970s-style model that matched the feel of the truck but was generally useless. Erin turned the tuning knob with her fingers as she moved through the dial. It was static mostly, the sound of stations long since forgotten. She listened anyway, catching scratches of music and voices she could not quite decipher. She made a right at the intersection and put the school behind her as she headed north toward the hospital. Along the way the reception improved, and she found something she could listen to, a song whose lyrics she almost remembered. She turned it up, tapped her fingers on the steering wheel, and rolled through the town as if it still belonged to her.

3

(March 1996)

ROSE PERRY CROSSED THE DINER, THE SOLES OF HER WHITE SHOES squeaking on the part of the floor she'd already mopped. She was carrying a coffeepot in her right hand and the weight of the last twenty minutes of her ten-hour shift in the rest of her short, slim frame. They were playing "Wonderwall" by Oasis on the radio, a song that had come out a few months back and was still climbing in popularity. She'd been on her feet since ten A.M., cleaning up from the breakfast crowd and then soldiering on through lunch and dinner. Thursday was her late shift, when her fifteen-year-old daughter spent the evening with her ex-husband, Jim. The marriage had lasted six years, and only one of them had been good. Katey was the best thing that had come from that time, and it was peculiar, she thought, how the best part of her life was so entwined with the worst.

"Fill that up for you, Bob?" she asked, placing a hand on the man's shoulder.

Bob Cannon turned his head and smiled. "Just a splash," he said. "I can take the check whenever you're ready."

Rose poured the coffee, then fished the slip of paper from

the front pocket of her apron. The meal came to $11.05. Bob would leave her thirteen dollars, a little more than the standard fifteen percent. She'd been serving him long enough to know.

"Cold out tonight," he said. "Supposed to drop to fifteen below by morning."

Rose turned her gaze toward the window. Light from the interior of the diner was reflected in the glass, creating a mirrored image of the two of them at the table. She saw a woman in her late thirties holding an almost-empty pot of coffee. Her face looked weary, not just from this shift but from all the ones that had come before and from the years of similar work that still lay ahead. *I'm young,* she told herself, but she wasn't *that* young and it was hard to reconcile the assertion with the image in front of her. It was 1996, getting close to the turn of the century, and she wondered if she would be here in two decades, clearing tables and pouring coffee at the Old Town Grill. Staring at the glass, she could almost see her face changing, the corners of her mouth turning downward, the lines around the edges of her eyes sinking deeper into the flesh. Rose turned away from the window and tried to eradicate the thought. It was hard to shake it, the idea that her best days were already behind her.

Bob leaned to the left and reached back with his right hand to retrieve his wallet from his back pocket. "I should be getting home," he said, placing a ten and three ones on the table in front of him. "Millie will be worried."

Rose smiled. She doubted that Millie—Bob's twelve-year-old dachshund—would be awake when he got home, much less worried. "Nice to see you again," she told him, and she stepped back from the table as Bob put on his coat and made his way across the diner.

The bell jingled as he opened the front door and stepped

outside. Rose watched him cross the parking lot, his feet spread wide for stability on the frozen asphalt. She listened to the *chunk* of the driver's door as it closed, then cleared the table as the diesel engine roared to life. Headlights illuminated the snow as Bob put the vehicle in gear and pulled out onto Fourth Avenue. Rose crossed the room and listened to the engine until it faded into the night.

The diner's owner had already removed most of the money from the register for the evening. Rose deposited Bob's cash, minus her two-dollar tip, and straightened up the area behind the counter. It took another fifteen minutes to wash the few remaining dishes and to finish mopping the floor. When everything was clean and in its place, she switched off the radio, hung her apron on a wooden peg on the wall, turned out the lights, and exited through the front door.

The cold wrapped itself around her. It nibbled at her ears and the tips of her fingers as she jiggled the key in the lock, trying to get the dead bolt to turn. When it finally did, she circled her scarf once more around her neck, stuffed her hands into the pockets of her coat, and headed for home.

The snow had stopped falling by midday, leaving an extra three inches on top of yesterday's base. It was late March, and today's storm was nothing compared to the one they'd been hit with the month before. A young girl, eleven-year-old Angela Finley, had gone missing during that one. Mayor Brody had organized a search party. It was a massive effort, covering a twenty-mile radius in all directions. Rose herself had been out there, along with almost every other able-bodied citizen of Wolf Point. She'd gotten frostbite on one of the toes of her right foot, wading through the waist-deep snow in the hope of finding the child. But if Angela Finley was out there, they hadn't found her that day or the next. Two weeks later they called off the search. "When the snow melts, someone will find her," people said, but Rose hated to think about that, the girl getting lost in the storm, her body still lying beneath the snow.

The wind gusted, kicking up a thin film of white powder that snaked across the intersection at Fourth and Fallon. She stopped and watched it for a moment beneath the incandescent glow of the streetlamp. She lived six blocks from here and could've driven. The toe that she'd damaged three weeks ago ached within the confines of her shoe. It had been stupid to walk, but gas was expensive, and these days the less she spent the better. "Every little bit counts," she'd told herself this morning, leaving her car keys hanging from their hook on the wall. "You can either drive to work this month or pay the electric bill, but you can't do both."

She lowered her head and hunched her shoulders against the wind. The snow muffled the sound of her footsteps, and she was limping now, keeping her right ankle flexed upward so she wouldn't have to push off with her toes.

Her daughter, Katey, was with Jim tonight. Rose missed her when she wasn't home. The house was too quiet, the silence reminding her of the mistakes she had made that could never be corrected. *My daughter lives in two homes,* she thought, and Rose picked up the familiar guilt of that and walked with it down the snow-covered sidewalk.

She tried to think of a happier time, and the memory that came to her was from a decade earlier, when Rose had taken Katey to Disneyland and the beaches of Southern California. Katey was only six, and it was the first time either of them had seen the ocean. Rose remembered the crash of waves and the call of seagulls as the sunlight danced along the surface of the water. She could feel wet sand against the soles of her feet, and she watched as Katey ran to the edge of the water and then scampered back again. "Now you, Mommy," her daughter shrieked, giggling, and when the next wave struck the shore, Rose took a few steps forward and allowed the ocean to wrap around her ankles as her feet sank beneath the—

THUD!

It hit her from behind like the hand of God himself.

Her head snapped backward, her teeth clicking together. For a moment she was airborne, weightless in the vacant fabric of the night. Then the left side of her face slammed against the asphalt and she slid along it, the ice and salt grinding into her skin.

What is it? What just happened?

Rose opened her eyes, but she couldn't see out of her left eye and the image through the other one was blurry. She could make out the fingers of her right hand, though, and a small patch of roadway illuminated by a light that was coming from behind her. She moaned, but the sound was drowned out by the harsh idle of an engine and the hurried crunch of footsteps, someone coming to help.

"You okay?" a man asked. She couldn't see him, but his hand was on her shoulder, his voice close to her ear.

"I . . . don't . . ."

"You walked into the street. Didn't you hear me coming?"

Rose opened and closed her mouth. Her lower lip felt weird, as if part of it wasn't there. She searched for it with her tongue, but tasted only salt from the roadway, felt a few bits of gravel on the corner of her mouth.

"Can you move? I can help you up if you want?"

"I . . . don't . . . know. I can't feel . . . my legs." A few droplets of blood sprayed from her mouth as she said this. In the glow of the headlights, tiny red dots littered the white backdrop of snow.

"You're hurt. I'll get you to the hospital."

Rose tried to raise her face off the asphalt. *My skin will stick to the ice,* she thought, but she was able to lift her head a few inches off the road before an immense pain awoke in her pelvis.

"*Aaaaaaagh.*"

"What's the matter?"

"Something's broken."

She clenched her teeth. The agony was a brick wall that pressed against her, a presence she couldn't escape. Rose closed her eyes and tried to breathe through it, the way she'd done during childbirth.

"I'm going to pick you up. It might hurt a little, but—"

"*No, wait.* Call . . . an ambulance."

He was silent for a moment, and Rose tried to gather herself, to get out from under the crushing weight of the wall pressing down on her.

"No phone," he said. "I can't leave you like this." He paused to think it over. "I have a van, though. I can put you in the back and drive you myself."

Rose's muscles went rigid. "No. I can't take the—"

"It'll just take a second," he said. "You can bite on this." He stuffed a large piece of cloth deep into her mouth. It tasted like oil and rusted metal, made her gag as he pushed it down. "Going to get you to the hospital now," he said, and rolled her onto her back. She screamed as he lifted her, but the sound was choked off by the dirty rag and the noise of the engine. The pain was everywhere, and she retreated to the beach, to the place where she had been before any of this had happened.

He carried her to the van and rested Rose's butt on his thigh while he opened the side door. She could hear it sliding back on its track, another wave tumbling against the shore. She screamed again when he moved her, dug her hands and feet into the sand and tried to skitter backward, away from the water. "Now you, Mommy," Katey called out, but Rose couldn't see her, couldn't make out the shape of her daughter beneath the harsh glare of the sun.

Please, she thought, but she couldn't remember what she wanted. Her thoughts were jumbled, falling into each other like empty bodies, churning in the surf.

"We'll get you fixed up, okay? You don't need to worry."

Beneath her body, the sand was a cold, hard surface, rigid as glass. She heard the sliding noise again, followed by the *chunk* of a door slamming closed. A surge of vomit flooded the back of her throat. She choked it down and gagged once again on the thing lodged near the base of her tongue.

("Now you, Mommy. Now you.")

I . . . can't . . .

The surface beneath her began to move, and the pain rose up again, more than she could bear. She closed her mind off from it, tried instead to focus on her surroundings.

"Gonna get you all better," a voice said, and she struggled to place it, to make sense of what was happening to her.

The surface shifted to the left, and as she rolled onto her right side, the bone in her hip crunched beneath her weight.

The pain is far away. I can breathe through this. The important thing now is to find my daughter.

A radio clicked on in the darkness. "That was John Michael Montgomery with 'I Can Love You Like That,' and you're listening to KVCK out of Wolf Point, Montana. The latest weather report says it's twelve degrees outside with a forecast of more snow this weekend. There's plenty of ice on the roads, so be careful if you're driving out there and stay home if you can. And if you're missing that special someone this evening, here's a song for all you folks who can't help but wonder about the one who got away. This is Garth Brooks with 'What She's Doing Now,' and this is 107.1 FM, the Wolf."

The Wolf, she thought. It was the radio station her ex-husband used to listen to. Rose reached up with her left hand and pulled the rag from her mouth. She stretched her hand out in front of her to see if anyone else was there. Her fingers touched metal, and she moved her hand upward, probing its vertical ridges.

The surface beneath her bounced upward, jamming itself into her right hip and shoulder. She screamed, a tortured, plaintive sound that filled the small interior.

"Quiet now. I need to focus on my driving."

I know that voice. I've seen him at the market.

The tip of her middle finger touched the bottom edge of something plastic. She reached farther upward, wrapped the rest of her fingers around it. She pulled on the handle, felt it pivot in her grasp.

"Hospital's probably closed. It might be good to take you somewhere else for the evening."

Somewhere else, she thought, but it was hard to make sense of it. Where was she now? How long had she been here?

Rose pulled harder on the handle. She heard a click, followed by the sound of small wheels rolling along a metal track. Her hand fell away from the lever as a frigid blast of night air entered the compartment.

"What are you doing?"

The room lurched to the left, and Rose's body was thrown in the opposite direction, toward the open doorway. She put a hand out to stop herself, found only empty space, the wind buffeting her face. The compartment filled with a sudden light, the blare of a horn.

"Shiiiiiiiit."

The room jerked to the right, and she rolled left, away from the door. There was a strange sensation of the room floating, turning slowly on its axis, then a *whump* as it connected with something soft and slightly yielding. Rose slid forward and struck her head on something solid.

"*Goddamn it*. We're in trouble now. Just *look* at what you did."

She heard the creak of a door opening, the soft tramp of receding footsteps. She waited, listened to the engine as it idled.

I'm in the back of a van. I was hit by a car and now he's taking me to the hospital.

("Hospital's probably closed. It might be good to take you somewhere else for the evening.")

It was cold in the compartment. The song was still playing on the radio, but Rose could hear distant voices above the sound of the music. She could see light, too, a blinking red reflection off the surface of the snow. *Hazard lights,* she thought, *from the vehicle we almost hit.*

She lay on the floor of the van and tried to listen to the conversation. It was too far away, too difficult to make out above the radio and the deep grumble of the engines.

(*You should call for help. You should let the other driver know you're in here.*)

Rose used her elbows to slide her body toward the open door. The pain was still with her, gnawing at the bones of her pelvis like a cluster of rats, but she could feel the lift of adrenaline pushing her forward, making movement bearable. She focused on the opening, on the blinking red glow that synchronized with her heartbeat.

"Help," she said. "Please, help me."

"—get her to the hospital," the man said, and as Rose's head cleared the opening, she saw both of them walking toward the van.

"What in the hell happened?" asked the man in front. He was tall and thin and wore a brown leather jacket with the zipper open, as if he'd put it on in a hurry on his way out the door. It was not the same voice as the man who had found her lying in the roadway.

(*He didn't just find you. He hit you. Drove up on the curb and hit you on purpose.*)

"Stepped right into the middle of the road," he said. "I don't know what she was thinking."

"Hey," the man in front said. "Hey, honey, you okay?" He reached the van's open doorway and bent slightly at the waist so he could get a better look at her. "Where are you hurting?"

"My hips and pelvis," she said. "Something's broken. I know it is."

For a moment, it was like she was lying on the road again, trying to figure out the parts of her that were shattered. She could see nothing out of her left eye, and part of her lower lip was missing. She had the urge to search for it with the tip of her tongue again, wondering if she would taste salt and gravel or if this time it would be different.

("I'm going to pick you up. It might hurt a little, but—")

"I need to get to a hospital."

"Yes," the man said. His eyes moved across the parts of her that she couldn't see. "We need to . . . call an ambulance." He glanced back at the man standing behind him. "You probably shouldn't have moved her."

"Couldn't leave her there in the roadway," the man said. "It wouldn't be right to do a thing like that."

The man in front nodded to himself, and in that moment she recognized him. This was Curt Hastings, a familiar face. He worked at the processing plant north of town. Rose was friends with his wife, Debbie. She'd been to their house for dinner.

"Curt. Curt, it's me, Rose."

"Rose," he said. "Rose Perry." He blinked a few times in rapid succession, as if he'd just woken up and was still trying to get his bearings. "I'm . . . sorry this happened to you. We'll get you fixed up. I've got a CB in the cab of my pickup. I can use it to call an ambulance."

She shifted her gaze upward so that she was looking over Curt's shoulder at the man standing behind him. The side of his face was illuminated by the blinking red glow of the hazards. "Curt," she said, and the words that came next tumbled out of her like building blocks. "Curt, you've got to be careful. I think he hit me on purp—"

But the man's hand was already raised above them. In it was the L-shaped outline of a lug wrench. He swung it hard, connecting with the back of Curt's skull. Rose heard the sickening crack of it and saw the look of dismay on Curt's face a second before he lost consciousness. He fell forward and on top of her, his face landing on her shoulder. *He's dead,* she thought, *or will be soon.* She could tell by the sound the wrench had made striking his skull, as well as the sheer lifeless weight of him.

The man shoved Curt's body in the rest of the way, then stood there looking down at her. "I didn't want to do that," he said. "It's your fault for opening the door."

"None of this is my fau—" she replied, but he slammed the door closed before she could finish.

The snow crunched as he walked around to the driver's side and hoisted himself into the seat. "If you open the door again," he said, "I will come back there and smash your head with this tire wrench. You hear me? Go on and see if I don't."

He turned the music up as he dropped the shifter into Reverse.

The tires will spin, Rose thought. *They won't have enough traction to get us off the shoulder and away from the snowbank.* But the wheels bit into the snow and the van lurched backward. There was more weight over the rear tires now, she realized. Two bodies instead of one.

She found Curt Hastings in the darkness, put her hand near his mouth and nose to feel if he was still breathing.

The man put the vehicle in Drive and pressed on the gas. The van skidded forward, and they began to roll again, picking up speed.

"It's fifteen minutes past the hour," the DJ said, "and we've got lots more great songs for you on the way. Chances are, you know a lot of them. Maybe, before the night is over, we'll introduce you to something new. Keep listening, Wolf Point. Because this next one'll take you back. And that's not such a bad thing, is it? Everyone comes from somewhere. And you belong right here on 107.1 FM, the Wolf."

4

TRINITY HOSPITAL WAS LOCATED AT THE NORTH END OF THE CITY.
Erin drove up Fourth Avenue, crossing the railroad tracks
and passing several blocks of suburban homes. She recognized
some of them, the places where her friends had lived when they
were younger. Emily Soto's house was the split foyer with dark
green siding. Melissa Perez had lived two blocks away in the
tan ranch-style house with purple drapes; only, the drapes were
gone now, just an empty window looking out at the street.
It was hard to shake the feeling that some of them still lived
here—not the adult version of their former selves, but the way
they were when they were children. If Erin stopped the truck
and knocked on the front door, Meghan Decker would open
it, her red hair tied in pigtails, the sun glinting off her recently
fitted braces. Deirdre McKinney would greet her, lollipop in
hand, her left arm in a sling and wrapped in plaster from the
time she fell from the school monkey bars and broke her elbow.
And Erin herself would be younger as well, asking them if they
could come out and play or go bike riding down by the quarry.
It was ludicrous to think that way, she realized, to imagine that
it would be as simple as pulling over and walking up to their

houses, as if that previous life was still playing out, the outcome not yet decided.

Erin shook her head. She hadn't kept up with her friends. Maybe, like many families from Wolf Point, they had moved on to other places. *No,* she decided. She did not want to be a child again. She did not want to return to a time when most of the bad things were still ahead of her.

She pulled into the hospital parking lot and took Diesel for a walk around the back of the building. The few scattered trees were devoid of leaves, their skeleton limbs jutting up against the gray backdrop of November sky. Rows of winter wheat lay dormant in the field to the north.

At the end of the dirt road was an abandoned fruit stand with a wooden placard that read CLOSED FOR THE SEASON. Under those words someone had scrawled, "Everything hear is roten." It bothered her, the misspellings as much as the message. It was nothing, Erin told herself, the impulsive scribbling of a kid who'd thought it was funny. It made her think of their faces, though. Greg Cannon and Jeremy Grissom. Tony Shifflet with his big slouched shoulders and slow, taunting drawl. And Vinny Briggs, the leader of the group, a wild-eyed kid with a taste for recklessness and violence, as if he'd been born with a swarm of bees in his head that buzzed and stung and flitted their angry little wings and grew crosser every year. Of all the people who had gone missing back then, none of the rotten ones were touched by it. And whether it was irony or the inexplicable will of God or just the way things tended to work, the outcome was the same. Erin's mother was gone, but the Vinny Briggses of this world lived forever.

They turned around and walked back to the truck, and she opened the driver's door for Diesel to jump up into the cab.

"Gonna have to leave you here for a bit," she said, and the dog watched from the bench seat as Erin made her way across the parking lot.

The hospital had been here for decades, but Erin had been only vaguely aware of its existence when she was younger. With its single-story brick exterior, it was not much larger than the veterinary clinic she'd worked at near Boulder. The automatic sliding glass door at the entrance opened as she approached, and she walked to the information desk and smiled at the young woman behind the counter.

"May I help you?" the woman asked. She was wearing a white shirt with a faded red vest. There was a name badge— *K. Anderson,* it read—pinned against her chest.

"I'm here to see my father, David Reece," Erin told her. "He's under the care of Dr. Houseman. I was told he's in the intensive care unit."

"Yes, ma'am. The critical care room, just next to the emergency department. Let me give you a visitor badge and I'll show you the way."

"Thank you," Erin said, peeling the adhesive tag from its backing and sticking it to her shirt.

"It's this way," the woman said. She got up from her chair and led Erin down a narrow hallway with faded yellow walls punctuated by a series of black-and-white photos of Wolf Point at various moments in its history. Erin wondered how far the city dated back. It was the kind of thing she ought to know but didn't, like the birthdays of colleagues or distant cousins. She made a mental note to look it up.

The woman in front of her turned her head. "You're Erin Reece, David Reece's daughter. You used to live here, up until the end of high school, I think."

"Yes," she said, "a long time ago."

"Must be strange coming back. I don't know if you remember me. I'm Katey Perry, or at least I was back then, before I got married. I was a few years ahead of you in school."

Erin searched her memory, a dusty collection of furniture in an attic she hadn't explored since childhood. There were things in there long since forgotten, stacked on top of one another and lost in the shadows. There were things in there that could hurt her if she let them.

"Katey, yes," she said. "I remember."

Do you? Erin asked herself. *Because everything in here is connected. You shouldn't start opening drawers unless you're ready to see it all.*

"I go by Kate now," the woman said, "and my last name's Anderson, although I almost didn't change it, on account of my mother."

"Your mother," she said, and in her mind she could hear one of the drawers sliding open.

"Yes. My mother, Rose. You lost your mother, too. I'm sure you can understand why it was so hard for me to let go."

Erin stopped in the hallway. "Your mother was Rose Perry."

The woman stopped walking and turned around to face her. "That's right," she said, and nodded, like a teacher encouraging her slowest pupil.

"She was the second person to go missing."

Again, Kate nodded. "Her and Curt Hastings, yes. They were the second and third people to disappear that year. But they weren't together that night like some people said. My mom and dad were separated by then, but Curt was married. My mother wasn't having an affair."

Erin frowned. "No. Of course not."

"Well, that's what *some* people said. The kids at school, for instance. They used to tease me about it. Can you *believe* that?

My mother was taken from me, and all they could say were nasty things that weren't true."

"*Who* said that?"

"It doesn't matter. None of them ever amounted to anything."

Everything hear is roten, Erin thought. She flashed to the day she found them down by the quarry, the four of them pinning Robbie Tabaha against the rocks. She hadn't known him that well yet, not the way she would come to know Robbie in the years that followed. But it had seemed to her that four on one was the recourse of cowards, that any one of them would crumble if pulled away from the others.

"Kids can be cruel sometimes," she said.

Kate smiled. It was the kind of smile that people use when there is nothing left to smile about. "Cruel kids become cruel adults," she said. "Most of them anyway." She sighed. "My mother was walking home that night after a shift at Old Town Grill. The police told me that Curt Hastings left his house about twenty minutes later after a fight with his wife. They found his truck the next morning, its front end buried in a snowbank near the railroad tracks east of town. The keys were in the ignition and the diesel engine was still running. He left the driver's door open, as if he only intended to get out for a second and didn't know he wouldn't be coming back."

"But there was no sign of your mother."

She shook her head. "They found the keys to the restaurant lying on the front steps of Assembly of God Church at the intersection of Fallon Street and Fourth Avenue North. It's a long way from where they found Curt's truck. That's how I know they weren't together."

Erin nodded.

"I always felt it was strange for the keys to have ended up

where they did," Kate said. "It was like God reached down and snatched her up but returned the keys later. He dropped them right out of the sky onto the steps of one of his churches to let me know that he was with her. I'm thankful for that. It gives me peace. She's in a good place now where nothing else can hurt her."

Erin placed a hand on her upper arm. "I'm so sorry."

Kate shrugged. "It was a long time ago. It happened to a lot of us. It happened to you, Erin. I understand the pain you must've felt in losing your mother." She turned and started walking again, and Erin followed her down the hall, their footsteps echoing, as if it was more than just the two of them. Erin's eyes turned to the people in the pictures on the walls. Most of them were dead by now, but there were stragglers maybe, with the fading memories of all that had come before.

They turned left and proceeded down another hallway until they came to a man in a police uniform. He was sitting in a chair, reading a copy of the newspaper. "This is Officer Mike Brennan," Kate said. "Mike, this is David Reece's daughter, Erin."

"Ms. Reece," Officer Brennan said, rising from his chair and extending a hand. He was a slim man, slightly taller than Erin, with prominent cheekbones and dark eyes that were set deep into his face. His hair was dark as well, kept short with a bit of scalp peeking through at the sides. Erin shook his hand. There was a door behind him, and she caught a glimpse of an EKG monitor through its small rectangular window.

"I'm going to head back to my desk now," Kate said. "I'll contact Dr. Houseman and let him know you're here. His office is right across the street." She started down the hall, then stopped and turned around. "I know they'll find the person who took my mother and bring him to justice. It's been twenty-two years since she went missing, but I've always believed in that." She hesitated for a moment and glanced at the officer before she looked back at Erin. "Maybe now the tide is turning," she said. "The Bible tells us that the Lord loves the just and will not forsake his faithful ones. But those who bring evil unto the world will be destroyed, and the offspring of the wicked will perish. That's Psalm 37, verse 28. You should look it up sometime. It's one of my favorites."

Erin nodded. "It's important to have faith, and I appreciate what you said about my mother. There were times when I was away that I got to thinking that maybe my father and I were the only ones who still remember her."

"I remember," Kate said. "Welcome home, Erin. I always figured you would find your way back someday."

She gave them a brief smile and walked away, and Erin and Officer Brennan stood there in the hallway, not speaking, as the sound of her footsteps faded down the hall.

"He's doing okay?" Erin asked eventually, turning to the officer.

"I don't know, ma'am. I'm just assigned to sit with him."

"Why is that?" she asked. "Why has a police officer been assigned to watch over my father?"

Officer Brennan shifted his weight from one foot to the other. "Lieutenant Stutzman asked me to give him a call when you got here. I'm sure he can answer all of your questions." He gave her a brief smile, then turned and took a few steps down the hallway.

"I'm allowed to go inside?" she asked.

"Oh yes," he said. "I'm sorry. You must be eager to see him."

She watched the officer for a moment longer. There was a portable radio clipped to his utility belt, but instead of using it, he pulled a cell phone from its leather case and began typing.

Erin stepped forward and opened the door to her father's hospital room. And there he was, lying on a bed with raised side rails. There was a cardiac monitor perched above his head, and its green digital display kept vigilance over her father's vital signs. A bag of saline and a bottle of white milky substance hung from an IV pole to his left. Lines of IV tubing ran through a pump and then snaked their way beneath his gown, just below the collarbone. David's eyes were closed. A breathing tube exited his mouth and was attached to a ventilator. The soft rhythmic sound of the machine filled the room as it shuttled oxygen and carbon dioxide in and out of her father's lungs.

In the corner of the room, a woman rose from her chair as Erin stepped inside. There was a bedstand in front of her and papers were spread out on its surface. She wore blue scrubs, and her blond hair was pulled back into a ponytail. A red stethoscope was draped over her shoulders.

"Hello," Erin said, and she introduced herself before they turned their attention to the man lying on the bed in front of them. "How's he doing?" she asked, and there was a brief silence as the woman reached forward and adjusted the sheets at the foot of the bed.

"Much better than when he first came in," the nurse said. "When he arrived in the ER five days ago, he had a low blood pressure and was having trouble breathing. He was intubated and put on the ventilator almost right away. Dr. Houseman thinks it's pneumonia or maybe influenza. The flu swabs came back negative, but . . . they're not always accurate."

"You've been giving him antibiotics?"

She nodded. "Two of them, plus a drug for influenza. His blood pressure's stabilized, and his oxygen level is better now." She pointed to the monitor. "His heart rate's been a little fast, and he's anemic. He received a blood transfusion three days ago."

"What was his hematocrit?"

The nurse frowned. "Let's see, I've got it in the chart." She turned to the table, shuffled through some papers. "You have some medical background?"

"With animals, not people," Erin said. "I'm a veterinarian."

"Oh, wow. That's great," she said. "It must be hard, seeing animals hurt and sick like that. I had to put my cat to sleep two years ago. Kidney failure. He was sixteen years old."

"I'm sorry."

"One of the saddest decisions I've ever had to make. I don't know how you deal with it on a daily basis."

"Euthanasia is a small part of the job," Erin told her. "We see young and old, sick and healthy. We have a lot of success stories, too."

"Yeah," she said, "good things and bad, just like with people." She picked up a piece of paper. "Here it is. Hemoglobin of 6.2 grams per deciliter and a hematocrit of eighteen percent when he got here."

Erin frowned. "I know the normal hematocrit for cats and dogs. For people, I assume it's . . ."

"Somewhere around forty percent. A little higher for men and a little lower for women."

"So why was my father's red blood cell count so low? Was he bleeding from somewhere?"

She shook her head. "Not that we could figure out. No injuries, and there was no evidence of bleeding from his intestinal tract."

"Eighteen percent," Erin said. "I don't like the sound of that."

"Well, he's up to twenty-five percent after two units of

packed cells. Dr. Houseman thought he might benefit from another unit, but he wanted to discuss it with you first, now that it's not such an emergency."

"Erin? Erin Reece?" a man asked from the doorway.

Erin turned and saw a tall thin figure dressed in slacks and a tan blazer. Like David's nurse, he was wearing a stethoscope around his neck, although his was black, the same color as his hair. The bell of the stethoscope rested against a white shirt and canary-yellow tie, and the top of a pen protruded from his shirt pocket like the head of a prairie dog checking to see if it was safe to leave the protection of the tunnels.

"Mark?" she asked, surprised by how different he looked from the meek and quiet boy she remembered. He was maybe six-four, and he stooped a bit when he took her hand. He still had the cowlick, she noticed, and when he smiled his face looked younger, more like the one she'd envisioned when she spoke to him on the phone.

"My God," he said. "How long's it been?"

"Fifteen years," she said. "I graduated from high school, took a little drive, and just kept on going."

He looked at her, his big hand still wrapped around her fingers. "I wish I could say a lot's happened since then," he said, "but it hasn't. Wolf Point is pretty much the way you left it. Smaller, maybe. Fewer people."

"Where did they go?" she asked, and then immediately regretted the question.

"I don't know," he said, and his smile faded. "They wandered off, I guess. Just like you."

A motor clicked on, followed by the steady whisper of forced air filling a container. Beneath the sheets, something crackled.

"Sequential compression device," the nurse told her. "We call them squeezers. It pumps air into sleeves wrapped around your father's legs. Helps with circulation and prevents blood clots from forming."

Erin nodded, and looked back at Mark. "How bad was it?" she asked. "It sounds like he came pretty close to dying."

The doctor frowned. "He gave us a bit of a scare. One of your father's employees found him lying on the ground next to a trench on his farm. If he hadn't stopped by and found him, if your father hadn't gotten here when he did . . ." He shook his head. "David is a stubborn son of a bitch, and always has been. An underground irrigation pipe on his farm had ruptured. He was trying to tend to it himself while he was in septic shock with a fever of a hundred and five and a blood pressure in the toilet. Most people can't get out of bed when they're that sick. Your father"—he looked at him, lying there beneath the blanket—"was out in the fields in early November trying to fix a water main."

"Dad," she said, shaking her head. She went to the bedside and laid a hand on her father's forearm.

"He's lucky to be alive," Mark said. "The ER crew did a great job, and Shelly here is one of the best nurses we have. You have her to thank more than anyone."

Erin turned to the nurse. "Thank you," she said. "I appreciate your taking such great care of him."

"You're welcome," she said, and looked down at the floor.

"Your father will survive this, barring any unexpected complications. Trinity Hospital has exactly one critical care room, and this is it. Ordinarily, we don't keep critically ill patients here beyond the initial resuscitation. We ship them out to Billings Clinic or to St. Vincent. But in David's case we decided to make an exception, mostly because he was getting better. We expect to take him off the ventilator soon. After that, he'll be moved to a regular hospital bed."

Erin reached down and placed her palm on the back of her father's hand. "I'm sure he'll be happier waking up in Wolf Point."

"And he'll be glad to see you when he does," a man said, and they all turned to the figure standing in the doorway. "Hello, Erin," he said. "I'm Jeff Stutzman. We knew each other growing up."

"Jeff." She stepped forward and shook his hand.

He smiled briefly and looked around the room, his eyes settling on David Reece before he turned his attention back to Erin. "Today you're a popular person," he said. "You have more to discuss with the doctor, I'm sure. Take your time. And when you're done, if it's not too much trouble, I wouldn't mind having a word with you myself." He glanced again at the man lying on the hospital bed. "We can meet at the station, whenever you're ready."

5

LIEUTENANT JEFF STUTZMAN OPENED THE DOOR TO HIS OFFICE and held it for Erin as she stepped inside. "Please, make yourself comfortable," he said. He went to the window, adjusted the wooden blinds to let in as much of the dim afternoon sunlight as the day would allow, then moved around the desk and took a seat.

Erin sat down as well. There wasn't much to the office, just the desk and two chairs on either side. A metal file cabinet stood in the corner. To the left of it, mounted on the wall, was a sign displaying the police department's insignia. It was the same emblem as the shoulder patch on Jeff's uniform, a badge and a wolf in front of a cloudy night sky, the full moon rising in the background. Erin tried to recall if she'd noticed it as a kid, the way the wolf's pupils were directed upward, as if whatever the animal was looking at was standing behind you, looming over your shoulder. It was strange that the town had designed it that way, but maybe not that strange considering its history.

Jeff leaned forward in his chair and rested his forearms on the desk. He had been on the high school football team, she remembered, and his neck and shoulders were thick and well defined beneath the uniform. His hair was cut short, only a few millimeters above the scalp, and his face had retained much of its youthfulness. He glanced toward the window with its plastic slatted blinds, the shadows falling across the room in thin blades of darkness. It was 2:45 P.M., and already the sun was low on the horizon.

"I'm sorry to pull you away from your father's bedside," he said. "It must be difficult for you to see him like that."

"Mark says he's doing better."

"That's good. Thank God for that."

"My father's too stubborn and too independent to lie there for any longer than he needs to. He'll want to get back to his farm as soon as possible."

Jeff nodded. He glanced once more toward the window.

"And yet here I sit," she said, "in the Wolf Point police station, wondering what the hell is going on, and why there's an officer stationed outside of my father's hospital room."

Jeff frowned. He ran the palm of his hand across the desk's lacquered wooden surface. "There's been a . . . complication."

"Yes," she said. "I gathered that. Is he behind on his property tax? Is the bank trying to repossess the place?" She sighed. "He operates on a slim margin, Jeff. Some years are leaner than others. If it's money he needs, I might be able to help him out with that."

The lieutenant shook his head. "It's not money. It's nothing like that."

"What then? He's gotten himself into some sort of trouble?"

"I don't know," he said. "We're at the beginning of it. We're just trying to figure things out . . . here in town and out at the farm."

The farm, she thought, and it was strange how those two simple words evoked such nostalgia and trepidation, sorrow and longing. It was the place of her childhood and a land that defined her father. In the years following her mother's disappearance, Erin found that she could not stand in the kitchen without hearing the soft hum of her mother's voice and the clink of dishes as she washed them in the sink and returned them to the cupboards. It was a place of ghosts, and even when Erin had been living there, it had been hard to shake the feeling that she and her father were among them, wandering the rooms like lost souls in search of a purpose.

The farm was mostly a dairy operation—about a hundred and fifty head of cattle—but David also grew wheat and barley, and had a small alfalfa patch in the rear of the property. His hobby was beekeeping, and he'd set aside an area for vertically stacked hives from which he harvested honey that he sold to the local grocery store. It kept him busy, and the time he spent with Erin when she was younger revolved around the endless tasks and repairs necessary to keep things running. The place was everything to him, drawing his attention in a way that Erin never could, or so it had seemed when she was younger. She resented the farm for that, for the parts of her father it had taken away from her. After her mother was gone, things had only gotten worse.

"Here's what I can tell you," Jeff said, and Erin looked up, realizing that her hands had been balled into fists in her lap.

Jeff leaned back in his chair. It squeaked a bit in the hushed silence of the office.

"At the time he collapsed," he said, "David was working on fixing an underground water pipe that had ruptured. It serviced his irrigation system and spanned about three hundred yards along the back end of the property. There's a long trench there now, one he created to access the pipe. He seems to have isolated the leak and replaced the broken section. That much he did before he was taken to the hospital."

"Okay."

"He has a farmhand, Travis Cooper. I don't know if you know him."

"No," she said. "My father never mentioned him. He must've hired him after I left."

Jeff nodded. "Travis works for David part time. He helps with harvesting and some of the manual labor. He's originally from Illinois and moved west to Wolf Point about five years ago."

Erin listened from the other side of the desk. She tried to imagine where this might be leading.

"A ruptured water pipe causes a lot of trouble," Jeff said. "Finding it was one issue, fixing it another. The trench had to be filled in, but there was also a large section of earth that had become saturated with water and was caving inward."

"A sinkhole."

"Yes," he said, "a sinkhole. It was about fifty feet in diameter."

"Sounds like a mess."

"It was. And . . . well, now it's even worse."

"Why is that?"

"We've been digging," he said, "uncovering as much as possible."

"Why would you do that?" Erin asked. "Let the ground dry out. You can fill it in—"

"We found something," Jeff told her. "Or at least Travis found it, down there in the mud."

Erin sat perfectly still, watching him.

"It was a skeleton," Jeff said, "the remains of a body. I'm sorry to be telling you this, Erin, but we think it's human."

Erin leaned forward in her chair. She fixed her gaze on the surface of the desk. The room faded in and out, the way lights sometimes do when a building's about to lose power. It was actually fake wood, she noticed, some kind of plastic laminate. The overhead light reflected off its shiny surface, the darker lines blending together like tiny strands of rope.

"Erin?"

She looked up.

"I'm not saying your father has anything to do with this. I've known David a long time."

"He killed your brother," she said. Her voice was little more than a whisper.

"An accident. I've made my peace with it."

"He ran him over with the Bronco in the middle of the street."

"It was raining. Kenny ran out in front of the truck. David told the officers he didn't even see him. There was nothing he could've—"

"He'd been drinking."

"Two drinks an hour before at Old Town Grill," Jeff said. "By the time they tested him, the alcohol barely registered in his system. *He wasn't drunk, Erin.* It was the storm more than anything."

"He was convicted, Jeff. As much as I missed him during that time, he deserved to go to prison."

"None of us deserved the things that happened."

They sat there in silence, each of them angry for their own separate reasons.

Jeff leaned forward in his chair. "Listen," he said, "this isn't about that."

Erin couldn't look up at him. She kept her eyes focused on the desk between them, on the way the lines of imitation grain separated and came back together.

"You have an officer," she said, "stationed outside of his hospital room."

"Precautionary," Jeff told her. "David could be a witness. Right now he's in a vulnerable condition. We have a responsibility to protect him."

She looked up. It was strange how things could change so quickly, how the course of your life could be derailed in a single conversation. *They had found something. Down there in the mud.* She kept coming back to that, turning it over in her mind.

"Whatever happened to that body," she said, "you don't think he was respons—"

"No, I don't," he said, and frowned. "But we've uncovered a body. We have to investigate. If you want me to recuse myself from the investigation, I will. David has the right to an unbiased—"

"Who else do you have?"

He thought about it. "Nobody, really. The chief, I guess, or one of the patrol officers." He shrugged. "We're a small department, Erin. Nine officers total. I'm the only one who handles this sort of thing. But that's *our* problem, not yours. I could bring in someone from the state or federal level."

"Someone who doesn't understand Wolf Point," she said. "Someone who wasn't here during the time that all those people went missing."

"Yes," he said. "It would be someone from the outside. There are protocols for situations like this."

She shook her head. "I don't want someone from the outside. I want one of us."

One of us, her mind echoed, and that was the heart of it. She'd been back in Wolf Point for only a few hours, but already she had become *one of them* again, as if they'd been waiting all this time for her to return to them, as if part of her had never really left.

Jeff nodded and laced his fingers in front of him. "This guy

Travis," he said, "he's not from around here. He rents a room from Margery Turner, who says he keeps pretty much to himself. I've listened to his story, and there's something about him that makes me wonder what a guy with no ties to the area is doing here in the first place. People don't move to Wolf Point unless they've got a pretty good reason."

Erin tried to concentrate on what he was saying. She glanced again at the police insignia mounted on the wall behind his desk.

("It was a skeleton, the remains of a body.")

"What did you do with it?" she asked.

"What did we do with what?"

"The body."

"Oh," he said. "The bones were sent to the state crime lab in Missoula. They'll try to determine the cause of death, the identity of the deceased, and how long the remains have been there. They have two medical examiners and perform about three hundred autopsies per year. There's quite a backlog. I'm told the results could take weeks, maybe months."

"And in the meantime?"

"In the meantime, your father needs you," he said. "There's a reasonable explanation for all of this, and I'm confident we'll get to the bottom of it. The important thing right now is for David to recover."

"Yes," Erin said. "I'm sure you'd like the opportunity to question him."

"To be honest," Jeff said, "I just want him to get better." He looked at Erin. "I've known your family for a long time," he said. "You've been away for a while, but this town hasn't changed. We look out for each other. When one of us suffers, we all do. You remember how it was back then."

"Of course."

"And I don't blame you for going away. I can understand why you wanted to be rid of this place."

"I went off to college and got a job in Colorado."

"And never came back," he said, "until now."

"That's right," she told him. "I wanted to be done with it."

"We all did. But the people here haven't forgotten, Erin. The things that happened back then are still part of this community. We carry it inside of us, and a body discovered on your father's farm is going to rekindle a lot of those emotions."

"Who else knows about this?"

He crossed his arms in front of him. "People know. We tried to keep it quiet, but . . ."

"News travels fast in Wolf Point."

"Yeah. And the *Wolf Point Herald News* ran an article."

"So you're sharing details of the investigation with the paper?"

"No," he said. "'Anonymous sources,' they cited. I still don't know who leaked the information."

Erin shook her head. "So everyone knows by now, and you thought you'd warn me."

"I didn't want you to be blindsided."

"And a police officer is watching over my father. Just in case."

He shifted in his chair. "Like I said, it's just a precaution."

Erin nodded. She could hear the hiss of air coming through the heating vent in the far corner. It reminded her of the ventilator, of the noise it made every time it filled David's lungs with the contents of its churning mechanical circuits.

Jeff reached across the desk and touched her forearm. "I'm glad you're here, Erin. I know you'll do everything you can to help us get to the bottom of this."

"Of course."

The lieutenant rose from his chair. He seemed relieved, less somber than he'd been when they first arrived. "I assume you'll be staying in town for a week or two?"

"Is that your way of asking me not to leave?"

He shook his head. "It's my way of saying, 'Welcome home. I hope you decide to stay for a while.'"

Erin stood up and followed him into the hallway. She waited while Jeff pulled a set of keys from his pocket and locked the door to his office.

They left the building, walking around the corner to where Erin had parked her truck. Diesel was waiting for her in the cab of the vehicle, his black nose pressed against the glass.

"I wish your father a speedy recovery," Jeff said. "If you need anything"—he pulled out a card and jotted something on the back—"this is the number to my cell phone. Give me a call anytime."

"Thank you," Erin said, and she tucked the card into her pocket. She opened the truck's door, climbed inside, and started the engine. Diesel turned his body in a tight circle and lay down on the bench seat, his muzzle resting on her thigh. She placed a hand on his head and stroked the coarse fur between his ears as she pulled out onto the street.

The trip back to the hospital took less than ten minutes, but Erin registered none of it, her thoughts sifting through the things Jeff had told her.

("We found something . . . down there in the mud.")

("You remember how it was back then.")

("I'm sorry to be telling you this, Erin, but we think it's human.")

She tried to picture her father, the way he'd been when he was younger. It was a turbulent time for them, and like always, David had sought refuge in the farm. Crops and cattle needed tending. When everything else was falling apart, there was clarity in the work, in the steady unrelenting pace of it. She could picture him digging, his calloused hands wrapped around the wooden handle of a shovel, the muscles of his back bunched with effort.

"What are you doing, Daddy?" she asked aloud in the cab, and Diesel whined and looked up at her.

She kept her foot on the gas, and the truck rolled through the neighborhood. When she passed the homes where her childhood friends once lived, this time she didn't look at them. Instead, she kept her eyes focused on the road ahead. *There is a way through this,* she thought. *I can move forward without going back.*

But the image was with her now, the silhouette of her father working the land, the sound of the shovel scraping the earth, and the hunch of his shoulders as he filled in the dirt.

6

SHE KNEW HIM FROM SCHOOL, BUT THAT WAS IT. ROBBIE TABAHA was the kind of kid who kept to himself, which was a good idea, in Erin's opinion, because he was shy and awkward and different from the rest of them. He was small for his age for one thing, with dark hair that hung in his face and offered him something to hide behind. He sat in the second row, two seats down from Erin, and answered the teacher's questions only when called upon. At recess, he hung out beneath the tree with his brown leather notebook, drawing pictures of things that no one asked about.

Northside Elementary covered grades four through six, and this was the first year at the school for both of them. They'd attended Southside Elementary together from kindergarten through third grade, but he wasn't in her circle of friends and she hadn't paid him much attention. She might not have noticed him now, either, but by the time they got to fourth grade Erin had discovered that some of the kids were turning mean, and Robbie Tabaha seemed to draw their attention like potato salad attracts flies on a hot summer day.

The fifth graders were the worst, she thought, and there were four of them that Erin had learned to watch out for: Greg Cannon, Tony Shifflet, Jeremy Grissom, and Vinny Briggs. Vinny was the nastiest by far, but they traveled in a pack—what she came to think of as the Briggs gang—and to see any one of them heading your way meant the others would be there soon enough.

The problem with Robbie was that he was small and quiet and always by himself. Erin had seen enough nature videos in Ms. Loran's science class to know that those were the ones the predators go for first. Even the most vulnerable creatures know that there's protection in the group, and wandering off by yourself is a good way to get eaten.

It wasn't as bad as it could've been. Teachers kept an eye out for bullying, but the school year was drawing to a close and everyone was getting a bit lazy. Lately, the Briggs gang had discovered that one of them could get the teachers' attention by causing trouble on one side of the schoolyard while the rest of them went after a kid on the other. Erin's father had taught her about wolves—the way they hunt in packs, the way they work together to set up an ambush—and she started to think of Vinny Briggs and his gang as a pack of wolves, always hungry, always drawn to the outsider.

There were no teachers to watch out for them on the weekends, and Erin came across the five of them while riding her bike one afternoon down by the quarry. It was a Saturday afternoon in late May, and she'd ridden into town hoping to catch Meghan Decker or Deirdre McKinney at home and up for something fun. No one had answered when she'd knocked on their doors, however, and there was no one home at Emily Soto's house, either. In her head, she ran through a list of her other friends, checking each of them off by name. Melissa

Perez hadn't been to school on Friday, and her parents' car was gone from the driveway. Erin walked up to the front door anyway, but there was no answer, just the patient silence of a house waiting for the return of its people.

There were others she could've tried, but four strikes was one more than her favorite baseball player, Kirby Puckett, was allowed, and she decided to head out on her own rather than waste what was left of the day.

The quarry was in a remote area west of town, just south of the city landfill. It was a wide hole in the ground about the size of a football field, and the sides were stacked with boulders that kids could climb on. There was a lake at the bottom of it, home to toads and fish and other creatures left to the imagination. During the week the quarry was busy with trucks coming and going, but on the weekend it was quiet, and the sign that read NO TRESPASSING was so battered with rocks and bullet holes that it looked like a half-eaten carcass rotting in the sun.

Erin laid her bike down at the lip of the quarry and descended the sidewall hand over foot, being careful to test the smaller boulders to be sure they wouldn't roll away from her. Two weeks ago, she'd spotted a snake twisting along the surface of the water, and she wanted to see if she could find it again. It was strange how all the animals made it here, how fish could wind up in the middle of a man-made lake as if they'd fallen from the sky or hitchhiked across the plains from the Missouri River. Her father said that people stocked it, that they put fish and other animals here on purpose, but it was hard to shake the image of critters standing along the roadway, hoping to catch a ride.

It was such a big area that at first she didn't see them: the small bronze-skinned boy scrambling across the rocks at the far end of the quarry while the others chased after him. They were yelling, though, the two chasing him, and when Erin's eyes focused on Robbie Tabaha, the first thing she noticed was that he was fast. He moved along the boulders like a stone skipping across water, leaping from one rock to the next without settling on any of them. They couldn't catch him, that much seemed certain, and Erin's initial concern turned to admiration as she watched him move across the terrain.

She hadn't been thinking about wolves, though—the way they hunt in packs, the way they work together to set up an ambush—and Erin felt her stomach dip when Jeremy Grissom appeared along the lip of the quarry ahead of him, cutting off Robbie's escape and hurling a barrage of stones in the boy's direction.

They had him trapped now—two behind and one in front—and Robbie couldn't move as fast with the stones flying around him and his hands raised in front of his face to protect himself.

Jeremy had the aim of someone who'd never thrown a baseball in his life, but he threw enough stones to make some of them count. One of them caught Robbie in the right wrist, and another struck him in the left kneecap. Erin heard a popping sound with the second one, like the snap of bubble gum. Robbie grabbed his knee and cried out in a language she didn't recognize. They repeated it—not exactly as he had said it, but close enough—mocking him.

He'd given up running and crouched instead behind a boulder to shield himself from the attack. Vinny Briggs had been lying in wait at the top of the quarry, but he showed himself now, scrambling across the rocks like the others. There was nowhere for Robbie to go, with the water behind him and the boys closing in from every direction.

He's going to take a beating, she thought, and Erin's stomach turned in her midsection. The only fights she'd seen were on

TV or in the movies. She'd never watched someone get beaten up in real life before, and she realized—too late to turn away from it—that she did not want to see it now.

"*Swim!*" she yelled, and they all stopped for a moment to look in her direction.

It was a horrible idea, both getting involved in this and yelling for Robbie to jump in the water. Her father had warned her not to go swimming in the lake down by the quarry. "They dump all kinds of poisons in it," he'd told her. "It'll make you sick, and there are things beneath the surface—trash and big hunks of metal—that'll cut you or pull you under."

She'd nodded and done as he'd told her. But now she was yelling for Robbie to go in there, and it occurred to her a few seconds later that she didn't even know if Robbie *could* swim. "People have drowned in that lake," her father had told her, and she could suddenly picture them, still in there, with hair like seaweed and fingers that stretched upward through murky water. *Wait! Don't go in there!* she wanted to yell, but Robbie was already waist-deep in the water.

By the time the kids reached the edge he was swimming with long powerful strokes that took him into the center of it. They continued to throw rocks at him, and it was only a matter of time until one of the stones struck him in the head or he just got too tired to make it back.

He can swim to the other side, she thought, but the boys were fanning out now, circling the water's edge in an attempt to surround him. Robbie was a good swimmer, but he wouldn't make it, not before Vinny Briggs got to the other side. He'd be stuck in the middle, and it was Erin's fault that he was out there. She felt the guilt of it, knowing she had made things worse instead of better. He couldn't tread water forever. Eventually he'd be forced to swim to shore.

The rocks got bigger, and they made a game of it, seeing how close they could get to him. Greg Cannon launched a big one that came up short, and he followed that with a smaller one that sailed over Robbie's head. Vinny took to skipping the stones along the surface, and Robbie had to duck a few of them, his head dipping below the water for several seconds at a time.

"Hey, Vinny, it's like Whac-A-Mole," Tony Shifflet called out from the other side of the lake, and they all laughed as Robbie continued to duck and dodge the projectiles.

If it had only been a standoff, she could've biked into town and gotten help from the first adult she could find. It was worse than a standoff, though. It was a drowning in progress. And because Erin was at least partially to blame for this, she couldn't leave him and couldn't stay here and watch as they tried to kill him. She could hear her father's voice, telling her that people had drowned in this lake and that there were things below the surface that could pull you under. Again, she could picture them, the bodies or maybe just the souls of those who had died here, reaching upward with arms covered with algae, their legs trapped beneath something heavy in the muck.

They will get him, she thought, and it wasn't the boys she was afraid of anymore but something much worse. He would be dead because Erin had told him to go out there.

She picked up a rock and threw it. The stone arced through the air and landed at Vinny's feet. He looked back at her, just as she released another one that flew low and fast toward its target, covering the distance in just over a second.

The rock struck him in the left shoulder, and Vinny staggered backward with a look of surprise on his face, his right hand going to the place where the stone had connected with the flesh.

"That was a mistake—" he started to say, but Erin unleashed another one, and this one struck him directly in the forehead.

He took two steps backward, and on the second step the heel of his shoe got snagged on a boulder and he plopped down in the water. She heard his teeth snap shut, and saw a trickle of blood running from his lower lip that mixed with the blood already flowing from his forehead.

They all watched him to see what would happen next, and Vinny sat there for about ten seconds, as if trying to decide whether it was even worth getting up again. Erin stood there and watched him, and for a brief moment it seemed that maybe that was the end of it. But she'd forgotten what she was dealing with, the way wolves use distraction to set up the ambush, and Erin didn't notice that Jeremy Grissom was circling around until he was almost behind her.

Vinny got to his feet and smiled. There was blood on his teeth and his hair was sticking up in the middle. His eyes were wild and gleeful, as if he'd just gotten an electric shock and decided that he liked it. Erin broke right and scrambled up the hill. She could hear them coming after her: the quick sound of breathing; the chatter of loose pebbles as tennis shoes slapped against the rocks. She did not know what was happening with Robbie Tabaha, but there was no time to look back now.

Erin made it to the lip of the quarry and sprinted for her bicycle. She was not as fast as Robbie, and she knew that Vinny and Jeremy were close behind her. *If they catch me before I get to the bike . . .* she thought, but she didn't finish that thought because all the possibilities were bad ones.

Her Schwinn was lying on its side in the dirt. She scooped it up, pointed it in the right direction, and ran alongside it for a few steps before throwing herself onto the seat. Her right foot missed the pedal, and the bike swerved and almost toppled before she regained control. Then she was pedaling as hard as she could, down the dirt road that headed back into town.

"*Go back and get him!*" she heard Vinny yell, and that was bad news for Robbie because there was nothing she could do to help him now.

Erin chanced a look over her left shoulder. The road was full of dust, swirling in the air and blocking her view of what was behind it. *There could be no one,* she thought, and that was a bad thing because it meant that they had all turned back for Robbie.

She pedaled hard, picking up speed on the gradual descent. When she got into town, she would find a grown-up to come back with her. Robbie was a good swimmer. He could fend them off in the meantime.

"*Rrrrrrrr . . .*"

Erin looked back, just as Vinny Briggs exploded through the dust on his own bike. He was leaning forward over the handlebars, his hair pushed back by the wind but still sticking up in the center, where it was clumped and matted with blood. He was gritting his teeth, and the sound coming out of him was more like a growl than anything else. Vinny bore down on her, legs pumping as he stood up on the pedals for maximum speed. He was about fifty yards back but gaining rapidly, and it was sheer terror more than any physical ability that forced Erin to pedal faster.

Gonna catch me, gonna catch me, she thought, and she scanned the road in front of her, hoping for an approaching truck or the intersection where Eleventh Avenue met Cascade Street and the closest neighborhood began.

There was nothing that she could see, only the empty road stretched in front of her and the sound of their tires on the dirt.

Erin's thighs burned as she pedaled. There was sweat in her

eyes, and her palms were slippery on the handlebars. *Why did I get involved in this?* she asked herself, but she couldn't remember the details now, and it didn't really matter. Vinny Briggs was going to catch her. He was going to smash her face into the ground and kick her in the ribs until all of them were broken. He would pop her eyes out with his thumbs. Maybe he would drag her by the hair back to the lake, where he would introduce her to all those other people whose bodies were still trapped along the bottom, their hair like seaweed and arms stretched upward toward the surface.

". . . *rrrrRRRRRRRR* . . ."

Erin glanced over her left shoulder and he was right behind her, his lips pulled back to show two rows of slanted teeth. It was like looking into the grille of a big-rig truck, the massive chassis bearing down on her. "*Gonna . . . kill you,*" he said, and Erin believed it. Vinny Briggs was going to kill her, and it didn't matter if he tossed her in the lake when he was finished. *It'll be better that way,* she thought. Her mom shouldn't have to see the results of the things he was about to do to her.

"Whoooooo-hooooo!"

She blinked away the dust, and there were two of them now, only, one of them was smaller, with dark hair that hung in his eyes, giving him something to hide behind.

"*You!*" Vinny said. His eyes were wide, and his mouth hung open as he turned his face to the left to study the boy riding next to him.

"Hello, jackass," the boy said, and he smiled, as if the two of them were the best of friends and hadn't seen each other in a very long time.

Fast, Erin thought. *He got out of the lake, made it to his bike, and somehow managed to catch up with us.* Had she ever seen anyone this fast? Had she ever been happier to see anyone in her life?

"I'll . . . I'll kill the both of you," Vinny said, but Robbie's smile never changed. And they rode that way for a couple of seconds—Erin in front, looking back, and the two of them side by side and close behind her.

Don't stop pedaling, she told herself, but she was slowing down, waiting for the next thing to happen.

"I brought you something," Robbie said, and he let go of his right handlebar for a second and tossed it to Vinny.

It was a plain old stone like all the rest of them, half the size of Robbie's fist. Erin followed its arc with her eyes as it passed from one boy to the next, its smooth surface glinting in the sun.

Vinny let go of the handlebar with his left hand as he reached out to catch it. He should've ignored it, Erin thought later, and let it drop to the ground. But it was the most natural thing in the world, catching something that was tossed to you. The stone slapped into the palm of his hand just as Robbie reached out with his foot and gave him a hard shove to the right.

There was no stopping it. Vinny realized what was happening too late to do anything to save himself. His bike swerved once as he tried to correct. Then he was onto the shoulder and into the rocks, and the front tire turned sideways as he flew over the handlebars, taking the bicycle with him.

Erin heard him go down behind her: the clatter of flesh, metal, and bone. For a moment she actually felt sorry for him, but there was nothing to do but ride like the wind, because if Vinny got up from that, or if one of his buddies caught up with them, Vinny really would kill the both of them for sure.

She rode with Robbie around the curve of Eleventh Avenue, past West Cascade Street, and into the neighborhood. They both lived in the agricultural section east of town, and they rode in silence for another twenty minutes until they pulled up in front of his house, a ranch-style home with white siding on a dirt road between Highway 2 and the railroad tracks.

"Thanks for helping me," he said as he got off his bike and dropped it in the grass.

Erin nodded. "You helped me, too."

Robbie looked down and toed his back tire with a sock that was coated in dirt and still soaked from the lake.

"Where's your shoe?" she asked.

"I lost one of them in the water."

Erin laughed and shook her head.

"What?" Robbie asked, and he put his hands on his hips, tired of being laughed at.

"It's just that . . . you had only one shoe," she said, "and you caught up with us anyway."

Robbie wiggled his toes. "That's the one I kicked him with," he said. He glanced up at her, and suddenly they were both laughing.

"Revenge of the sloppy sock," Erin said, and she went to her knees and rolled in the grass.

Robbie lowered his voice to sound like Vinny. "It was the last thing I saw before I met my maker."

Robbie's mother opened the front screen door and looked out at the two of them.

"Hi, Mom," he said.

She gave them a perplexed smile and waved. "You have a friend," she said, and it was almost a question. Thinking back on it later, Erin wondered if maybe she was his *first* friend, or at least the first one he'd ever brought to the house, and it was a confusing thing to think about because the idea made her happy and sad at the same time.

"Does your friend want to stay for dinner?" Mrs. Tabaha asked, although it wouldn't be time for dinner for another couple of hours.

"Thank you," Erin said, "but I should be getting home."

Robbie's mother nodded. "Yes, of course," she said. "It was nice to meet you . . ."

"Erin," Robbie told her. "This is Erin Reece, Mom. We go to school together."

"Oh," she said, and her hand went to her mouth before she could stop herself. "Your mother . . . lives up the way a bit."

"Yes, ma'am."

"On the farm off Highway 13 and Route 1."

Erin nodded. *And my father, too,* she wanted to say. Only, her father didn't live with them these days. He was living somewhere else for a while because of something that had happened that he couldn't take back.

Mrs. Tabaha glanced at her son. "You're a mess," she said. "You should come in and get cleaned up a bit."

"I'll see you later," he said, turning to Erin. He lowered his voice to a whisper. "My dad's gonna whoop my ass when he finds out about the shoe."

"Come on, then," his mother said, and she stood in the doorway, looking past them at the yard.

"I'll come back tomorrow," Erin told him, but she suddenly wondered if she really would. Maybe it was better for Robbie to steer clear of a girl whose father was locked away in prison. Maybe it was better if Erin wasn't friends with someone who'd gotten her in trouble with Vinny Briggs.

She got back on her bike and rode the rest of the way home, thinking of all the ways that this could end for them. "My dad's gonna whoop my ass when he finds out about the shoe," Robbie had told her, and she thought about that most of all, how there had always been a beating in store for him, no matter the outcome.

7

(March 1992)

"WAKE UP. IT'S TIME."

Erin sat up in bed. She rubbed her face with the palm of her hand. The skin of her left cheek was soft and warm from the pillow, the traces of a dream still shifting in her head. The bedroom was dark, but there was light coming from the hallway behind him. She could see the outline of her father standing in the doorway, his broad shoulders spanning the width of the doorframe, a tuft of uncombed hair silhouetted by the light. He took a step backward into the hall. He was wearing jeans and the same tan thermal long-sleeved shirt that he'd worn earlier that day, the neckline a shade darker than the rest of his shirt. It was strange to see him this way, with his hair uncombed, dressed in the previous day's clothing. Her father was an early riser, up by 4:15 at the latest—showered, shaved, and out the door before the first light of day.

In the hallway now, he looked at her for a moment before turning to go. "Get dressed," he said. "Meet me in the barn."

Erin brushed away a crust of sleep from the corner of her right eye. She pulled back the covers, swiveled her body until her legs were free of the sheets, and dangled them over the side of the bed, the soles of her feet two inches above the dark wood of the bedroom floor. An area rug covered the center section of the room, but it had been worn down and flattened over the years until it was almost as hard as the floor itself. She stood up, the sole of her left foot pressing against the cool wood while her right foot settled upon the rug. She grabbed jeans and a T-shirt from her dresser drawer, a flannel button-down from the closet, and dressed quickly, sensing the urgency with which her father had awoken her.

It's time, he'd said. But time for what? Her father preferred to work by himself in the morning, seldom waking her for milking. Her usual chores began at six, but her internal clock told her it was much earlier than that. She ran through the other possibilities in her head. Her thoughts were sluggish and muddled with sleep. They clung to her, thick and sloppy, like the mud along the riverbank that sucked at her shoes when she got too close to the water's edge.

Erin's baseball cap was hanging on the bedpost. She looked at it but decided she didn't need it. There was work to be done, and all work was the same in the middle of the night, a problem that needed to be dealt with. *It's time,* she thought again, and now the specifics seemed less important. Whatever it was, she and her father would handle it. On the farm, it was always time for something.

Her mother was in the kitchen making coffee, and it was strange to see her doing it in the middle of the night. There was a warm, familiar scent to it, though, an aroma that made Erin want to linger, to sit in a chair and watch as she set out the mugs and the small ceramic bowl of sugar. At almost seven years old, Erin didn't much care for the taste of coffee, but she liked the smell of it, the way her mother would hum to herself while she set the table: a soft melody from a song with no name. The notes expanded and contracted. They followed Helen Reece around the room like a purple ribbon that unfurled behind her and rippled in the morning sunlight.

There was no sunlight coming through the kitchen window now. Beyond the panes, Erin could see only the blackness of night and a ring of frost that had formed along the exterior edges of the glass. She looked up at the clock mounted on the wall, saw it was 2:35, a time with little context and no particular meaning. Erin turned her head and looked out the window again, the darkness like an empty chalkboard waiting to be filled.

"What's happening?" she asked. Her coat was hanging from the back of a chair at the table. She slipped it on, but left the front of it unzipped, the way her father did on early spring mornings, when the temperature could go from freezing to fifty degrees in the space of an hour.

Her mother took a step forward and wrapped her arms around her. She kissed the top of Erin's head and released her hair from under the collar of the jacket. "Miss Pepper is calving," she said. "Your father is already in the barn. You should get out there and help him."

Miss Pepper. Calving. The words made her stomach lift and fall, the way it did when she swung high on the tire that hung from the limb of the oak outside. Erin was awake now. The two-year-old heifer had been born on Erin's fifth birthday. She had been there for the delivery, helped her father feed the newborn calf, and tended to Miss Pepper—a name she had given her because of the speckles of black around her mouth and nose—in the small plastic hutch where the calf had lived for the first eight weeks of its life.

"Why do we take her away from her mother?" Erin had

asked, and her father had explained that it was the best way to keep track of Miss Pepper's health during the initial two months of life.

"Their bodies and immune systems are weak," he said. "If one of the calves gets sick, we don't want it to spread to the others."

"What's in a moon system?"

"What?"

"A moon system. Why don't we want it to spread to the others?"

Her father smiled. "Immune system," he corrected her. "It's part of the body that fights off sickness. When calves are born, their immune systems aren't strong enough to protect them. If they get sick, they can die. We don't want that. We want Miss Pepper to grow up to become a happy and healthy cow like her mother."

"But doesn't her mother miss her baby?"

Her father thought about this. "I don't know," he said, "because I'm not a cow. But . . . I don't think so." He looked toward the pasture. "People assume that humans and animals think in the same way. But cows and people are very different."

"*How* are they different?"

"In all sorts of ways," he said. "Cows spend a lot of time chewing their cud." He looked at her and scrunched up his nose. "Does that sound fun to you?"

"Maybe," she said. "I never tried it."

Her father laughed. "That's because you're not a cow."

She was quiet for a moment. "It doesn't matter. I still think they miss their babies."

"Maybe they do," he said, and he lowered himself to one knee and put a hand on the top of her shoulder. "We don't separate them to be mean," he said. "We separate them because we're responsible for their well-being. We think it's best for the health of the calf."

She looked back at him and nodded.

"Miss Pepper will be joining the herd in a few months," he continued. "She'll get to see her mother then." He paused and studied his daughter. "But . . . Miss Pepper is *your* calf now. She's your responsibility. If you think it's best to put her with the adults, then that's what you should do."

Erin thought it over. In the end, she decided on the hutch. It was warm in the small plastic shed, warmer than it was in the open pasture. She hand-fed Miss Pepper colostrum at birth, held the bottles of milk for her to suckle twice a day until she completely transitioned to the calf starter meal. Erin's father taught her to watch for scours, loose stools that could herald infection and rapid dehydration in a young calf. They vaccinated Miss Pepper against clostridial diseases and common respiratory ailments. At eight weeks, she was moved to a pen with other calves her age, and eventually she joined her mother in the herd, just as Erin's father had promised.

Now, two years later, Miss Pepper was calving. For nine and a half months, Erin had imagined what the moment would be like, to watch Miss Pepper—*her* cow—give birth to a baby of her own. And although she had witnessed lots of deliveries on the farm, somehow *this* was different, something new and scary and exciting all at the same time. "She's getting close," her father had told her two weeks ago, studying the heifer as she grazed with the others. But *close* wasn't the same as *now,* and the moment had snuck up on Erin and caught her by surprise in the middle of the night.

But maybe I've missed it already, Erin thought as she hurried across the open field, crunching the frozen grass beneath the rubber soles of her boots. She stumbled in her haste and took a few lurching steps forward until she regained her balance, the coldness of the night air slicing into her lungs, pressing itself against the naked skin of her face. She moved faster, breaking into a run. The barn was another fifty yards away, past the chopping block and the silent bulk of the tractor, past the tire swing that hung silent and lifeless from the lowest branch of the oak where her father still pushed her when he had the time.

At first the lever on the metal handle of the barn door wouldn't budge when she pressed down on it with her thumb. She grasped the handle with both hands and tugged until the lever loosened in its catch. A moment later, the door opened, revealing cones of light from the overhead lamps, an animal on its side, Erin's father kneeling beside it.

"Come in and close the door," he said, not bothering to look back at her. "Take off your jacket and get over here."

Erin closed the door behind her. It was warmer in the barn than it was outside, but not by much. She shucked off her coat, went to her father's side, and squatted down next to him.

"Miss Pepper wants to do this lying down," he said. "What's wrong with the way she's lying?"

Erin looked at her cow. Miss Pepper was pregnant, her sides bulging outward. The heifer turned her head sideways to look back at her, and Erin put a hand on her warm flank. The straw behind the cow was brown and wet.

"Her water broke," she said. It was the only unusual thing she noticed.

"About an hour ago," her father replied. "What else do you notice?"

Erin pressed her lips together, concentrating.

"It's not something small," he told her. "It's something obvious."

"She's . . . lying on her right side."

"What's wrong with that?"

"It's harder for Miss Pepper to deliver her calf."

"Why?"

"The rumen is on the left," she said. "When she lies on her right side, it presses down on the calf. It makes it harder for the calf to fit through the birth canal."

"So what do we need to do?"

"Turn her."

"How are we going to do that?"

Erin stood up and walked around to the other side. She tucked Miss Pepper's rear legs forward, keeping them close to the body. "Now we have to push," she said.

David Reece shook his head. "Push yourself. This is your cow. You're going to do this."

Erin circled back around. She put her hands on Miss Pepper's right flank, dug her boots into the loose hay as best she could, and gave her a shove. The hay shifted beneath her. Her feet slid backward, away from the cow, and she tumbled to the ground.

"Get up. Stop wasting time."

Erin tried again, putting everything she had into it. The cow was heavy, more weight than she could move herself.

"I . . . can't," she grunted. "I'm not . . . strong enough."

"It's not about being strong, it's about knowing what you're doing. You've got to get lower. Put your hands on the side of her pelvic bone, not up by her backbone. That's right," he said as Erin adjusted her position. "Give her a good shove. Tell her she's gotta help you if she wants to get this baby out."

"Come on, Miss Pepper," Erin said. Her voice was high-pitched and fluttery. The sound of it embarrassed her in front of her father. She cleared her throat, tried to sound tougher.

"Help me get you turned over, girl. We've gotta get you in the right position if you want this baby out."

Erin pushed hard, and when she went to her knees she kept pushing, putting the side of her head against the cow's flank and driving forward with her shoulder. Miss Pepper shifted and swatted Erin in the face with her tail.

"Don't let up now. You've almost got her."

The weight of the cow was moving away from her, and all at once Miss Pepper was on her left side, not lying flat exactly but sort of propped up with the bulk of her weight shifted to the left.

"That's it. Get the back legs away from her belly. Good." He turned and walked a short distance away, sat down on a bale of hay, and motioned for her to come over and join him.

"What's next?" he asked.

"Now the calf comes out."

"How long should it take for us to see something?"

"Not long. Half an hour, I guess."

"Maybe," he said, "but heifers can take longer. It could be another hour or two. We'll give her some time and see how things go."

He leaned backward and put his back against the wall. Erin sat on the hay bale and kicked her feet, her heels softly thumping against the hay.

"Quiet now. Let her concentrate."

Erin stopped kicking. She looked down at her father's hands, where the dark veins coursed beneath the skin. Her own hands were small by comparison, the skin smooth and hairless and a little pink from the cold. She turned them over and searched for a hint of the veins that stood out so prominently on those of her father. There was nothing that she could see, the resemblance either buried deep inside of her or lost completely. She tapped the hay again with the heel of her boot, then reminded herself that she was supposed to be quiet.

It was hard to know how long they sat that way, neither of them talking. There was no clock in the barn, no way to mark the passage of time except for the sound of their breathing and the rustle of hay as Miss Pepper nuzzled the ground, just like she would do to the baby when it finally emerged.

At some point, Miss Pepper began pushing. Her body tensed with the effort, her sides moving inward. The first few contractions were brief and spaced apart by long intervals, but they eventually became more regular, the time between them shortening.

"Pretty soon now," her father whispered, and Erin watched for the glistening sac, the appearance of hooves that would herald the impending birth of the calf.

Miss Pepper continued to labor, the contractions coming once a minute, a short enough span for Erin to count out the seconds in her head. The cow was quiet through all of this, not mooing or bellowing. At most, a soft grunt accompanied some of her contractions, the noise a person might make when lifting something heavy.

Erin had heard descriptions of human childbirth, the way women screamed and suffered terrible pain when the baby was coming. Her friend Deirdre McKinney said that *her* mother told her it was the worst pain she had ever experienced, and it lasted for *eighteen hours*. That was enough for Erin to know that she never wanted children of her own. In comparison, having a baby didn't seem too uncomfortable for Miss Pepper, and she thought again of her father telling her that cows and people were very different, that they probably didn't see things in the same way.

"Something's wrong. We'd better check her."

Erin straightened up, the pace of her heart quickening. She

watched her father walk across the barn to a small box that was sitting on a shelf against the wall. He pulled out four disposable shoulder-length gloves, walked back over to where Erin was now standing, and handed two of them to his daughter. "Put these on," he said, and he applied some lubricant to the clear plastic sleeves.

The gloves were too big for Erin's hands. Her fingers moved freely, the plastic enveloping her hands like mittens, the extra material bunching around her upper arm and shoulder.

"She's labored long enough. We should be seeing something by now," he said. "You'll have to reach in and see if you can feel the calf."

"I don't know how to do that."

"I'll show you," he said. He walked over to Miss Pepper and got down on his knees behind her. Erin followed, her heart thudding like a tom-tom in her throat.

"What part will you be feeling for?" he asked. "What part comes first?"

"The front legs," she said, "with the head just above them."

"Right," he said. "Now reach in there and tell me what you feel. It's important to know if the calf is in the right position."

Erin hesitated, her hand across her chest. "Go," her father told her, and she reached inside, feeling the slick warmth of the cow's body wrap itself around her.

"What do you feel?" he asked, but she couldn't feel anything—or rather, everything felt the same, like a vat of warm jelly, with nothing recognizable to grab on to.

"If the forelimbs aren't right there, you'll have to go deeper. Go as far as you need to go."

She pushed her arm in deeper, turned her body sideways as if she was kneeling at a fence and reaching past the posts for an object just beyond her grasp.

"Anything?" he asked, and then she felt it: the broad surface of something firm and unyielding. Was it the head or the back end of the calf? It was hard to tell. And where were the legs? She moved her hand around, tried to feel everything about it. She felt the jut of bone—*maybe a hip bone,* she thought—then followed it down to what felt like a limb lying along the floor of the birth canal. She moved her hand over, found the other one: two limbs extending toward her.

"I found the legs," she said, "but I can't feel the head. I think . . . I think maybe it's breech."

"Maybe it is," he said. "Do they feel like front legs or back legs?"

"I can't tell."

"Can you feel the hock?"

She followed the course of one of the limbs with her fingers. "I don't . . . think so."

"Okay," he said, "let me see what I can feel."

She pulled her arm out and stepped to the side. Her father reached in and felt around for a moment. "Front legs," he said. "There's no hock, and the hooves are facing down." He frowned. "I don't feel the head, either," he said, "but it's not breech."

She watched his face for clues as to what this could mean. His expression was distant, his gaze on the far wall as he worked.

"I can feel an ear," he said. "It's a head-back dystocia. The calf's head is turned sideways and trapped against the bones of her mother's pelvis. What you were feeling earlier was the side of its neck."

Erin stood there, shifting her weight back and forth from one foot to the other. "Miss Pepper can still deliver her baby, right?"

"Maybe," he said, "but it's gonna be tough. A head-back

dystocia is one of the hardest ones to correct. And I have to warn you. Calves in this position are often dead."

"Not Miss Pepper's baby. Not *this* one," Erin told him, but her father wasn't listening. Instead, he had changed arms, reaching in with his left so that his back was toward her. She didn't like that, needed to see his face, and so she circled around to the other side, put a hand on Miss Pepper's flank as he worked.

"It's going to be okay, Daddy. You're going to get this calf out."

"I don't know," he said. He looked worried, and maybe even a little scared. It was a look she hadn't seen on his face before, the realization that things were going badly and that there might not be anything he could do to stop it. She felt her stomach lift and fall, like she was back on the tire swing, the air buffeting her ears as the tree's limb creaked but held fast above her.

Her father gritted his teeth and sank his arm deeper into the cow. Miss Pepper swung her head around and tried to shift her body away from him.

"It's okay, girl," Erin whispered. "We're going to help you." But she wasn't sure if they *could* help her, and Erin had only a vague and horrible idea of what would happen to Miss Pepper and her calf if they couldn't.

"You've got to . . . hook the lip . . . or the eye socket with your finger."

"Not the eye, Daddy, not the eye."

"It's okay," he said. "It doesn't hurt them." Part of the left side of his chest was in the cow now, as if he might suddenly be swallowed whole. He scrunched up his face. "I've got it," he said. "I've got a finger inside the corner of its mouth. Now I've got to push the body back in, to make room for the head while I try to swing it around."

Both of his arms were inside the cow now, and he was

sweating, the muscles of his shoulders working as he tried to get the calf facing in the right direction. Erin tried not to think of what he had told her, that calves in this position are often dead. Instead, she moved to the front end of her cow and told Miss Pepper that everything was going to be okay, that her baby would be out soon. "My dad can handle this," she told her. "He knows what to do." And she wasn't just reassuring Miss Pepper but was reminding herself. There was no situation that her father couldn't handle. There was nothing broken that he was unable to fix.

"There," he said. "The head's . . . facing in the right direction."

Erin looked back at him. He was breathing hard, the sweat rolling down his face in large droplets that collected along the angle of his jaw like birds on a telephone wire. The front of his shirt was streaked with blood and grime, and it was hard to tell where the shoulder gloves ended and the rest of him began.

"Bring me the calving chains," he said. "Let's get this calf delivered."

Erin ran to the wall where the chains were hanging. She brought them over and held them out to her father.

"Reach in there and put them on the forelimbs," he told her, "one loop above and one loop below the fetlock."

She was still wearing her gloves, but the excess plastic got caught up in the metal links as she tried to manipulate them. She hung the two thirty-inch chains around her neck like a pair of stethoscopes, pulled off her gloves, and made a loop at the end of one of the chains by threading it through the large end link. She reached into Miss Pepper with the loop of chain, found the calf's left front leg, and slid the loop over it, cinching it down above the joint. With her hand still inside the cow, she made another loop that she slid over the limb, snugging it down below the joint. She repeated the process with the other chain, looping it around the right forelimb.

"Good," he said. "Now wait until she has another contraction before you pull. If you just start pulling, you're going to tear her uterus. She could bleed to death or die of infection."

Erin wrapped the chains around her hands and waited. It seemed to her that the contractions had slowed, or maybe even stopped, while her father was trying to get the calf facing in the right direction. She tensed her muscles, readying herself, but nothing happened. The minutes ticked by in her head. "What if she doesn't have anoth—"

"Okay, *pull!*" he said. "Here's the next contraction."

Erin pulled, the muscles of her arms and back tightening as she dug into the earth with her heels.

"*Good. There are the front hooves.*"

Erin kept pulling, putting everything she had into it.

Her father put a hand on her shoulder. "Stop," he said. "The contraction's over."

Erin rested, the chains going slack.

Her father put a finger under her chin and tilted her head upward until she was looking him in the eyes. His face looked tired but proud, satisfied with the work that they had done. "You've almost got this calf delivered," he said. "Whether it's alive or dead, we did the best we could. It's in God's hands now. We've got to let him take it from here."

Erin nodded. She looked at the hooves protruding from its mother and promised herself she wouldn't cry, no matter what. Cows and people were very different. If the calf was dead, they would bury it. She would stand next to her father and fill in the dirt. This was night work, and all work was the same in the middle of the night, a problem that needed to be dealt with.

Miss Pepper mooed, a long and tapered sound that receded

into the night. When the final contraction came, Erin was ready. She pulled hard and brought the calf into the world for as much time as God would allow. As it turned out, the calf was alive, and Erin sat with her father on the bale of hay and watched as Miss Pepper nuzzled the newborn and coaxed it to stand.

"You did good," he told her on the short walk back to the house. "Let's give them some time to say hello to each other."

"Okay," she said, and after a shower and an early breakfast, they returned to the barn and sat for a while on a bale of hay, watching Miss Pepper and the new life she'd delivered. Sunrise was more than an hour away, and Erin rested her head against the side of her father's chest until eventually she fell asleep.

In her dream, things turned out differently. She left the house and crossed the yard in search of her father, but when she got to the barn, the place was empty. The animals shifted restlessly in the darkened fields as she passed, and Erin walked her father's farm until she found him digging a hole at the rear of the property. The body of the calf lay lifeless on the ground beside him. "We did the best we could," he told her. "It's in God's hands now. We've got to let him take it from here."

Erin awoke with a start to find herself alone on the hay—her father, the calf, and its mother all gone—with morning sunlight spilling through the open doorway.

8

MARK HOUSEMAN RAN HIS MEDICAL PRACTICE FROM AN OFFICE ON the north end of town, just across from the hospital. His father, Bruce Houseman, had been Erin's doctor growing up. Except for breaking her arm at the age of seven, she'd been a healthy kid, more or less. She remembered the office, though, the anxiety she felt every time her mother dragged her here for a routine physical or childhood immunizations. The sign out front hadn't changed, she noticed: the white background with brown lettering, the paint faded and flaking now, but still holding up after all these years. HOUSEMAN FAMILY PRACTICE, it read, and it occurred to Erin that the name could be interpreted both ways, as a general family practice but also as a business run by the family, passed down from father to son. If Mark had children of his own, maybe one of them would step into the role of small-town physician someday. If so, what would their father tell them of the times that came before, of the things that still lingered in the town's collective consciousness? People had gone missing, torn away from their families in broad daylight and in the small hours of the night. She could picture them, names and faces that rose to the surface from the dark waters of her memory. Angela Finley. Marian Montgomery. Rose Perry. Helen Reece.

No, Erin thought as she nosed the Chevy into a space in the small parking lot. *There are some things that shouldn't be passed on from generation to generation. There are some things that need to be over.*

The afternoon had turned cold. Her suitcase was in the passenger footwell. She opened it and pulled out a jacket before taking Diesel for another walk and returning him to the cab of the truck. A bell jingled as she pushed open the front door of the medical office and stepped into the reception area. It was much the way she remembered—the sterile scent, a line of chairs against the wall to her right. A woman was sitting in one of them, reading a magazine. She looked up briefly when Erin entered, smiled, and went back to her article. Another woman sat behind the receptionist's desk, her eyes on the paperwork in front of her. Dim light spilled through a window to Erin's right, and the blinds organized it into scalloped rows of tombstones on the floor. She didn't recognize the furniture, couldn't recall if these were the *same* chairs she and her mother had sat in when she was a child. Most likely they weren't. Two decades was a long time. Things wore out and needed to be replaced. She wondered who had cared for the place during all those years, whether Mark's mother still mopped the floors at night the way she'd done for her husband, or whether it was Mark himself, closing up the office at the end of each day and getting down on his hands and knees to scrub at the spots that never seemed to come clean.

"May I help you?" the receptionist asked, and Erin looked up, realizing she'd been staring at the floor, at a small discoloration in the linoleum near the coatrack.

"Yes," she said. "I'm here to see Dr. Houseman."

"Do you have an appointment?"

"No, I . . . I'm Erin Reece. My father, David Reece, is a patient of Dr. Houseman's. I spoke with the doctor earlier today in the hospital."

"And you need to speak with him again?"

"Yes, please. I had to . . . attend to some other business. He asked me to come by the office when I was finished."

The woman nodded. "He's seeing a patient right now," she said. "If you want to have a seat, I'll let him know you're here."

"Thank you," Erin said. She crossed the room and sat down in one of the chairs. Someone had left a copy of *National Geographic* lying on the seat next to her. She picked it up and turned it over in her hands.

"You're Erin Reece."

She looked up. The woman to her right was studying her.

"Excuse me?"

"You're Erin Reece, David Reece's daughter. Isn't that what you said?"

"Yes," she replied, getting a better look at the woman's face. She appeared vaguely familiar, but the specifics were fragmented and difficult to recall, like a dream that scatters in the morning light.

"I'm Betty Doyle," the woman said. "From the Roosevelt County Library. Or at least I *did* work there around the time when you were growing up. I'm retired now, but I still volunteer for the children's reading hour on Tuesdays and Thursdays."

Erin smiled. "It's good to see you."

"You don't remember me, I can tell," she said. "And that's fair enough. Truth is, I didn't recognize you, either, not until I heard you say your name. But Erin Reece, now that's a name

I remember. You used to come in with your mother. She was an avid reader. The books she'd check out were fiction mostly: mysteries, thrillers, romance . . . even horror." She made a face. "At least that's what I remember."

"She read to me sometimes. She could get lost in a story." Erin pictured it in her memory, the stacks of books her mother used to keep on her bedroom nightstand. Erin had asked her once how many of them she was reading, to which her mother had responded, "All of them."

"But how can you read *all of them* at the same time?" she'd asked her mom.

Helen smiled. She brushed back a lock of blond hair from her daughter's forehead. "You have more than one friend, don't you? Just because you play with Deirdre doesn't mean you can't hang out with Emily the next day."

Erin frowned. She had gotten into an argument with Deirdre McKinney the day before. "I don't have many friends," she said.

Her mother had laughed. "Yes you do. You have more friends than I can count on my fingers and toes." She leaned forward and gave her daughter a tickle, her fingers scampering along the sides of Erin's body like furry caterpillars. Erin giggled and slinked to the floor.

"You have more friends than peacocks have feathers," her mother said, "and they're all a little different, aren't they. You don't get them confused with one another?"

"No."

"And you're able to spend time with all of them?"

Erin looked up at her mother, her head resting on the floorboards. "When is Daddy coming home?"

Helen Reece looked away from her for a moment. "I don't know," she said. "That's not for us to decide."

"Who decides?"

"A group of people at the prison. In four months they'll meet again and decide if Daddy can come home early."

"—father was in the hospital."

"Hmm?" Erin blinked and looked over at the woman.

"I said I was sorry to hear that your father was in the hospital."

"Oh. Thank you."

"Some kind of a respiratory illness, I heard. It sounds like he's pretty sick."

"Yes," she said. "I guess everything's common knowledge here in Wolf Point."

The woman shrugged. "Small community. People talk."

Erin nodded. "I've been away for a while. I'd kind of forgotten."

"I'm neighbors with Bill and Margery Turner. They rent a room to your father's farmhand, Travis Cooper. They heard it from Travis, and I heard it from them." Betty Doyle looked down at the open magazine resting on her lap. "Seems to me like your father's got some questions to answer."

"Right now he's on a ventilator."

"Yes, I understand that. We're all wishing him the best."

Erin was silent for a moment, watching her.

Betty looked up from the pages. "Everyone knows what they found on your father's farm," she said. "I think we have a right to know whose body it is and how it got there."

The room went still and quiet. Betty's eyes were upon her, and the receptionist was watching her as well. Erin's heart thudded in her chest. She could hear it in her ears, could feel the *whump-whump-whump* of it in her teeth. She tried to draw in a breath, but it was like pulling air from a vacuum.

"I would caution people not to jump to conclusions," Erin said, and it was strange how calm her voice sounded, as if it was coming from someone else.

The woman leaned forward in her chair. "People don't know *what* to think, but they have a right to ask questions." Her fingertips turned back the pages at the corner of her magazine, lifting and releasing them like a stack of cards, the order never changing, each shuffle coming out the same. "And if it turns out to be what it looks like, I'd watch yourself, Erin. People will expect justice, and some of them might not want to stop at just that. This isn't a safe place for you. You decided a long time ago that you don't belong here."

Erin shook her head. "I was eighteen years old. I had my reasons. I left and you stayed. That doesn't make you better than me."

"No," Betty said, "it doesn't make me better." She returned the magazine to the rack, stood up, and walked to the door with a limp that favored her right hip. She placed her hand on the doorknob, then paused with her head lowered before turning once more in Erin's direction. "This town has been through a lot since you left. Businesses shut down. People moved away. Those of us who stayed found a way to carry on. But we're smaller now. It's not the same place as the one you left behind." She sighed, and the sound of it blended with the wind as it gusted against the side of the building. "We all have our own way of dealing with things," she said. "You left and I stayed. It doesn't make me better. It just"—she opened the door and straightened her body against the cold—"makes me a different kind of survivor."

9

"MY RECEPTIONIST TELLS ME YOU GOT INTO IT WITH BETTY DOYLE,"
Dr. Houseman said as he closed the door to his small office and
took a seat behind the desk. "I'm sorry about that. Betty was
grumpy when she was younger, but she's even worse now."

"She left without seeing you."

"She'll be back," he said. "I'm the only doctor in town.
Betty Doyle isn't going anywhere."

Erin nodded. "I was hoping to make a good impression on
the people I haven't seen since childhood. I don't think I'm
doing a very good job of that."

"Don't worry," he said. "It's gossip, a bit of small-town
chatter. People talk, that's all. By late this evening, everyone
will know you're back. Then they have to decide what to
make of you."

"Any words of advice?"

"Be yourself. What else can you do?"

"Betty tells me I should be careful."

"You should concentrate on your father's recovery. Getting
him better is our top priority."

Erin was silent for a moment, recalling the image of her father
in the hospital, his breathing supported by the ventilator, a line

of plastic tubing running from an IV pump to a catheter that disappeared beneath the blue-and-white fabric of his hospital gown. He'd appeared weak and vulnerable, an older and thinner man than he'd been when she last saw him.

"Will they arrest him, once he's well enough to leave the hospital?"

"I don't know," Mark said. "I hope not. Right now they don't know what they're dealing with."

"What do *you* think?"

"I'm your father's physician, not his attorney."

"But I respect your opinion."

"I don't have one to offer," he said, "not on any legal matters."

"You think I should hire someone—an attorney, that is?"

He shrugged. "He hasn't been accused of a crime yet."

"Not formally, no."

He looked down at his desk, then back up at her. For a few seconds, neither of them spoke.

"It's not my area of expertise," he said. "If you need the name of someone, I can ask around. There's a guy in town who does some defense work, but"—he shrugged—"maybe it's better to get someone from outside of Wolf Point."

"Hard to separate the town from the person? Hard to find someone who isn't already biased?"

"Something like that."

There was a knock on the door. They both turned in its direction.

"Come in," Mark called, and the door opened halfway to reveal the receptionist.

"Will you be needing me anymore this evening, Dr. Houseman?"

"No, Candice. Thank you. Have a good night. I'll lock up when I leave."

"Okay. Have a good night, Dr. Houseman. Good night, ma'am."

"Good night," Erin said, and the door closed, leaving the two of them alone once again in the office.

Erin leaned back in her chair. "By tomorrow morning the whole town will know I stayed after hours to chat with you in your office."

Mark smiled. "Right."

He picked up a small instrument from the surface of his desk and turned it over in his hands. It looked like a drawing compass, with two thin metal arms that tapered to sharp points at the ends. He glanced up at her. "Calipers," he said, "for measuring intervals on an EKG. Do you use them in veterinary medicine?"

"Rarely," she said. "I don't have any in the office."

Mark nodded. "It was a gift from my father." He brought the arms together and returned it to the desktop. "There's something else I need to talk to you about," he said. "We discovered it during your father's diagnostic work-up."

Erin straightened herself in the chair. "He had sepsis, pneumonia . . . and the nurse said something about anemia."

Mark nodded. "He had all of those things. We've been giving him IV fluids and antibiotics, so the sepsis and pneumonia seem to be under control. The anemia's better, too, after the transfusion." He laced his fingers together. "We're heading in the right direction. I'm pleased with the way he's responded."

"That's good," she said. "It sounds promising."

"Yes," he said. "You see, we've . . ." He looked down at his hands, then back up at her. "There's a mass in your father's right lung. The first few chest X-rays didn't show it very well. It was hidden beneath the pneumonia. Now that the infection is clearing, it's more distinct on the follow-up films."

"A lung mass. A tumor," she said. The words tasted sour in her mouth.

"Yes, a tumor. I ordered a CT of the chest, just to be sure. There's a tumor sitting in the right middle lobe of your father's lung. There are some enlarged lymph nodes in the mediastinum, and a smaller nodule in the left lower lobe."

Erin sat in silence, trying to wrap her mind around the things he was telling her. "Lung cancer," she said. "You're sure."

Mark shook his head. "No," he said. "There are other possibilities. We'd need a biopsy to be certain."

"What other possibilities?"

"It could be anything. Scarring from a previous infection, for example. Tuberculosis. A pulmonary abscess. Or it could be something benign and of no concern. The point is, we don't know. That's why we need the biopsy."

Erin drew in a deep ratcheting breath and let it out. As a veterinarian, she'd had similar conversations with the owners of her own patients. It was difficult to deliver bad news all at once. More tests were usually needed. In this case, her father needed a biopsy. They couldn't make a definitive diagnosis without it. And yet she could tell from Mark's demeanor that he was pretty certain already.

"—have a friend from medical school who's a pulmonologist," he was saying. "He works out of Billings, but he's agreed to fly up here this weekend to do a bronchoscopy."

"He's flying all the way up to Wolf Point just to do a bronchoscopy?"

"He owns a Cessna and has his private pilot's license. It'll give him a chance to get out of the office and log some flight time."

Erin was quiet. It was hard to come to terms with the things Mark was telling her. She wanted to argue that it didn't make sense for the pulmonologist to fly all the way to Wolf Point to perform a single bronchoscopy. Why not send the patient to the doctor, instead of the other way around? But no, the argument ran deeper than that. How had she suddenly ended up in a world where her father had cancer?

"He never smoked," she said. "Not that I know of."

Mark nodded. "Smoking is only one risk factor. There are people who smoke for most of their lives who never get cancer, and there are people who never smoke who do. Part of it is genetic," he said, and Erin winced. "Or other exposures," he added quickly, "a whole host of factors we know little about."

"Some chemical he used on the farm, perhaps? A carcinogen he wasn't aware of?"

"Could be." He cleared his throat. "Most of the time we never know, not for certain anyway."

She stared at the surface of the desk. It was the second one she'd studied in the space of a single afternoon, the second time she'd been handed a revelation about her father she did not want to accept.

"He's a good man," she said, "the best man I've ever known."

"Yes," he said. "Wolf Point is lucky to have him."

"It gets everyone, doesn't it?"

"Hmm?"

"It gets everyone, everyone who's ever lived here. My mother. My father. It's only a matter of time until the town takes what belongs to it." She laughed, but there was no humor in it, just a sound that filled the room and was gone, like many of the lives that had passed through this very office. "It's had a piece of him for years. I shouldn't be surprised that it's decided to take the rest."

"Erin, listen to me."

She looked up.

"I know this comes as a shock," he said. "It's going to take time to process. Right now we're at the beginning of it. There are many steps in front of us. My advice is to try not to worry about all of them at once. It's hard to see around the corner. The road ahead is never as straight as we think it is."

"The specialist," she said. "You called in a favor and pulled some strings to get him up here."

Mark shrugged. "Dr. Kowalski is a good friend. It's easier for him to do the bronchoscopy now while your father is still sedated with an endotracheal tube in place."

"Thank you. I appreciate the way you're taking such great care of him."

"Of course," he said. "You should try to get some rest. Do you have a place to stay for the night?"

"I was initially planning on staying at my father's house, but Lieutenant Stutzman tells me that's not an option at the moment."

"I'm afraid I don't have a room to offer you," Mark told her, "unless you'd like to share one with a three-year-old."

Erin smiled. "As tempting as that sounds . . ."

"Other than that, it's the Homestead Inn. The other place closed five years ago."

She nodded. "Then the Homestead it is. Do I have time to visit my father again this evening?"

"Visiting hours are from nine A.M. to eight P.M." He glanced at his watch. "It's six-thirty. You have time to see him again if you'd like."

"Thank you," she said, and Mark walked her out and said good night.

The wind was blowing hard from the west as Erin crossed the street to the hospital. She found the room on her own this time, and her father appeared unchanged from earlier that day, only now she had a better understanding of what he was up against. David's illness had unearthed more than just an unsettling discovery on the farm. It had uncovered something ominous lurking inside of him. There was a chance that one of these things—the tumor or the human remains they'd discovered on the property—might get him before the other. But Dr. Houseman was right. It was hard to see around the corner, hard to know for certain what lay ahead.

Erin leaned over her father's body and kissed him on the forehead, something her mother had done to her each evening when she tucked Erin into bed. "Good night, Daddy," she whispered, but the words caught in her throat. It was painful to see him like this, dependent and helpless, waiting for whatever came next. Still, she was glad she had come. Her father needed her, more than she'd realized. Maybe he always had.

She sat there for a while longer, her left hand cupped around the top of his forearm. Erin closed her eyes and listened to the sounds of the hospital until her breathing fell in step with the steady cadence of the ventilator. *There is a way through this,* she thought, but she kept hearing the sound of the shovel striking the earth, the scrape of metal against the dirt. She woke to a hand on her shoulder, her father's nurse telling her that visiting hours were over.

"Sorry," she told Diesel as she climbed into the truck. She keyed the ignition, and the engine turned over twice before it caught. "Homestead Inn," she said, and she put the Chevy in gear, pulled a U-turn in the middle of the empty street, and got them heading in the right direction.

The streets seemed different in the dim, artificial glow of the headlights. Yards and houses she'd recognized earlier that day were indistinct shapes now, the shadows shifting and merging, a congregation of souls gathered along the roadside to watch her pass. She turned left too early and ended up in an unfamiliar neighborhood. Erin pushed onward instead of turning around and heading back. Her phone with its GPS was in her front pocket. *But, no,* she told herself. *Even after all those years away, I should know how to move through Wolf Point in the darkness.*

You don't know this place, an inner voice responded, *not the way you used to.* And beneath that was Betty Doyle telling her that the things that happened here had changed this town for good, that the people who left were different kinds of survivors than the ones who'd decided to stay.

"Right now, we're at the beginning of it," Mark told her. "There are many steps in front of us."

"I know," Erin whispered, and she drove deeper into the heart of it, searching for something familiar.

10

CONNIE GRIFFIN SAT IN THE FRONT ROW OF THE SMALL ASSEMBLY of funeral-goers gathered at Wolf Point Cemetery. They sat by the burial site, facing west, and even though it was only two-thirty in the afternoon, the sun was already low on the horizon in front of them. Connie focused her eyes on the grass and tried to concentrate on the words of Pastor Kimble's eulogy. *He's talking about my son,* she thought, but it wasn't real yet, the grief trapped beneath the sudden shock of losing him. Two kids had come across his body floating in the reeds along the northern bank of the river four days after Miles had gone missing. His neck had been broken, and Chief Ward suspected that it was the injury that had killed him, not the river. "The broken neck and a bump on the back of his head were the only signs of trauma," he said. "The medical examiner is ruling this an accidental death."

"An accidental death," she repeated. They were sitting in her kitchen, and she reached out and touched the side of the ceramic teacup in front of her. It was cold, she noted, and she tried to remember whether she had made the tea or if Chief Ward had prepared it for her.

"I suspect he fell off the bridge. You know how the kids are always playing there." The chief cleared his throat. "If he struck one of the girders on the way down, chances are he was rendered unconscious before he even hit the water."

"He was sixteen," she said.

"Yes," he replied. "I understand he was at a party the night he went missing?"

"That's right. He was at Charlie Husker's house."

"Well," he said, "that's not too far from the river. If he was intoxicated when he walked down to the water . . ."

"What about the fire? The barn on the Turner property burned to the ground on the night my Miles went missing."

"Thankfully, there was no one inside. The firefighters searched the place thoroughly, both during and after the fire."

"Why did it burn?"

He shrugged. "There are lots of possibilities. An electrical short. A spark from one of the machines. Oily rags left sitting around can spontaneously combust under the right conditions. There was hay in the loft." The chief sighed and shook his head. "All it would've taken is a small flame to get things started."

"My Miles didn't drown. Someone killed him and threw his body in the river."

"I'm sorry," he said, "but there's no evidence of that."

"They did it to my father," she said. "He was left in the bed of his pickup and was found dead the next morning."

"That," the chief said, "was a long time ago. Your father was in a bar fight. There's nothing linking the two."

"Miles Griffin was a kind and generous boy," Pastor Kimble told the small congregation gathered at the graveside. "He was loved and admired by all who knew him."

Connie let the words wash over her. She wanted to believe

the things the pastor was saying, but she'd been hard on her son, charging him with responsibilities that should've been those of his father.

It wasn't fair, really. Their father had been a fifteen-year-old boy. Connie had seen him in school but met him only once herself, and at first it was sweet, the way he said nice things to her and listened when she told him about the death of her father eight years before. She had cried a little, and when she was finished, he had leaned over and kissed her, a soft brush of the lips that sent tingles down her spine. It had never happened before, a kiss like that. And even at fourteen years old, Connie knew that it was something she'd remember forever. He had stood up and taken her by the hand then, leading her beneath the bleachers, and her heart had raced at the idea of it, how you could fall in love with someone in a single afternoon and then lie down beside them in the grass and let them hold you. This was the thing the older kids talked about, and it was happening to *her* just when she least expected it.

She didn't understand the way it was supposed to work, and Connie flinched and put her arm in front of her when he reached up and touched her breast. "It's what makes it special," he said, and Connie wanted this to be special, so she moved her arm and let him reach under her shirt where there was only a bra between them. He traced his fingers along the fabric, and he was breathing faster now. She could feel his body changing, becoming excited and urgent. He undid the button of her pants and pulled down on the zipper. "Wait," she said, and grabbed at his hand as she tried to squirm out from under him. He was bigger and heavier than she was, even though some of the kids called her *piggy,* and before she knew it her pants were down around her knees and he was pressing himself against her, shoving at the hips.

She didn't remember much of what happened next, but she remembered the sound of laughter, and when she looked up, she saw people's faces peering down on them from between the slats of the bleachers. "Oh my God, I can't believe you porked her!" someone yelled. "How did you get *in there* with all that fat?"

"He porked the pork chop!" someone else said, and there was more laughter and a few piggy snorts as the boy rolled off her and pulled up his pants.

Connie put her hands over her face and rolled onto her side so she couldn't see them. There was pain in her belly and blood on the grass and on the inside of her thighs. She could still smell the sweaty animal scent of him on her body, and when she touched her lower lip with her tongue she found that it was cracked and bleeding.

They dropped pebbles down at her from above. The tiny stones landed on the white flesh of her buttock with a soft plop because it hurt too much for her to bend at the waist and rake up her pants to cover herself. Eventually they went away—even the one who'd told her that it would be special—but Connie lay there for another hour until the pain subsided and she felt strong enough to stand.

Mother will be angry, she thought, and when she got home, she was relieved that her mother hadn't returned yet from her job at the deli. Connie took a shower and put her clothes in a trash bag. She left her house and carried them to the dumpster behind the gas station.

No one has to know, she thought, but by the next day it seemed that everyone in school had heard the news. "Jason Fisher porked the pork chop!" someone had scrawled on the bathroom stall, and there was a picture to go with it. In this depiction of the event Connie was drawn as the pig that she was, with a snout, floppy ears, and a curly tail sticking straight up into the air. "Oink, oink," they had written in a word bubble coming from Connie's snout, and that was the last time she ventured into the girls' bathroom. If she had to pee, she would hold it until she got home.

She wore baggy clothes and tried to keep the baby from coming, but six months later it was obvious that she had gotten herself "knocked up," as her mother put it, and Connie dropped out of school and stayed with her mother's cousin in Minnesota until she gave birth to not just *one* boy but twins, whom she named Miles and Abel.

Pastor Kimble lifted his right hand in the air, his palm facing the huddled cluster of attendees. "We surrender this body to the earth," he said, "but Miles Griffin has already risen into heaven and dwells in the house of the Lord our Father. It is there that he will live out the promise of life eternal, and each of us, in our own time, will someday join him."

Life eternal, she thought, and she glanced at Abel, who sat next to her, rocking in his chair.

"He's slow," her mother said when Connie returned to Wolf Point with the children. They were toddlers then, far enough along to tell that there was something wrong with Abel, who had gotten turned around in the womb and had to be delivered by C-section, forty-five minutes after the birth of his brother.

Abigail Griffin folded her arms across her chest as she watched them from the living room doorway. "They look the same," she said, "but the second one doesn't act like his brother."

The second one, Connie thought. That's what her mother called him.

"This is what I warned you about," her mother told her. "'If you don't give the child away for adoption, nothing good will come of it.' Isn't *that* what I told you?"

"There's *nothing* wrong with him," Connie had countered, but as the years went on, it became obvious that her mother was right. Abel was a sweet child, quiet and obedient, but broken just the same.

And you decided to keep the broken one, her mother would have said if she hadn't died of a stroke two years ago. And it was strange, Connie thought, how people kept right on talking, even after they were gone.

"Please stand," Pastor Kimble said, and they all stood up but Connie, the mother of the fallen one.

"Mom. Mom, we're supposed to stand."

"I know. I can't. Leave me alone."

"But the man said. We've *got to.* He's talking about Jesus."

Tug on her sleeve. A hand in her armpit, lifting her upward.

"*Stop it.* Leave me alone. Can't you leave me alone for *just this once?*"

He let go of her, and she slumped back into the chair.

("This is what I warned you about. 'If you don't give the child away for adoption, nothing good will come of it.' Isn't *that* what I told you?")

Stop it.

("Do you wish it was the second one? If it *had* to be one of them, wouldn't it be better if it was *him* lying there in the . . .")

No. It wouldn't. She loved them both the same.

Connie got to her feet. At thirty-one, she was still a young woman, but today she felt old, worn down by all of the things that could've been but weren't. She cupped her hand around her son's arm for support.

"In the name of God the Father, we commit the body of Miles Griffin to the earth and his soul to everlasting life."

They watched as Pastor Kimble let three handfuls of dirt sift through his fingers. The soil struck the lid of the coffin with a soft and hollow sound that reminded her of the patter of a child's footsteps in the hallway.

"I invite each of you to step forward," he said, and the funeral-goers did, one after the other, letting the dirt fall from their hands as they filled the grave in tiny increments.

11

JEFF STUTZMAN SAT AT THE KITCHEN TABLE, EATING WHAT WAS left of his dinner. It was the kind of meal that was packaged in a partitioned plastic tray and could be kept frozen for weeks or even months if necessary. Not that the frozen dinners ever made it that long. He cycled through them pretty quickly.

Almost as quickly as the beer, he thought, although he was careful to limit those to two a night. There was a half-empty one on the table in front of him—his first for the evening—and he lifted it to his lips and took a sip.

(*You ought to clean your service weapon.*)

Yeah, he thought. It had been a while. A few days, in fact.

The Glock 17 was lying on the counter next to the sheet of cellophane he'd peeled from the tray of meatball marinara. Last night it had been Cajun shrimp and chicken. The portions were modest and never really filled him up. Still, he had gained ten pounds since the academy, not enough for a come-to-Jesus moment, but enough to realize how easy it would be for ten pounds to turn into fifty.

Come to Jesus, he thought, and Jeff shook his head. It was interesting the words that popped into your skull when you weren't thinking about anything in particular.

He stood up, walked to the trash can, and threw out the remains of his dinner. *Remains,* he thought, *something to get rid of.* He turned and leaned against the counter, studying the handgun.

"You keep your weapon clean and it'll save your ass when you need it," Uncle Clayton told him on the day Jeff graduated from the academy. By then, Clayton Crowe had twenty-two years on the force and the experience to prove it. He'd been shot once in the line of duty, taking a round in the vest at almost point-blank range during a routine traffic stop on Highway 2. He'd gotten up and returned fire, killing both of the car's occupants and earning himself a Medal of Valor. He could've risen to any position after that—chief of police, even mayor if he had wanted to—but Uncle Clayton saw those as politicians' jobs, and he chose something smaller but just as good. "Detective first class," he said, "that's good enough for me," and Uncle Clayton remained in that position until he retired twelve years later.

Jeff picked up the Glock and carried it to the table. There was gun oil, a towel and rag, strips of cloth, and some cleaning tools in a metal box below the sink. He fetched those as well and brought them over.

Jeff sat down and finished off the rest of his Budweiser. In the early days, he never would've handled the gun if he'd been drinking. But he'd been on the force for ten years now and the Glock had been his companion through all of it. It soothed him, the feel of the grip in his hand and the familiar weight of the weapon. He removed the magazine, racked the slide three times in rapid succession, and inspected the chamber.

Empty. Safe to dismember.

Dismantle, he corrected himself. The gun was safe to dismantle.

He field-stripped it and laid the parts on the towel in front of him. Slide, barrel, frame, and recoil spring with guide rod. The parts were simple and consistent. They came out the same every time.

("Jeffrey, I need to talk to you.")

Jeffrey. The name his uncle used to call him as a kid.

"It's about your brother," Uncle Clayton said, and in Jeff's mind he was seven years old again, standing in the living room in his bare feet and pajamas. He'd woken up that morning to a silent house, and had sat on the couch and watched cartoons until he heard the sound of his parents' car pulling into the driveway.

Jeff started to look up, but his uncle squatted down in front of him. He put a hand on Jeff's shoulder and gave it a squeeze.

"There's been an accident," he said. "Your brother was hit by a truck out on Main Street."

Main Street, Jeff thought. He wasn't allowed on Main Street. Too busy. Too many cars. But Kenny was three years older and allowed to do whatever he wanted. Sometimes his uncle even took him on rides in the unmarked police car so Kenny could use the siren and turn on the flashing lights on the dashboard. It wasn't fair, really. Just because he was older shouldn't mean that Kenny got to do everything.

Jeff looked past his uncle to where his father was standing in the living room doorway.

"Mom says there's too much traffic on Main Street."

His father turned his back on them. His shoulders were hunched and shaking, like he was laughing at something but trying to pretend that he wasn't.

Uncle Clayton waited until he had Jeff's attention. "He was running across the road," he said. "The driver—he didn't see him. It was raining and he just . . . didn't see him."

Jeff nodded. He could picture Kenny lying in a hospital bed, his arm and leg wrapped in casts and propped up on the pillows. "Hello, dipshit," his brother would say when Jeff stopped by the hospital to visit. "You gonna sign these things or just stand there looking stupid?"

"I'll sign 'em," he said, but the words died on his lips as he sat there by himself at the table.

Nothing to sign, he thought. *His head was crushed, but he didn't stop breathing until he got to the hospital.*

"An accident," he'd told Erin Reece earlier that day. "I've made my peace with it."

("He ran him over with the Bronco in the middle of the street.")

"It was raining," he said, and Jeff glanced at the kitchen window to see if it was true.

Uncle Clayton reached out and lifted Jeff's chin with his finger. "I know this is hard on you, buddy. I need you to be strong for your family."

Jeff ran a piece of cloth through the cylinder of the gun barrel. Had he done that? Had he been strong enough for his father? His aunt Amy?

And what about your mother? he thought. *Were you strong enough for her?*

"I was seven," he said, but there was no one left in the room to listen.

Jeff held the slide with the muzzle end pointed downward. He picked up the toothbrush and worked the bristles along the breech face.

No, he thought. *I won't accept responsibility for that.* His brother had been killed by accident. Six months later, his mother swallowed enough pills to have her own come-to-Jesus moment.

(*You miss them, don't you?*)

"Yes," he said. "Of course I miss them."

(*So what are your plans for the evening?*)

"Nothing," he said. "I go to bed, get up tomorrow, and do it all over again."

(*Kenny wanted to be a police officer.*)

"I know."

(*Now it's just you.*)

"Yeah," he said. "Now it's just me."

He finished up with the gun and put it back together. It wasn't necessary—wasn't even *good* for it—to clean it this often.

(*It soothes you. It feels good to hold it in your hands for a while.*)

"It's nothing," he said, but it felt like something familiar. He'd been here before, hadn't he, drinking beer and staring down the barrel of his service weapon. The discovery of the body on David Reece's property had started it all over again.

He slid the gun back into its holster. He was tired. If he could get some sleep, maybe tomorrow things would feel better.

Jeff looked down at the box of cleaning supplies. He thought about returning it to its spot beneath the sink, but decided to leave it on the table where he could get to it more easily in the morning. Just in case he wanted to go through the ritual all over again.

("Hello, dipshit. You gonna sign these things or just stand there looking stupid?")

"I'll sign 'em," he said. "I'll sign 'em as soon as I see you."

He rose from the table, turned out the kitchen light, and walked down the hall toward the bedroom.

12

ERIN PEDALED HARD, THE ROAD BLURRING BENEATH HER. UP AHEAD, she could see Robbie, standing on his pedals as he crested the small hill. He let out a whoop when he reached the top, then sat down on his seat as he dipped below the horizon.

Erin squeezed the rubber grips on her handlebars and leaned forward in her seat. The muscles in her thighs burned with exertion. She wasn't far behind him, and she gave it everything she had as she climbed the incline, the sun on her back, the breeze light and feathery, like the gentle tug of her mother's fingers in her hair.

It was mid-September and still warm, the summer holding on for a little while longer. Today was Saturday, the *best* day of the week. She'd finished her chores early before riding her bike to Robbie's. She'd found him in the backyard, hunkered down in front of the maple tree.

"Hey," she said, walking up behind him. "Whatcha doin'?"

He turned his head and looked at her. It had been three weeks since the fight. The cuts across the bridge of his nose and lower lip were almost healed by now. There was still a shade of a bruise around his right eye, but he looked like himself again, only better.

Erin plopped down beside him. She ran her thumb over the spot at the base of the trunk where he'd been carving his name.

"You forgot the *e*," she said.

"Haven't gotten to it yet." He turned the pocketknife around in his hand, the blade clasped between his thumb and forefinger. "Here," he said, holding it out to her. She took it by the handle and let it rest in her lap for a moment before pressing the tip of the blade into the trunk.

"It's really dull," he said. "I should get another one."

She started in on the last letter of his name, sketching a thin line at first, then tracing it over and over, being careful not to slip, not to mess up what he'd already started.

"Curves are harder than straight lines," he said. "The *e* is almost all curves. It's the hardest letter."

"What about *s*?" she asked.

"The curves on the *e* are tighter, like water circling a drain."

"I tried knocking on your front door."

"My dad's sleeping. Mom says he's got a headache. He was up late last night watching the ball game."

"Who played?"

"The Twins lost to the Oakland A's. Brent Gates hit a one-run homer in the bottom of the ninth." Robbie pressed his index finger into the dirt. "My dad gets mad when the Twins lose. He was pretty mad last night."

Erin nodded. "Did you catch a beating?"

"No," he said. "I'm still recovering from my last one."

"That was different."

"Yeah," he said. "That was different."

They were quiet for a while. Erin dug into the tree with the pocketknife. Robbie was right. The letter *e* was the hardest, like water circling a drain.

"You wanna go someplace?" he asked.

"I've gotta finish the *e*."

"Finish it later."

"Okay," she said, and folded the blade into the handle. "Where do you wanna go?"

"My grandpa's place. He lives on the reservation—not in Wolf Point, but on the *real* reservation. It's a few miles north of town."

She hesitated. "I don't know."

"Come on. It'll be fun. He's old, but he's real nice. He carves things and sells them to the tourists."

"What tourists?"

"I don't know, the *tourists*. There's a cultural center in Poplar, a place where people can learn all about Native Americans."

"Meghan Decker says the reservation's a scary place. Her older brother drove out there one time with his friends. He said there were dead bodies lying on the side of the road."

Robbie scrunched up his face. "That's stupid. There are no dead bodies. He was just trying to scare her."

Erin turned the pocketknife over in her hands. "They don't have any laws or anything. People can do whatever they want."

"What are you *talking* about? Of course they have laws, just not the same laws as the rest of the country. There's a tribal government. We have our own courts and jails and stuff."

"Is your grandfather Native American?" She paused as a thought occurred to her. "Wait," she said, "are *you*?"

Robbie rolled his eyes. "My last name's Tabaha. What do you think?"

She shrugged.

"My family's from the Lakota tribe. That's Sioux. We've been living here a really long time."

"How long?"

"Nobody knows for sure. We were here long before the settlers came to America."

She nodded.

"You don't know much about Native Americans, do you?" he asked.

"They teach us about them in school."

"Yeah, but not everything. You know the Battle of Little Bighorn? Custer's Last Stand? That was the Lakota tribe. They teamed up with some other tribes to beat the U.S. Army."

"They killed a lot of soldiers."

"We were protecting our people. My grandpa can tell you all about it."

"I don't know if I'm allowed to go all the way out there."

"Geez," he said. "You wanna go home and ask your parents? Fine with me."

"It's just my mom and me. My dad's in prison, remember?"

Robbie flinched at that, his face taking on a miserable expression. "Right," he said. "Sorry, I forgot."

"He goes before the review board later this month. There's a chance they might let him out so he can come home to us."

Robbie reached out and put a hand on her shoulder. "That's great, Erin. I sure hope that's what happens."

"Thanks." She brought her knee to her chest and wrapped her arms around her shin while she thought over his proposal. "I don't have to ask permission for everything. I can pretty much go where I want."

"Yeah?"

"Yeah," she said. "Let's go. If there are dead bodies, I wanna see 'em."

They had ridden their bikes, and it had taken only fifteen minutes to get to the place where Wolf Point ended and the rest of Fort Peck Indian Reservation began. A single road stretched north through the countryside, the brown sunburnt grass standing tall on either side. At first they went slow, weaving back and forth across the roadway. A pickup truck approached from behind, the engine rattling like a washing machine beneath the hood, and they moved over and allowed it to pass.

"There used to be bison," Robbie said over the rush of the wind. "Back when my grandpa was a kid there were thousands of them." He swiveled his head to scan the open plains all around them. "Now there are almost none."

"Where did they go?" Erin asked.

"Gone," he said. "Hunted by fur traders and the government." He stood up on his pedals and searched the horizon. "Every once in a while you'll see one. But most times, no." He sat down and continued to pedal. "Things that get hunted too much disappear and don't come back. That's what my grandpa says." He looked at her and said something else, but the words were lost in the wind, carried away from the two of them and across the grasslands, where there used to be bison for as far as the eye could see. She could imagine them standing there, scattered across the fields like a collection of dark stones, their massive heads lowered toward the earth, the distinct hunch of their shoulders pressed upward against the blue backdrop of the sky.

Robbie was pulling ahead of her now, standing up on his pedals and *putting some muscle into it,* as her father liked to say. She tried to keep up with him, standing up on her own pedals and forcing her feet to go faster. The pedals spun in gerbil-wheel circles a few inches above the road, but Robbie was stronger than she was and the distance between them widened. He crested the small hill, let out a triumphant whoop—*like the day he rode up behind us,* she thought, *the day he kicked Vinny off his bike*—and disappeared from view as he descended the other side.

She pedaled harder, tightening her grip and leaning forward over the handlebars. Her breath was quick and focused, her eyes on the road. She didn't know exactly how far ahead of her Robbie had gotten, but she was impressed by how fast he could be when he wanted to. *Some people are like that,* she thought, *normal until you see the part of them you never knew existed.*

By the time she was nearing the top of the hill and could finally see him on the other side, Robbie had stopped along the roadside and was looking back at her. He waved his hand and yelled something, but he was too far away and she couldn't make out the words. There was a rising noise, a steady growl that became louder with every passing second. Robbie cupped his hands to his mouth and yelled again, and this time she heard part of it. "—*aaarr,*" he said, but a moment later it was upon her, a dark black chassis that reached the summit at the same moment she did.

If she'd been in the middle of the road, it would've struck her. The vehicle was going fast, the engine roaring. Erin was on the right side of the roadway, near the shoulder, but she was close enough to feel a blast of air as the car hurtled past. She jerked the handlebars to the right and the bike wobbled, the front tire feeling loose and unpredictable on the pebbled shoulder as she fought for control. She saw a flash of it—the bike coming down on top of her, the crack of her head as it struck the asphalt—but she leaned left and was suddenly back on the roadway as the bike straightened out and picked up speed on the decline.

Erin was vaguely aware that she was sweating. The tiny hairs on the back of her left forearm were bolt upright, as if the gust of air from the car's passing had blown them to a standing position. She coasted for the remainder of the distance, not hurrying now but simply appreciating the fact that she was still in one piece. Robbie was waiting for her. She slowed as she neared him, pulled up alongside, and came to a stop.

"You okay?" he asked.

"Yeah," she said, shaken and embarrassed. "He didn't even come that close. Just surprised me, is all."

"It looked close from here."

"It wasn't."

"Right." He toed a pebble with the tip of his sneaker. "He came close to hitting me, too. Seemed to swerve right at me."

"He was probably messing with the radio."

"You saw him?"

She shook her head no. She'd been startled by the car. After that, her attention had been focused on not crashing.

"I don't know about this place," she said. "It's kind of creepy. There's nothing out here."

Robbie rolled his eyes. "There's *plenty* out here. You just have to know where to look."

"People drive too fast. Don't they know that kids can come out of nowhere? Sometimes you don't see them until it's too late."

"It's okay," he said. "He missed us, right?"

"It's *not* okay." She stepped away from her bicycle and let it fall to the ground. "If you run someone over, you can't take it back."

He nodded.

"I *mean* it."

"Okay," he said, and grew quiet, watching her.

Erin picked up a rock and threw it. "What's *wrong* with this place anyway?"

He straddled his bike and said nothing.

She chucked another rock low and hard, which skittered across the asphalt.

Robbie turned away from her to scan the landscape. "Hey, Erin."

"What?"

"You see it? Over there to your right?"

She turned. "See what?" There was a small stone still clutched in her hand.

"Jackrabbit," he said. He pointed and she saw it, a medium-size rabbit in the brush. It stood on its back legs, the front legs held close to its chest. Its black nose twitched as it sampled the air, searching for scents of food and predators.

"Yeah, I see it. So?"

"You said there was nothing out here. That's *something*."

"One jackrabbit. Big deal."

"What about that big old rattlesnake?"

Erin spun around. "*Where?*"

Robbie cracked a smile. "I don't know," he said, "but you should keep looking because they're out here, too."

Erin shook her head. "That's not funny. I don't like rattle-snakes. I almost got bit by one when I was younger."

"You almost got bit by one now. Don't you see it over there, coiled up next to your front tire?"

"No," she said with a scowl, "and you don't, either."

"You're right. I see two. There's another one over there in the grass—"

"Shut up," she said, although at this point she was smiling.

"—and a third one on top of your head."

Erin snorted. "I'll use it as a hat."

"It looks good," he said. "I'm gonna get my mom one for her birthday."

Robbie's mother was a thin, stern woman whose favorite pastime, as far as Erin could tell, was smoking cigarettes and peering at people through the haze. She imagined her doing this with a coiled and dried-out rattlesnake on her head, a gift from her precious son.

"She'll like it," she said, laughing.

"She'll wear it to church," Robbie told her, and Erin laughed harder, picturing Mrs. Tabaha standing in the front row holding a hymnal, her heavily sprayed hairdo sagging under the weight of her new snake-hat.

"S-she . . . goes to church?" Somehow it was hard to imagine.

"Not really," he said. "But she *would* if she had a new hat."

Erin wiped the tears from her eyes. "Here," she said, "you can give her mine."

"A used hat. She won't like th . . ." He trailed off, his smile fading.

"What?" she asked.

"He's back," he said, and Erin knew what he was talking about before she even turned to look.

The car was facing them now, perched on the summit of the small hill behind them. Sunlight glinted off the chrome of its grille, the vertical lines looking like long thin teeth that stretched from the hood to the jut of its front bumper. The sun reflected off the windshield, too, making it difficult to see through the glass. They watched as it sat there, the black body hunkered over the tires like a panther crouched low against the earth. Erin could hear the steady rumble of its engine, an idling drone of metal and oil.

"What's he doing?" she asked, but Robbie was silent and unmoving beside her.

The engine revved. Once. Twice.

"Get your bike," he said. "It's time to go."

Erin looked at him. "We can't outrun that thing."

"No," he said, pointing his bike toward the dirt field to their right. "Not on the road anyway."

She looked out across the open field, a wasteland of shrubs and small stones, nothing large enough to stop a car.

"Come on," Robbie said, and he started pedaling, the dirt crunching beneath his tires.

Erin snatched up her bike and headed after him. She ran with it a few steps, then mounted it and started pedaling. The front tire bounced over a small rock, the jolt traveling through the frame and into her arms and shoulders. She tried to control her fear and kept her eyes on the space in front of her. Robbie was ahead of her, standing up as he pedaled, the way he'd done when he was climbing the hill. She remembered how he had pulled ahead of her, how fast he could be when he wanted to. He was doing it now, opening the distance between them. If the car came for them—if it hurtled across the stretch of rocks and scrub brush and tried to run them down—she would be the first one to get swept under its grille.

It's not going to do that, her mind told her. *The driver just turned around to make sure the two of you are okay.*

Right, she thought, and Erin imagined how they would laugh about it later, two kids hauling ass across the open field. *What the hell are those crazy kids* doing? the driver would think. But right now it didn't *feel* crazy. It felt like the car was coming, and it was only a matter of seconds until it ran her over.

"*Wait up!*" she called out to Robbie, and he stopped when he heard her, hitting his brakes hard enough to send plumes of dust into the air from beneath his tires.

"Come *on,*" he said. "There's a ditch up ahead. We should get to the other side of it."

"*Is he coming?*" she asked as she barreled toward him, her voice tight and panicked. She brought her bike to a stop beside him and turned to look back at the roadway.

The car had descended the hill and was parked near the spot where they'd taken to the field. She could see the driver standing beside it, an indistinct shape partially obscured by the car itself.

"What's he doing?"

Robbie shrugged. "Don't know. Maybe he just wants to say hi."

"He should go away. How close are we to your grandpa's place?"

Robbie turned his head to the right, squinting under the glare of the sun. "If we were biking on the road, it'd take us another twenty minutes. Out here, it'll take longer."

"I'm not going back to the roadway."

"Don't have to," he said. "There's an irrigation ditch ahead of us. It brings water to the farms and goes a long way, miles maybe. We should cross to the other side of it. He won't be able to get to us then."

Erin turned her head to look for it. She could see it now, another fifty yards ahead of them. She glanced back at the road. The car was still there, its engine idling. The air rippled above the dark black exterior, a mirage of water that shimmered above the long stretch of asphalt.

They pushed their bikes toward the ditch, looking back every few seconds to be certain he wasn't coming. Twenty seconds later they got to the lip of it, a wide concrete channel about eight feet deep and ten feet across. It stretched in both directions as far as her eyes could see.

"It's an aqueduct," she said.

"A what?"

"An aqueduct. A concrete channel for moving water. There's one close to my father's farm as well."

"I call it a ditch."

"A ditch is different."

"Whatever," he said. "We should get to the other side of it."

"Maybe," she said, and looked back at the car, thinking.

"What's the matter?"

"Nothing," she said. "It's deep enough. If we climb down there, he won't be able to see us. Not from the roadway. We could ride our bikes in either direction." She looked at her friend. "We could head back into town if we wanted to."

They were silent for a few seconds, considering it.

Robbie chewed on his lower lip. "It'll be harder to get away from him if we're down there. If he catches up to us, we won't have time to pull each other out."

"It's better this way," she said. "It's better if he can't see us."

"Okay," he said. "We go down."

"Which way do we go? Back toward town?"

"Uh-uh. Not a good idea. It doesn't go all the way to town. It's a dead end. If he catches up to us . . ."

"Does it go all the way to your grandpa's?"

"I think so."

"You *think* so?"

"Yeah. It does."

"Are you *sure*?"

"Yes."

"Because you didn't *sound* sure a second ago."

"I'm sure," he said. "It goes all the way to my grandpa's. It goes way past that."

"Okay," she said. "We'll go that way." She got down on her stomach and held on to the lip of the aqueduct with her hands as she lowered herself into the channel. With her arms fully extended, her feet dangled three feet above the bottom. Erin let go and dropped the remaining distance onto the concrete surface. She landed on her feet, stumbled slightly, and took a half step back to steady herself.

"Here," Robbie said, lowering her bike into the pit.

She reached up and took it, laid it down next to her, and held her arms up for his bike as well.

"Oh man."

"What?" she asked.

"This is not good. This is *definitely* not good."

"What's the matter?"

Robbie looked down at her. "He's coming," he said. "He's walking over here *right now.*"

"*Get down here!*"

"No."

"What do you mean *no*?"

"You go. Bike fast. I'm gonna slow him down. I'll catch up with you."

"Robbie," she hissed. "Robbie, *no.*"

She couldn't see him now. When she looked up, there was nothing but a cloudless sky above her. She could hear him talking, though, taunting the guy in a voice that was trying to sound brave and almost succeeded.

"*Hey! Hey, jackass, whatcha following us for, huh? Why don't you leave us alone?*"

Erin grabbed her bike and ran with it, wheeling it along. She stopped a short distance down the channel and looked back. It was hard to know what was happening, hard to know *anything* from this vantage point. There was just the straight, smooth-walled passage in either direction. It seemed to go on and on, the gullet of a concrete beast that had swallowed her whole.

A few sticks and small rocks lay in scattered clusters along the floor of the aqueduct. Erin held her breath and listened, her heart walloping in her throat.

"You shouldn't be riding along the road like that." It was a man's voice, deep and rough.

"Fine," Robbie said. "We're not on the road anymore, okay? We're just out here playing. My dad's coming by in a few minutes to pick us up."

There was a short pause, the space of a single heartbeat. "That's a lie."

"It's not a lie. He's a cop in Wolf Point."

"Is that right?"

"'Course it's right. Sometimes he takes us on patrol with him during the weekend."

"Hey, girl."

Erin looked up. The man was standing over her, looking down into the aqueduct. The sun was above him, and Erin squinted into it, making out the general shape of him, a baseball cap with its brim pulled low. She could see stubble on his neck and chin, the slanted upturned corner of the left side of his mouth. The rest of his face was lost in shadow.

"Next time I see you out here I'm gonna take that bike," he said. "Next time I see *either* one of you out here, you're gonna regret it."

She backed against the far wall of the channel.

The man turned his head and looked at Robbie. "What are you *doing* out here with a girl anyway?"

Robbie was silent, but the man stood there waiting for an answer, the upturned corner of his mouth never changing, as if he had tasted something bitter and couldn't decide whether to swallow it or spit it out.

"Hey! I asked you a question."

"Leave us alone."

The man laughed, a flat angry sound that was there and then gone in the space of a second. "Leave you alone? Is that what you want?" He looked down at Erin. "What about you? You want to be left alone? You want to be out here all alone with this *boy*?"

Erin gripped the handlebars to keep from shaking and focused her eyes on the spot where the tips of the man's boots—brown and scuffed with dirt—protruded past the lip of the aqueduct. *Bike fast,* Robbie had told her, but Erin couldn't do it. She stood there frozen, the bike no more useful than the twigs at her feet.

"Okay," he said, turning quickly, and Erin heard the sound of Robbie's bike clattering to the ground above her. "I'll leave you alone if that's what you want." The man stepped away from the lip of the aqueduct, disappearing from Erin's view. "You be careful out here. Don't go biking on the road again." He paused. "You hear me, boy?"

"Yeah."

"Yeah, what?"

"Yeah, we hear you. We'll stay off the road from now on."

The man was silent for a few seconds. Erin readied herself, swinging one leg over the frame of her bike and using her foot to turn the pedal backward to a position where she could get the most leverage. If the man came after her—if he turned around and dropped into the aqueduct—she would *bike fast* like Robbie had instructed her. She would stand up on her pedals and *haul ass* down the concrete channel.

What will you do if he goes after Robbie? she asked herself. *What will you do if he grabs him and starts dragging him toward the car?*

She could hear it in her mind, the sudden scuffle from above, the sound of Robbie being dragged across the field as she struggled to claw her way out of the pit.

"Good," the man said, and the sound of his voice made her jump. "Just wanted to make sure the two of you were okay, that's all." Erin could hear his boots on the dirt, the hard grind of it as he walked away. "Oh yeah," he said, "and I haven't seen your father the police officer returning for you yet. I'm sure he'll be along shortly."

Erin listened to the receding sound of his footsteps, to the shushing sigh of the wind as it moved above her. Eventually she heard the car door slam, the growl of the engine as it sprang to life. Even then, neither of them spoke. They just stood there silently—one above the earth and one below—waiting until they were alone again.

"What a jerk," Robbie said, lowering his bike into the channel.

She reached up and took it, then waited as he swung his hips over the lip and dropped down beside her.

"He gets off on scaring kids," he said. "You could tell that right away."

"You know who he is?"

"No," he said, "I don't think so. He was wearing a hat. It was hard to get a good look at his face."

"What about the car?"

"I haven't seen it before." Robbie mounted his bike and started pedaling.

Erin got on her bike as well. There was enough space to avoid the scattered debris as she pedaled after him. They were headed north, away from town, and he didn't go fast this time, just cruised along at a steady speed. She was able to keep up with him, but Robbie glanced back a few times just to be certain. The sun was high above them, and the shadows they cast were small and shapeless pools beneath the tires. In the years that followed, it was the same with Erin's memory of that day, her mind condensing it into something minor and inconsequential, until eventually she was able to put it on the shelf with everything else.

13

THE HOMESTEAD INN WAS A TWO-STORY MOTEL AT THE INTERSECTION of Second Avenue North and Highway 2. A driver could follow the highway west all the way to Seattle, or east to Lake Huron if they wanted. In Wolf Point it was mostly local traffic, though, and Erin watched the cars go by from the window of her room.

She stood up from her chair and stretched. She had not slept well. From the sagging mattress to the faded sea-green carpet, the place was a stark reminder that she was home but not *all the way* home. During her drive north from Colorado, she'd anticipated spending her nights in her old bedroom in her father's house on the farm. It wasn't far from here, a few miles from the inn, but it was inaccessible now, cordoned off with police tape and occupied by a team of investigators. What would it be like to be there now, she wondered, looking out through her bedroom window as the men moved across her father's yard? She leaned forward and pressed her fingertips against the glass. She could almost see them gathered in huddled groups, pointing to the place where the ground was open beneath them.

("We found something . . . down there in the mud.")

Erin closed her eyes, but she could see it anyway: the pale luster of bone peeking up from the muck.

She put on her jacket and grabbed the keys to the Chevy off the nightstand. The truck was one of only three vehicles in the parking lot. A light frost had settled on the exterior, and the driver's-side door groaned loudly when she opened it, a sound she heard so often that she no longer heard it at all. She had walked Diesel two hours ago, her muscles stiff from a fitful night on the mattress. It had been dark then, a good forty-five minutes before the November sun crested the horizon. There was sunlight now, though, and it glistened off a thin layer of ice on the windshield.

She stepped aside as Diesel jumped into the truck's cab, then climbed in herself so she could start the engine. There was a trick to starting the Chevy on cold mornings like this one. She kissed the key twice, said a short prayer, inserted it into the ignition, and listened to the engine turn over for a few seconds before pressing down on the accelerator. It was more of a good-luck ritual than anything grounded in the physics of automobile mechanics, and like all good-luck rituals it worked only about fifty percent of the time.

The engine sputtered twice and came to life.

"Good girl," Erin said, and leaned over to open the glove compartment. There was an ice scraper inside, and she used it to clear the glass before setting off for the hospital.

From its exterior, Trinity Hospital appeared unchanged from the day before. Erin had hoped the same officer would be stationed outside her father's room, but the face was different this time and she introduced herself again as the daughter of David Reece. The man nodded, asked for identification, and studied her Colorado driver's license with a bit of skepticism before writing her name down on a small pad of paper he retrieved from the front shirt pocket of his uniform.

A different nurse was in the room as well. Her name was

Donna, and Erin asked if there had been any changes in her father's condition from the night before.

"Not since seven A.M., when I started my shift," she said, "and the night nurse told me your father had an uneventful evening."

"Has Dr. Houseman been by to see him this morning?"

"Yes. He stopped by shortly after change of shift."

Erin nodded. Her father was lying on his back, his eyes closed, as if he was sleeping. The ventilator made soft shushing noises that coincided with the slight rise and fall of his chest. Someone had tucked a pillow under his left forearm.

"His breathing is easier this morning," Donna said. "I'll be moving his extremities through passive range of motion. It helps to keep the muscles loose and the joints lubricated. Normally a physical therapist would do that sort of thing, but Wolf Point doesn't have any physical therapists so . . ."

"It falls on you."

"That's right," she said. "We've got to make do with what we have."

"Anything I can do to help?"

Donna was silent for a moment, hesitant.

"I won't get in your way," Erin assured her. "It's just that . . . I'd like to put myself to use if I can."

The nurse shrugged. "A little help is always appreciated." She moved to the opposite side of the bed. "We'll start with the legs, one leg at a time. I'll do this one and you can do the other."

Erin followed the nurse's directions as they progressed from one extremity to the next. Her father's limbs were heavier than she expected, like sacks of grain that needed to be rotated.

"What's he in for?" Donna asked, and Erin looked up at her, surprised by the question.

"What do you mean?"

The nurse shrugged. "It says 'pneumonia' in the chart. Most people with pneumonia don't end up on a ventilator."

"He was septic," Erin said. "The infection spread to his bloodstream."

Donna nodded. "It happens sometimes, mostly with the elderly or people with a suppressed immune system."

"They found something," Erin said, "a growth in his lung that needs to be biopsied."

"Yes, I heard about that. He wasn't a smoker?"

"No."

"And there's no family history of lung cancer?"

"Not that I know of."

"It's strange," she said as she lifted David's left arm, gently raising it above his head. "It's hard to know what to think about that."

"Sometimes bad things happen to good people."

"Yes," she said, and looked over at Erin. "Sometimes bad things happen to all kinds of people."

Erin placed her hands on the rail of the hospital bed. "There's a police officer stationed outside the room. I know how that must look."

Donna flexed David's arm at the elbow, paused for a moment, then brought it back to its original position.

"You've probably heard some rumors," Erin said. "News about my father seems to have traveled faster than a fire in high wind."

Donna shook her head. "No, ma'am, I haven't. I do my best not to listen to rumors. As for the police officer stationed in the hallway, if your father has done something wrong, then God will be his judge, not me." She returned David's arm to its resting place on the pillow. "You lost your mother," she said. "You were just a kid back then, but . . . I remember."

Erin sat down in the chair next to her father's bed. She could feel her throat tighten, the old pain rising to the surface.

"For all these years you've wondered what happened to her," the nurse said. "It's hard to get closure on a thing like that. It's hard to put it to rest." She walked around to the other side of the bed. Gently she lifted David's right arm, her fingers folded around his wrist and elbow. "My Jimmy went missing. Did you know that? He was six years old when it happened."

Erin looked up at her. She put a hand to her lips. She hadn't recognized her. The woman was older now, her hair graying at the roots.

"For a long time I prayed for a miracle," Donna said. "I asked God to bring my boy back to me." She looked down at the bed. "I was desperate. I was willing to do anything."

"You're . . . Donna Raffey. I'm sorry, I . . . I didn't . . ."

"The last name's different now. I got divorced and remarried. These days I'm Donna Kensington." Her eyes focused on the wall for a few seconds before clearing. "But Raffey, yes. I guess I'm that woman, too."

"I'm so sorry," Erin said. "I was older than Jimmy. I didn't know him well. I think I only saw you once, at the funeral."

"It was a memorial service," she said, "not a funeral. I guess it doesn't matter. We treated them like they were dead, Jimmy and all the others."

Erin swallowed. It had been a long time since she'd thought about that day. Her parents had taken her to the service. She'd worn a dark blue dress because she didn't have one that was black. Erin had felt self-conscious about it, telling her mother that she wanted to remain in the car. "Why do I have to be here anyway?" she'd asked. "I barely knew Jimmy Raffey." Helen Reece had turned in her seat and looked at her. "We aren't here for Jimmy," she said. "We're here for the people he left behind."

"I didn't give up on him," Donna said, and Erin jumped at the sound of her voice. "I prayed to God for a miracle. 'Bring him home to me,' I pleaded. 'Bring him back to Wolf Point where he belongs.'"

Erin took a breath. It rustled in her chest like the wings of a bird before it settled.

"It's a funny thing about miracles," Donna said. "When they do happen, it's never the way we expect." She moved David's arm through its range of motion, flexing and extending the joints as if the act itself brought her comfort. "My Jimmy never did make it back to me. It was the Lord's will that I would never see him again." She returned David's arm to his side. The hospital gown had slid down at his shoulder, and she adjusted it, smoothing out the fabric where it had gathered in the middle.

Donna stepped away from the bed. "Something was buried in the earth for a long time, and now it's not. When you think about it, *that's* a kind of miracle, don't you think?" The corners of her mouth turned downward, a brief current of sadness that was there and then gone in the space of a second. "All those unanswered questions. All that we lost and never found. We've been trapped in the past for too long, Erin. Maybe finally we can be free."

"It won't bring them back," Erin told her, but the nurse just smiled and shook her head.

"I don't expect it to," she said. "It'll bring *us* back. It's enough, isn't it?"

14

IT WAS ANOTHER TWO HOURS BEFORE ERIN TURNED RIGHT ONTO the dirt road off Highway 2 about half a mile east of the city line. Like most of Roosevelt County, this was an unincorporated area composed mostly of farmland, and the Tabaha residence looked much the same as she remembered, a modest ranch house with a few distant neighbors. The color of the gray siding had faded over the years, and the yard seemed smaller, the grass sparse and patchy. The small front porch faced west toward Wolf Point, and the property was backed up against a dry riverbed that twisted like a desiccated serpent across the open plains.

Her father's farm was two miles east of here. The fastest bike route between the two places was along the dirt shoulder of the BNSF railroad tracks, a journey she'd made countless times during her youth. Back then, the freight trains had passed through with more regularity, long processions of tankers, boxcars, and open hoppers. Biking along the tracks, she'd been able to hear them approach for five minutes before they trundled past her, the steel wheels shrieking against the rails, the ground vibrating beneath her. She'd ride alongside, her legs pumping as she tried to keep pace while the roar of the train reverberated in her skull and her heart thudded in her chest like her body's own persistent locomotive.

Erin parked the truck in the dirt driveway, opened the door, and stepped outside. The yard was silent and empty, the only sound coming from the occasional murmur of passing cars on the highway. From what she could see through the front windows, the interior of the house looked dark and vacant. She took a step forward, her eyes moving along the exterior of the building. The maple tree in the backyard had shed its leaves for the winter, but a few of its branches poked above the roof line. She had the urge to walk around back and get down on her knees to search for the name they'd carved into its trunk. The *e* was the hardest letter, she remembered, the way it circled in on itself like water in a drain.

Maybe he's back there, she thought. *Maybe he's still kneeling in the dirt at the base of the tree.* She closed her eyes, picturing it, the way the speckled light had filtered through the branches and fallen on his shoulders.

I could go back there. I could kneel down beside him and we could start over.

Erin stepped onto the porch. The boards creaked beneath her as she curled her right hand into a fist and rapped her knuckles on the door.

"Coming," a man said, and she could hear footsteps on the floorboards, the sound of someone approaching from the hall.

Don't let it be him. Please don't let it be him.

But you came here to see him, a voice reasoned, and she winced, aware of the mixed truth in that. Maybe she *had* come here to see him. Then again, maybe she hoped to find him gone, moved to someplace far away, married with a few kids and doing just fine without her. Maybe *that* was her reason for coming, to assure herself that the boy she once knew wasn't still back here hunkered down in the yard, whittling his name into the bark.

The doorknob turned. She looked down at it and waited.

"May I help you?" the man said from the other side of the threshold. His face was creased and tanned from the sun, the outer corners of his eyes marked by crow's-feet. He was not yet an old man, but he was well on his way, at least twenty years older than Erin herself.

"Matta," she said. "Mr. Tabaha. It's—"

"Erin," he said. "Erin Reece." He stepped forward and embraced her, his arms thin but strong, like the branches of the tree she'd seen peeking above the roof line.

Erin closed her eyes. *Home,* she thought, but this wasn't home. This was the place to which she'd chosen to escape. She could feel the pedals beneath her sneakers, the press of the handlebars against the palms of her hands. The ground vibrated as the train rattled along its tracks, bearing down on her, chasing her away from her father's house and the ghost of her mother. "You came back," Matta said, but Erin tasted the shame of it, the familiar guilt of standing in front of *this* doorway instead of the one that belonged to her parents.

He took a step back and held her at arm's length. "You've grown up," he said, looking at her, and he laughed, as if the reality of it surprised him.

She smiled. "I couldn't stay a child forever."

"No," he said. "I suppose not. Still, it's . . ." He shifted his gaze to the Chevy pickup parked in front of his house. "You've got a passenger," he said, nodding in that direction.

Erin glanced back over her shoulder. "My dog," she said. "Rhodesian ridgeback. His name's Diesel."

"Diesel."

"Yeah, I'm a veterinarian now. Someone dropped him off

at my office two years ago after he got hit by a truck. It was one of those tractor-trailers with a big diesel engine. The guy who brought him in saw it happen; only the truck driver never stopped. So this six-month-old puppy had a fractured pelvis, broken ribs, and some blood in his lungs that rattled when he breathed. Sounded like a diesel engine himself when I listened to him with the stethoscope."

"He's lucky he survived."

"Yes, he is," she said. "We didn't name him until it became clear he was going to make it. That may sound harsh, but a lot of these animals don't. No sense in naming a dog that dies within the first twenty-four hours of being carried through your doors."

Matta nodded. "So he became Diesel, and you adopted him."

"Right. Normally, in cases like that, we label it *HBC,* or *Hit By Car.* In this case it was a truck, so my technician labeled it *Dog vs. Diesel* on the chart, and the name kind of stuck. That was two and a half years ago. I've had him ever since."

"Well, don't leave him in the truck," he said. "Bring him in. My twelve-year-old coonhound passed away a few months ago. I've got a box of Milk-Bone biscuits in the closet that I haven't been able to bring myself to throw away yet. With your permission, Diesel can have a few if he wants them."

"Thank you," she said, "I'm sure he'd enjoy them," and Erin went back to the truck to let him out.

Matta swung the door wide and stepped to the right as they entered, giving them a view of the hallway and the family room beyond. He closed the door behind them, then turned and proceeded down the hallway, his movements deliberate and careful, like a man who no longer trusted his own body to serve him as it should. Diesel ran ahead, and Erin followed at a short distance, taking in the blank walls of the hallway, the dim lighting of the family room with its cluttered coffee table and dated furniture. A sliding glass door offered a partial view of the backyard—and *yes,* there was the maple tree the way she remembered. It was an old tree when she was a child, the trunk dividing about five feet up into two primary limbs that stretched horizontally like a man's outstretched arms before turning skyward and giving rise to the other branches. From October through early November, the leaves would turn yellow and then bright orange before falling to the ground in a trickle of smoldering embers. She had missed it by two weeks, she figured, and Matta or a hired worker had wasted no time in raking them up. There were still a few of them scattered in the grass, she saw, ones who had outlived their siblings or had simply been left behind to be blanketed by snow in the coming winter.

Matta stopped in the kitchen to fetch the box of biscuits. "Can I offer you a drink?" he asked. "I no longer keep alcohol in the house, but I have juice and water. If you'd like some coffee, I'd be happy to brew up a pot for the two of us."

"No, thank you," Erin said. "I stopped off for lunch at the Old Town Grill."

"The Old Town Grill," he said. "Does Kimberly Mathus still work there?"

"I don't know. The place was pretty empty. The name of my waitress was . . . Ophelia, I think. Something that started with an O."

"Olivia," he said. "Olivia Palmer."

"Yes, that's it."

"Sweet girl. Lost her mother to cancer a few years back."

"I'm sorry."

"It's okay," he said. "She's a friend of the family." He was standing over his recliner, the box of biscuits in his hand. "Now, how many of these do you think he'd like?"

"No more than two," she said. "He's still young, but his previous orthopedic injuries make him prone to arthritis. Best to keep him trim and healthy."

"Two it is," he said, "one for now and one for later." He reached into the box, withdrew a biscuit, and broke it in half. Diesel's ears perked up at the sound of that, and he approached Matta and took it gently from his outstretched hand.

"Have a seat," he told Erin, and Matta lowered himself into his chair. The cushion wheezed as he sat down on it. He leaned back until he found the position that was most comfortable for him, then held out the second half of the biscuit until Diesel took it from his hand and made it disappear like the first.

Erin sat down on the couch. She turned her body sideways to face him.

"How's your father?" he asked. "I read about what happened in the paper."

"He's getting better," she said. "Dr. Houseman hopes to get him off the ventilator soon."

"Ventilator. Now *that* sounds serious."

"He's recovering nicely. By the time I got here, the worst of it was already behind him."

Really? she asked herself. *Is that what you think, that the worst of this is over?*

"—s a good doctor," Matta was saying. "Keeps telling me that I need a hip replacement. But hell, I'm kind of attached to the one I've got."

Diesel had taken up residence beside the recliner. Matta reached down and ran his hand along the dog's right flank.

"You've come to see Robbie," he said. "We named him Kohana, his mother and me. It's a Lakota name, in honor of his great-grandfather."

"Funny," she said, "Robbie never told me that."

"Kohana," he repeated. "It means swift or light-footed."

"It's fitting," she said. "He could always outrace me. He was the fastest kid I knew."

She turned her head and looked out again at the yard through the sliding glass door. *I knelt there once,* she thought. The ground was puckered around the tree base where its roots had dug themselves into the soil.

Erin was quiet for a moment. "Robbie doesn't live here anymore, does he?"

"No," he said. "He has a place of his own. It's out on the reservation, where his grandfather used to live."

"I remember the place," she said. "He took me there a few times."

Matta nodded.

"He's okay?" she asked.

Matta took a moment to answer, and Erin found herself holding her breath as she waited.

"People change," he said. "He's not the same person you remember."

"Change," she said. "How do you mean? Is he sick? Has something happened to him?"

He looked down at his hands and thought it over. "Yes," he said. "I believe that it has."

"What?" she asked, and she sat there in silence, waiting for the response.

Matta shook his head. "You'd have to ask him," he said. "He won't speak to me. I wasn't a very good father, you know. When Robbie's mother passed four years ago, I thought . . .

well . . . I thought maybe he might come home and live with me for a while."

"I'm sorry to hear about your wife. I didn't know."

"She lives on," he said. "That's what we believe in. People pass from one plane of existence to the next. We lost her brother the following year. It was cancer that got the both of them."

"I'm so sorry."

He shook his head, dismissing it. "You will go to see him, then? Robbie, I mean. You will try to talk to him?"

"Yes," she said. "I will."

"Good," he said, and he seemed genuinely pleased by the idea. "If anyone can get through to him . . ."

Erin looked down at her hands. "So much has happened. I should've come back sooner."

"You're back now. Maybe that'll be enough." He reached into the box and retrieved the second biscuit. "Do you have a place to stay while you're here in town? I ask only because—"

"They won't let me stay at my father's farm. If you know he's in the hospital, I assume you know the rest of it."

Matta looked down, embarrassed.

"I'm staying at the Homestead Inn," she told him.

"Oh," he said. "I didn't know they allowed dogs."

"Actually, they are pet-friendly, so I'm able to take him into the room with me."

"If you'd rather, you could stay with me," he said. "I'd be happy to have you."

It was a tempting offer, and Erin took a few seconds to think it over. It was nice to see Matta again. If he had an opinion about what had been unearthed on her father's farm, he had apparently decided to keep it to himself. But when it came to that particular development, it seemed to Erin that Matta was in the minority. "People will expect justice," Betty Doyle had told her, "and some of them might not want to stop at just that." Was it right to drag Matta into this? Did she want to accept the responsibility for making him guilty by association?

"I appreciate the offer," she said, "I really do. But there are some things I have to take care of, things that are better sorted out on my own."

"You don't want to bring the wrath of the town upon me," he said. "A swarm of locusts and a plague upon my house. Is that what you're worried about?"

"Or just a bunch of angry people looking for a scapegoat."

"I see," he said. "But the invitation stands if you change your mind. You know you're always welcome here. You and Diesel both."

"Thank you."

He looked down at the dog. "If you want to leave him with me rather than keep him cooped up in the truck and the hotel room, I'd be fine with that, you know. I've got the space, and I could use the company."

Erin shook her head. "It doesn't feel right," she said. "I couldn't ask you to—"

"It's no trouble," he told her. "Over the past ten years, I lost my son, my wife, and my dog. It's too quiet here with just me. You let me watch Diesel while you're tending to your father and you'd be doing *me* a favor, not the other way around."

Erin looked at Diesel. Driving up from Colorado with the dog lying on the bench seat beside her, she had imagined them staying at her father's house with the full expanse of the farm at their disposal. Diesel was a good dog, but she couldn't leave him in the hotel room during the day, and leaving him in the truck didn't seem fair, either. She'd been trying to come up with a solution, and here it was, unexpected but reasonable.

"Are you sure?" she asked. "It's a lot to ask of you."

"I'm sure," he said. "We'll get along fine. I can tell already."

"Maybe we can try it out for a few days," she said. "I'll stop by every day to check on you. If it becomes too much . . ."

"Then it's back to the Homestead Inn." He stood up, and Diesel got to his feet as well.

"I have bowls and food for him in the truck."

"Perfect," he said, and they waited until she returned with the items and placed them in the kitchen.

"I wish your father a speedy recovery," he said as they stood at the front door. "It's difficult circumstances, I know, but . . . I'm sure things will work out for the best."

"Thank you," she said, and she knelt in front of Diesel and ruffled his ears before clipping the leash to his collar and handing it to Matta. "You're gonna stay here for a while," she told her dog, and he sat at Matta's feet as she stroked the fur on the side of his neck.

Erin stood up and gave Matta a hug. "Thank you," she said. "I appreciate you helping us."

"Of course," he told her, and as she turned toward the truck, Erin noticed that the golden hue of late afternoon was already fading. It would be dark in just over an hour—*and how had it gotten so late so quickly?* she wondered. Only, it wasn't late. It was mid-November, and the daylight was weak and fleeting.

I'll go to see Robbie tomorrow, she decided.

"Good luck," he told her. "I hope he'll talk to you. I remember the way the two of you used to whisper, like you were sitting down to tea with a kettle of secrets."

She smiled. "It's good to see you."

"It's good to see *you,* Erin," he said, and he paused and looked down for a moment before continuing. "Tell him I miss him. Tell him the door to this house is always open."

"I will," she promised, and she turned and walked back

to the truck. *Robbie doesn't live here anymore,* she thought, but that wasn't exactly true. She'd felt his presence as much as his absence in the empty hall and dimly lit family room. She'd looked through the glass doorway and imagined him hunkered down at the base of the tree, and Erin had no doubt that Matta could sense him, too: his child standing at the bathroom sink and brushing his teeth before bed; the thump of his son's shoes as he ran through the house. He was everywhere, and he was nowhere. It had been the same way with her mother.

Erin started the truck and backed away from the house. "Tomorrow, then," she told herself, and put the vehicle into Drive.

He was still standing in the doorway with Diesel, watching her, and Erin lifted her hand before she left. Matta waved back, but she lost sight of them in the rearview mirror as she moved down the road, the man, the dog, and the house disappearing in the dust.

15

MARIAN MONTGOMERY TURNED OUT THE KITCHEN LIGHT, CROSSED the living room, and settled into her leather recliner in front of the television. Between her thumb and forefinger, she held the upper corner of a bag of Orville Redenbacher's Naturals Light popcorn, which she had removed from the microwave but had not yet opened.

She opened the bag carefully, pulling outward at two of the opposing corners. A plume of steam rose through the opening, and Marian leaned forward (being cautious not to burn herself) and breathed in the warm buttery smell. She waited until the steam had dissipated, then reached into the bag to retrieve a piece. It was salty against her lips, but not too salty. She chewed, swallowed, and retrieved another.

Everything you need to know about popcorn was contained in the number two, she thought. A box of six bags of Orville Redenbacher sold for two dollars and twenty-five cents at the Town Pump Food Store, where she worked as a checkout clerk. With her ten percent employee discount, that came to two dollars and two cents, a sign from God if she'd ever seen one. It wasn't just the popcorn, either. Marian loved the number two. In many ways, it defined her life. Several years ago, she'd purchased a small ranch-style home on two acres at 246 Rodeo Road. She was one of two sisters, and she'd been born on February 22, 1960. She'd been married for only two years before her ex-husband, the son of a bitch, left her for another woman. *Not that it mattered,* she thought. She had a sixteen-year-old son who decided to move in with his father two years ago, but other than that she'd given up on men altogether. These days she lived with her two cats, Milo and Otis.

Marian tore the corner of the bag and extended it halfway down for easier access. She plucked out three more pieces and ate them, one at a time. It was ten-thirty at night and time for *The Tonight Show with Jay Leno.* The TV was already on, and she sat through a few commercials as she waited for the show to begin. The local news anchor came on for a fifteen-second teaser for the late-night news. There were reports that a U.S. Air Force plane had crashed in Croatia, FBI agents had arrested a man named Ted Kaczynski, and there were no signs yet of Angela Finley, Rose Perry, or Curt Hastings, all of whom had disappeared from Wolf Point during recent storms over the past two months.

Marian shook her head. Montana winters could be brutal, the snow piling up until almost nothing was recognizable. If you wandered off and lost your bearings, you didn't stand a chance.

She caught a blur of movement in her peripheral vision, and suddenly the cat was on her lap, purring loudly and sniffing at the bag of popcorn.

"Where's your brother?" she asked the orange tabby, but Milo didn't answer. Instead, he settled down on her lap and prodded the bag with the tip of his nose.

"Oh no," Marian told him. "Popcorn is not good for cats." She did not know if this was true or not, but Milo had a sensitive stomach, and she did not want to clean up a mess later. Marian stroked the top of the feline's head and turned the volume up on the remote so she could hear Jay Leno's opening monologue over the cyclical hum of Milo's purring.

KA-THUMP.

Marian and Milo turned their heads simultaneously.

"Oh great. What's your brother up to?" Marian reached over and turned the volume down on the remote.

KA-THUMP-RUM.

"Otis?" she called out. "You'd better not be up on the dresser again."

Milo jumped down from her lap and disappeared into the kitchen. Marian paused with her finger on the remote. "Otis," she said, "what are you doing back there?"

On the television, Leno was interviewing people on the street. "Why does the moon orbit the Earth?" he asked an auto mechanic. The man thought about it. "To get to the other side?"

Marian shivered. There was a draft coming from the hallway, and that didn't make any sense because there were no doors back there, just her bedroom and the bathroom.

She placed the remote and the popcorn bag on the book table beside her. It was irritating to have to get up like this. She did not like to miss the first part of *The Tonight Show*. Later would've been better, during the musical number.

"Our guests this evening include football Hall of Famer Terry Bradshaw."

There was another sound from the bedroom, a scraping noise, like the leg of a chair sliding along the floorboards.

"What in *the hell* have you gotten into?" she asked, and she hustled down the hallway, worried now that perhaps the cat was injured. She could picture it in her head, the large wall-mounted mirror or perhaps even the dresser toppled over and lying facedown on the floor. And Otis, trapped beneath it, using the nails of his front paws to try to pull the back end of his body out from under it.

She passed the closet in the hallway, then rounded the corner and stepped into the bedroom. The dresser was standing in its usual position, the mirror still hanging from its hook on the wall. There was nothing broken and lying on the floor, no injured cat pulling himself across the room. She checked the adjacent bathroom. Her toothbrush stood upright in its holder next to her blow dryer, and the door to the vanity mirror above the sink was closed as it should be. The toilet seat cover was down so the cats wouldn't be tempted to drink from the bowl. It was her fear that they might fall inside headfirst and drown in the water. *Had such a thing ever happened?* she wondered. Maybe not. But Marian had an active imagination, and sometimes it got the best of her.

She checked anyway, lifting the toilet lid to make sure that Otis wasn't trapped inside. The bowl was empty, just a small puddle of water at the bottom. Marian turned and looked at the shower curtain, a scattered array of sand and seashells.

What if there's someone standing there on the other side?

She shuddered, victim again to her own imagination. She could even picture him, a large man with dark black hair and broad shoulders. She would pull the curtain back to find him grinning at her, his eyes wild and void of reason. *Nonsense,* she told herself. *There's no one in this house but me and the cats.* But she looked around anyway and picked up the closest weapon she could find. *And what will I do with this?* she wondered, looking at the toilet bowl plunger with its long orange handle and black rubber cup. She turned it around, stick end forward, and readied herself to jab it in the face of anyone standing on the other side of the curtain.

This is my house, she thought, summoning her courage. She reached out, her hand hesitating at the edge of the curtain, and yanked it open. She let out a small battle cry as she did this. It rose from her midsection like the vocalization of an opera singer and died on her lips when she saw that the shower was empty.

Marian slid the curtain closed and returned the plunger to its plastic stand next to the toilet. *How stupid,* she thought, *to think that anyone would care about breaking into* this *house.* She had almost nothing of value, just her television and her cats and a few trinkets that meant nothing to anyone but her. Her life was small, and it had gotten smaller over the years instead of bigger. Ten years ago, she'd seen her current situation as a brief stopping point on her way to something greater. These days she saw it for what it was: a trivial, insignificant existence with little promise of anything better. And the only thing that really bothered her (during the rare occasions when she thought about such things) was that it didn't bother her at all.

"Otis," she said. "Otis, where *are* you?"

She turned out the light and left the bathroom. She was irritated now, angry that she'd missed the first portion of *The Tonight Show.* She didn't care that much about Terry Bradshaw. She wasn't a sports fan and was only vaguely aware of his accomplishments. She liked Jay Leno, though, the way he could banter so easily with almost anyone. It was part of her evening routine: popcorn, Leno, and time spent reading until her eyes grew heavy and she fell aslee—

She stopped in the middle of the bedroom. The book on her nightstand had been moved. It was near the edge now, on the opposite side from where she usually kept it. And there were her reading glasses, lying on the floor next to the bed. She walked over, picked them up, and placed them back on the book where they belonged. There was an analog alarm clock on the nightstand as well, an antique she had picked up at a flea market a few years back. She adjusted its position, noting that the big hand was on the number nine. *Quarter of eleven,* she thought. She was missing the best part of the show.

Marian looked around the room once again. It was warmer now than it had been when she'd first entered the bedroom a few minutes ago.

"Otis?" she called. "You leave my books alone, do you hear? If you want to read something, I'll get you a book of your—"

She stopped, staring at the window. It was open, just a crack. She could feel cold air seeping into the room through the opening.

How long has it been this way? A day? Maybe more? It was expensive to heat the house in the winter. She couldn't afford to be leaving the windows open in early April.

Marian pushed down on the upper rail, closing the window. She had cleaned the windows a week ago. Had she forgotten to lock this one? Had it been open since then?

That's not the only thing. Look at the closet.

Marian took a step toward the bedroom closet. The left bi-fold door was open—not completely, but enough for one of the cats to sneak inside. She knew better than that. It was too easy to close the door and inadvertently trap one of them inside.

"You've gotten careless," she told herself. Otis had gotten in there and knocked over the ironing board. That was the thud she'd heard. Maybe it fell against the wall and slid to the floor a few seconds later. That was the scraping noise and the second thud.

She pulled the left bifold all the way open, then tried to open the right one as well. Some of her shoeboxes had toppled over, and they caught in the place where the right door folded in on itself. She got down on her hands and knees and reached behind the door to push them out of the way.

The closet was packed with clothes and dresses that hung from the rack above her. She got the right door open and restacked the boxes the way she liked them. The bottom of one of the boxes was wet, and she put it aside to dry. There was some water on the floor of the closet—*or urine,* she thought. She leaned over and sniffed. Not cat urine, just water, and a few bits of melting snow.

What's going on here? she asked herself, but she could feel the hair standing up on the back of her neck, the gooseflesh erupting on her forearms.

She removed the shoeboxes. With the clothes in the way, it was hard to see everything, but here was the ironing board, folded up and still leaning against the wall of the closet in its usual position.

"Otis, you come out now. That's enough hiding for one evening."

There was a rustling noise, something shifting in the closet.

Marian looked up. The clothes above her started to part, pushed aside by the massive shape of a man who ducked under the wooden bar and took a shuffling step toward her.

Marian screamed and scuttled backward across the floor. The back of her head contacted the nightstand, and the thing wobbled a moment on its wooden legs before settling.

The man pushed through the clothes and stepped into the room. Several of the garments pulled loose from their hangers and slid from his body like sloughed skin. He wore jeans caked white with snow, a dark green jacket the color of sewer sludge, and a brown winter cap that barely covered the tops of his ears. There was a two-day growth of stubble on his face, and dark eyes that seemed to look right through her.

Marian opened her mouth and screamed again, as loud as she could. The man took a step forward, leaned over, and slapped her.

"Stop now," he said. "You need to stop doing that."

He put his hands around her left calf and began pulling her toward the center of the room.

He's going to rape me. He's broken into my house and is about to rape me.

Marian clutched at the legs of the furniture. Her fingers closed around a vertical pillar and the nightstand tipped over and crashed to the floor. Her book, reading glasses, and alarm clock scattered in all directions.

"Stop it," he said, and he sounded annoyed. He pulled her again, and she slid across the floor and away from the bed, her right cheek scraping the floorboards.

He let go of her leg, but a moment later he was looming over her, stuffing her mouth with a roughly textured fabric that tasted of sweat and motor oil. She gagged and wrapped her left hand around his wrist, trying to push him away.

"No," he said. "You asked for this." But his face was one she recognized. It was only her fear and surprise that had prevented her from recognizing him sooner. She tried to tell him so, but the rag was in her mouth, gagging her, his fingers stuffing it deeper.

I will not be raped and strangled on the floor of my own house, she thought, and she brought her right arm up and struck him in the face. To Marian's surprise, there was a satisfying ring to it, a distinct *ching* at the moment she made contact. The man let go of the cloth and tilted backward. There was a cut on his left cheekbone, the skin there turning fire-engine red.

Marian looked down to find that she was holding the alarm clock. The big hand, she saw, was between the ten and eleven.

The man reached up and put a hand to the left side of his face. A trickle of blood ran beneath his palm and stopped at the jawline.

His weight was on her right leg, pinning it against the floor, but Marian's left leg was free. She brought it up as far as it would go and kicked out at him, striking him in the chest and shoving him backward.

He struck the closet door, knocking it from its attachments. The door clattered down on top of him, landing across his body.

Marian scrambled to her feet. Her right leg felt numb and unreliable, a collection of pins and needles that tingled when she shifted her weight onto it. She used it like a crutch, putting just enough weight on it to propel her forward. She made it to the hallway before she heard the sound of the man coming after her—quick and heavy steps that filled her with panic.

Can't breathe, can't breathe, she thought, and Marian was halfway down the hallway before she realized that the cloth was still in her mouth. She yanked it out, drew in a ragged breath, and stumbled onward.

CLOMP, CLOMP, CLOMP, CLOMP.

(*He's coming for you! He's coming for you down the hallway!*)

The alarm clock was still in her hand. She threw it back at him without turning around, just hurled it over her shoulder as hard as she could. It hit the wall and clattered to the floor.

Doesn't matter. Get to the kitchen.

She passed the easy chair and the coffee table, Jay Leno on the television introducing his next guest. There was the remote and the bag of popcorn next to her chair, and big fat

Otis crouched low on his haunches under the dining room table.

You were never in that room, she thought, and Otis looked back at her as if to say, *I never told you that I was.*

She rounded the corner, lurched into the kitchen, and saw a blur of orange fur at her feet as Milo shot past her. Marian stumbled over the cat. Her right hip caught the hard edge of the countertop.

"Damn it," she hissed, but Marian shuffled forward anyway and came to a stop at the far end of the room. There were carving knives in the wooden rack. She grabbed two of the longest ones by the handles and spun around to face him.

Breathing hard. Sucking air into her lungs in deep greedy gulps that made a high-pitched noise on the way out, like tiny screams that fell away to nothing.

"Heeeeee . . . heeeeee . . . heeeeeeeeee . . ."

CLOMP, CLOMP, CLOMP.

He stopped just outside the kitchen. She could sense him standing there, just around the corner.

"Whatcha got there?"

Marian's body tightened. She could see the silhouette of him now, standing in the entryway. "Go away. I've already called 911."

"You *did*? What did you do *that* for?"

She stood in the corner, shaking. Each breath was a dagger sliding in and out of her.

"Please. I'm warning you."

He was quiet for a moment, watching her.

"What do you *want*?" she asked. "I don't have any money."

"I don't want your money." He took a step toward her.

"*No,*" she shrieked. "Don't come any closer."

"I want you to come with me," he said. "We can be friends. You and me, we have a lot in common."

"No, we don't. I don't have anything in common with anyone."

He laughed at that. "Yes, you do. You're special. Just like me."

"*Please,*" she said. "You don't have to do this."

"I'm just trying to be friendly," he told her, and he sounded hurt that she wasn't returning the sentiment. "Remember when that was the most important thing? Remember when we spent most of our time just trying to get people to like us?"

"Nobody likes me," she said. "Nobody even notices."

"I like you," he said. "I like you a *lot.*"

"Then go away. If you like me, leave me alone."

"Leave you *alone*? How are we gonna be friends if I leave you alone?"

Marian pressed her back against the counter. *I'll kill him,* she thought. *I'll kill him if he comes any closer.*

"Are you gonna stab me with one of those knives? I come here asking to be your friend and *that's* the way you treat me?"

"I don't want to," she told him. "I want you to go away."

"I can't do that. Then *I'd* be the one getting into trouble."

"Why? Because I saw your face? It was dark in the bedroom. I don't remember."

He shook his head.

"*It's true,*" she said. "Leave now and I *promise* I won't say a word to anyone."

He stood there, one hand resting on the counter.

"You should put those down," he said. "This isn't the way I wanted it."

"I'll *kill you* if I have to."

He sighed, turned around, and left the room. She could hear him walking down the hallway toward the bedroom.

What's he doing? Where is he going?

Marian looked to the right. The sliding glass door to the backyard was right here, next to the kitchen. There was snow out there, two feet of it, but there was also more space to run, a chance to get away. If she went now, before he came back, she'd have a good head start. Maybe she could even find a place to hide.

No, she thought. *He'll catch me. He's stronger and faster and dressed for the snow.*

Marian touched her wrist to her nightgown and felt the cool caress of the tile floor on the naked soles of her feet.

I'll die out there. Even if he doesn't catch me.

The front door, then. The truck was parked in the driveway and the keys were hanging from the hook on the wall. Could she get to them before he returned?

(*Maybe he's waiting for you, just around the corner.*)

She paused to think it over, and that was when she heard it: the scraping noise she'd heard earlier. It started at the far end of the hallway and drew closer, a low-pitched dragging sound that built in volume and authority until it came to a stop just around the corner.

She could see him, just the front edge of his body in profile. He turned his head slowly to face her.

"I'm sorry about this," he said. "I've got something bad and you're not gonna like it."

"*Please,* can't you just leave me alone?"

"No," he said. "The rules are clear. I can't come back without it."

"Without what?" she asked.

He looked at her and lifted the axe. It stood out against the background of light from the living room.

"You," he said, and then he was upon her.

16

LIEUTENANT JEFF STUTZMAN TURNED ON HIS SIGNAL, SLOWED THE
Chevy Suburban, and made a left onto Route 13 off Indian
Highway. It had been a pretty drive through Montana farmland, but his mind hadn't registered much of the quiet stretch.
Instead, he'd been thinking about the phone call he'd gotten
on his cellular thirty minutes earlier from Todd Pitsinger, the
owner of the contracting company they'd been using to exca-
vate David Reece's property.

"It could be another body," Pitsinger had said, and Jeff's
mind flashed to the way the first one had looked in the bottom
of the sinkhole: the skeletal remains lying on their side and
partly buried in the mud, the open jawbone half visible, the left
eye socket black with sludge.

The Reeces' property was half a mile east of Route 13 and
six miles east of Wolf Point. The BNSF Railway ran north of
here, and the Missouri River was within walking distance to
the south. Technically, this was the town of Macon, but there
was nothing out here, just farmland and open sky, the smell of
cows and dirt and vanishing economic opportunity.

There was a time, Jeff thought, when people had made a decent living here, when a place like David Reece's farm could

turn a profit most years, and even the lean years weren't *that* lean. It was different now. Montana had been slow to adapt to changes in technology. The evolution of large corporate farms made it difficult for many of the smaller operations to compete. People discovered easier ways to make a living, and some of them— especially the young folks—had left Montana for better oppor- tunities elsewhere. Erin Reece had been one of those people, and she was not alone. There were fewer families with children now, and smaller class sizes at the local elementary school. Jeff's daughter, Kayla, was one of only thirteen students in her fifth- grade class. When Jeff attended Northside twenty-three years ago, there were at least twice that many. There was something horrible in those numbers. What did it mean, he wondered, when a town could no longer hold on to its children?

Jeff turned onto the dirt driveway and followed it back. It ended at a single-story farmhouse whose white wooden exte- rior looked as if it had been recently painted. It had a wrap- around porch, dark blue shutters, and a porch swing hanging from a set of chains to the right of the front door.

It was a small farm by Montana standards, a hundred and eighty-six acres. With Erin's permission, they'd moved the cattle and other livestock to a neighboring property, where David's farmhand, Travis Cooper, could continue the dairy operation in the midst of the investigation.

He grabbed his brown wide-brimmed hat from the passen- ger seat and stepped out of the Suburban. There was a tractor not far from the house near a large oak tree, and a rope and tire swing dangled from one of the tree's branches. He counted three men standing next to the tractor, two of them leaning on shovels. A fourth man, Pitsinger, was walking toward him.

"Thanks for coming out," Todd said. "I don't know what we've found yet, but . . . I think it might be something."

"What is it?" he asked as they walked toward the spot where the men were congregated.

Todd didn't answer right away. Instead he joined the others standing at the lip of an excavated section of earth. The hole was about ten feet across, fifteen feet in length, and six and a half feet deep.

"The GPR picked up a disruption in the layering of the soil here," he said. "At first we figured it was a root from the oak tree. It didn't make sense for a body to be buried so close to the house."

Jeff glanced over at the GPR machine. "Ground-penetrating radar" was the technical term for it, but it looked more like a lawn mower than anything else. Todd's company used it to identify underground utility lines and other potential hazards at a work site. It could be used to look for other things as well, however—bodies buried in the earth, for example. Granted, it was an imperfect science. The radar detected shifts in the horizontal layering of the soil. A blanket or a coffin could cause such a disturbance, but so could a rock, tree root, or any other object buried in the ground.

"The first body was discovered at the rear section of the property," Todd said. "If there's anything else out here, it stands to reason that he would've buried it in the same general area." He lifted his head and pointed to the young man standing to his left. "Joshua here's the one who found it."

Jeff nodded at the slim, pimple-faced boy who barely looked old enough to vote. The kid looked up long enough to give Jeff a crooked smile, then dropped his gaze. "I was calibrating the instrument and getting a baseline. The tree root helps with that."

"But you didn't find a tree root, did you? You found something bigger." Jeff focused his eyes on the thing at the bottom of the hole. "A piece of wood," he said. "You've identified the corners."

"Yeah," Todd said, "those are the corners. It's six and a half feet down—the top of it anyway. We used the tractor's back-hoe to dig the first four feet, then switched to shovels for the rest of it."

"Good," Jeff said. "It's important not to damage it."

"Right," Todd said, "although I wasn't thinking about the wood. I didn't want to slice through the remains of a body with the backhoe."

They were silent for a while, looking down at it.

"It's the top of a wooden rectangular box," Jeff said. "That's what you're telling me."

"Yes. That's what it looked like on the GPR. That's what got us digging."

"What are the measurements?"

Todd put a hand on his hip. "The section we've exposed is seventy-two inches long by twenty-eight inches wide."

Jeff thought about it for a moment. "It's short for a coffin."

"Is it?"

"Yes," he said. "A standard coffin is about eighty inches in length."

Todd frowned. "There's nothing standard about this one. There are nails around the perimeter, hammered into the lid. If you ask me, I'd say there's a pretty good chance the thing was built right here on the premises."

"Why here?"

Todd looked at him. "Because if you're killing people and burying them on your property, it's a bad idea to have profes-sionally made caskets delivered to your house."

Jeff reached up with his left hand and adjusted his hat. "No," he said, "that's not what I'm asking."

"What then?"

"We found the other one toward the back of the property. Why is this one all the way up here?"

"Hell if I know. Maybe there's another twelve of them spread out around the property."

"Maybe," he said, "but like you said, it doesn't make sense. And assuming there's a body inside, why is it buried in a coffin? The other one wasn't."

"That's for you to figure out, Lieutenant."

Jeff put his hands on his gun belt and looked down at the box.

"It could be nothing," Todd said. "Maybe somebody buried their dog here. You want us to open it? I've got a hammer in the truck. We could pull those nails out for you. Wouldn't take but a minute."

"No," he said. "Let's take our time with this. I need to call my boss and get some more people out here. He'll want photographs, forensics . . . the whole nine yards."

"And if the thing is empty, or the only body is the remains of a bloodhound from days gone by?"

Jeff looked at him. "I *hope* it's empty. I want it to be empty. Don't stop looking, though. The presence of this . . . thing . . . increases the likelihood that you'll find others." He reached out and put a hand on Todd's shoulder. "Find me some more," he said. "Find me everything that's out here."

Todd nodded and walked with him back to the truck.

"You okay?" Jeff asked. "You think you and your boys can finish this?"

"Yeah," he said. "It's just that . . . I mean . . . all those nails . . ."

"What about them?"

"It's like he wanted to keep something out. Or maybe," he said, "he was trying to keep something in."

There it is, Jeff thought. It was something he'd wondered about, too. *If he's right, there will be scratch marks on the inner surface, and bloodstains from fists pounding on the wood.*

"Listen," he said, "we'll get some folks out here to take a look. Once we get that lid off, we'll see what we find. Until then, I don't think there's any need to let our imaginations get the best of us."

"Okay, we'll get on with it then." Todd paused a moment, as if he wanted to ask something else or maybe quit the job altogether.

"You can do this," Jeff told him. "Just try to stay focused."

"Yeah," he said. "I mean . . . it's just another job, right?"

"No, it's not. These are people's lives we're dealing with. It's their chance to be found."

"Right."

Jeff opened the Suburban's heavy metal door, but he stood there for a moment with his hand on the roof. "The more I do this job, the less I believe in justice," he said. "It's not that it doesn't exist. It's just . . . so much different than what you want it to be." He shook his head. "Find everything you can. If there are more bodies out here, they deserve a proper burial. The families of these people have suffered enough."

Jeff started the engine, turned the truck around, and accelerated down the driveway. He would talk to the chief first, but he wanted to do it in person. On the drive back, he spoke with Maggie from dispatch and asked for an officer to be stationed at the entrance to the property. "No access in or out without prior authorization," he instructed, and for the rest of the trip he thought about David Reece lying in his hospital bed, and how the past is never buried as deeply as we imagine.

17

ERIN PULLED THE CHEVY ONTO THE DIRT SHOULDER AND CAME TO a stop. The tires kicked up a cloud of dust that enveloped the truck for a few seconds before drifting eastward across the open plain. She killed the engine, swung the driver's door open, and stepped out beneath an afternoon sun that was already descending toward the horizon. This morning's weather forecast had predicted a high of forty-one degrees, and she guessed that it was colder than that by now. She zipped her jacket, stood in the middle of the street, and looked north along the flat stretch of roadway that extended as far as she could see. Behind her was the hill she and Robbie had ascended on her first visit to the reservation. It had seemed taller and more formidable when she was younger, something she'd had to stand on her pedals to summit, the weight of her body shifted forward over the handlebars. Robbie had been ahead of her as he crested the hill, the sunlight beating down on his black hair and slim shoulders, the well-worn fabric of his faded red T-shirt rippling in the wind.

"*Wait up,*" she called out to him, but the words fell from her lips and were gone like a jackrabbit in the brush.

Erin pushed her hands into her pockets and slid the sole of her right boot across the asphalt. It was about here where the car had parked and its driver had gotten out to watch them. A black Dodge Challenger. A muscle car. She remembered the way its grille had gleamed in the sunlight, the hot shove of air as the car sliced past her on the roadway.

Almost hit me, she thought. *Would've killed me if he had.*

("You okay?")

("Yeah . . . Just surprised me, is all.")

Erin walked across the field and felt the turn of pebbles beneath her boots. She kept going until she came to the aqueduct. The floor of the concrete channel was littered with debris. Branches, mostly, but there were also a few beer cans and two black plastic bags, one of them caught on a stick and flapping in the wind. Farther down she could see something bigger, lying on its side. *It's a bike,* she thought, and her stomach did a slow roll, as if she'd just spotted the rotting carcass of an animal lying in the sun.

She walked along the lip of the aqueduct until she was close enough to see what it really was: an old rusted shopping cart that was missing one of its wheels. There was nothing inside it, no clue about its final cargo or how it wound up here, miles from the closest grocery store.

("Oh man.")

("What?")

("He's coming.")

("*Get down here!*")

("No . . . You go . . . I'll catch up with you.")

Erin closed her eyes. She could feel herself pedaling, her heart racing in her chest.

What if he had gotten caught that day? What if the man had taken him?

"He didn't," she said, but it wasn't the first time she had almost lost him. That day at the quarry had been the first. The reckoning with Vinny Briggs had come three months later.

"I don't want to fight him," Robbie had told her at the beginning of that summer, and Erin had answered that it didn't matter whether he wanted to or not.

"Just beating you up won't be enough for him," she said. "Vinny aims to kill you. And even if he doesn't kill you, you'll *wish* you were dead. It'll happen if you let it, not just one day but many. The only person who can put a stop to it is you."

"I can't stop it. I can't do anything."

"Yes, you can. His arm is in a cast now. It'll take time to heal. We'll practice all summer if we have to. When he finally comes for you, you'll be ready."

Robbie shook his head. "I'm no good at fighting. You're going to get me killed."

"'You fight them once or you fight them every day.' That's what my dad told me. He had to do the same thing when he first got to prison."

"Vinny's bigger and stronger than I am."

"Doesn't matter. You just have to be the last one standing."

"Forget it," he said. "I'm not fighting him. We'll think of something else. I'll move to China if I have t—"

She jumped on him then, bringing him to the ground. They rolled in the dirt, and Erin punched him in the ribs over and over as hard as she could, her fists pounding away at the side of him. Robbie wrestled himself free of her, got to his feet, and when she came at him again, he stepped to the side and shoved her to the ground.

"*Stop* it," he said. "What's *wrong* with you?"

"Nothing. I'm Vinny Briggs and I'm coming to beat the *shit* out of you." She charged him again, and this time he blocked some of her punches and threw a few of his own.

She hid her bruises from her mother for the rest of that summer, and Erin returned to Robbie's house day after day, dogged by the guilt of having made things worse for him and convinced that it was her responsibility to make things better. They stuffed their clothes with padding and learned to spar without hurting each other. They did push-ups and sit-ups and fought in the dirt. *He'll be ready,* she told herself, and she saw the change in him, the way he believed in it, too.

"And then the summer was over," Erin said to herself, and she stood there at the lip of the aqueduct, looking out across the terrain and remembering the rest.

"Get up. Get up if he knocks you down. Do you *hear* me?"

Robbie stood in front of her and nodded. A loose circle of kids had gathered at the soccer field to watch. More of them were coming, drawn to the impending fight like gnats to a porch light.

"You can do it," she told him. "Remember what we practiced. The winner is the one who keeps getting up."

"Enough talk," Vinny said. He walked over, grabbed Robbie from behind by the back of his shirt, slung him around, and sent him sprawling to the ground.

"Get up!" Erin yelled, but Robbie was slow getting to his feet.

Vinny walked over and kicked him hard in the ribs. "That's for the quarry," he said, "and this is for my broken arm, you *nasty little creep.*" He kicked Robbie again with the toe of his boot, connecting with his right shoulder.

Robbie grunted and rolled away from him. He got to his feet and took a few shuffling steps backward. There was blood on his knees, and he kept his right arm tucked against his ribs, like a bird with a broken wing.

He's faster than this, Erin thought, but his movements were sluggish, as if he'd already decided that the best course of action was no action at all.

Vinny took two steps forward. "You're a *freak,*" he said. "Everyone knows your dad's a drunk." He threw a haymaker and Robbie ducked it, but Vinny drove his knee upward into Robbie's face. There was a loud crunch as it slammed into his nose.

This isn't working, she thought. *All that practice over the summer didn't prepare him for* this.

Robbie was still standing, but his guard was down and there was blood gushing from a cut across the bridge of his nose. His right eye was already swollen, she noticed, *and how could a kid be expected to fight if he couldn't even see?*

The circle of spectators had tightened, and Vinny strutted around the periphery. "This is what happens when you try to mess with us," he said. "*I* didn't want this. *I* was gonna leave him alone." He pointed to Erin. "His girlfriend here is the one to blame. 'Just the two of you,' she said. Well, here we are, just the two of us, and one of us is getting his ass kicked." He stopped and looked at Erin. "You satisfied, or do you want me to beat him up some more?"

She opened her mouth and shut it. There was nothing she could say to make this better.

Vinny shook his head, turned, and walked over to his opponent. Robbie threw a punch—his first of the fight—but Vinny batted it down and socked him hard in the stomach.

Her friend doubled over and vomited on the ground.

"Oh, gross," Vinny said. "You gonna piss yourself next?" He put his hands on Robbie's chest and gave him a shove.

Robbie stumbled backward into the crowd. They pushed him away frantically, as if he was contagious, and sent him back into the center of the circle.

Vinny was there to meet him. He grabbed him by the hair and punched him twice in the face.

Robbie fell to his knees and the larger boy circled around behind him. He hooked one arm under his neck while he landed punches to the side of Robbie's head. "Don't you ever, ever, EVER disrespect me again," he said, and the sound of each impact was like the flat side of a board striking water.

"*Stop* it!" Erin yelled. "That's *enough*." She ran out into the middle of the circle and gave Vinny a shove.

"What are you *doing*?" Vinny asked, straightening himself. "Just him and me, that's what you wanted. You jump into this fight now and *all three* of *my* guys get to do the same."

"He's *done*," she said. "Can't you *see* that? You're gonna kill him."

"Maybe," he said. "Maybe he *wants* to be killed, the way he runs around picking fights. I broke my arm because of this dimwit. Two months in a cast over the summer. It's time for a little payback."

"You've done enough," she said. "It's over."

"It's over when I say it's . . ." He stopped and put his hands on his hips. He was looking past her now.

She felt a hand on her shoulder, and Erin turned around to face him.

Robbie's right eye had swollen shut and blood was still flowing from the deep gash across the bridge of his nose. His lower lip was split down the middle. He was leaning to the right, protecting his ribs, and the eye that was still open looked lost and confused, as if he'd suddenly woken up in the middle of this and was trying to make sense of what was happening.

"I'm not done," Robbie said. He looked at Erin, focusing on her face. "Last one standing, remember?"

She shook her head. "No. That's enough. I was wrong. I'm not gonna stand here and watch him kill you."

He put his hand on her chest and pushed her aside. "Let's go," he said to Vinny. "Ain't nothing you've done to me that hasn't been done a hundred times before."

"Boy," Vinny said, "you don't know when to quit." He stepped forward and popped him in the face.

Robbie's head snapped backward. He took a few sideways steps before collapsing in the dirt.

"*Stay down,*" she told him, but already he was trying to get back up. He looked over at her and smiled. There was blood in his mouth. It ran down his chin and dribbled on the ground.

Vinny spat in the dirt. "Your girlfriend's right, boy. You oughtta stay on the ground if you don't wanna end up in a casket."

Robbie got to his feet. A string of bloody saliva hung from his lower lip like a necktie. "You don't scare me," he said. "I've had much worse than you."

Vinny put his head down and charged. He was coming in fast, growling like a mongrel.

This is my fault, she thought. *Whatever happens is my responsibility.*

Robbie dropped to his hands and knees a split second before their bodies connected. Vinny struck him with his lower legs and his momentum carried him forward, launching him into the air. He did an awkward half somersault and landed on the side of his head and his left shoulder, his face scraping across the earth.

"You dumb shit," he said, getting to his feet, but there was something wrong with his shoulder, the way it drooped and wouldn't move.

"Come on, then," Robbie told him, and Vinny charged again. Robbie stepped to the side and punched him once in the face. *Thwack!* The impact sent the older boy sideways. He took a few steps and sprawled into the dirt.

"Dirty fighter," Greg Cannon said, and he stepped into the circle.

Robbie whirled on him. The string of bloody saliva snapped and fell to the ground. "Let's go," he said. "Last man standing."

Greg looked around at the faces in the crowd. They peered back at him, the many kids he and his crew had terrorized along the way.

Robbie took a step toward him. "I'm ready," he said. "I'm ready for *all* of you."

Greg held up a hand. "Take it easy, little man. This is between the two of you. Dirty fighter, is all I'm sayin'."

"You ready for *this*?" Vinny asked. He was back on his feet and standing behind him. He swung with his good arm as hard as he could.

Robbie tried to duck, but it got a piece of him, the fist glancing off the side of his head. He spun around and struck Vinny twice in the face—*whip-whap!*—and it was Vinny's turn to stumble backward.

Erin stood there with her mouth open. It was the *fear* that had slowed him down. Now that it was gone, he was *so much faster* without it.

He stepped forward, dodged a haymaker, and smashed Vinny twice more in the face.

The larger boy staggered but did not fall. He let out a primal scream and leaped forward, grabbing Robbie with his good arm as the two of them toppled to the ground.

They rolled over each other as they tussled in the dirt, both of them throwing punches. Vinny ended up on top, pinning Robbie against the ground. The larger boy was on his knees and breathing hard, the sweat rolling off his body. His left arm still hung at his side like a forgotten satchel, but he raised the other one high above his head. He had a large rock in his hand, buried in the splayed claw of his fingers. He raised it higher and readied himself to bring it down on Robbie's head.

"Game over," Vinny said, but Robbie sat up suddenly and planted his forehead into Vinny's face.

There was a crunching noise as bone met cartilage. Vinny let go of the rock. It dropped to the ground and rolled a short distance before coming to a stop. The boy went with it, falling forward and to the right. He was dead weight now, unconscious, and Robbie had to roll him over in order to get out from under him.

"That's it," he said. "That's all I can do." He stood up and walked into the crowd, and instead of shoving him back into the circle they embraced him now, propping him up so he wouldn't fall and clapping him on the back.

His left eye searched their faces. He was looking for the rest of them—Greg Cannon, Tony Shifflet, and Jeremy Grissom.

"Robbie," she called out, pushing through the mass of kids that had gathered around him. They were everywhere, shouting and jabbering all at once. She lost sight of him in the crowd and had to stop and look around.

Their voices faded, and Erin discovered that she was still standing near the lip of the aqueduct. She glanced to her left and saw him: a body, lying crumpled and unconscious on the ground. She took a step toward it. *But no,* she realized, it was the metal carcass of the shopping cart, lying on its side. It had served out its purpose, its body now broken and useless. Someone had decided that *this* was all the burial it needed.

The wind kicked up from the east, and Erin squinted into it, the air cold against her skin. She stood there for a while, looking out across the emptiness of the landscape, before she turned and made her way back to the truck. The heater was one of the few things that worked well in the Chevy, and she cranked it up during the short drive to Robbie's grandpa's place. *Except his grandpa's not around any longer,* Erin reminded herself. *It's just him now, and if he doesn't want to see his father, what makes you think it'll be any different with you?*

Erin slowed the truck and made a right onto the dirt road that led to the spot where she'd accompanied him as a child. She drove about a hundred yards before coming to a small wooden bridge that spanned the aqueduct. It was wide enough for the Chevy, but the bridge was missing a few planks and had seen better days. The trailer was on the other side of it. Next to it was an old Jeep Wrangler, its windshield cracked and caked with dirt.

Erin turned off the ignition and got out of the truck. She walked across the wooden bridge, a hodgepodge of multilayered boards that clunked and shifted beneath her boots. The aqueduct stretched below her, its long concrete spine like the remains of a dead animal lying in the dust.

The trailer was a silver Airstream, a thirty-foot RV propped up on jacks and dual-axle tires. There were a couple of windows, all of them curtained from the inside, and a door that faced the bridge. On either side of the trailer, hundreds of acres of barren land unfolded for as far as she could see. There were no fences to mark the territory, just the aqueduct behind her and the surrounding span of the distant horizon.

"Robbie," she called out, "it's Erin Reece. I'm back in town for a while. Your father told me I could find you out here."

Erin stood in front of the Airstream, waiting for a response. There was no sound of movement from the interior, no inquisitive parting of the curtains. Except for the tired hulk of the Wrangler parked outside, there was no indication that anyone lived here. The wind gusted, and a thin film of sand blew across the yard at the level of Erin's feet.

She waited another thirty seconds, then stepped forward and knocked on the door. Her knuckles made a hollow, supplicant sound against the trailer's aluminum exterior.

"Robbie? You in there?"

She heard a noise on the other side of the door, the clunk of an inanimate object being propped against the wall.

Maybe it's a shotgun, she thought. *People change. Isn't that what his father told you?*

She could picture Matta leaning forward in his easy chair, warning her that his son was not the same person she remembered.

Erin took a step back from the door. She was not afraid of Robbie. She'd known him too well for that.

Be cautious, then. Not afraid, but cautious.

"Robbie," she said, convinced that even if he wouldn't open the door, her friend was in there, listening.

"I really want to talk to you. I *need* to talk to you." She swallowed. "I don't know if you're mad at me or disappointed. I always meant to come back, you know. But once I left, I got it in my head that maybe it would be better if I stayed away for a while. After that, time just . . . got away from me. I shouldn't have left you here to deal with things on your own. I realize that. I'm sorry," she said. "I don't expect you to forgive me."

Erin stood there in the front yard, staring at the door to the trailer. "That's it," she said. "That's all I came here to say. If you change your mind, I'm staying at the Homestead Inn. Come and see me if you want. I really wish you would."

She turned and walked back to the truck. Along the way, she counted her footsteps, waiting for the sound of a trailer door swinging inward on its hinges.

She turned around when she got to the truck, hoping to find

him standing there on the other side of the bridge, studying her with those dark eyes, the faintest hint of a smile on his lips.

That was some speech, he'd say. *How long did you practice it in front of the mirror?*

"Shut up," she told him, but there was no one there, just the empty yard and the things she should've never left behind.

18

THE LIGHTS WERE TURNED UP IN THE WOLF POINT JUNIOR SENIOR High School auditorium as people filed in for the special town meeting. With a seating capacity of five hundred and fifty and standing room for another hundred or so in the back, the auditorium was already packed. Most of the townspeople had attended classes here themselves when they were younger. They all knew one another, but there was no interest in the usual pleasantries as people jostled for position.

Mayor Zachary Brody climbed the steps and walked to the microphone perched on the metal stand in the center of the stage. He was a rotund man with a receding hairline and a tendency to bend forward slightly at the waist, looking downward, when he walked. In his front shirt pocket, he carried a pair of glasses. He was always in the process of pulling them out, fiddling with them, and returning them to his pocket without ever putting them on. Whether he used them for reading or distance or just plain appearances was a topic of some conjecture among the locals.

"Please," he said, "if we can get settled, I think we're about ready to begin."

Most of them were already in their seats, but there were a few stragglers. He waited for them to find a spot at the back of the room.

"I'm sure—" He was interrupted by feedback from the speakers, and he adjusted his position in front of the microphone. "I'm sure we're all aware of the reason for this meeting. Over the past four and a half months, we've had an increased number of missing person reports filed with the Wolf Point Police Department. There are currently several ongoing investigations, and I wanted to take this opportunity to update you on the state of affairs and to discuss strategies to reduce the risk of related incidents moving forward."

He reached into his front shirt pocket, pulled out his glasses, and turned them over in his hands.

"Chief Martin Ward has been kind enough to join us for tonight's meeting, and before I turn it over to him, I just wanted to assure you that we're taking this matter very seriously and have asked our law enforcement officers to utilize every resource possible in the search for these individuals."

Donna Zemke was sitting in the front row. She raised her hand and stood up at the same time, intent on asking her question. "Excuse me, Mayor," she said. "You mentioned that the disappearances started four and a half months ago, but the body of a young man was discovered in the river in October of last year. Is there any reason to think that the incidents are related?"

Mayor Brody returned the eyeglasses to his pocket. "Well now, you see, all evidence suggests that *that* incident involved an accidental death. Obviously it was a very tragic event, but I've discussed this question extensively with Chief Ward, and there's just no evidence linking the death of Miles Griffin with any of the individuals who have gone missing since early February. Now, if we can turn our attention to—"

"I'm sorry to interrupt you, sir," she said, "but Miles Griffin and Angela Finley were both students in our school system. I teach fifth and sixth grade math, and I can tell you that a lot of parents have come to me with serious concerns about the safety of our young people. My question for you is this: What, if anything, is being done to ensure that our children are safe?"

Mayor Brody nodded and motioned for her to sit down. "Thank you for asking that very important question, Donna. And what I can tell you is that your elected officials are deeply invested in the safety and security of *all* of our residents, young and old alike. Now, there may be some differences in how we address those concerns—"

"But it could happen," Mike Flannigan called out from the fifth row. "It could happen to any of the families here tonight."

"Not mine," Bob Cannon piped in from the back of the auditorium. "I keep a loaded shotgun in the house, and I'd invite *anyone* to try to break in and—"

"This isn't about home defense, Bob," Mike said from his seat near the front. "These people are being taken right off the street."

"Now, hold on a second," the mayor said. "No one's suggesting that these missing individuals have been taken by *anyone*. To the best of our knowledge, these are folks who have gone missing under nonviolent circumstances, and it may just be that there's a logical expl—"

"What about Curt Hastings?" someone yelled. "He left his pickup in the middle of the road with the engine running. You think he went out for a midnight stroll and forgot where he parked?"

There was a bit of nervous laughter, but not much.

"Those circumstances were a bit different," the mayor said, "but I still think that—"

"You don't know *anything,* that's the problem," Mike yelled. "And neither do the police. What's the point of holding a meeting if you ain't got nothin' to tell us?"

"Okay, order now. *Order!*" The mayor held up his hand. "Let's wait to be recognized and speak one at a time so we can hold a civil discussion." He frowned. They were talking among themselves now. It had been seven minutes since the start of the meeting and already he'd lost control of it.

". . . what's it gonna take to . . ."

". . . sitting on their hands and waiting for . . ."

". . . law enforcement isn't prepared to . . ."

". . . never faced anything like this before . . ."

"Please," he said. "If we can't conduct this meeting in an orderly fashion, I'm going to have to call it off."

"Just like you called off the search for my daughter?" Dan Finley called out from the corner of the room.

They all turned their heads and looked back at him.

"Now, Dan, you know that we put every resource into finding her—"

"Not enough, as far as I'm concerned."

"—and half the people in this audience volunteered for the search. With all due respect, I don't think it's fair to say that we—"

"She was too young to vote in your next election," Dan said. "Is that why you called off the search?"

There was a buzz of chatter from the people in the audience, and Mayor Brody stood there on the stage in front of them. He opened his mouth to reply, then closed it again.

Brian Cray was standing in the back as well. "That's going

too far, Dan," he said. "The mayor's right. We searched for your daughter for *two weeks* over a twenty-two-mile radius. What more do you expect?"

"I expect you to *find* her. We don't give up on our children."

"No one gave up on your daughter," he said. "It's just a matter of facing reality."

"Oh yeah? And what reality is that?"

"That maybe she's not out there to be found."

More rumblings from the crowd. Dan Finley took a step toward him.

"Is that right? What would *you* know about it?"

"That two weeks is all the information we have. Maybe she ran off. Maybe she's buried in the snow. Either way, you can stop blaming others. These people went out of their way to help you."

"I know what people did and I'm grateful for it," Dan said. "But let me ask you something: Where were *you* on the night Angela went missing?"

"I was home watching television," Brian said. "Are you *accusing* me? Do you even *hear* what you're saying?"

"If the shoe fits . . ."

"What in the hell is *that* supposed to mean?"

"Oh, come on, Brian. It wouldn't be the first time you were accused of ditching a body."

"Now, listen . . ." Mayor Brody said, but they drowned him out with their voices.

He glanced over at Chief Ward. Dan was referring, of course, to Gerald Griffin, a man who'd been an agitator with the union at the Columbia Grain processing plant twenty-six years ago. One evening he'd gotten into a bar fight at Stockman's 220 Club and was struck in the head with a bottle. He was found dead the following morning, lying in the bed of his pickup. Twenty-

year-old Brian Cray had been in the bar that night, but none
of the patrons were willing to testify to anything else. Maybe
it was because they'd been drinking and couldn't remember.
Then again, maybe it was because Brian's father, Vincent Cray,
was chief of police at the time.

"*Order! Order now!*" Mayor Brody bellowed into the microphone, but nobody was listening.

"You've got a big mouth," Brian said. "How about if I come
over there and close it for you."

Dan took another step toward him. "You can try," he said.
"It's about time you got your teeth handed to you."

The men charged each other, and people scattered, giving
them room.

"*Jesus Christ,*" the mayor said, and he motioned for Chief
Ward to get over to the men and put a stop to it. "This meeting
is *over,*" he announced into the microphone. "We're not gonna
have chaos here in Wolf Point."

"Shut up! Go to hell!" they yelled as he walked off the stage.
And for the first time that night, Mayor Brody began to worry
about his *own* safety at the hands of the people he'd been elected
to represent. There was *one* police officer in the place, and that
was Chief Ward, who was currently wrestling Brian Cray to
the floor. *One cop,* he thought, *and an old one at that. Why didn't
we anticipate this? What the hell is* wrong *with these people?*

He went backstage, found an exit, and took it. His car was
in the parking lot with everyone else's, but there was *no way*
he was going out there, not after a meeting like that. Instead,
he made a beeline for the United Dakota Presbyterian Church,
whose doors were always open to the public. It was right across
the street, the best place that he could think of to lie low for a
while and wait this out.

19

"JACOB'S FIELD, RIGHT? YOU GOING?"

"Yeah. Who else will be there?"

"Me, Deirdre, Robbie, Emily, Meghan." Erin shrugged. "I don't know who else."

Angela sighed. "I have to shovel the driveway before I go. I'll meet you there."

"Can't you do it tomorrow?"

"No," she said. "I have to do it today. Otherwise it turns to ice and my dad gets mad."

The windows of the bus had fogged up the moment they climbed aboard. Angela wiped hers with the palm of her hand and looked through the glass at the falling snow. "You could help me," she suggested.

Erin frowned. "I don't know. Robbie and me, we're supposed to pick up the sleds and go straight from his house. The others will be waiting."

Angela wiped at the glass again and looked out at the neighborhood. There was a man dressed in a dark green coat and mittens standing in one of the yards. He looked up at them and waved as they trundled past.

"Stranger," Angela said with a start. She sucked in her breath and pulled back from the window.

"Where?" Erin asked, but they had moved down the street and the man was gone.

The bus slowed and Angela stood up. "Doesn't matter," she said. "He'll get me soon enough." She grabbed the strap of her backpack and slung it over her shoulder.

"So we'll meet you there. Jacob's Field, right?"

Angela nodded. "It would be nice if I had a buddy, someone to make sure I got there safe."

Erin looked down at the floor. A single blade of grass lay crumpled near the aisle, left behind by the sole of someone's shoe. She heard the door close and looked up to find herself alone with the bus driver. She was the first kid on in the morning and the last kid off at the end of the day. She stood up, walked to the back of the bus, and used the fleshy part of her hand to wipe at the window. It was hard to see anything through the glass, just hints of color in the vague alien landscape sliding past them.

"I was supposed to have a buddy," a girl said. It sounded a lot like Angela Finley.

"I'm sorry," Erin whispered. "I didn't know."

"Those are the rules," she said. "Tell someone where you're going, always travel with a buddy, and never, *ever* . . . talk to strangers."

Erin woke with a start. There was something in the room with her, clawing its way up the sheets from the foot of her bed. She squirmed away from it and put a hand out to push herself backward. There was open space below her, and she tumbled out of bed and onto the floor. Even then, the dream world still tugged at her. She could hear the girl breathing, peering out at her from beneath the bed.

Erin flew across the room on hands and knees that barely touched the floor. Her head bumped into the dresser, and she yanked open a few of its drawers before realizing what she was up against. She could hear it, the sound of the girl pulling herself across the floor on her stomach.

Erin found the doorknob and flung the door open. It banged against her wall, a firecracker in the stillness of the house. She got to her feet and ran down the hallway and through the kitchen to her parents' bedroom.

"*Mom. Dad.*"

The door opened. It was her mother.

"Honey, what's the matter?"

"I had a nightmare. I thought . . . there was someone else in the house."

"What's wrong?" her father asked. She could see him lying in the bed, the upper half of his body propped up on a pillow, his chest bare. He sounded awake, not groggy like her mother.

"She had a nightmare," her mother told him. "She thought there was someone in the house."

"Why would you think that?" her father asked. "Did you hear something?" He was on his feet now next to the bed, wearing only pajama bottoms.

Erin shook her head. "No, I . . . I think I was dreaming."

"Well, let's have a look, then." He walked to the closet and retrieved his shotgun and a flashlight.

"Babe, do you think that's necessary?" her mother asked.

"I'd rather have it and not need it than the other way around." He racked the gun, then crossed the room and handed Erin the flashlight. "Where did you hear someone? What room was it?"

"My bedroom," she said, "but I think I was just dreaming."

"You probably were. But we'll check it out, okay? There's no harm in checking, is there?"

Erin shook her head. "Do you want me to turn on the flash-light?"

"No," he said. "Just hang on to it in case we need it."

"Be careful, David," her mother said. "Don't accidentally shoot yourself. Or her."

He looked back at her for a moment before returning his attention to the hallway in front of them. "Let's go," he said to Erin, and he stepped into the hall. He had the muzzle up, pointed ahead of him. Erin lagged back a little, giving him space. Her father had taught her about guns from a young age. She'd helped him load and unload the shotgun, had sat on the front porch swing and watched him clean it. He had a hunting rifle in the closet as well, and she'd seen him use that to scare off the coyotes, who occasionally visited the farm in search of an easy meal. The firearm did not scare her, but what did frighten her was the way he moved through the house with it—muzzle up, safety off, the butt plate tucked in tight against his shoulder—as if he actually expected an intruder to jump out from around the corner at any moment.

Adults seem nervous these days, she thought. Five people had gone missing since February. The last one disappeared a month ago, an eighteen-year-old kid who had just graduated from high school and had a football scholarship to Montana State. Her friend Deirdre McKinney said that Angela Finley might've gotten kidnapped by a *perv.* "What's a perv?" Erin had asked, and Deirdre had rolled her eyes like Erin had just arrived on the planet yesterday. "It's short for pervert," she said. "You know, *sickos.* They do all kinds of things to kids that you don't even *wanna* know about." Erin nodded. That was how it was with Deirdre. She seemed to enjoy giving Erin new things to worry about.

Her father stopped in the doorway to her bedroom. Erin almost bumped into him.

"Window's unlocked," he said. "You leave that open?"

Erin tilted her head to see around him. Her window was open half an inch, letting in the night air.

"I like to have it open when it's warm enough," she said. "It helps me sleep better."

He leaned the gun against the wall in the corner of the room, then took the flashlight from her hands and slid the window all the way open. "Turn out the light in the hallway," he said. Erin did as she was told, and her father turned on the flashlight, sweeping the yard with the beam.

"There's a raccoon out there by the tree," he said. "You see it?"

Erin looked through the window screen at the yard beyond. The raccoon was out by the oak tree, his fat body wobbling from side to side as he hustled across the grass. He turned and stared into the beam of the flashlight, the white circular orbs of his eyes standing out in the darkness.

"He was probably sniffing around your window," her father said. "You heard him out there and it woke you up." He sighed. "For the time being, let's keep the windows shut and locked at night, okay?"

"Yes, sir."

"Good girl," he said, and put a hand on her shoulder.

"Dad?" she asked. "Is everything okay here?"

"What do you mean?" He sat down on her bed, and Erin sat down beside him.

"I feel like people are scared. Adults even."

"Well," he said, "I guess some people *are* scared, or maybe just worried about the people who are lost."

"Is that what you think happened to them? You think they got lost?"

He was quiet for a while. Erin sat there and waited.

"I don't know," he said at last. "Nobody seems to know *what* happened to them. That's what scares people more than anything I think, the not knowing." He turned, slid the window closed, and locked it. "I want you to feel safe," he said. "Your mother and I, we will do whatever it takes to protect you."

"Hey, you two. How's it going?"

They looked up to find Erin's mother standing in the doorway.

"Raccoon," he told her, "looking for an evening snack."

"He was at my window keeping me company," Erin said.

Her father put his arm around her and gave her a sideways hug. "Good night," he said as he stood up and crossed the room, retrieving the shotgun on his way out. "House is all clear. I'm gonna go to bed. I'll see you at breakfast."

"Good night, Dad. Sorry to bother you."

"It's no problem. You can always come to us, Erin. No matter what."

Erin's mother put a hand on her father's chest. "I'm gonna tuck her in," she said, and she kissed him on the cheek.

Her father nodded and made his way down the hallway. Erin listened to the sound of his footsteps until they receded into nothing.

"You messed up your bed," her mother said. Erin stood up and watched as her mother straightened the sheets, tucking them in along the sides. "You need a glass of water?"

"No, ma'am."

"Well, let's get you in bed, then. Morning will be here before you know it."

Erin climbed into bed, sliding her bare feet between the sheets. Her mother folded them over at the level of her shoulders. "Comfy?" she asked, and Erin nodded.

She leaned over and kissed her daughter on the forehead.

"Mom?"

"Yeah."

"Will you stay with me for a while, until I fall back to sleep?"

Her mother ran her fingers through Erin's hair. She lay down next to her and rested her head on the edge of the pillow. There was a clean, crisp scent to her, like freshly washed linen drying in the summer sun. "You want a story?" she asked. "I could tell you one that I used to read to you as a child."

"No, thank you," Erin said, "I'm a little old for that." She removed her right arm from under the sheets and draped it across her mother's body. They lay that way for a while, silent except for the slow and rhythmic sound of their breathing.

At some point, Erin's mother began to hum. As always, Erin could picture the notes in her mind, a purple ribbon that unfurled itself in the space above them until it filled the room. She closed her eyes, and the ribbon was inside of her, too. The silky caress of its fabric wound through her body, encircled her head, and brushed against her skin with the softness of spring tulips after the rain. She fell asleep, and there were no dreams to meet her this time but only music, following her down until she emerged on the other side into the soft and slanting light of a new day.

20

"THANK YOU FOR COMING," DR. HOUSEMAN SAID. HE WALKED around his desk to greet her and folded Erin's hand into his own. "This has been a difficult week for you. You must be exhausted."

"I'm just getting used to it," she said. "I feel like I've been playing catch-up since I got here."

"Yes," he said, "I can imagine." He motioned for her to take a seat and closed the door to his office. Instead of returning to the chair behind his desk, he grabbed the one next to her, turned it around so he could sit facing her, and lowered himself into it.

"The biopsy," she said, "it's bad. That's why you asked me to come here."

He shook his head noncommittally. "I asked you to come here so we could discuss the results. In these situations, it's best to keep an open mind and to remember that this is just information—neither bad nor good. I like to think of it as a starting point that will guide us toward the best possible course of action."

She took a deep breath and let it out. "Tell me what you found."

Mark nodded. He was quiet for a moment, organizing his thoughts.

"The procedure itself went well," he said. "Dr. Kowalski was able to complete the bronchoscopy and obtained tissue samples of the mass in question. He was also able to perform some needle aspirations of several local lymph nodes. There was minimal bleeding. Your father tolerated the procedure without difficulty."

"That's good," she said. She'd been worried about the bronchoscopy. It wasn't commonly performed in veterinary medicine, and she hadn't done one herself since vet school. Still, she knew about the risks. If things went wrong during the procedure, the complications could be serious.

Mark shifted in his chair. "Yes," he said. "I was pleased that it went so smoothly."

They sat across from each other, so close that their knees were almost touching.

"Dr. Kowalski took the samples back with him," he said. "He had them evaluated by a pathologist in Billings—a specialist in cytopathology. He's the best they've got."

"Thank you."

Mark put his hands together in his lap. "Unfortunately," he said, "this does appear to be lung cancer—squamous cell carcinoma to be exact."

Erin stared at him. After a few seconds she realized she was holding her breath.

"It's a non-small-cell lung cancer that accounts for about a third of all pulmonary malignancies. There is a strong association with smoking, but it can also be caused by other factors, such as age, genetics, and exposure to certain minerals and metals. Asbestos and radon are common contributors."

"Okay," Erin said. She could feel her heart walloping in her chest.

"Staging was the next step," Mark continued. "In your father's case, Dr. Kowalski was able to obtain cell samples from lymph nodes on both sides of the mediastinum. Unfortunately, several of them were positive, which gives us a diagnosis of stage 3B squamous cell carcinoma."

"Stage 3B," she said, trying to make sense of the information.

"This is"—he sighed—"an aggressive form of cancer. Because of the involvement of lymph nodes on both sides of the chest, surgery is generally not recommended. Radiation and chemotherapy are both reasonable options. In addition, recent studies have also shown that treatment with certain tumor-targeting antibodies or medications to enhance the immune system have both been effective in shrinking the tumor and improving life expectancy in some patients."

"What are the . . . I mean . . . why would he . . . ?"

"I don't know why this happened to him," Mark said. "We look for answers, but most of the time we just have to . . . deal with what's in front of us."

Erin's vision blurred as her eyes welled with tears. She tried to draw a breath, the cartilage of her throat lifting and falling, but it was like pulling air from a vacuum. A tear rolled down her cheek and spilled onto the back of her wrist, and when she looked down, she saw that her hands were balled into fists in her lap, the nails biting into the flesh.

Erin put her face in her hands and cried. It was the only sound in the small confines of the office, and the sobs ripped through her like jagged chunks of metal. Of all the shitty things to happen to her father . . . of all the horrible things he had been through already . . .

Mark reached over and put a hand on her shoulder. "I'm sorry," he said. "I really wish I had better news."

Now that the tears had started, it was hard for Erin to get

control of them. She let them come. A storm had been building up inside of her since she'd gotten Mark's initial phone call, the one telling her that her father was ill and she needed to come home to Wolf Point. Everything had gone wrong since then. Had she really expected this to be any different?

"What's the prognosis?" she asked, and she looked up at Mark as if there was a chance for something hopeful and un-expected.

He shook his head. "It's impossible to say. Estimating these things is always tricky."

She grabbed a tissue from a box on Mark's desk. "How much time does he have, statistically speaking?"

"Statistics tell us how the *average* person will do," he said. "Nobody's average. Your father's certainly not average."

Erin nodded. This is what she told the families of her own patients when the diagnosis was a bad one. *Renal failure. Feline leukemia. Cardiomyopathy.* They were just words until you knew how to interpret them. "How much time does he have?" a cli-ent would ask her, and Erin would look down at the animal and envy the fact that it would never comprehend the details of this part of the conversation.

She looked back at Mark. "You've got to tell me," she said. "If I don't have much time left with him, I need to know."

"Erin . . ."

"*Please.*" She took him by the hand. "I'm going to find out anyway. I'd rather hear it from you."

He swallowed. "These days people can look it up on the internet. It's not good for them. It doesn't paint the complete picture."

"I understand all of that," she said. "How long?"

"The median survival for all stage 3 non-small-cell lung

cancer is fifteen months from the time of diagnosis," he said. "Stage 3B is worse, about twelve months."

"Twelve months," she said.

"Half of stage 3B patients live longer than that."

"And half of them die sooner," she said.

"Yes." He'd been leaning forward, and he slid back in his chair a bit. "As I said, it's difficult to predict."

Erin sat back herself. She looked down at her hands. "Goddamn it," she said.

They were quiet for a moment, neither of them talking.

"He helped me deliver a calf once," she said. "He walked me through the process one step at a time."

"That's how we do this," Mark told her, "one step at a time."

"What's the next step?" she asked. "Where do we go from here?"

"We could transfer him to Billings," he said. "We don't have an oncologist here in Wolf Point. You should talk to your father. We both should. We don't have to decide right away."

"I can't talk to him. He's on a respirator, remember?"

"Not anymore," he said. "We removed the breathing tube an hour ago. Your father's breathing on his own now. He's weak—deconditioned from lying in bed so long—and he's pretty groggy. We were giving him a sedative while he was on the ventilator. It takes time for it to clear the body. It'll be another few days until he's ready for a lengthy conversation. But you can talk to him. He'll understand what you have to say."

"He's awake?"

"He's conscious, yes. He might be sleeping now, but he'll wake up if you talk to him. We'll get him up and moving around soon. His muscles have atrophied. He'll need some time to recover. This is the tough part," he said, "helping

David to climb out of the hole we dug for him." Mark winced, realizing too late that he couldn't have picked a worse analogy.

"I'm worried," Erin said, ignoring his comment. "He's stubborn, my father. What if he decides that he doesn't want the treatment?"

"You'll talk him into it," Mark said. "Or you won't. There's no perfect solution here. It's a decision that the two of you have to make together."

21

LIEUTENANT STUTZMAN MADE A LEFT OFF PALMER STREET AND parked the Suburban in front of the Montana State Crime Lab. It had been an eight-hour drive across the state from Wolf Point to Missoula, broken up over the span of two days. Last night he'd stayed at a Days Inn in Great Falls. From the window of his hotel room, he'd been able to see the Missouri River, the same body of water that passed through Wolf Point and along the southern boundary of David Reece's property. Seeing the river so far from home had given him a sense of disorientation, as if he'd been driving for half the day and had wound up right back where he started. There was some truth to that, he supposed. This was a case twenty years in the making. He'd read through the reports by the officers who'd investigated the disappearances back then—typed and handwritten notes on paper yellowed with age that he'd found in cardboard boxes in an off-site storage shed. The place had smelled of mildew and neglect. The bottom of one of the boxes—damp and weakened by decay—had given way when he lifted it, the papers spilling out onto the concrete floor. Jeff had gotten down on his knees to collect them, gathering the files and loose papers in his hands as if they were the mortal remains of the victims themselves.

Oh, but you have those, too, he thought. *One of them's been riding with you all the way from Wolf Point.*

He glanced in the rearview mirror, as if it might be sitting up and staring at him from the back seat, the remnants of the skeleton they'd discovered in the rectangular wooden box buried on David Reece's property.

Jeff took a shuddering breath and ran his hand across a three-day growth of stubble on the side of his face. He hadn't shaved since Pitsinger's crew had unearthed the box on Wednesday.

"It's not Kenny," he said to himself. "Whoever these bones belong to, it's not your brother. We buried him in a plot at Wolf Point Cemetery. Remember?"

Yeah, he thought. *I remember. I wore a black suit and tie and stood there with Dad, Aunt Amy, and Uncle Clayton. Mom was there, too, drugged up on Valium and staring at the coffin.*

"You take care of this thing," he told himself. "You take care of this *one thing* and maybe it'll be better."

Jeff unfastened his seat belt, climbed out of the truck, and stood there beside the open door. The Montana State Crime Lab was a one-story structure that shared a parking lot with several other buildings. Behind it were a medical clinic and the Missoula County Detention Center, with its chain-link fence and coils of barbed wire that stood out against the light blue backdrop of the morning sky. The parking lot was mostly empty. He'd arranged to meet the medical examiner here this morning with the remains of the second body. The autopsy of the first set of bones had already been completed, but Jeff wanted to see it for himself, to take some photos of the things the pathologist had discovered.

Jeff closed the driver's-side door, opened the rear hatchback, and pulled out a large black duffel. He locked the truck and walked to the front door of the building, ringing the bell when he found it locked.

A minute later, a thin man with short dark hair and wire-rimmed glasses came to the door and unlocked it from the inside. He was dressed in tan khakis and a button-down shirt. Jeff recognized him from a newspaper photo he'd viewed online the night before. The doctor looked to be in his mid-thirties, younger than Jeff had expected for a man in his position.

"Dr. Lester?" Jeff asked as the man swung the door open to let him inside.

"Yes. Call me Owen," he said, and extended a hand.

"Jeff Stutzman," the lieutenant said. "We spoke on the phone."

"Yes, we did. You made a long drive to meet me here on a Saturday. I appreciate that." He glanced at his watch. "You arrived a bit earlier than I expected."

"I got on the road early this morning," Jeff told him. "It was hard to sleep with this thing in the room with me." They looked down at the duffel bag Jeff was holding in his left hand. "I put everything in a plastic body bag that I sealed myself. I have photos of the way we found it."

"Excellent. We'll log what you have into evidence first."

There was a welcome desk in the front lobby, and the pathologist walked around to the other side of it. "We keep a physical and an electronic log of all the evidence that comes through here. You took a photo of the seal?"

"Yes." Jeff unzipped the duffel bag's side pouch, reached inside, and pulled out a series of Polaroids. He handed the first one across the desk, and the doctor took it, making note of the number on the seal.

"Fill out as much as you can," he said, placing the logbook

on the counter. When Jeff had finished, Owen initialed it and placed the open logbook where the intake clerk would see it when she arrived on Monday. "Please bring the bag with you," he said, and he led Jeff down a hallway and into the west wing of the building.

"Been working here long, Doctor?"

"About six years," he said. "I grew up in western Montana but did my residency in Seattle and worked at a hospital there for a year before returning home." He looked back at Jeff and gave him a smile that subtracted another couple of years from his face. "Sooner or later, we all return to our starting point."

Owen held his ID badge in front of an electronic reader on the wall next to a door marked PATHOLOGY. The pad beeped and he opened the door, holding it for Jeff as he stepped inside.

The lab was smaller than Jeff had imagined. A single stainless-steel table occupied the center of the room. To their right was a metal counter and sink. A scale hung from a hook in the ceiling, and a microscope sat in the corner of the room. To their left was an office, a small room with an internal window between the office wall and the lab. Owen stepped inside, retrieved a file from his desk, and walked to the counter on which the microscope was sitting. "This is the forensic report from the first set of remains," he said, and motioned for Jeff to join him at the counter.

Jeff placed the duffel bag on the floor and crossed the room.

"The lighting is better in here than in my office," Owen said. He opened the file and flipped through thirty or forty pages of catalogued descriptions of every bone and marking. Jeff caught glimpses of words he couldn't pronounce and didn't understand. There were pictures, too, color photos with notations beneath them. "Here," the doctor said. "This is a summary of the findings."

Jeff looked down at the page, a dense paragraph of tightly packed medical jargon. "Maybe," he suggested, "you could summarize the summary."

"Yes, of course," he said, and adjusted his glasses. He was quiet for a moment before he began. "The initial set of skeletal remains was, in fact, human. A young male in his late teens or early twenties."

"A male," Jeff said. "You're sure."

"Well," Owen said, "the thing about science is that you can never be absolutely sure of anything. Males and females can be differentiated based on the shape of their pelvic bones. Females have shorter and more rounded pelvic bones. The hips are wider and the shoulders are narrower than their male counterparts. There are other differences as well, but those are the big ones. There are always exceptions, but yes, I'm fairly certain that this was a male."

"There weren't that many males who went missing back then. It was mostly women and children." Jeff looked down at the pages in front of him. "I was a kid myself. I remember what that was like. It can paralyze a community when one of its members goes missing, even if it's just one. In our case there were—"

"Fourteen women and children," Owen said, "plus the two men. Sixteen souls were lost over the span of three years."

Jeff looked at him, surprised that he knew the numbers.

"I looked it up," Owen said. "I was pretty young back then myself, but I remember hearing about the story from my parents. People know about Wolf Point—people in Montana anyway. It's one of the reasons I prioritized your case."

"We had a hard time of it," Jeff said. "We'd like it to be over."

"I can understand that. I'm here to help if I can."

"I appreciate that," Jeff said. "You mentioned that the first set of remains was from a person in their late teens or early twenties. You can tell that from the bone structure as well?"

"Yes," he said. "We look at the surface of the teeth for wear and tear. Dental development is especially helpful in determining the age of children and adolescents, since different teeth come in at different ages. Three out of four of this specimen's wisdom teeth had already erupted. That puts him between seventeen and twenty-five. Children's bones also have growth plates that become fused in adulthood. The clavicle is typically the last bone to stop growing, and that happens at about twenty-five years of age. The growth plates of the clavicles from these remains were not yet fully closed."

Jeff nodded. "So we know the gender and approximate age of the individual. Is it possible that he was buried long before the disappearances ever took place? What if he died a hundred years ago? Maybe we just happened upon him now."

"That gets a bit trickier," the pathologist said. "Traditional carbon dating helps archaeologists estimate the age of fossils buried between five hundred and fifty thousand years ago. Old stuff, in other words. Historically, it's been of limited use in dating remains buried more recently."

"Well, that's a problem," Jeff said. "I need to know if he was buried twenty years ago."

"Exactly," he said. "The difficulty with using radioactive carbon is that it decays very slowly. It doesn't vary much over the span of a single century. Unless, of course, humanity does something to change that."

"What do you mean?"

"The nuclear age," he said. "During the 1950s and early 1960s, governments started testing nuclear weapons, and atmospheric radioactive carbon levels skyrocketed. Fortunately, we came to our senses. In 1963, the United States stopped aboveground testing of nuclear weapons, and radioactive carbon levels have been dropping back toward their natural levels ever since. As a result, we can date people who were born over the past six decades by the amount of radioactive carbon present in their tissues."

Jeff frowned. "People who were born in the 1950s and 1960s tend to glow in the dark. Is that what you're telling me?"

He smiled. "That's one way of looking at it. And people born during the decades that followed glow less. Again, we can look at the teeth. Adult teeth are formed during certain ages, and the level of radioactive carbon can be measured in the enamel. If we match this up with the known levels during a given year, we can deduce the year of birth."

"Radioactive teeth. You're shitting me."

"No," he said, "I'm not. For teeth formed after 1965, the amount of radioactive carbon in the enamel can predict the year of birth to within one and a half years."

"Jesus," Jeff said, "that's the scariest thing I've thought about all day." He sighed. "And I've been driving around with a skeleton in my duffel bag."

"It's unsettling," Owen agreed, "but it does give us an answer. Our office works closely with University of Montana's anthropology department. Most of the forensic autopsies on human remains are actually performed there."

"And? What did you find out?"

"Based on the samples we obtained, this man was born around 1979. If we estimate his age to be twenty at the time of his death, that means he died in 1999, plus or minus a couple of years."

"The turn of the century," Jeff said. "Twenty years ago."

Owen nodded.

"There were two adult males who went missing back then," Jeff said. "Curt Hastings and Abel Griffin. Curt was a thirty-five-year-old guy who got in an argument with his wife and went for a drive in his pickup. The Ford F-250 was found in a snowbank the next morning. The driver's door was open and the diesel engine was still running. It was the same night that Rose Perry went missing. Two unrelated victims. Neither of them were ever seen again."

"This isn't Curt Hastings," Owen said. "This guy was much younger than that."

"Abel Griffin, then," Jeff said. "He went missing in June of 1999, four years after the death of his brother Miles."

The doctor frowned. "Two from the same family, spaced four years apart? But that makes *three* adult males, not two. Unless, of course, Miles was younger."

"He was sixteen," Jeff said, "and he didn't go missing, not for long anyway. His body washed up on the banks of the Missouri River a few days after he disappeared. It was ruled an accidental death."

"Accidental," he said. "Did they do an autopsy?"

Jeff shook his head. "Not a formal one, no. The coroner back then was an elected official, not a physician. He had the body examined by one of the local doctors."

"Were there any signs of trauma?"

"The report noted a broken neck and a bump to the back of his head. There's a bridge that spans the river not too far from where the body was discovered. Kids play on it all the time. It was felt that the boy must've fallen from the bridge and struck his head on a girder on the way down."

"How did they know he had a broken neck?"

"X-rays. I can get you a copy of the report. It's pretty minimal."

The pathologist nodded. "He could've been killed first and then thrown in the river. I'm sure you considered that."

"Yes," Jeff said, "but it doesn't fit the pattern of the others."

"Because he was found?"

"Exactly. None of the others were ever seen again. If someone did this to him, I don't think it was the same person. They didn't make any attempt to hide the body. It was in the river, yes, but there was nothing tied to it to weight it down."

They were quiet for a moment, considering the possibilities.

Jeff touched the pages spread out on the counter between them. "How did *this one* die?" he asked.

Owen looked at him through the circles of his spectacles. "Head trauma," he said. "The frontal bone was fractured. It was a long weapon, and slightly curved." He sorted through the report, found the page he was looking for, and placed it on top of the others. It was a picture of a skull with a long diagonal crack through the forehead. "The fracture extends through the patient's left orbit and cheekbone," Owen said. "It appears to have been a single strike. There was a lot of force involved. A fist couldn't have done this."

"A long, slightly curved blade. Any ideas about the weapon?"

"Some sort of tool would be my guess."

"And a big man," Jeff said, "someone who could swing it hard."

Owen shrugged. "A long handle multiplies the force of the blade during the arc of the swing. You don't have to be strong. You just have to know how to swing the thing."

"A farmer," Jeff said, "someone who works with his hands."

"I can tell a lot from human remains," Owen said, "but I can't tell you the occupation of the person who did this."

"Okay," Jeff said, "so where do we go from here? How do we identify the body?"

"Well," he said, putting the pages back in order, "DNA testing would be the next step. Are there any living relatives?"

"Yes," he said, "Abel's mother, Connie. She runs the local movie theater in Wolf Point."

"That's good," he said. "We can do kinship matching then. A buccal smear from the inside of her cheek should be sufficient. I'll give you a kit to take with you."

"Thank you," Jeff said. He pointed to the black duffel bag resting on the floor. "Do you want to take a look at this?"

"Sure," he said. "Let's see what you've got." He walked over, retrieved the plastic body bag from the duffel, donned some latex exam gloves, and opened it on the stainless-steel table. The doctor hummed to himself as he spread the bones out in front of him. The lower section of the spine was still attached to the pelvis.

Just another day at the office, Jeff thought to himself, and he had to look away for a moment as the pathologist lifted the spine and rotated it in his hands.

("It's about your brother. There's been an accident.")

"No," Jeff muttered, and the doctor turned and looked back at him.

"Pardon?"

"Nothing," he said. "Sorry, I was . . . just thinking about something else." He turned and put his hands on the counter.

"You okay?" Owen asked.

"Just tired," he said. "I haven't been sleeping well."

"Understood. It's a tough case to investigate."

"Yeah. I'll be glad when it's over."

"I don't know if you want to see this," the pathologist said, "but this pelvis belonged to a female. On preliminary exam, I can tell you that there are some mild degenerative changes to the vertebrae. For most people, that starts to happen in their thirties and forties."

"An adult," Jeff said. "Definitely human?"

"Yes," he said. "This is human."

"Can you tell the cause of death?"

The doctor was quiet for a moment, and Jeff kept his eyes focused on the counter in front of him.

What's wrong with you? It's an adult female. You heard that, didn't you? Turn around and take a look at what he has to show you.

"Nothing obvious," Owen said. "I don't see any fractures to the skull or long bones." He put the skeletal remains back on the table. Jeff could hear the clunk of it from where he was standing.

Owen zipped up the bag. He removed his gloves and tossed them in the trash can. "I'll need some time to make a thorough assessment," he said. "I'm going to take this over to the university. We'll see if we can get some carbon dating as we did on the other specimen. I'll contact you in a week or two, as soon as I know something."

"Thank you," Jeff said. Beads of sweat had formed on his forehead. He wiped them away with the sleeve of his shirt before turning around. "I can't emphasize enough how helpful this is."

The medical examiner nodded and walked with him to the parking lot. "It's what we do here," he said. "Sometimes the evidence talks to us." He held out his hand and Jeff shook it. "But it's a poor substitute for the living."

22

(October 1998)

HELEN REECE OPENED THE DRIVER'S DOOR OF THE WHITE DODGE Dynasty, slid behind the wheel, and waited for Erin and Robbie to climb into the back. "Seat belts, please," she said as she turned the key in the ignition. The engine fired up immediately, already warm from her drive over here. In the winter it was a different story. She kept a pair of jumper cables in the trunk just in case.

Mrs. Tabaha was standing in the doorway, watching them. Helen gave her a wave before putting the car in Reverse and backing out of the driveway. She pressed down on the accelerator, and the tires kicked up small plumes of dust that took to the air behind them.

Helen liked the Dodge. It was ten years old, and the only vehicle she'd ever owned. Her father had bought it for her in 1988, and she'd done her best to take good care of it. The Dodge had outlasted her old man, in fact, who died of a heart attack a week after Helen's twenty-ninth birthday. She'd become obsessive about its upkeep since then, changing the oil herself every three thousand miles and taking it to the shop twice a year for preventive maintenance. The car had its share of quirks, but Helen felt closer to her father when she drove it, and that was reason enough to keep it running.

"How are you this afternoon, Robbie?" she asked.

"I'm fine, Mrs. Reece."

"I haven't seen you since school started back up again. What've you been up to?"

"Not much," he said. "Getting ready for Halloween, I guess."

She glanced at him in the rearview. "Are you going trick-or-treating this year?"

"I don't know," he said. "My mom wants me to stay home. She doesn't like the idea of us running around the neighborhood after dark."

Helen put on her blinker—a habit more than a necessity in this empty stretch of road east of Wolf Point—and turned left onto the highway. "You could come over to our place this Halloween," she said. "We'll tell scary stories and eat fistfuls of candy corn until our eyes pop out of their sockets."

"*Mom.*"

"What?" She glanced in the mirror in time to see Erin roll her eyes, an expression she'd picked up earlier this year. There had been none of that when she was younger, but Erin was thirteen now, a tough nut to crack.

"That chicken you like had a brood of chicks last week," Helen told Robbie. "She's got eleven of them following her around the yard."

"That's great," Robbie said, smiling. She could see it in the rearview.

"Peep, peep, peep," Erin said, and Robbie's smile broadened, his dark eyes glancing toward her daughter.

Helen returned her attention to the road in front of her. It was a rural area, the occasional homes nestled far back from the roadway. They drove in silence for a while, entering Wolf Point and passing the Agland Co-op on their right. The parking lot was mostly empty on this Saturday afternoon in mid-October. These days, people did their shopping in the morning, while the sun was still climbing in the sky.

Helen slowed the car, turned left onto Fourth Avenue North, and continued south beneath the railroad overpass. There was graffiti here, indecipherable scribblings mostly, but someone had drawn nine tally marks in broad red strokes on the concrete with plenty of room for more.

Nine disappearances over a year and a half, she thought. *In the beginning, we searched for our missing. These days we simply add another mark to the wall.*

There was a man standing at the corner with a cardboard sign in his hand. "Will work for anything," he'd written. Helen took her foot off the brake and made a right without stopping.

"Maybe this isn't such a good idea," she said. "Things have changed for the worse on this side of town."

"Mom, we'll be fine. We hardly *ever* get to do anything anymore. Do you expect us to hide in our house for the rest of our lives?"

She's got a point, Helen thought. *I used to be the one she'd come to when she wanted to feel safe from the monsters. These days, I'm more afraid of the boogeyman than she is.*

"I'm just looking out for your well-being," she said.

"Mom."

"What?"

"Wolf Point is fine in the daytime."

"Is it?"

"Yeah. There hasn't been a disappearance in months."

Three months, Helen thought, *as if that's something to celebrate.* She sighed. There was a time when Erin used to ride her bike to Robbie's house, but Helen had put a stop to that more than a year ago following the fifth disappearance. There had been four more since then, and another accidental death when Henry Rosen mistakenly shot a neighbor who'd stopped by his house to watch Monday-night football.

It's more than just being afraid, she thought. The disappearances had changed the way they lived. Helen no longer talked to people at the grocery store, and David preferred to stay on the farm even on Sundays, when they used to go to church. At his insistence, Helen now kept a .38 caliber revolver in her glove compartment, and her husband had made certain she knew how to use it.

She pulled up to the curb in front of Prairie Cinemas. It was a two-story structure with movie posters displayed outside and a sign with the name of the establishment above the front entrance. Bolted to the brick exterior of the second story, the decorative silhouettes of two cowboys leaned against imaginary posts, facing each other, the brims of their hats tipped low over their faces.

Helen put her right hand on the backrest of the seat beside her and turned her head to look at her daughter. "You have the money I gave you? There should be enough for tickets and drinks for the two of you."

"Okay, Mom."

"Do me a favor and ask Ms. Griffin what time the movie lets out. I'll come by and pick you up when it's over."

She watched as they got out of the car and walked inside, disappearing into the dim interior. They had come to see *Antz,* an animated movie that was doing pretty well at the box office, but it made her nervous to let them do this. Everything these days felt like an unnecessary risk. Still, it had been two and a half years since the first disappearance, and on some level her daughter was right. Helen couldn't expect them to forfeit their childhood. She didn't want their recollection of these years to be defined by fear.

The front passenger door popped open, and Helen jumped.

Erin leaned into the car. "Ms. Griffin says the movie is eighty-three minutes," she said. "There are some previews beforehand, so . . ."

Helen looked down at her watch, a birthday present that David had gotten her the year before. "It's four-thirty," she said. "I'll pick you up *right here* at six o'clock when the movie's over. Stay in the theater until I get here. No wandering around after dark."

"Okay," Erin said.

"Do you want me to go in with you?" Helen asked. "I wouldn't mind seeing it myself."

"No, Mom. We'll be fine."

"Are you sure?"

"Yes. Don't worry."

"I'm your mother. It's my job to worry." Helen blew her a kiss. "Have fun," she said. "Don't give Ms. Griffin any trouble."

"We won't," she promised, and Erin closed the door and headed back into the theater.

Helen sat there for a while, uncertain of where to go. The idea occurred to her that she could just stay put until the movie was over, but eighty-three minutes plus previews was a long time to spend in the car with nothing to do.

She flipped on the radio and turned to 107.1 FM, the Wolf. The voice of the new DJ was younger and less raspy than the one who'd held the job for the past eight years. The new guy didn't chatter much, just played the songs one after the other, a combination of country music and classic hits: "hits from yesterday," as the guy liked to put it, as if everything good was already behind them. And maybe it was, at least for a while. The DJ's predecessor, Mike Flannigan, had taken an indefinite leave of absence two days after his seventeen-year-old daughter went missing. There was an investigation, but no search party. *Just another tally mark on the underpass wall,* she thought. No one talked about people getting lost in the snow anymore. By now they pretty much knew what they were dealing with.

She pulled away from the curb and drove with the window down. Cool air buffeted the side of her face and neck, and Bruce Springsteen headed into the final verse of "My Hometown," a song that had always struck her as more fatalistic than nostalgic. Her parents were gone now, her father from a heart attack and her mother a year later from a broken heart in the space of his absence. She had a brother, Jason, but he'd left Wolf Point at the age of eighteen to join the military, and chances were he was never coming back. It was just her and her family now, in a town she no longer trusted.

Helen pressed down on the accelerator as she crossed the city line. She watched Wolf Point grow smaller in her rearview. *Maybe that's what we should do,* she thought. *Go someplace else, at least for a while.* But there was the farm to think about. What would they do with the livestock and machinery, the two decades of work David had already put into a business he'd inherited from his father? It would crush him to lose it, and it would ruin them financially. Putting the farm up for sale wasn't a realistic option, either. No one was looking to move here. There was no sense in building a life in a place that was already dying.

She heard a *whump,* and the steering wheel pulled hard to the left.

"*Damn it.*"

The wheel jerked in her hands. She could feel the car tilting, the right-side tires losing contact with the road.

Jesus, don't flip, she thought, and she lifted her foot off the brake.

The car lurched forward. There was a jolt as the tires returned to the pavement. She pressed down on the brake again, more slowly this time, and brought the Dodge to a shuddering stop.

Helen sat there for a moment, settling herself. Her hands were shaking. She put the car in Park and turned off the ignition.

The Dodge had come to rest diagonally across the roadway, but it was mostly farmland out here, nothing but the railway to her north and the small airport about half a mile back. She opened the door and got out of the car.

The left front tire was shredded, she could see that right away. Whatever she'd hit, it had been more than just a nail. She reached inside and pulled the lever to pop the trunk. It would take her less than ten minutes to change the tire. Her father had been strict about making her learn how to do it—not just on sunny afternoons, but in the dark and rain as well. "A tire waits for the worst possible time to go flat on you," he used to tell her. "Learn how to do it in these conditions and you'll never be stranded."

She walked around to the trunk, and that's when she noticed that the left rear tire was flat as well.

What the hell did I hit? she asked herself, and she looked back at the vacant stretch of roadway behind her. There was nothing that she could see, just flat asphalt and a skid mark where she'd applied the brake too hard.

Helen squatted down to inspect the rear tire. There was a piece of metal embedded in the rubber. She tried to work it free with her fingers, but it was sunk in deep and wouldn't budge. She stood up, went to the front one, and inspected that as well. There was no hunk of metal sticking out of the tire, but she'd definitely hit *something*—construction material that had fallen off a truck, maybe. Whatever it was, there was probably more of it back there, lying in the roadway.

Helen walked along the road in the direction from which she'd come. She'd passed the airport less than a minute ago. That meant she was about three miles from home, close enough to walk if she had to. Whether she could make it home, pick up David's truck, and get back to the theater by six was another matter. *I should get going,* she thought, but first she wanted to make sure there wasn't anything else back here. If she didn't, the next car to come along might end up in a similar predicament.

Helen followed her skid marks. There was something lying in the road, about fifteen yards from where the first skid mark started. She walked until she was standing over it, an L-shaped metal angle projecting three inches off the surface. Helen reached down to pick it up and was surprised to find that she couldn't. She hunkered down to get a better look. The angle had holes in it, places for bolts to pass through, and two bolts secured it to the asphalt. It was construction material, all right, designed to connect wooden joists and framing, but this one had been filed down to a point at the angle sticking up from the ground.

Helen looked up. There was another metal angle a short distance away. She walked over and nudged it with her foot. It was bolted into the road like the first, although this one was a bit loose. Maybe it was the one she had hit with the front tire. Her rear tire must've picked up another.

Helen looked around. There was no one out here. The only house was a hundred yards off the roadway.

These didn't just fall off a truck. They were bolted into the road on purpose.

She started back toward the car. There was only one spare

in the trunk and no way to change out *both* of her tires. It was time to set out on foot, but there was something in the glove compartment she wanted to grab first. She'd feel safer, having it in her hand. When she got home, she'd contact the police.

Helen heard the vehicle before she saw it, a white van approaching from the road ahead. It got to the car before she did, and came to a stop as the driver flipped on his hazards.

A man stepped out of the vehicle. He was wearing sunglasses and a baseball cap with the brim pulled low.

"Hey, lady. You okay? Did you get into an accident or something?"

Her heart rate kicked up a notch. "There's some metal in the road. It punctured two of my tires."

The man walked around the car and glanced at the tires. "*Aww, geez,*" he said. "It did a number on 'em, didn't it? I mean, *one* you could change, but *two* . . ." He shook his head. "That puts you in a tough spot, I guess."

"My husband will be here in a second," she said. "I called him from that house over there."

The man looked over his shoulder. "*That* house?" he asked. "The one all the way over there?"

"That's right."

"That house belongs to Roy Shifflet. You knocked on old Roy's door and asked to make a phone call? Is that what you did?"

Helen swallowed. She could feel her heart thudding at the base of her throat. The gun was in the Dodge's glove compartment. Why hadn't she pulled it out and taken it with her when she left the car?

(*Because you didn't know what this was. But you do now, don't you?*)

Yes, she thought. *Now I know.*

The man was walking toward her. She took a few steps backward, and he stopped.

"Last I heard, old Roy was visiting his mother in Wisconsin." He placed his hands on his hips. "Of course, you're telling me he's back. He let you into his house to use the phone and that's when you called your husband."

Helen pressed her lips together. The muscles in her thighs were shaking. She took in a breath through her nostrils and held it in her chest before letting it out. She was in trouble. She was in . . . *a tough spot.*

"Please," she said. "You don't have to do this. I have a daughter. I'm somebody's mother."

"I know who you are," he said. "You're Helen Reece. Your husband ran over a kid in the middle of Main Street. You think he's paid his price for that? You think three years in prison is good enough?"

"It was an accident. The child ran out right in front of him."

"Oh, an accident," he said, and looked down at the roadway. "Well, okay. This is an accident, too. You run, and I'll get in the truck and try not to hit you."

Helen turned around and ran, back toward the city of Wolf Point. It was barely visible on the horizon, a cluster of buildings crouched low against the earth. Her daughter was back there, but in her panic, Helen couldn't remember where. She left the roadway and cut a jagged path across the plains, like a child running from the boogeyman. *Gonna make it,* she thought, but there was so much space ahead of her, and she could hear him coming, the growl of the engine gobbling up the distance between them.

23

"TWO TICKETS TO THE FOUR-THIRTY SHOW OF *ANTZ*, PLEASE." ERIN dug into her pocket, pulled out a crumpled ten-dollar bill, and placed it on the counter.

Connie Griffin looked down at the money. She was a tall, heavyset woman, a little older than Erin's mother. Her gray hair was pulled into a loose bun that sat like an oversize jelly doughnut on top of her head. She wore a solid blue dress with a collar of white lace and three-quarter-length sleeves that stopped just south of her generous elbows.

"Two tickets for *Antz,* you say." She scooped up the money and placed it into the register. "Can I interest you in snacks or a beverage?"

"Yes, please. A medium Coke and a medium popcorn."

The woman nodded. "And butter on the popcorn?"

Erin nodded.

"Of course you'd like butter. Popcorn without butter is like . . ." She paused for a moment, thinking it over. "Is like a sandwich with no bread. And what do you have then? Just a bunch of meat and cheese." She placed the refreshments in front of them. "The matinee is two dollars and fifty cents apiece. With the Coke and popcorn, that comes to eight dollars total." She plucked two dollars from the register and laid it on the counter in front of them. "*Antz* is playing in Cinema One. That's the theater on your left. You've got the whole place to yourselves. You can sit in the front row for half of the movie and in the back row for the other half. I'll go upstairs and get it started."

"Thank you," Erin said as she and Robbie turned and walked toward the doors of the theater.

Ms. Griffin lifted a hinged section of the counter and walked across the lobby to the door leading to the stairwell. "Thank you both for coming to Prairie Cinemas," she said. "Please take your seats. The show is about to begin."

Erin and Robbie entered the theater. The overhead lights were still on, revealing a large screen and seven rows of chairs upholstered in a red velour that matched the color of the carpet in the entryway. They chose center seats in the third row and waited for the lights to dim and the projector to flicker on.

"*Bride of Chucky* is playing in Cinema Two," Robbie whispered. "We should go see that instead."

Erin shook her head. "It's rated R."

"So?"

"She'll catch us. We're the only ones in the theater, remember?"

"Yeah, I'll bet she's lonely," he said. "Nobody comes to the movies anymore."

"Nobody does *anything* anymore. I'm amazed your mom let you out of the house."

He reached over and grabbed a handful of popcorn. "You just have to annoy them enough. Then they're like, 'Okay, get out. Go bother somebody else for a while.'"

On the screen in front of them, an ant talked about how he didn't feel like he belonged in the colony. They sat in silence for a few minutes, munching on popcorn.

"This is kind of boring," Robbie whispered.

"Shhh. I'm sure it gets better."

"Okay." Robbie leaned forward and took a sip of Coke. "I got two straws," he said, "in case you're worried I have cooties or something."

He handed her the second straw in its wrapper. She looked at it, shrugged, and put it in her lap.

"Let's do something," Robbie said.

"What do you mean?"

"I don't know. This is boring. Let's get outta here."

"We can't get into the other movie, I already told you. She'll catch us for sure."

"Let's go someplace else, then."

"Like where?"

"I don't know. Down by the river or beneath the railway overpass. We can go exploring at the city dump. Except for school, my parents haven't let me out of their sight for the past three months. I don't even get to leave my yard."

"That's because of—"

"I know, I know," he said. He leaned over and took another sip of Coke. "But the people who went missing, they were adults mostly."

Erin turned around to glance at the rows behind them. They were still alone in the theater.

"Some of them were kids."

"*Two* of them were kids. Seven adults."

She shook her head. "We can't just . . . my mother would *kill me* if she found out."

"So don't let her find out." Robbie scooped a handful of popcorn from the bag. He tossed a kernel in the air and tried to catch it in his mouth. It bounced off his nose and fell to the floor. "We can leave through the exit door and come back later."

Erin stared at him in the darkness. "It'll lock behind us. We won't be able to get back in."

"Sure we will," he said. He tossed another kernel in the air, and this time he caught it in his mouth. "I'll wedge a quarter between the door and the frame so it stays open a crack. The movie's got at least another hour. We'll be back before then."

"I don't know," she said. "My mom, she's trusting us. If we get busted, I'll be grounded for life."

"What's the difference? Your parents keep you at home, same as me. You might as well be grounded already."

He put his index finger in her ear. She swatted his hand away, spilling some of the popcorn.

Robbie smiled. "We're not gonna get busted, okay? We'll be gone for less than an hour. But . . . if you want to watch the rest of the movie, that's okay, too. I don't want you to be mad at me if we get in trouble."

She was quiet for a while, thinking. "He's out there, you know, the person who's doing this."

"So what? Big deal. People should be patrolling the streets, making it safer, not staying inside and hiding behind the curtains. This is *our* town, not his. Doesn't anyone care about that anymore?"

"I care."

"Great. So let's go."

"We're gonna patrol the street?"

"We'll look for clues." He picked up a kernel of popcorn and bounced it off her right cheek.

Erin chewed on her lower lip. "You think there's an alarm on the emergency exit?"

"Nope," he said. "I've opened it before."

"When?"

"Lots of times."

"*Lots* of times?"

"Okay, once," he said. "I pushed on it to see what would happen. It opened and closed, no problem. No alarm. Nothing."

"When was this?"

"About a year ago. I was with my mom."

"Your mom let you mess with the emergency exit?"

"Not exactly," he said. "I left my jacket on the seat and had to go back for it. I grabbed the jacket, left through the emergency exit door, and ran around to the front of the building to surprise her."

Erin got up and walked to the door. She stood there looking up at the exit sign.

Robbie walked over to join her. "Go ahead and push it," he said. "Nothing's going to happen."

She reached her hands out and pushed on the horizontal bar. The door opened outward into the waning daylight.

"See?" he said. "No alarm. I told you." He removed a quarter from his pocket and stuck it between the door and the jamb.

"It doesn't close all the way," Erin said.

"That's good."

"No, it's bad," she said. "It lets in light. It's obvious that the door is open. If she looks down from that window"—she pointed to the projectionist booth—"she'll notice."

"Okay," he said. "What do *you* think we should do?"

She stepped back and studied the frame of the door, then reached forward and toggled the latch with her finger.

"We break off a piece of plastic from the cup," she said. "If we put it over the latch, the door shouldn't lock when we close it."

Robbie went back to retrieve the cup. He exited the building, popped the lid off the cup, and dumped its contents on the pavement. With the empty cup lying on its side, he stepped on it. The plastic cracked into several pieces. He picked up the biggest one. "Will this work?"

"Probably," she said. "Put it over the latch and shut the door. I'll stay inside until we know it isn't going to lock us out."

"Okay," he said, and positioned the plastic between the latch and the latch plate as he shut the door. Once the door was closed, the plastic remained in place, wedged between the edge of the door and the doorjamb.

"Can you open it?" she asked through the door.

"No," he said. "There's no handle on the outside. I can't get a grip on it."

Erin pushed on the bar and the door opened. The plastic shard dropped to the ground. "Don't shut it as far as it will go," she said. "Leave a little bit of an edge so you can get a grip on it."

"Got it," he said, and tried again. This time he was able to open the door from the outside, and Erin caught the plastic before it fell.

"How was that?" he asked.

"Pretty good," she said. "Are you sure you want to do this?"

He frowned. "*Of course* I'm sure. Let's go. We've gotta be back here in an hour."

"Fifty minutes," she said, and he shrugged.

Erin stepped through the doorway and waited as Robbie positioned the plastic.

Inside the theater, the movie played to an empty auditorium. Five miles to the east, Helen Reece watched as the driver of a white van turned on his hazards and came to a stop on the other side of her Dodge Dynasty. It was ten minutes after five, about an hour before sunset, and the city of Wolf Point was shutting down for the evening.

24

BRIAN CRAY LOOKED AROUND THE LIVING ROOM AT THE FOLKS packed into the small house on Dawson Street. Debbie was sitting in her favorite chair near the window. She'd let him do most of the talking so far, but this was her place, and the gathering had been *her* idea.

"Bring them out to the house," she'd told him two nights ago after dinner. "It's time this town had a discussion about what to do with David Reece."

Brian had been sitting on the couch, smoking a cigarette. "What do you mean?" he asked, although he'd known her long enough to have a pretty good idea about where this conversation was heading.

Debbie stood in the doorway to the kitchen, drying her hands on a dish towel. Her shirt was tight across her chest. It was the kind of thing she usually wore when she wanted him to do something for her.

"They found a second body. You know that, don't you?"

He lifted the cigarette and took a drag. "I heard."

"So he killed those people," she said. "He killed Curt and Rose Perry and Angela Finley and little Jimmy Raffey. I can remind you of the names of the other twelve in case you forgot."

Curt. Her dead husband. *Not dead but missing,* Brian corrected himself. Even now, after fifteen years with her, Brian could still feel the man's presence in the house, as if Curt Hastings had just stepped out for a pack of smokes and would be walking through the door any minute.

Brian glanced at the front door, a habit a long time in the making. "I know who they were."

"Seems to me like a lot of people want to forget."

"One of them was David Reece's wife. You figure he killed her, too?"

"Why not? It's usually the husband who does it. I'm sure they'll find her buried on that farm with the rest of them."

He took another drag from the cigarette. "It's over, then. People can finally put it behind them."

"The hell with that," she said. "What about justice? What about retribution?"

He looked at her. Debbie looked good in that shirt. He had to give her that.

"You wanna tie a noose around his neck and hang him from the nearest tree. Is that it?"

"No," she said. "I'd like to torture him for a few days first. All those people buried in the ground. A monster like that doesn't deserve an easy death."

Brian shook his head. "He's on a ventilator. Who knows if he's even gonna make it."

"He's *off* the ventilator," Donna Raffey announced, and Brian blinked. He was sitting in the living room with the rest of them now, and it suddenly occurred to him that *he* was the outsider, the only one among them who hadn't lost someone at the hands of David Reece.

Kate Anderson shifted in her chair. "He's getting better," she said. "He could be discharged by the end of the week."

Debbie nodded. "And now he lies there in a hospital bed with people wiping his ass and arranging his flowers."

Brian brought a hand to his face, covering a smile. *Wiping his ass and arranging his flowers,* he thought. Nice touch.

Bill Stutzman stood in a corner, leaning against the wall. "He'll be arrested as soon as he's discharged from the hospital." He looked over at Mike Brennan for confirmation.

"Maybe," Debbie said, "and maybe he'll get a fancy lawyer and a change of venue and drag the case through the courts for eight years. God, Bill, who knows if you'll even be alive that long."

"Screw you, Debbie."

"That's not on the menu," she said. "Besides, I don't think your heart could take it."

Bill ignored the comment and looked at the rest of them. "*If* this is what we think it is, he'll be found guilty and go to prison for the rest of his life."

Debbie laughed. "You think they're gonna try the case here in Wolf Point? It'll happen in another town far away from here. Most of us won't even be able to attend the trial. Does that sound like justice to you?"

Vinny Briggs tipped back in his chair. "He could get the death penalty," he said, and he smiled, pleased with the idea.

Mike Brennan shook his head. "It's unlikely. Montana hasn't executed anyone in over twenty-three years."

"So he'll live out the rest of his miserable days in prison," Bill said. "That's good enough for me. It's got to be. I mean, what are we talking about here?"

"Do you speak for all of us, Bill? What's good enough for Bill Stutzman is good enough for the rest?"

Bill turned to Donna Raffey. "That's not what I'm saying, and you know it."

Dan Finley put a hand to his temple. "Excuse me, Bill, but your situation is a bit different than ours. When Kenny was hit by that car, it was a tragedy, but you know what happened to your son. That's not the same for the rest of us. If they find the remains of my daughter buried on David Reece's property, I'll kill the man myself."

"I can understand you feeling that way, Dan, but—"

"It's not that I'm *feeling* that way, Bill. I'm telling you that I'll kill him." He turned to Mike Brennan. "Maybe you could lock me up just for saying that, Mike. But a threat is just a threat until it's carried out, and you can't lock me up forever."

Mike raised a hand. "I won't be locking up anyone tonight. You're just blowing off steam as far as I'm concerned."

Bill took a step forward. "So we're making blatant threats on the man's life now?" he asked. "That's the solution? That's what we've come here to talk about?"

"We're discussing our options," Debbie told him. "That's all."

Bill shook his head. "We don't *have* any options. We sit back and let justice take its course. We don't go off half-cocked and decide to take matters into your own hands. I mean, *Jesus,* haven't we lost enough people already?"

"Listen, Bill," Vinny said, "you have the right to your opinion, and we have the right to ours."

"It's not an opinion. It's the way things *have to* be. You lost your brother. I understand that you're angry."

"Oh, I'm more than angry, old man. I'm ready for some payback."

"You're *always* ready for some payback," he said, "even if it's you who caused the trouble in the first place."

"Ain't no trouble if people stay out of my business. You should do yourself a favor and remember that."

Bill took a step forward. "Is that a threat? I may be old, but I can still beat the crap out of a punk like you."

Vinny jumped to his feet. "Well, let's see it then. I'll throw your fat ass through the window."

"*Stop* it," Mike said. "Sit down, Vinny. Or I'll drag you out of here and beat the crap out of you myself."

Vinny turned to him. "Come on, Mike. You heard him. The old man wants to fight."

"Sit *down*," the cop said. "I won't tell you again."

Vinny plopped himself back down in the chair. He scowled at Mike and kicked the leg of the coffee table with the heel of his boot.

"Thank you," Mike said. "We're gonna keep this civilized. We're not here to fight each other. Bill has some objections and I think we should hear him out."

"I've said everything I have had to say," Bill told them. "I know what you're considering, and I can tell you it's a mistake— not just for me, but for *all* of you. You wanna come together as a community? That's fine. Hold a memorial service for the people we lost. But don't make the error of deciding that evil deeds require evil deeds in response. We're better than that. Wolf Point is better than that. It's the only thing that keeps us human. Don't you see?" He searched their faces for signs of understanding. "It's the only thing we have left."

They were quiet for a moment, none of them looking at the man in front of them.

"Thank you, Bill," Mike said. "I appreciate your perspective. We all do. A memorial service is a good idea. A candlelight vigil, maybe. That's the way we ought to handle this." He walked over and put an arm around the man. "We'll let these folks work out the details, but it's your suggestion and we won't forget that. Thanks for reminding us of who we are."

They nodded and murmured their agreement.

Mike walked Bill to the door. "The two of us came together," he told the group. "I've got an early shift in the morning, so I'm gonna drive Bill home and then get some sleep myself. Thank you, Brian and Debbie, for inviting us out here this evening. It was a good idea to talk this over." He put his hand on the door. "No one gets behind the wheel until they're stone-cold sober. I have your word on that?"

They looked at him and nodded.

"Well, that's fine then. You folks have a pleasant evening," he said, and the two of them walked out together.

A minute later they heard the sound of two car doors closing and an engine starting in the street. They listened as it faded away into the night.

"You shouldn't have invited a cop *and* the father of a cop," Vinny said. He leaned back in his chair again, raised the bottle to his lips, and finished off the last half of his beer.

Debbie got up from her chair and went to the window. "Doesn't matter," she said, looking out at the night. "Let's get back to business. What are we really going to do about David Reece?"

25

ERIN LEANED FORWARD AND PUT A HAND ON HIS FOREARM. DAVID made a noise in the back of his throat, as if agreeing with something his daughter had said. She hadn't said anything, though, not in the last two hours. She'd been sitting beside the bed for most of the morning, listening to the unfamiliar sound of her father's breathing without the ventilator.

"Mmm," he said, and he muttered something else that Erin couldn't decipher. The flesh beneath his eyes was pink and puffy, and he swallowed with a bit of effort, his Adam's apple rising and falling.

"Dad. Are you awake?"

"Hmm?"

"It's Erin. I've come back to see you."

He turned his head in the direction of her voice.

"I know you're not feeling well," she said. "You're in the hospital. You were sick for a while, but now things are getting better."

He opened his eyes a bit, the upper lids lifting a few millimeters.

"Do you want to sit up?" she asked. "I can raise the back of the bed if you want." She leaned forward and pressed a button on the bedrail. A motor whirred to life, and the head of his bed began to elevate.

"Nnnnn-oo."

She let go of the button.

Erin watched as he drifted off to sleep. Thirty minutes later she left the hospital, got into the truck, and drove down to the high school, where she parked along one of the side streets. She and Robbie had come this way on the day her mother went missing. Erin headed south, retracing their steps, as if the childhood version of herself was still out here, wandering the neighborhood, and everything that happened that day could be undone if she could just find her.

She passed Jacob's Field. The house, she saw, had fallen into a state of neglect. The exterior siding looked as if it hadn't been painted since Erin left fifteen years ago, and the shingles on the roof were broken and crumbled. She wondered if Mr. Jacob was still alive, and for a moment Erin had the urge to walk up and knock on the door. *He would remember me,* she thought, but there was no comfort in the idea, just another face looking out at her from the faded recesses of her past.

Instead, Erin continued south until she made it to the tree line overlooking the Missouri River, where she sat down on the hillside and watched the water circulate below her. There was part of her younger self here as well, and the thought occurred to her that she might never make it out of Wolf Point. Had she known that from the beginning? Had she left her house in Colorado knowing that she was never coming back?

The sun glinted off the water. She shielded her eyes, and Erin caught a glimpse of a child standing at the water's edge, skipping rocks across the surface. Was it Angela Finley, Jimmy Raffey, or maybe even Robbie Tabaha skipping stones down by the quarry? She stood up to get a better look, but the shoreline was empty, just a long stretch of undeveloped land that fell away beneath her.

"I'm sorry," she whispered, but there was no one left to hear her.

26

THEY WALKED WEST ALONG MAIN STREET UNTIL THEY GOT TO THE high school, a silent brick building just south of the railroad tracks. A row of streetlamps stood in formation along the vacant semicircle that buses used to drop off the students. There was still light in the sky, but one of the bulbs flickered on in the approaching dusk as Erin and Robbie crossed the street.

The athletic field was unoccupied on this Saturday evening, the oval-shaped track flanked by empty rows of metal bleachers. They continued south toward the river until they reached Jacob's Field, a stretch of open farmland on their right. Mr. Jacob lived in a single-story house set back off the roadway, and this evening they could see light from one of its rooms shining through a small square window at the front. To the rear of the house, a modest porch overlooked a broad congregation of crops that were currently dormant. A collection of pine trees marked the ridgeline at the back of the property. Beyond that, the earth sloped sharply downward for about eighty yards until it flattened out along the northern bank of the Missouri River, whose dark waters flowed eastward toward her father's farm.

The children continued walking until they got to the other side of the pines. From this vantage point, they could no longer look back and see the city, just the river below them and miles of open land to the south. Robbie gathered a handful of stones, and they spent a few minutes hurling them down the hillside, seeing if either of them could make it to the water's edge.

"Last one down is a rotten egg," Robbie said. He dropped to the ground and rolled down the hillside with his arms tucked tight against his chest.

Erin watched him for a moment, then got down on the ground and rolled after him. Robbie beat her to the bottom, of course, and by the time she came to a stop, he was already hauling ass up the hill.

"Last one to the top is a chump," Robbie said, and he stopped, ripped up a handful of dirt-caked grass, and threw it back at her.

She got up and ran after him, knowing she could never beat him but happy to try.

"Look out below," he said, rolling down the hill, and Erin had to jump over him to avoid getting taken out at the legs.

Robbie won the first two sprints to the ridgeline. On the third one, however, Erin stopped rolling, reached out, and grabbed his foot as he ran past her up the hill. He fell forward, doing a face plant into the grass. "*Ooommff,*" he said as Erin got to her feet, put the sole of her sneaker between his shoulder blades, and pushed off. She leaned forward into the ascent, her legs pumping. She was dizzy from three rolling trips down the hillside, and was laughing so hard that she almost didn't make it to the top. Robbie was on his feet in a second, snorting and lumbering after her. "Here I come!" he said. "I'll show you what it's like to be stepped on."

"*No, no!*" she called back to him, collapsing in the grass at the top of the hill. She covered her head with her arms and pulled her body into a protective ball as he gathered handfuls of pine needles and dumped them on her head.

"Be one with the trees," he said, and got down on his hands and knees to collect some additional arsenal.

Erin jumped to her feet, shook off the needles, and ran. She could hear his footsteps closing in on her, and she cut a jagged course through the pines, trying to keep at least a few of them between her and the next shower of needles.

She was near the eastern edge of the tree line, almost back to the path they had taken to come here, when a man stepped out in front of her.

Erin screamed and skidded to a stop.

"What's going on here?" the man asked. He was wearing overalls and a baseball cap pulled low across his face. "What are you doing on my property?"

Robbie came to a stop behind her. Erin could hear him breathing.

The man was holding a flashlight in his right hand. He raised it and trained the beam on Robbie's face. Twenty minutes ago he wouldn't have needed it, but it had gotten dark in a hurry since then. Had they lost track of the time, Erin wondered, or was it just darker here beneath the towering canopy of the pines?

"Is this boy bothering you?" the man asked. He took a step forward.

"Yes," she said, "I mean *no.* We were just playing, that's all."

The beam of light swung to her face. "Playing," he said. "Do your parents know you're out here?"

"Yes," Robbie answered. "They told us to be home by sunset. We were just getting ready to head back."

"You're trespassing," the man said. "I've turned a blind eye to it for years, but . . . things have changed. I can't have kids on my property no more. If one of you goes missing, it's me they'll come after."

"Mr. Jacob," Robbie said, making the connection. "We weren't—"

"There's no discussion here, young man. I want the both of you off my land right now. Tell your friends not to come back here neither. You're gonna have to find a different sledding hill. This one's closed for good. Do you hear me?"

"Yes, sir," they said, answering in unison.

"And don't trample through my crops," he told them. "Use the road. You can go around the long way."

Erin squinted into the light. "I'm sorry we disturbed you, Mr. Jacob."

"Don't be sorry," he said. "Just leave." He narrowed his eyes. "Are you sure your parents know you're out here? You shouldn't be out this late in the evening. Ain'tcha got no sense in your heads? Don'tcha know what's been goin' on in this town?"

Robbie reached forward and grabbed Erin by the forearm. "Come on," he said. "Let's get going."

They retreated along the ridgeline toward the dirt road at the far side of the property. Erin could feel Mr. Jacob watching them. She looked back once and saw him standing there, where the trees merged with his precious field of crops.

"He's not very nice, is he?" she whispered. "I *knew* we were going to get in trouble."

"Ain't no trouble," Robbie said. "Just a little bit of trespassing, is all." He lowered the pitch of his voice, mimicking

Mr. Jacob. *"I want the both of you off my land right now. Tell your friends not to come back here neither."*

"Me and my friend are supposed to be at the movies."

"Whatcha doin' out here, then?" he asked. *"Ain'tcha got no sense in your heads? Don'tcha know what's been goin' on in this town?"*

"Shut up. This was *your* idea."

"Hey, I had nothin' to do with it. Last thing I remember, I was enjoying a movie and some popcorn. You said you wanted to go take a walk."

"I did not."

"What time is it anyway?" he asked. "It got dark quick."

"I don't know," she said. "You promised to get me back in less than an hour."

"Did I?" he asked. "I must've forgot when you tripped me and made me slam my face into the ground."

"Come on," she said, and Erin broke into a jog as they got to the dirt roadway that bordered the property.

They hustled along in the shadows. Erin could picture her mother, standing in the lobby of Prairie Cinemas with Ms. Griffin. *I don't know where they went,* Ms. Griffin would tell her. *They propped open the emergency exit door with a piece of plastic cup. It's against the law, you know. I have half a mind to report this to the authorities.*

"Hold up a minute," Robbie said, and stopped running.

"What is it?" she asked. "Hurry up. We're really late."

He took a few steps into the high grass to the left of the road, bent over, and fished something out of the grass.

"What are you doing?"

He turned around and tossed something to her. Erin reflexively trapped it against her chest. It was soft and light, like a Ziploc bag of moist cotton balls. She looked down, saw the finger, and almost dropped it. Robbie had discovered a severed hand in the bushes. But *no*, she realized, it wasn't a hand, just a mitten, dirty and torn in a few spots, as if an animal had chewed on it before deciding it wasn't something it could eat.

"Whose is it?" she asked.

"Don't know," he said. "I don't see the other one."

"Why did you pick it up?"

He shrugged. "What's it doing out here, right across from Mr. Jacob's house?"

"Maybe it's his."

"It's too small for him," he said. "It belongs to a kid, maybe one of the ones who went missing."

"You don't know that."

"No," he admitted. "Someone could've accidentally dropped it. But it *is* out here . . . near our sledding hill."

"Our *ex*–sledding hill," she corrected him.

"Right," he said. "Our ex–sledding hill. He sure was determined to run us off. I guess he doesn't want people snooping around on his land."

She looked down at the mitten. In the dim light, it was difficult to make out its true color. It was ripped, the surface caked with dirt. *It's been out here for a while,* she thought, *years maybe. It belongs to one of them, one of the kids who went missing.* Now that Robbie had put the idea in her head, it was impossible to think of it in any other way.

"It could be evidence," she said. "You shouldn't have touched it."

"What was I supposed to do?"

"Leave it here. Ask the police to come take a look at it."

He shuffled his feet. "Well, I can't put it back now."

"Why not?"

"He probably saw me pick it up."

"*Who? Mr. Jacob?*"

"Yes," he said. "I'm sure he's still watching us."

She turned her head to look back at the house.

"*Jesus, don't look,*" he said. "You want him to know that we suspect he might be a murderer?"

"Don't be creepy."

"I'm serious," he said. "The less he knows, the better."

She handed him the mitten. "I still think you should put it back where you found it."

"If I do, he might take it. When the police come out here, they won't find anything. It'll be his word against ours. Who do you think they're gonna believe? A weirdo loner like him, or two honest kids like us?"

"Him," she said. "We snuck out of the theater and jammed a piece of plastic cup in the emergency exit door."

"Well," he said, "when you put it like that . . ."

"Keep it, then," she said, "but let's go. The longer it takes us to get back, the worse it's gonna be for me."

They ran the rest of the way at an all-out sprint. The sun had fallen below the horizon, and the sky was a deep tumultuous purple they might have considered beautiful under different circumstances.

The emergency exit door was just as they'd left it. With his fingers gripping the edge, Robbie was able to pull it open, and Erin caught the plastic shard before it hit the concrete.

It was perfect timing. The credits were rolling as they stepped into the theater. They closed the door, took their seats, and waited until the projector came to the end of the reel and there was nothing but white light on the screen in front of them.

"Let's go," Erin whispered, and they stood up and made their way to the aisle.

It was still dark in the theater, which is why they didn't see her in the seat closest to the exit until she spoke to them.

"Did you enjoy the movie, children?" Ms. Griffin asked, and Erin felt her stomach drop as the projectionist of Prairie Cinemas stood up, turned around, and led them into the empty lobby.

27

JEFF STUTZMAN PULLED UP IN FRONT OF THE ONE-STORY BUNGA-
low and shut off the engine. The road to the modest dwell-
ing was dirt like so many others this far from town, but it
had rained the night before and the dust along the half-mile
driveway had been minimal. Connie Griffin drove a tan Jeep
Cherokee that was parked at an angle in front of the house.
Jeff had called ahead to make sure she'd be home, and as he
climbed out of the Suburban, he looked up to find her standing
on the front porch waiting for him.

"Good morning, Connie," he said. The sun was to his right,
and his body cast a shadow that stretched halfway across the
yard toward a dry creek bed thick with weeds. He'd been
out here in the spring when water from the melting snow-
pack flowed through the shallow channel, transforming it into
something young again. With the approach of winter, it was
good to remember that, he decided. Life still coursed through
the veins of Wolf Point, and there was no telling what another
season might bring. *Nothing,* Jeff thought, *lies dormant forever.*

There were four steps leading up to the front porch, and he
ascended them slowly, wishing there was some other reason for
him to be here. When he'd left the Montana State Crime Lab

four days ago, Jeff had forgotten to take the DNA collection kit with him. Dr. Lester had shipped it to him by FedEx, but Jeff had still waited a few days to contact Ms. Griffin. This was the hardest part of his job, delivering bad news to unsuspecting people. He'd become accustomed to everything else, but visits like this one never got any easier.

Connie smiled at him as he stepped up onto the porch. "Your boots are dragging this morning, Lieutenant. It's a good thing I just brewed a fresh pot of coffee."

"I can use it," he said. "I'm never fully conscious until the second cup."

"Then three cups it'll be, two for you and one for me." She turned and headed back into the house, and Jeff followed her into the kitchen.

The interior was mostly wood, but sunlight streamed through a bump-out window above the sink, and small dust particles hung in the shaft of light, suspended in the air like fireflies on a summer evening.

"I don't have a special cup for officers of the Wolf Point Police Department," she said, "but I do have one with a Boy Scouts of America logo on it. I suppose that's the best I can do. Were you a Boy Scout, Lieutenant? I can't remember."

"No, ma'am," he said. "I kind of went the other way. Got into some fights, played hooky, and came pretty close to getting kicked out of school before I pulled my act together." He smiled. "I guess you could say I'm a reformed juvenile delinquent."

She gave him a stern look. "I do not remember that, Lieutenant. You were always a *good* boy. That's what I remember."

"Well then, your memory serves me well." He pulled out a chair and took a seat at the table. Jeff watched as she stood at the counter and poured the coffee. She reminded him of his own mother, the way she'd been before the death of his brother. His mother was dead now, the victim of too much grief and too many pills in the medicine cabinet. He wished things had been different. He wished she'd had the courage to stick it out.

Connie settled into the chair across from him and gave him a brief smile as she arranged the items. She'd placed the coffee mug—*Boy Scouts of America,* it read, just as she'd promised—on the table in front of him. There was a jar of sugar and a small white ceramic pitcher with creamer, and she'd set out a folded napkin and a spoon for each of them.

"I'm not supposed to have too much sugar," she told him, "on account of my diabetes. Half a scoop is all I allow myself, and no sweets in the morning, just a slice of toast and a pat of low-fat butter." She sighed. "The things I would eat if my body only allowed it."

"You look good. I don't think you're giving yourself enough credit."

"Hogwash," she said. "I'm fifty pounds overweight, and that's not likely to change in *this* lifetime." She paused and looked at him. "Help yourself to the cream and sugar, Lieutenant."

"None for me, thank you." He lifted the mug to his lips and took a sip. It was hot, but not scalding. He swallowed it down, and the comforting warmth of it filled his stomach. He took a second sip. It was almost good enough to make him forget why he had come here.

"So," she said, as if reading his mind, "what brings you all the way out here to see me, Lieutenant?"

Jeff put his coffee mug back down on the table. He watched as she lifted the top of the sugar jar, scooped out half a spoonful, and submerged it in her coffee. She looked down at the spoon as she stirred. It clinked along the inside of the ceramic cup like a wind chime.

"You're a busy man," she said, "and although you've been out here before for social visits, that was a long time ago. I don't imagine that's the purpose of your visit today."

"No, ma'am. I'm sorry to say that it isn't."

She stopped stirring, removed the spoon, and placed it on her napkin.

"You've found something on David Reece's farm."

"Yes, ma'am," he said, and his heart ached at the sound of it.

"And now you're here. Because it involves me, doesn't it? One of the bodies you discovered buried in the ground."

He leaned forward in his chair. "I don't know if it involves you or not," he said. "That's what I'm here to talk to you about."

She stood up and went to the window, leaving Jeff alone at the table. He looked across at her empty chair, at the small dark stain where the head of her spoon was resting on its napkin.

"I almost told you not to bother coming," she said. "He's been gone for two decades. I've found a way to come to terms with that."

Jeff folded his hands on the table in front of him. He couldn't think of a single thing to say to make it better.

"He had a place of his own, but he used to visit me every Sunday," she said. "When two Sundays came and went without him walking through that door, I knew he was gone." She shook her head. "Abel was a *good* boy, like you, Lieutenant, but he was always slower than his brother. It wasn't his fault. He got turned around in the womb and had to be cut out of me. By the time he made it into this world, the damage was already done."

She leaned forward and looked out the window, as if she thought he might be walking up the driveway, returning home at this very moment.

"'Dimwitted,' people called him, and as much as I hated them for saying it, I have to admit that it was accurate. Kids leave when they get older, but not Abel. He relied on me. He couldn't make it on his own. That's how I knew, Lieutenant. That's how I knew that something terrible had happened."

"We don't know that it's him," Jeff said. His voice was soft, as if he was calming a child. "The age seems about right, but . . . there were a lot of people who went missing back then. It could be any one of them."

"You know it's him," she said. "You know or you wouldn't be here."

He took a deep breath and let it out. "We're not certain. The pathologist gave me a DNA specimen kit. I'm supposed to ask you for a sample."

Connie stood there with her back to him. He could hear her whispering to herself, a prayer that began with "Dear God" and became fiercer and more personal after that. She was in her mid-fifties, and her shoulders were more rounded than the last time he'd been out here. Jeff tried to remember when that had been. It was difficult to pin down, the years since then tumbling together.

He waited until she was finished praying, until the whispering stopped and she was just standing there, looking out the window. "I'll come back later," he said, and when he stood up to go, the legs of his chair squawked against the floorboards.

She turned her head. "Tell me at least that you have enough to prosecute."

"We're working on it."

"That's not good enough."

"We're being careful," he said. "We want the charges to stick. We need to gather as much evidence as possible."

"And a DNA sample from me will help you with that?"

"Yes, ma'am. Just a quick swab from the inside of your cheek."

"Take it, then," she said. "Collect your sample and then bury this man the way he's buried the rest of us. And if his daughter had anything to do with it, you can bury her, too."

"We're looking into it. We haven't ruled out any possibilities."

Connie turned and looked at him. Her eyes were red and puffy, but her jaw was set and her lower lip protruded from her face. Again, she reminded Jeff of his mother, Avery, and the determined look she'd had on the night she checked out forever.

"I know this is difficult," he said. "If it ever becomes *too* difficult, if you ever start to have thoughts of hurting yourself—"

"I'm not like that, Lieutenant," she said. "I'm a survivor. I keep going. It's the only way I know how."

He nodded.

"If you find out that it's my Abel who's buried in the ground there, I don't want to know," she said. "You can do me that courtesy, can't you?"

"If that's what you want," he said. "You might hear about it from the others, but you won't hear about it from me." He looked down at the floor. "The kit's in the truck," he said. "I'll go get it. We'll take the sample, and then we'll be done with this."

"Okay," Connie said, but she had turned and was looking out through the window at the long stretch of driveway leading up to her house.

28

THEY SEARCHED FOR HER MOTHER IN SILENCE, THE DAYS AND weeks blending together as the sun traveled in tightening arcs against the horizon. Erin sat beside him in the passenger seat of the pickup, staring forward through the windshield at the road ahead or down at the footwell, where the stock of the shotgun rested against her feet. She could feel the weight of the weapon pressing against her left shoulder, the hard metal separating her from her father. She sat on the bench seat and listened to the creak of the shock absorbers as the truck's frame rattled along dirt roads and uneven pavement, her father muttering to himself as he guided the vehicle through vacant backstreets and familiar neighborhoods.

At night he sat on the porch swing and stared out across the open land. Erin watched him from the kitchen window. Sometimes she would make him coffee because her mother was not around to do it, and she would take it to him in a mug that he'd hold in his lap until it was too cold to drink. There was no place for her on that porch. Her father's pain took up every square inch of it. She retreated to the interior of the house until it was time for her to go to bed. She walked the hall or sat at the table. Sometimes she would visit her parents' bedroom to lie on the floor with her face buried in one of her mother's dresses.

On some nights she heard the truck start up again, the diesel engine coming to life, the sound of the tires rolling across hard-packed dirt and pebbles on the driveway. Light from the headlights swept through the house as her father turned the truck around, and she listened as he drove away, the sound of the engine diminishing with distance.

They found the Dodge Dynasty on Indian Highway, about half a mile east of the airport. The left two tires were flat, and a large hole had been torn into both of them, as if a prehistoric creature had reached up from the earth and clawed at the rubber. The police investigator found some smaller holes in the roadway. It was his guess that whatever pierced her mother's tires had been drilled into the asphalt—the work of a different kind of monster.

Her father never blamed her for what happened. He never uttered the words that it was *her fault* that her mother was gone. Still, Erin knew that it was. She had asked to go to the movies, and her mother had driven them because she didn't want them traveling the streets on their own. They had done it anyway, though, running through the city in the gathering dark, and Erin thinking only about herself instead of the people who risked their lives to keep her safe.

During the months that followed, as the sky turned gray and the ground became dense and frozen beneath them, Erin discovered that there was more than one way to disappear in Wolf Point. Sometimes it was the ones who were left behind who disappeared the most. She erased herself that winter, and her father did the same, sitting on the front porch with his untouched coffee, driving through the streets in search of a person who no longer existed. They faded into themselves, and there was no one left to bring them back.

For four months they searched for her, covering every road and trudging through every patch of brush in search of her body. They spoke to anyone who might have seen her on the day she went missing. Finding her mother was the only thing that mattered, and the intensity of this futile quest kept most of their grief at bay, until one day her father announced that they had finished searching.

"I guess that's it then," he said after breakfast, and he stood up from his chair at the kitchen table, grabbed the shotgun leaning against the wall, and disappeared into a bedroom that he no longer shared with his wife.

Erin heard the click of the door as it latched. She looked across the table at his abandoned seat, and her eyes settled on a half-eaten piece of toast near the edge of his plate.

She sat that way for a long time, listening for the sound of him, until eventually she got up and cleared away the dishes. Erin washed them by hand, the way her mother had taught her, and dried them with a towel before returning them to the cabinet. When she was done, she walked around the table and scooted in her father's chair, being careful to lift it slightly so the legs wouldn't scratch along the floorboards.

It was quiet in the house, as quiet as she had ever heard it. Erin stood in the kitchen and waited, and when nothing else happened, she turned and went to her own bedroom, closed the door, and climbed back under the covers.

It was seven-thirty in the morning. She closed her eyes and fell asleep, and dreamed of a purple ribbon unfurling above her, the hint of a song that tapered into nothing until she awoke ten hours later and opened her eyes in the darkness.

We can let her go now, she thought. *We can figure out how to be a family with just the two of us.* Only, they never would. Not really. They would become careful with each other instead of honest. They would focus on daily chores instead of the notion that they were still standing over her grave and that part of them was buried there as well, a part they could never talk about.

When she left for college four years later, it was these things that filled her with the most regret. She had let go of him too easily, and he had done the same with her. And the thing that was missing was no longer her mother, but a fight for each other in the wake of her absence.

29

DAVID WAS SITTING UP IN BED READING THE PAPER WHEN SHE EN-
tered, and Erin's first impulse was to snatch it from his hands so
he wouldn't see the article with the headline QUESTIONS LINGER
FOLLOWING DISCOVERY OF SECOND BODY—an article that all but
accused him of being a mass murderer.

He looked up and smiled at her, though, as if all was right in
the world. "Erin," he said. He removed his reading glasses and
placed them on top of the newspaper. "I was wondering when
you might stop by. It's good to see you."

She stepped forward and wrapped her arms around him.
"Dad . . . I was so worried about you." She buried her face in
the side of his neck, taking in the scent of him. He'd been in
the hospital for almost a month, and still he smelled like hay
and fresh-cut grass, and under that, the scent of their kitchen
on summer mornings with the sun streaming through the window and eggs and bacon frying in the skillet.

"You brought something good to eat, I hope."

"I can get you something," she told him. "What do you want?"

"Let's start with getting me out of here. You've got the get-
away truck parked out front?"

"No passengers today," she said. "I spoke with Dr. Houseman

on my way in here. He wants to keep you in the hospital for one more day."

"Mark Houseman lost two hundred bucks to me in a poker game six years ago. He sees this as a perfect opportunity to get it back."

"He saved your life, you know. Up until a short time ago, you were on a ventilator."

"That's what they tell me. My nurse, Shelly, described it as"—he leaned over and glanced at a pad of paper on the bedstand—"'circling the drain.' 'Mr. Reece,' she said, 'when they dragged you in here, you were circling the drain.'"

Erin shook her head. "You looked horrible. You should've gone to see Dr. Houseman sooner."

"Nah, it'll take more than that to do me in." He coughed. "I've still got this lingering tickle in the back of my throat, though. Too much recycled hospital air, I think. It'll feel good to get back out into the sunshine."

Erin took a ratcheting breath and nodded, her smile fading. "You saw the newspaper article, I guess."

"Yeah," he said. "It's amazing how they can get so much wrong in so few words. They spelled my name right, though. That's gotta count for something."

"This is serious. They could put you away for the rest of your life. Or worse," she said. "As far as I know, Montana still has the death penalty."

"The death penalty," he said. "*Now* you're talkin'."

"Please don't make light of it."

"I'm not making light of it," he told her. "It *is* ironic, though. They snatched me back from the brink of death just so they can kill me good and proper."

She looked at him, and he looked back, his smile never faltering.

"What will you tell them?" she asked.

"The truth," he said. "I murdered half the town and buried the bodies in my backyard."

"Stop it."

"What? That's what they want to hear, don't they?"

She took in a deep breath and let it out. "You think they won't execute you or give you back-to-back life sentences?"

He shrugged. "Better me than somebody else. Besides," he said, "the doc says I've got lung cancer. How much longer have I got to live anyway?"

Erin took a step back. "He told you?"

"Of course he told me. Like I said, he's got a lousy poker face."

She pulled the chair to the bedside and collapsed into it. "Damn it," she said. "I wish he hadn't . . . I wanted to be here when he told you."

David reached out and took her hand. Even now, all these years later, her own hand looked like a child's when it was enfolded in his.

"Don't blame the doctor, honey," he said. "I've been coughing up blood for a couple of months now. I figured it had to be something."

She looked up at him, her eyes wide and disbelieving. "A couple of *months,* Dad? Why didn't you go to see him sooner?"

David turned the newspaper over in his lap. "Why would I do that?" he asked. "I've been coughing up *blood,* Erin. You have a medical degree. What does that mean to you?"

"It could mean a lot of things. Not all of them are bad."

He shrugged. "This one is. Lung cancer," he said, shaking his head. "I've never smoked a day in my life. How's that for a kick in the teeth?"

"There's an oncologist down in Billings. Dr. Houseman said he's—"

"Hold on a second," he said, and he let go of her hand. "Oncologist? Who said anything about treatment?"

"Dad—"

"They'll be coming for me, Erin, now that the bodies have been discovered. I asked about the cancer because I wanted to understand my time frame. I wanted to know if it was worth the fight."

She groaned. "Stop talking as if it's already over."

"It is over," he said. "It's better this way. I killed those people. I deserve whatever punishment the justice system has in store for me. I'm glad it's finally out in the open."

"Dad. I can't let you just—"

"*Be quiet, child!*" he exploded, and his glasses fell from the bed and clattered onto the tile floor. "I've made my peace with it, and you should, too. They're going to bury me, Erin, one way or the other."

30

ONCE IT WAS OVER, NOBODY TALKED ABOUT THE MISSING. IT WAS an unspoken pact carved into the town of Wolf Point, as if the thing that had taken so many of its residents could be awakened again by the mention of its name. It was strange how quickly Erin had gotten used to that as an adolescent, and how easily she had fallen into the habit of avoiding the subject with her father. She had returned fifteen years later to find that the spell hadn't broken, that the people of this town had gone right on living that way, half awake and half asleep, their eyes cast downward instead of focusing on one another. It was a *quiet* town, she thought, not in the usual ways of small-town America but because of the implicit admonition that nothing dormant and evil should ever be disturbed.

Now that two of the bodies had been discovered on her father's farm, however, the rest of the missing came bubbling to the surface of the town's collective consciousness. CANDLELIGHT VIGIL, the flyer announced in large red letters across the top of the page. Under that it gave the date and time—tomorrow at 7:30 P.M.—and the simple words "In Memory of Those Who Were Lost." There was no further explanation, and none was

needed. This was Wolf Point's wake-up call, a chance to acknowledge the dead as they were pulled from the earth.

Erin encountered the flyers everywhere that day. One had
been pinned to her windshield beneath the blade of one of her
wipers. The words were facing inward toward the cab of the
truck. Someone had been thoughtful enough to add a handwritten note—"This is your invitation, bitch, so come to the
party!"—that she read a few times before folding the paper and
placing it into her back pocket.

She started the truck and pulled out of the parking lot with
no particular place to go. She'd visited Matta and Diesel earlier
that morning. The two of them were getting along well, and
the interior of the house felt brighter and more full of life with
each passing day. She'd gone to Robbie's after that, but there
was no answer when she knocked, and short of breaking and
entering, she felt her chances of seeing him seemed to have
dwindled to almost nothing.

She headed west now, beyond the outskirts of town, not
knowing where she was going until she had pulled up to the
curb in front of it, a small and sad little house sitting by itself
at the end of the road. The weeds grew tall around it, as if the
house itself was sinking into the earth. Erin was surprised that
it was still standing. She'd imagined it bulldozed and replaced
by something else. But here it was, lost to a state of neglect but
still calling out to her, reminding her of the first time she had
come here.

"It's over," she said, but it didn't *feel* like it was over. It felt
like the house had been waiting all these years for her to return
to it.

Erin reached into her back pocket, pulled out the flyer, and
unfolded it in front of her. "'Candlelight vigil,'" she read,

speaking the words aloud in the silence of the cab. "'In mem-ory of those who were lost.'"

She looked up at the house. The thirteen-year-old version of herself was in there somewhere, peering through a dirt-caked window at the yard beyond. "It doesn't own you," she said, but she'd returned to it anyway, and Erin wondered if she'd ever have the guts to go back inside.

31

(April 1999)

THE WEATHER TURNED EARLY THAT YEAR, BRINGING NOT JUST LON-ger days and warmer temperatures but the hope that most of the bad things were already behind them. It had been six months since the last disappearance—since *her mother's* disappearance—and there was mounting consensus among the people of Wolf Point that there might not be another. The perpetrator could have died or moved out of the area, they reasoned. He'd gotten spooked about getting caught or had simply lost his stomach for the work. Then again, maybe the disappearances had stopped for the same reason they'd begun: for no reason at all. Could it be that random? they wondered. Could the world fall apart and come together again without logic or explanation?

Her father had ended his search two months before, and Erin responded to this betrayal in the only way she knew how. She kept right on looking.

Robbie helped her through most of it. From the perspective of an outside observer, they were two kids in their early teens who spent most of their time hanging out together. But they never stopped searching for clues to the whereabouts of Erin's mother, and everything they did was in service of that singular, relentless pursuit.

They took the mitten they'd found on Jacob's Field to the police department, and when the officer there wasn't interested, they took it to Angela Finley's mother. She recognized it immediately, took it into her hands, and sobbed uncontrollably for fifteen minutes. Then she got in her car and drove the three of them back to the police department. Erin and Robbie sat outside of the chief's office on a wooden bench while Mrs. Finley spoke with the commander. "He's going to reopen an investigation into Nathaniel Jacob," she told them on the ride back, "and if I don't hear from Chief Ward personally within a week, I will go to that farmhouse myself."

Nothing came of it—at least as far as Erin and Robbie were aware—but the fact that they'd been able to *do something* to help the investigation bolstered their confidence and sense of purpose.

They searched the online newspaper archives for any mention of Helen Reece or her maiden name, Helen Fisher. They went to the library and photocopied a map of the city and the surrounding area. The librarian, Betty Doyle, helped them create a poster-size image that they pinned to the wall of Robbie's bedroom. They used colored thumbtacks to mark the approximate location where each of the victims had gone missing: blue for men, red for women, and green for kids. Erin's mother was given a special color—purple—and they listed the names of the missing people in a notebook in chronological order of the date of their disappearances. The rest of the notebook was used to document things they'd observed or uncovered in their investigation—"Mr. Felton works late at night; Janice Trujillo moved to Wolf Point three years ago"—and places they had already searched. On the cover of the notebook, Robbie had written "We Will Find Her" in black permanent marker.

Their weekend activities and after-school hours were filled with the task of finding Erin's mother, but sometimes the two of them just sat and thought. On this Thursday in late April, they biked to one of their favorite spots, the Lewis and Clark Bridge across the Missouri River, and were sitting on a metal girder with their feet dangling twenty-five feet above the water. The sun was setting to the west, the golden shimmer of it reflecting off the moving surface of the river. There were hawks circling in the sky overhead, and they watched as one of them plunged toward the riverbank and snatched up a fast-moving rodent before once again taking to the sky.

"He's hiding," Erin said. "That's what I think."

Robbie leaned over and spit. The small white glob fell like a pebble until it reached the water.

"He's afraid. He knows we're on his trail," Erin continued. "That's why he hasn't taken anyone in a while."

Robbie nodded. "That chickenshit oughtta come out and fight."

The girder they were sitting on was below the level of the deck. A truck passed above them. They could feel the vibration in the metal.

"He's a hawk, not a chicken," she said. "He drops from the sky and carries people away."

"So how do we catch him?" Robbie asked. "He only comes out when he's hunting."

Erin was quiet, thinking. A car passed above them. They heard the *thunk-thunk* of the tires on the expansion joint.

"We have to wait for him in the field," she said. "It's the only way to catch him."

"What field? What are you talking about?"

She leaned over and rested her head against his shoulder. He was fifteen now, and had grown six inches since the day she'd encountered him running from Vinny Briggs and his sordid gang of delinquents down at the quarry.

"I let him take me," she said, and Erin turned her eyes toward the bank of the river, where creatures darted back and forth between the sunlight and the shadows.

32

IT WAS NOT JUST A VIGIL BUT A PROCESSION. THEY ASSEMBLED
around seven P.M. at the Silver Wolf Casino, where parking
was plentiful, and each of them was given a white candle with
a small cardboard skirt to catch the wax as it melted. They
were dressed in suits and coats, in jeans and sweaters and hats
and earmuffs. They wore mittens and leather gloves, and some
of them wore no gloves at all. The roads along the way had
been sprinkled with salt and sand to reduce the risk of falls on
the black ice, and the path was marked by traffic cones, volun-
teers, and a few police vehicles. None of these details had been
spelled out in the flyer. The event had been organized in less
than thirty-six hours, the specifics coming together organi-
cally, without permits or committees. It was a testament to the
way small towns could work, the way they used to work before
bylaws and regulators.

Erin arrived with the rest of them, bundled in a scarf, jacket,
and gloves. She received her unlit candle from Betty Doyle and
took her place in the crowd among faces that were both familiar and unfamiliar, people she remembered from her childhood
and those she couldn't place. To her left was Kate Anderson,
the volunteer who had greeted her at the information desk

when Erin arrived at Trinity Hospital on her first day back in Wolf Point. She spotted Mark Houseman with a woman Erin presumed to be his wife. Donna Raffey was here, and so was Erin's old high school principal Jim Hastings, whose brother Curt had gone missing along with Rose Perry a month after the disappearance of Angela Finley. She saw Mike Flannigan, Deirdre McKinney, and the former mayor, Zachary Brody. To her right was a redheaded girl with pigtails and braces. She was about eight or nine years old, Erin figured, and she reminded her of Meghan Decker, although Meghan would be an adult by now, the braces long gone, the hair styled into something more appropriate for a woman in her early thirties.

"Good evening, friends," a voice said, and Erin turned to see a woman standing on a platform and holding a microphone. It was a face she didn't recognize, but they all turned to listen.

"We have gathered here this evening to honor the lives of those who are no longer with us," she said. "Like many towns, Wolf Point has suffered its share of tragedies. Two decades ago, sixteen people were lost over the course of three years. They were mothers and sons, husbands and daughters. They were the lifeblood of our community, and they were taken from us in a cowardly series of transgressions with no respect for human life or decency." She paused for a moment to look around at the sea of upturned faces. "We come together this evening to remember, and to reclaim what is rightfully ours. We are no longer a town broken by the things that have happened to us. We are a community that believes in justice and in the enduring strength of the human spirit. We look only to one another and to ourselves, and we march in unity on this night, in the name of those who have passed before us." She was holding a sheet of paper, and she looked down at it before proceeding. "Angela Finley," she said, and the crowd repeated the name, like a congregation responding to its pastor.

". . . Rose Perry . . ." she said, and the crowd responded in kind.

". . . Curt Hastings . . ."

"Curt Hastings," Erin said, and the name was like a sacramental offering on her tongue.

The list continued. She remembered all of them, the faces rising and falling in her mind.

". . . Marian Montgomery . . ."

". . . Valerie McBride . . ."

Erin recited the names, one after the other, and although she knew it was coming, her mother's name was still a shock when she heard it, spoken out loud and repeated by the crowd.

"Helen Reece," the woman said, and they echoed her name, same as the others.

There was one more name on the list, and after it was spoken and repeated, the night grew silent around them. Erin stood there, trembling, as if she had just received the news for the first time. She wanted to argue against it, to tell them that her mother *couldn't* be dead because Erin had just seen her folding clothes in the bedroom, humming softly to herself as she stacked them in neat little piles on the dresser. It was all a terrible mistake, but then they were moving, shuffling their feet in unison, like soldiers heading off to war.

She fell in step with the rest of them, and there was someone at the front of the pack helping to light the candles. A single flame became many, and people turned to one another and held out their candles for others to light the wicks. A man in front of her turned to the girl to Erin's right. She tipped her candle forward to catch the flame, then held it up for Erin to do the same. "Thank you," Erin said, lighting her candle and then holding it still for the person to her left.

They were all lit in less than a minute, and the congregation continued forward, moving with purpose into the street. They headed south toward the river, the stars hovering high above them. She could see the faces of people better now, but despite the light of so many tiny flames, the night seemed darker around them, as if nothing existed beyond the periphery of their huddled trudging mass.

They continued for four blocks, turning right and then left again. Erin followed along blindly, content to be in the thick of things instead of cast off as an outsider—or worse yet, to be looked upon like a malignancy that needed to be cut from their collective body.

Ten minutes into the journey, someone started singing, and like the flame it traveled rapidly through their midst. She swayed with the beat of it—they all did—and for the space of that time they were united, from the oldest to the youngest of them, from the ones who had suffered the ravages of those days to those who were too young to remember.

"*Swing low, sweet chariot,*" she sang, and the sound of the others carried her along like the current of the black and twisting water of the Missouri River itself.

There was a man to her right, at the periphery of the crowd. He was taller than the rest, with a deep baritone voice that seemed to hover above them as they walked. It was his voice that had started this, and he led them into the next verse as they marched on into the darkness.

"*I looked over Jordan, and what did I see?*" he sang.

"Coming for to carry me home," they responded.

"*A band of angels coming after me.*"

"Coming for to carry me home."

"*Swing low,*" they sang, going into the refrain, and they were heading north now, over the railroad tracks. Erin realized it then, their likely destination. They would end the procession at Wolf Point Cemetery at the northwest border of the city. There would be a memorial service there perhaps, in honor of the missing ones still waiting to be discovered.

"Bitch," she heard, a whisper to her right.

Erin turned her head, scanning the crowd, but the position of the people had shifted. The redheaded girl was gone now, replaced by an old woman whose gray hair peeked out from under a dark purple hat. She looked up at Erin and smiled. A single tooth protruded from her upper gumline.

". . . come here to bury the rest of us?"

She swiveled her head to the left, turned farther and glanced over her shoulder. It was hard to tell where the voices were coming from, whether it was just one person or several.

The song had come to a close, and they walked along, the sound of their feet loud against the pavement. The man with the baritone voice started in on another hymn, "How Great Thou Art," and a hush fell over the crowd as they listened.

> *O Lord my God, when I in awesome wonder*
> *Consider all the worlds Thy hands have made*
> *I see the stars, I hear the rolling thunder . . .*

They listened to the last line, then joined him in the refrain, a rising wave against the shore. Erin searched their faces, but in the flickering light none of them looked familiar. The wind picked up, and the flames rose instead of sputtered. They cupped their hands around their candles and marched together down the street.

> *Then sings my soul, my Savior God, to Thee*
> *How great Thou art, how great Thou art*

The flames grew higher to her right, a dancing monument against the sky.

". . . on fire . . ."

". . . her scarf. Someone better . . ."

". . . oh my God . . ."

The space around her head erupted in flames. Erin dropped her candle and beat at it with her hands.

"*Your scarf!*" someone yelled. "*Your scarf is on fire!*"

The crowd broke apart, separating around her. Erin stood by herself in the middle of them, the flame rising into the darkness.

I'm burning. I'm burning alive!

She tried to run from it, but the fire was everywhere, enveloping her head. The skin of her face rippled with the heat of it. Her nostrils filled with the stench of melting flesh.

"*Let her burn!*" someone yelled, but there were other voices, calling for someone to do something.

"*Get it out! Get the scarf off her!*"

Erin screamed. She pulled at the scarf and tried to unwind it from around her neck, but she'd created a loop with it and couldn't get it off. She yanked at the burning fabric with her gloves, but it pulled tighter instead of looser.

I'm going to burn to death. My head is on fire!

She spun around, scanning the faces through the flames. "*Help me!*" she shrieked, but they drew back from her, horrified by the sight in front of them.

". . . she's going to . . ."

". . . somebody get a . . ."

A sudden impact struck her from behind. Her teeth clicked together, and she was lifted off her feet for a second before she fell to the ground, a pair of arms wrapped around her. Erin landed on her knees as the two of them went down together, falling forward and onto her right shoulder.

I'm being attacked, she thought, but he was beating at her head, smothering her with his jacket. Everything went dark. The pocket of air around her reeked with the smell of her own burning body. She couldn't breathe, couldn't escape the char and smoke. Her eyes were on fire, but she couldn't get to them, couldn't reach them with her hands. Vomit rose in her throat. She gagged it back, tried to fight her way out from under the press of his body.

He pulled the jacket off her, and for a minute all she could do was suck in the coolness of the night air. She made a whooping noise with each frantic breath. Erin yanked off her gloves, loosened what was left of the scarf, and pulled it over her head. It was a scorched and ruined thing. She cast it aside before touching her face and the sides of her neck where the skin was raw and wet along the right side of the chin line. Her right ear continued to burn, as if part of it was still on fire, and Erin pressed her hand against it to smother any remaining embers.

There was a man kneeling beside her, breathing heavily. "Somebody call an ambulance," he barked, and there was a collective murmur as several of them reached into their pockets to retrieve their cell phones.

The man reached forward and helped Erin into a sitting position. Half of his face was lost in shadow, but she recognized him immediately as Robbie's father. She leaned into him, wrapping her arms around his shoulders.

"Thank you," she said, and she was sobbing now, unable to control the relief and horror as it bubbled up inside of her.

"Shh," Matta told her. "Everything's fine now. You'll be okay." He rocked her back and forth, as if she was a frightened child in the aftermath of a nightmare.

Erin sat there on the pavement and cried. When she closed her eyes, she could still see a flicker of flame against the inside of her lids, and she pulled away from it, her fingers reaching for a scarf that was no longer there. She could see their faces, too, watching her as she burned.

She shook her head as she cried, and the crowd was silent, studying her, until eventually Erin could hear a siren in the distance, the pitch of it swinging high and then low again, growing louder as it approached.

33

(June–July 1999)

THE DAYS CONTINUED TO GET WARMER, AND ERIN RODE HER BIKE along the vacant stretch of Indian Highway. She could see the railroad tracks to her right, and the L. M. Clayton Airport to her left as she drew closer to the city. When she got to Route 25, she turned around and pedaled back in the opposite direction. It was the same stretch of road where they'd found her mother's empty car, parked catty-corner across the eastbound and westbound lanes, its left two tires ripped apart and resting on the hubs.

Erin now came here every day, making the trip back and forth until her legs were too tired to pedal. On the first day she'd ridden her bike for forty minutes, but her muscles had gotten stronger since then and she'd built up her rides to two hours or longer. The sun beat down on her body, bleaching her hair and turning the skin on her arms and legs a deep bronze that was a bit darker than the shade of the earth on either side of the roadway.

She would sometimes talk to her mother as she rode. She couldn't see her, and her mother never responded to the things

Erin said or the questions she asked. It was more like writing a letter than having a conversation, but Erin told her about the things she was doing and reminded her that she was not forgotten. "If you can hear me, I want you to know that I'm coming," she said. "I'm going to find you and bring you home. You won't be alone forever."

If she had been an adult, people might have assumed that she was training for something, or perhaps that she had gone a little soft in the head. She was going nowhere, but it didn't matter to Erin. When she got thirsty, she drank from a plastic water bottle resting in a metal cradle attached to the frame of her bike. When she got tired or dizzy beneath the persistent rays of the sun, she stopped. And because she was going nowhere, it didn't matter how long it took her to get there. She rode with the expectation that she would get there eventually, whether it took weeks or months or even years for it to happen.

Sometimes people passed her in their cars and trucks along the roadway. Occasionally they would slow down and ask if she was okay. She'd nod and continue riding, and because word traveled fast in Wolf Point, it didn't take long for folks to start talking about the Reece girl, riding back and forth on her bike along the road where her mother went missing.

She continued on her quest for six and a half weeks before he finally came for her, just as she knew he would. He pulled up ahead of her and came to a diagonal stop across the road.

He was driving a white van, the color of heroes and good guys.

"Hey, girl," he said, leaning through the open window. "Whatcha doin' out here, riding around all day?"

"Nothing," she said, and coasted to a stop about five feet in front of him.

He shielded his eyes against the sun. "People think you're crazy. You know that, don'tcha?"

She shrugged.

He climbed out of the van, shut the door, and leaned up against it nice and easy. "It's all right," he said. "Sometimes they think the same thing about me. I guess that means we've got something in common."

She looked at him and turned the corner of her mouth up in a half-smile.

He shook his head. "You *are* a little crazy, ain'tcha? No matter. It's hot out here. I'm gonna head home where it's nice and cool and get me something to drink. You wanna join me?"

She took a deep breath and nodded.

He looked surprised. "Yeah? You wanna go?"

She nodded again.

"Well, okay then," he said, smiling. "Something cool sure would hit the spot right about now, wouldn't it?"

"Yeah," she said. "I think it would."

The smile faded. "You're all by yourself out here?" He stepped away from the van and took a look around.

Erin looked around as well. Her palms were sweaty. She wiped the right one on the side of her shorts.

"And you're agreeing to go with me. Is that right?"

"Right," she said, "for a cool place to get out of the sun and something to drink."

He ran a hand through his short black hair and looked around again. "I don't know," he said. "I don't wanna get in any trouble. People might not understand, a kid going back to the house of a grown-up she don't know."

"I know you," she said. "I've seen you around town before."

"Yeah, okay. You know me. But still, people could get the

wrong idea. Next thing you know, *I'm* the one who gets in trouble."

She stood there, astride of her bike, unsure of what to say. She hadn't expected him to react this way.

"I'm a nice guy, you know. I never did nobody no harm."

She nodded.

"But people, they don't understand when it comes to things like this. They wanna make me the bad guy."

"So, we're not gonna go?"

"No," he said. "No, ma'am. It . . . wouldn't be proper."

"Then why did you stop?"

"Why did I . . . ?" He turned and paced a bit. "Well, to make sure you were okay, that's all. There's a lot of bad things that've happened. Not everyone can be trusted. You ought not to be riding out here by yourself."

"I'm looking for my mother."

He stopped and turned to her, his mouth halfway open.

"She disappeared on this road somewhere," Erin told him. "I was hoping I could find her."

He stared at her, as if she'd suddenly transformed into something he'd never seen before.

"She was driving her car on the way home. Something reached up from the earth and snatched her."

"Snatched her," he said. "What do you mean by that?"

"Gone," she said, "just like the others."

He looked down at the ground and shook his head.

"She was very special to me," Erin told him. "I'm afraid I'll never see her again."

The man went back to pacing. "Well," he said, "I don't know nothing about that."

"I've been out here looking for her. I was hoping . . . maybe you could help me find her."

He snorted. "Me? How would *I know* where she is?"

"Please," she said. "I have to find her."

He stopped at the driver's-side door to the van and looked at her once again. "I'm sorry," he told her. "I don't know nothing about your mother." He opened the door and climbed back up into the vehicle. "I've gotta be getting home," he said. "You shouldn't be out here. It's not safe for a girl to be riding her bike all alone like this." He slammed the door and started the engine. "Don't be so eager to stop and talk to strangers."

"You stopped and talked to me," she said, but he wasn't listening. Instead he put the van in gear and made a wide arc around her, his right tires bumping along the uneven shoulder. He glanced at her once more through the open window, turned his attention to the road in front of him, and drove off without another word.

Erin stepped away from her bike and let it clatter to the asphalt. She stood there for a long time, watching, as he disappeared into the distance.

34

MATTA TABAHA PULLED HIS TRUCK TO A STOP NEAR THE WOODEN bridge across the aqueduct in front of the silver Airstream. The Jeep Wrangler was still here, unmoved from its resting place. Erin reached up with her right hand and touched the side of her neck and face with her fingertips. They'd applied a white cream at the hospital—Silvadene, Dr. Houseman had called it. It felt cool against her body, but underneath the skin was raw and blistered. The burns had been limited to a small area, thank goodness, and Dr. Houseman seemed to think they would heal without much scarring. If it had gone on much longer, though, if Matta hadn't tackled her to the ground and smothered the flames when he did, it could've involved her eyes and airway, the entirety of her face and head. She could've died while the rest of them watched, pretending it had been a tragic accident.

"Will you be arresting them for attempted murder?" she'd asked Jeff Stutzman when he arrived in the emergency department. Her tears had dried against the soot on her cheeks. She still smelled of burned hair and flesh.

"Who did this?" he asked. "Do you remember who was standing next to you or right behind you?"

She shook her head. "They were all shifting positions. Somebody must've seen it happen, though. Hasn't anyone identified the person who did this?"

"Not yet," he said. "We're still interviewing people. The wind kicked up shortly before the incident. If your scarf was dangling behind you, maybe it was just enough to—"

"Why did it happen to *me*?" she asked. "Why me and not someone else? This wasn't an accident, Jeff. Somebody *meant* for it to happen. Somebody made a conscious decision to hurt me."

"Who do you think it was?" he asked.

"I don't know," she said. "I feel like all of them wanted it. Matta was the only one who helped me."

And now he's brought me here, Erin thought, looking through the windshield at the familiar shape of the Airstream. Matta got out of the truck and slammed the driver's-side door. He walked across the wooden bridge toward the front of the RV, climbed the steps, and pounded on the door. She didn't understand it, why he'd insisted on coming *here* after her visit to the emergency department. Robbie didn't want to see either of them. What was the point of forcing the issue?

The cold air pressed itself against her as she slid down from the cab. Her entire body ached, not just the parts of her that had been burned. And something ached inside of her, too. Despite the warnings, she hadn't wanted to believe that she was in any *real* danger from the people she'd known since childhood.

Matta hammered on the door with his fist. "*Get up!*" he yelled. "*Open this goddamn door before I rip it off its hinges.*"

It was dark inside the trailer, and the thought occurred to Erin that maybe he wasn't home, that maybe Robbie was on a trip and hadn't been here *at all* over the past few weeks. *Wouldn't that be ironic,* she thought. *I've been standing out here calling to him for a month, hurt by the fact that he didn't want to see me.*

But the whole time the trailer's been empty. I've been calling to no one. I've been out here apologizing to myself.

Matta yanked on the handle. The door seemed to give a little, and he did it again. Erin recalled the way he had moved when she last saw him, an old man favoring his arthritis. There was no trace of that now, his body responding to the adrenaline. In the morning, maybe it would all catch up with him. But tonight he was young again, and he wasn't taking no for an answer.

Matta returned to the truck, fished around behind the seat, and pulled out a thin metal rod from the collection of tools used for changing a tire. He marched back to the Airstream with it, cursing beneath his breath, and wedged the tapered end between the door and the jamb.

"I think he wants to be left alone," she suggested, but Matta didn't even look back at her.

"I've left him alone long enough," he growled. "Now I'm here to kick his ass."

He pried at the door with the bar, adjusted his grip, and drove the bar deeper into the groove. He put his weight into it, giving it some extra torque, and the door popped open with a bang.

Erin took a step backward, uncertain whether she really wanted to go in there. Robbie had changed over the years. Isn't that what Matta had told her?

The man disappeared into the Airstream, and a moment later the lights came on. He passed in front of one of the windows, head down, surveying the interior.

Erin stood where she was. She heard the rattle of empty aluminum cans being kicked around the floor.

Matta appeared in the open doorway. "It's a mess," he told her. "Give me a minute to put some things away."

"Okay." Erin lowered herself to the ground, wrapped her arms around her shin, and pulled her right knee tight against her chest. She'd knelt that way at the base of the tree behind Robbie's house when she was younger. *The letter* e *was the hardest,* she thought, *like water circling a drain.*

Matta disappeared inside the RV once again. "Get up," he said. "The least you can do is to help me."

There was more conversation that she couldn't make out. In her mind, Erin could see Robbie in there, with his dark hair and wry, sarcastic smile. He was still eleven years old, the version she so often pictured when she thought of him. They had just finished riding down the aqueduct. He had brought her here to visit his grandpa.

"What are you *doing* here?" she heard a man say. "You broke my goddamn door."

There was a crash from inside, the sound of someone stumbling over something on the floor.

"Shut up," Matta said. "I brought someone with me."

"Who?"

"Erin. Erin Reece. She's been knocking on your door for weeks."

"You brought *Erin Reece* out here to see me? *Jesus, Dad. What were you . . . ?*"

He glanced out through the window. She saw him for a moment, a face held briefly to the glass. It was hard to make out his features—just that he was older now, a man instead of a boy. He pulled away from the glass, and there was more whispered conversation that she couldn't make out.

Erin stood up, tired of waiting. She walked to the trailer and ascended the steps.

The first thing she noticed was the mess. Matta had been right. He held a plastic garbage bag in his hand, already full of trash. She could see the bulge of a few pizza boxes and heard the rattle of aluminum cans as Matta bent to scoop something else off the floor. The interior walls of the Airstream were dark walnut. The space felt small and cramped with the two men standing inside. There was a modest sink set into a white countertop, but it was full of cups and food-caked dishes, and most of the countertop was covered with dirty clothes and newspapers. There was a separate space for the bedroom, and the door to it was half open. In front of it stood her friend, or what was left of him. He was wearing shorts that were hiked up on one side and a red shirt that was inside out and too small for him. It rose up a bit as he turned to look at her, revealing a half inch of flesh that pouched out above his waistband. His face was covered with stubble, and his black hair was sticking up in the places where it had been pressed against the pillow. Robbie looked both surprised and embarrassed to see her. There was a zip-up hoodie on the seat next to him. He grabbed it and held it in front of him.

"Erin," he said. "I . . . wasn't expecting you."

She glanced briefly at Matta, the person to blame for this awkward intrusion. He stood there with the bag in his hand, looking down at the floor.

"Hello, Robbie," she said. Her throat felt dry and tight. She tried to swallow, but there was nothing there, just the taste of all those years that had crept up between them.

"I know the place doesn't look like much," he said. "I was getting ready to clean it up before you got—"

She walked forward and wrapped her arms around him. He smelled like beer and unwashed hair, and he stood there while she hugged him, unsure of what to do.

"I've missed you," she said, letting go of him and taking a step back.

He stood there with the hoodie in his hand, his eyes searching her face to see if she was joking. "You look the same," he
said, although Erin knew that couldn't be true. "Your hair's a
bit shorter, but . . . you're just like I remember."

There was something on the front of his shirt that she hadn't
noticed before, and it took her a moment to realize what it was.
She reached forward and wiped it off as best she could, a bit of
Silvadene cream that had come off when she hugged him.

He lifted his hand and pointed to the side of her neck.
"You've got something . . ."

"Erin was burned this evening," Matta said. "She went to
the candlelight vigil and someone set her scarf on fire."

"Jesus," he said. "Are you okay?"

She nodded. "It hurts a little, but Dr. Houseman says it
should heal okay."

"I don't understand. Was it an accident?"

She shook her head. "I don't think so."

They stood facing each other, and silence descended between them.

"I'm sorry I didn't answer the door," he said. "I haven't been
feeling well."

"It's all right," she said. "I'm glad to see you now."

"Can I get you something to"—he glanced at his father—
"some water or something? I don't have a whole lot to drink.
Just beer and some other stuff."

"No, thanks," she said. "I'm fine."

"I could make you some tea," he said, and his face brightened with the idea. "I've got some around here somewhere."
He placed the hoodie on the counter beside him, opened a
cabinet, and began searching.

"I'm fine, really," she said. "I appreciate the offer, but . . ."

"No, no," he said. "It's no trouble." He stood on his tiptoes, found what he was looking for, and pulled out a box of tea bags from the back of the cabinet. "Cinnamon and spice," he said. "It's good. I'll make us some."

Erin felt a light touch on her upper arm. It was Matta, standing behind her.

"Do you mind helping me with something?" he asked, motioning toward the door. "It'll only take a second."

They descended the steps, and he closed the door behind them. He'd broken the latch, and it drifted open an inch before coming to rest.

"I should leave," he said. "The two of you have some catching up to do."

"Okay."

"I won't go if you don't want me to. I'd be leaving you here without your truck."

She considered the situation. "Does the Jeep run?"

"Yes," he said. "As far as I know it does. He could drive you back into town this evening. Or you could call me and I'll come pick you up."

"Either one is fine with me," she said. "I'll keep him company for a while."

"Okay. I'm sorry about the way things look."

"It's fine. I'll help him clean it up before I go."

Matta nodded and glanced back at the trailer. "He drinks too much," he said, "same as me when I was younger. It's gotten out of control. I'm sorry, but that's the truth of it."

"I understand."

"He's a good kid." He nodded. "I guess you already know that."

She gave him a hug. "Thank you, Matta."

"Yeah," he said. "Okay." He walked across the bridge to the truck and climbed inside. She watched as he drove away, his taillights disappearing into the night.

Inside, Robbie had placed the teakettle on the range for the water to boil. He'd cleaned up a few more things and cleared off a space for them to sit at the table. Erin washed the dishes in the sink and found a towel to dry them before putting them away in the cabinet. The place wasn't spotless by any means, but neither was her house in Colorado. It was habitable, and by the time they were finished, there were two steaming cups of tea on the table in front of them.

"So," he said, sitting down at the table, "what've you been up to these past fifteen years?" He smiled and took a sip of his tea.

He slid over and she sat down beside him. "I went to school, became a veterinarian, and moved to Colorado. That's it," she said. "That's fifteen years in a nutshell."

"A veterinarian. Wow," he said. "So you're Dr. Reece now. That's great. Your father must be proud."

She shrugged. "They're letting him out of the hospital tomorrow."

"He's getting better, then. That's good. I read about the farm in the paper."

She looked at him. "He's in a lot of trouble. They're treating the place as a crime scene. He can't go back there, not for a while anyway. Dr. Houseman invited us to stay at a place owned by his in-laws. It's quiet, he says, out in the middle of nowhere. We'd have the place to ourselves."

"That's real nice of him. He's a good guy, Dr. Houseman."

She nodded and took a sip of tea.

He lifted his cup. "Cheers," he said, and clinked their cups together. "To Erin Reece, doctor of the animals."

"To Robbie Tabaha," she said. "My best friend in all the world."

Her voice quivered at the end of it, and she looked away, embarrassed by the rawness of her emotion.

He set his cup down, and when she turned to look at him, she could see that his hand was trembling and he'd spilled some of his tea on the table.

"You okay?" she asked.

"Yeah," he said. "Just a heck of a lot clumsier than I used to be."

She was quiet for a moment, wanting to tell him but hating the words as they formed on her lips. "My father's been diagnosed with lung cancer," she said. "It's aggressive. Dr. Houseman wants him to see an oncologist for treatment, but . . . he doesn't want to go along with it."

Robbie looked over at her. He reached out and put his hand on her forearm. "Erin, I'm sorry," he said. "He's got to get treatment, doesn't he? I mean . . . you can convince him, right?"

"I don't know," she said. "He's stubborn. He makes his own decisions."

"Yeah, but . . ." Robbie leaned back and shook his head. "He can't just give up on a thing like that."

She leaned into him. She could feel the tremors, the fine hum of an electric current coursing through his body.

"You're shaking. What's the matter?"

"Nothing," he said. "I get nervous. I guess I'm a little nervous around you."

"You don't need to be nervous."

"I know."

Erin sat there and sipped her tea. She could hear a coyote in the distance.

"Do people call you Rob now, or is it still Robbie?"

"It doesn't matter," he said. "You should call me Robbie. It would be weird if you started calling me Rob."

She looked at him. "I'm sorry I left you. I'm sorry it's taken me fifteen years to come back."

"It's okay," he said. "You can see I've been keeping myself busy."

She nodded.

"I inherited this place from my grandpa. He passed away a few years ago."

"I'm sorry to hear that."

"Thanks," he said. "It happens. My mom died, too. It's just my dad living by himself now."

"And you're living here."

"Yeah. It's pretty nice. No one bothers me."

"Except me."

"Yeah." He smirked. "You're a real pain in the ass."

"So I've been told."

"I mean, people are lighting your head on fire. That's a sign they might not like you."

"It was just the right side," she said. "If it had been the whole thing, I'd be worried."

"That's true. Just the right side. That's not so bad." He gave her a sarcastic smile, the one she remembered so clearly from their childhood.

"Your dad would like you to visit him every once in a while."

"Is that what he told you?"

"Yeah."

"He broke my goddamn door."

"How else were we supposed to get in here to see you? I wanted this tea and I wanted it bad."

He laughed, and she could see the traces of him that she remembered: the dimpling in his chin through the stubble, the way his eyes looked up and to the left when she said something funny. She laughed with him, and it was like they were kids again, making fun of themselves for their own amusement.

The inside of the trailer grew quiet as their laughter tapered. He started to lift his mug and then stopped, placing it back on the table.

"I'm sorry I didn't open the door for you," he said, "and I'm sorry I didn't visit your father in the hospital." He was shaking again. It was getting worse instead of better.

"What's wrong?" she asked.

"Nothing."

"Are you having a seizure?"

"No," he said. "But I might. Sometimes it happens."

"Since when?"

He shrugged.

"Your father told me you drink. Are you going into withdrawal?"

"Yeah," he said. "I'm sorry, I . . . I don't want to have a seizure. Do you mind if I get up and get something else?"

She stood up and let him out of the booth. Robbie opened the cabinet above the sink, took down a bottle, and poured himself a glass of it. He swallowed it down in three gulps, his eyes watering.

"It's . . . not usually this bad," he told her. "I . . . don't know what happened."

She sat back down in the booth and watched as he poured himself another glass. He carried it to the table and slid in next to her.

"How long will that last you?" she asked.

"Four or five hours," he said. "After that, I start to get shaky."

"Can you sleep through the night?"

"Four or five hours at a time," he told her. "I keep a bottle on the nightstand, just in case."

"When's the last time you tried to stop?"

"A few weeks ago," he said, "just after you came here to

see me." He shook his head. "I started seeing things," he said, "snakes coming out of the walls and stuff. I couldn't make it, Erin. I couldn't make it half a day."

She put an arm around him. They sat that way for a long time, neither of them talking.

Eventually he sighed and pushed the empty glass away from him. "I'm sorry," he said again. "I don't know how things got this way."

"A little bit at a time," she said. "It's okay. I'm happy to see you."

"I guess you're pretty disappointed."

"No," she said, "I'm not."

He turned to look at her, but her eyes were closed, her head resting against his shoulder.

"Things got out of control," he told her. "I thought I could handle it, but I couldn't."

"It's okay," she said, and her voice was soft and without judgment. "You'll beat it. I know you will. Last one standing, remember?"

35

CHIEF MARTIN WARD LEANED BACK IN HIS CHAIR AND STUDIED THE two children. He knew Erin Reece from the investigation surrounding the disappearance of her mother. Her father had done time in prison. Martin had been in command of the department back then as well. He was less familiar with Robbie Tabaha, but these were the kids who'd found Angela Finley's mitten along a dirt road next to Nathaniel Jacob's place. They'd brought it here first, and unfortunately had been turned away by the officer they spoke with. Next they'd taken it to Angela's mother, who had driven down to the station personally to tear him a new asshole. Martin didn't appreciate being told how to do his job, but chief of police was still an elected position in this town, and as long as that was the case, he'd had enough sense to take her complaint seriously.

Still, he hadn't reached the point yet where he was willing to let two kids head up the investigation. He would quit or retire before he allowed *that* to happen. Martin looked from one face to the other and smiled at them, although he didn't feel like smiling. A familiar heaviness had settled in his chest—*a bit of heartburn,* he told himself, *from the stress of the investigation*—and although it would be another three days until the impending heart attack put an end to his time on this earth, right now he was focused on the two kids sitting in front of him. He leaned forward and placed his forearms on the desk.

"Tell me again why you think I should speak with him," he said. He was looking at Erin Reece, the one who did most of the talking.

"He wanted me to get into his van," she said. "He stopped while I was riding my bike and tried to get me to go with him."

"Did he say why?"

"Yes," she said. "I already told you. He said we could go to his house and have something cool to drink."

"And before he arrived, you'd been riding your bike back and forth on the road for how long?"

"About an hour."

"It was hot that day, wasn't it?"

"I guess."

"And he wasn't the only person who stopped to talk with you. We've received phone calls in this office about your riding back and forth on that road. It's not safe, you know. People have expressed concern about you being out there."

She looked back at him, but said nothing.

"How long would you say you've been doing this, riding back and forth on the road like that?"

"Six weeks. Almost seven."

"And *why* are you doing it? Is this about your mother?"

She nodded.

"What's the objective?" he asked. "What are you hoping to achieve by being out there?"

She shrugged.

Martin sighed. "You understand that people are sometimes going to stop and talk to you," he said. "They're concerned about you. They might even suggest coming inside and getting something cool to drink."

"It wasn't like that," she told him. "There was something different about him."

"Different how?"

She glanced at her friend, then back at the chief.

Robbie leaned forward in his chair, hands on his knees. "He started to get all nervous," he said. "There was definitely something weird about him."

Martin swiveled his chair in the boy's direction. It made a soft squeak, like a small animal in distress. "You were there with her? The two of you were riding your bikes along the road together? Before she said it was just her."

Robbie shook his head. "Erin was by herself. I was just watching with binoculars."

"You were"—the chief uttered a short laugh—"watching with binoculars."

"Yes, sir."

"And you could hear what they were saying?"

"No, sir. Not exactly. But Erin told me later."

Martin opened his mouth to say something, then decided to leave it alone and turned back to Erin. "What did you say," he asked, "when this guy invited you to come inside and get something cool to drink?"

"I said okay. I told him I would go with him."

"And then what happened?"

"He started to get all nervous about it, like Robbie said. He told me people might not understand and it wouldn't be proper. He was worried about getting in trouble."

"Well, that shows good judgment," he said. "Tell me, did he ever try to force you to get into the van?"

"No."

"And then he just drove off. Is that right?"

"Yeah."

"So why are you so convinced that he's the one responsible for the disappearance of your mother?"

"I just am," she said. "I know it was him."

Martin picked up a paper clip and started turning it over in his hands. "But *how* do you know? What *evidence* do you have? You see, in this country you can't just run around accusing people of things based on a hunch. It's important to have evidence. And so far, I haven't heard any evidence to suggest that it's him. He stopped out of a reasonable concern for your well-being. That doesn't make him a criminal. Does your father know that you're out there, riding back and forth on Indian Highway for hours at a time, day after day?"

"Yes."

"Is that the truth? Because I'm going to ask him. I'm going to talk to him about this."

"I don't want you to."

"I know you don't," he said, "but I have to. It's my job to make sure that you're safe. And it's his job, too. He can't do that job properly if he doesn't know you're out there."

Erin looked back at him, her lips pressed together in an expression of defiance.

"What would you have done if he did try to take you?" Martin asked. "Did you think that through?"

"That's why I was watching them," Robbie said. "I would've followed them to the house on my bike and then called the police."

"That's a horrible plan," the chief said. "A van is a lot faster than a bike. Do you really think you could've kept up with him?"

He nodded. "I'm fast."

"Not *that* fast," he countered. "Do you have access to a phone to call the police?"

"I could've gone to a neighbor's house."

Martin tossed the paper clip onto the surface of his desk. It did a quarter turn and came to rest halfway between the two children. "This is exactly what I'm talking about," he said. "It's a dangerous game you're playing. You're not police officers, and you're not detectives. You're *kids* with no understanding of the risks you're taking. I want you to leave the investigation up to us from now on. Don't go bringing mittens to the families of people who have lost their loved ones, and don't go around accusing people of horrible crimes when you have no evidence to support those accusations." He looked at them both. "Do you understand me?"

They nodded, but Erin leaned forward in her seat. "We don't mean to bother you," she said. "It's just that—"

"No," the chief said, "that's the end of it. I want the two of you to get out of here. Go be kids. Let the adults do their jobs."

They stood up and left the office. It was 3:15 P.M., but the streets were quiet around them.

Erin jumped on her bike and started pedaling. Robbie caught up to her, the two of them moving through the town as their shadows slid along the asphalt.

"What a *jerk*," she said. "'Let the adults do their jobs.' If they actually did their jobs, we wouldn't have to do it for them."

"Where are you going?"

"Nowhere. Back home, I guess."

"Hey," he said. "Let's go down to the water. We can skip rocks and go for a swim."

"No," she said, "I don't feel like it."

"Well, let's do something else then. You pick."

She kept riding, her feet moving faster on the pedals.

"Erin. Erin, what do you say we—"

She stepped down on her brake and came to a skidding stop. He did the same a moment later and turned to look back at her.

"Go yourself," she said. "You don't need to be hanging around me every second of the day."

"Erin—"

"You wanna go down to the water and skip rocks, that's fine with me. You don't need *me* to do that."

"I wasn't trying to . . . I was just—"

"This isn't a game to me. Do you understand that?"

He nodded.

"*No one* will help me find her. Not my father, not the chief of police, not even my own best friend."

"Hold on a second," he said, getting off his bike. "I've been helping you plenty."

"How?" she asked, ignoring the wounded expression on his face. "By pinning thumbtacks to a map? By writing stuff in a notebook? That's *not* gonna get her back, Robbie."

He let his bike fall to the ground and walked over to her. "We're *trying*, Erin. We're doing the best we can."

"No, we're not," she said. "We're wasting time. We're expecting the adults to do something and they won't."

"Okay, fine. So let's—"

"Forget it. You've done enough for me already. Why do you care so much about finding her anyway? It's *my* mother, not yours."

Robbie stared at her. He opened his mouth to say something and then closed it again.

"The chief's right," she said. "You should go be a kid. I can take care of this myself."

She pedaled past him and didn't look back. The light at the intersection was red, but Erin bolted through it without looking. A lady in a blue Subaru had to slam on her brakes to avoid hitting her.

Erin rode with a fury, her vision blurring with tears that tracked along the sides of her face as she shot down Main Street. She made the eight-mile trip to her father's farm in twenty-three minutes. The phone book was in a drawer in the kitchen, and she tore out the page that she needed. As for the other things, she already knew where to look. Her father was home, of course, but he was out tending to the cattle. Erin stood there for a moment in the kitchen as she considered leaving him a note, but decided against it. People who handled things themselves didn't leave notes for others to come get them if they weren't home by dark.

She was in and out of the house in less than fifteen minutes. Erin grabbed her bike, cinched the straps of her backpack tight against her shoulders, and headed west toward the city of Wolf Point.

36

THE HOUSE DR. HOUSEMAN HAD OFFERED THEM AS A TEMPORARY place to stay sat on fifteen acres along the southern border of the Fort Peck Indian Reservation. It belonged to Mark's in-laws, who were wintering in Arizona. "I'm sorry I wasn't able to let you stay here sooner," Mark told Erin as they stood on the porch step waiting for David to emerge from the house. "I could tell you I wasn't able to get in touch with my wife's parents until a few days ago, but the truth is that they took some convincing." He looked down at the yellowed grass in the front yard before looking up again. "They're good people," he said, "but they don't know you the way I do."

Erin reached out and put a hand on his forearm. "I appreciate everything you've done for us," she said. "I arrived in town to find that we had fewer friends in Wolf Point than I remembered. I'm so grateful that you're among them."

In the days that followed, Erin and her father settled into the place and began to establish a new sense of normalcy. The house was six miles west of the city, giving them enough privacy that they could walk the grounds without being seen from the road or adjacent farmland. David took to it well enough, although Erin could tell that he missed the farm. He was a man who was used to getting things done, and idle time seemed like wasted time. The restlessness got him up and moving, though, and his strength returned faster than she'd expected. It had been two weeks since he'd been discharged from the hospital, and he could now walk the property—once in the early morning and again just before sunset—for forty minutes at a stretch.

Now that they had some space and a place of their own, Matta had returned Diesel, who joined David on his walks and provided advance notice of any approaching visitors. "The dawn and dusk patrols," David called them, referring to their walks around the property, and Erin began to think of them that way as well, standing on the porch and waiting for their return whenever they took longer than she expected.

Jeff Stutzman had allowed David time to recover before asking for a statement. Erin had insisted upon hiring a lawyer, a fellow named Bill Casings who had flown in from Missoula. He'd been out to the house on several occasions already, but today he was there to be present at the questioning, and the kitchen was full of people. Lieutenant Stutzman was there, as well as Ronald Irving, who'd taken over the position of chief of police at the age of twenty-eight following the death of Martin Ward twenty years ago. There was the lawyer and a stenographer, as well as Erin herself. At the table sat her father, sipping coffee and looking more composed than any man should look when facing potential charges of multiple homicides.

"Let's get this show on the road," he said, and they took their places at the table.

The lawyer had a yellow legal pad in front of him. He'd introduced himself to Lieutenant Stutzman and Chief Irving already, but he did it again for the record. "My client, Mr. David Reece, is prepared to make a statement," he said. "In accordance with his rights under the Fifth Amendment of the

United States Constitution, I have advised him not to answer any questions. The statement should not be taken as an admission of guilt, but merely a telling of the facts surrounding the focus of your investigation. We reserve the right to amend and modify his statement at a later date to ensure accuracy." He looked at each of them in turn. "Are there any procedural questions before he begins?"

They were all quiet, waiting.

"Okay," Bill said. He turned to David. "You can begin when you're ready."

"Thank you, Bill," her father said. "That was very formal."

The two police officers smiled, but Erin didn't. She knew what was coming and how it would change his life forever. David would return to prison and he would die there, surrounded by people who saw him only in the context of the crimes he'd committed.

"My wife went missing in October of 1998," he said. "They found her abandoned car on Indian Highway. Two of its tires were ripped apart." He looked up from the table, but he was looking past them, at a place he hadn't visited for a very long time. "I've never lost anyone like that before," he said. "We searched for her, my daughter and me, for four months. We covered every road and talked to anyone who might have seen her. I was out of my mind with worry. I kept telling myself . . . if we looked hard enough . . ."

He closed his eyes, and the stenographer stopped typing. David's hands were on the table, his fingers interlaced in front of him. Erin looked at them. The skin was weathered and marked in a few places by scars he'd collected over the years, but they were still the hands she remembered from her childhood: strong and capable, the vessels dividing and connecting just beneath the surface.

"I knew from the beginning that she was probably dead," he said. "Still . . . I kept looking. Because I needed to find her. I needed to know what had happened. *Not knowing . . . that's the worst thing,* I told myself. But I was wrong. Knowing is worse. Knowing is always worse."

Erin looked up at her father's face. He was older now, but here were the parts of him that had sat in the truck with her during the time when he was still looking, before he had given up on her mother.

"It took me eight months to find her," he said. "It was only a hunch, really, the way I sometimes caught him watching me during the Sunday service."

"Who?" Jeff Stutzman asked.

The lawyer raised his hand. "Please," he said. "No questions. Remember?"

David looked across the table at the lieutenant. "Abel Griffin. The man you found buried on my farm. I put him there. I'm sure you know that already." He opened and closed his hands, the parts of his body that had held the shovel. "I didn't know for certain that he was the one who had taken my wife. Not at first anyway. But I suspected. It was the kind of suspicion that defies reason but builds slowly. I became more and more certain with time."

"How did you—"

"I never liked the boy. It wasn't because he was slow. He had a strangeness about him, a giddiness that made me uneasy. I would catch him studying me—not in the way that other people looked at me after Helen disappeared, but in a fascinated, emotionally detached way that made me feel like I was a bug in his collection. And that got me thinking: Does he have a collection?"

"Why didn't you tell someone?" Jeff asked, and the lawyer scowled at him.

"Tell them what?" David asked. "A feeling's not enough, Lieutenant. You of all people should know that. I needed evidence, something tangible. I needed to know that when I went to the police they would arrest him for the murder of my wife and all those others who went missing. The evidence needed to be strong enough to make the charges stick. I didn't want to give him the opportunity to get away."

He looked from one face to the next before lowering his eyes to the table.

"I skipped the nine-thirty service one Sunday and went to his house instead. The place was locked, but forcing open the back door was easy. It didn't take long for me to go through the place, opening dresser drawers and cabinets. Eventually I found Helen's necklace, the one she was wearing on the day she went missing. I walked out to the backyard and found the spot where the ground was soft. There was a shovel there, too, leaning against the back of the house. It didn't take long for me to dig her up, the loose dirt filling the blade of the shovel over and over as I worked. When I struck bone—when I uncovered her forearm—I should've stopped what I was doing and called the police. Instead, I pulled her out of the earth and sat with her for a while, rocking what was left of her body. Then I filled the hole back in, went to my truck, and retrieved a large blanket from the cab. I wrapped her body in the blanket and brought Helen home that day—back to the farm—and gave her a proper burial."

"Why didn't you call the police?" Chief Irving asked.

"Officers, *please,*" Bill Casings said, placing his pen down on his legal pad.

"It's okay," David said. "It's a fair question, and I'll answer it." He looked at the chief. "I considered contacting the police," he said. "It's what a sane man would've done. But no, my mind kept returning to the things he must've done to her."

Erin stood up from her chair and went to the window. She did not want to hear this. It was too much like the truth.

David was quiet for a moment before continuing. When he did start speaking again, his voice was calm and reflective, like a man recounting the details of a dream he could only half remember.

"I went back there later that night," he said. "I wanted to talk to him, to understand *why* he had killed her. I wanted to tell him about Helen, about how much we still loved her. He wasn't home yet, and so I sat in the living room . . . and waited."

The lawyer put a hand on David's forearm. "A point of clarification if I may, Mr. Reece. Did you go there intending to kill him?"

"No, I was going to talk to him, and maybe beat him to within an inch of his life."

"That's an expression," Bill Casings said. "Would it be more accurate to say that you were aware of the potential for violence, but that your intent was not to kill Mr. Griffin or even to render severe bodily injury? In fact, you didn't bring a weapon, did you?"

"Who's giving this statement?" Jeff asked the attorney. "Him or you?"

"I'm just trying to clarify for the accuracy of the record that Mr. Reece did not intend to kill Mr. Griffin that night. He was seeking verbal discourse. He wanted to understand—"

"He came home at nine o'clock," David said, interrupting him. "He was actually humming to himself when he opened

the door." David looked over at his daughter. "I'm not a murderer," he said. "I wasn't intending to kill that man, but he attacked me as soon as he saw me sitting there."

"*He* attacked *you*," the lawyer reiterated, "and you did what
you had to do to defend yourself."

"He grabbed a knife from the kitchen," David said, "and I
realized what a fool I'd been to confront him alone."

"What happened next?" the attorney asked.

"I ran," he said. "I ran out the back door. But I tripped on
the shovel that I'd left lying on the ground."

The lawyer nodded. "And he came after you, intending to
kill you?"

"Yes. Yes, I think that's what he intended."

"And then?"

"I got to my feet just as he was closing the distance."

"And he had the knife in his hand," the lawyer said. "You
could still see that."

"Yes, but there was something in my hand as well. I was
holding the shovel, and I swung it with everything I had."

"To knock the knife away."

"To defend myself and what was left of my family. I knew
he would come after Erin next. A man like that wasn't going
to stop with just the two of us."

"Mr. Reece, I know this is difficult for you, but if you could
just—"

"The blade of the shovel struck him in the head," he said.
"It sliced into his skull and became stuck there. He fell down
immediately. I think he was dead before he hit the ground."

"A single unpremeditated blow to the head," the lawyer said,
"in the act of defending yourself against a man who had murdered your wife and was clearly trying to do the same to you."

David nodded. "He lay there on the ground without moving.

And the shovel, it was still sticking out of his head. I had to put my foot on his chest to yank it free."

Bill put a hand on his arm. "I think it's clear now," he said. "You were in a state of severe emotional distress. You were concerned that the police might not believe that you acted in self-defense. In your mind, there was a perceived risk that you might go to prison or that your thirteen-year-old daughter could be taken away from you. For these reasons, you decided not to contact the police. You brought the body back to your farm and you buried it there."

"I'd been in prison before," he said. "I'm an ex-convict. Even if the situation was different, I don't think the police would've believed me."

"And so you buried him on your property."

"Yes," he said. "I buried him in the back. It wouldn't have been right to bury him next to Helen."

"And you've kept this secret for all these years. You didn't even tell your daughter."

"No," he said, "I never told Erin. I was afraid of what she might think of me."

They turned to look at her. She had backed herself against the wall by the front door. Erin shook her head, the tears flowing freely now. "No," she said. "I can't . . . I won't listen to this any longer."

Jeff rose from his chair. "Erin," he said, but she bolted from the room, flinging the door open hard enough for the knob to smack against the wall.

They heard footsteps on the front porch, the sound of the truck starting, the churn of the tires on the driveway.

"Someone should go after her," Jeff said, but David shook his head.

"Let her be," he told them. "It's a shock to her, I know. I haven't told her the truth of it until now."

The chief leaned forward in his chair. "You sure about that, sir? All these years and you never told her?"

David looked at the man. His eyes were clear, his voice as steady as the table between them. "I protected her as best I could," he said. "Tracking down her mother's killer was part of it. Keeping it a secret was the rest."

"You did this town a favor," the lawyer said. "Who knows how many more people he would've killed in the end."

David lowered his eyes to the table. "I went looking for answers and I found them," he said. "It's harder to know something than to not know it. It sits with you, and it never leaves. I've paid my price for the killing of Abel Griffin. I reckon there's not much more they can do to me now."

37

(July 1999)

SHE GOT THE ADDRESS FROM THE PHONE BOOK. IT WAS A SMALL single-story house that sat by itself about a mile west of town. Erin had never been here before, but she recognized the white van parked out front. The paint on the house's exterior was tan and flaking, and the walls seemed to droop outward, as if they had stood for too many years and were in desperate need of a rest. There was a small front porch with two steps leading up from the yard. The place looked nothing like her father's house, but there was something about it that made her think of home.

She left her bike at the curb and walked through the side yard to the back of the structure. The yard was overrun with weeds. Crabgrass and thistles clawed at her ankles and left thin red marks in their wake. In the rear, the land sloped gently downward toward a thatch of wild brush. She considered going back there, but turned to the house instead. There was a long-handled shovel lying on the ground next to the door. She tried the knob and found that it was locked.

"Hello," a voice said. "What are you doing here?"

Erin spun around to find him standing near the right rear

corner of the house. He was holding something metal and rectangular in his hand. It had little black wheels along the bottom, and he rolled them soundlessly across his palm as he studied her.

"I told you it wouldn't be proper for you to come here," he said, "but here you are, paying me a visit just the same." He looked down at the toy locomotive and gave its wheels another spin. "I was just making dinner," he said. "Spaghetti and hot dogs. Most people don't know this about me, but I'm a pretty good cook."

"Spaghetti and hot dogs?"

"Sure. And I think I've got some Oreos for dessert. Come on in if you want some. I don't get many visitors, so . . ."

He turned and disappeared around the side of the house without finishing his sentence.

Erin stood in the backyard, uncertain about what to do. She had come here to find him, and here he was, inviting her in for dinner.

She moved around to the side of the house just as he was rounding the front corner. She heard his boots on the porch, then a door as it opened and closed.

Erin walked around to the front of the house. There were two windows, one on either side of the door. She put her face up to one of them, but the interior was dark, the glass hazy and caked with dirt.

Don't go in there, she warned herself. *If you go in there, you'll never come out.*

She stood at the screen door and listened. The thicker, more formidable front door was already open. She could hear him moving around in the kitchen, the metallic clank of a pot as he set it on the range.

Erin hesitated, her hand on the door. She could run away now, hop on her bike before he even realized she was leaving.

Or I can go in, she thought. *I can go in and find out what happened to my mother.*

She fiddled with the straps of the backpack on her shoulders. He was singing to himself. She could hear that as well.

"Oh my darlin', oh my darlin', oh my daaaarrrllin' Clementine. You are lost and gone forever, dreadful sorry, Clementine."

Erin pulled on the handle and the screen door opened outward, its hinges creaking. There were a few holes in the screen itself. She stepped across the threshold and let the door clatter shut behind her.

"Hut-two-three-four. Come on in and close the door." He laughed at that, a quick brisk sound that was there and then gone again.

She was standing in a short, narrow hallway. The kitchen was off to her left. To her right was a living room with a faded orange couch, a coffee table, and a television sitting on a wooden stand in the corner. On the floor was a miniature train track. It wound its way under the coffee table and behind the couch. She could see a train station, small plastic trees on either side of the tracks, and tiny people standing on the platform. The train was stopped on the tracks: a locomotive, six boxcars, and a little red caboose.

It's the BNSF railroad tracks, she thought. *I ride alongside it all the time when I bike to Robbie's.*

"Do you like ketchup or butter with your spaghetti?" he asked.

She turned to see him standing in the kitchen doorway. He had a large knife in his hand. Behind him she could see the cutting board and a row of hot dogs that he'd chopped into small bite-size pieces.

"Butter," she said without processing the question. Instead, she was looking at the knife.

Those plastic people on either side of the tracks, she thought. *If I look closely, will I recognize anyone? Is there one that looks like Angela Finley? Is there one that looks like my mother?*

He turned and went to the refrigerator. Erin's eyes followed the knife as he opened the door and pulled out a small circular plate with a stick of butter.

"We can have Kool-Aid if you want," he said as he returned to the counter with the plate of butter.

There was a dining table in the kitchen, but he hadn't set it with any plates. The plates were on the counter, next to the cutting board. She watched as he scooped the spaghetti onto each of them, mixed in the hot dogs, and added two pats of butter to the top of both piles. There was a large pot of water on the range. A single strand of spaghetti looped over the lip of it and clung to the side like a tentacle. He turned with the plates in his hands and walked past her on his way to the living room. He'd left the knife on the counter, and she stared at the spot where the overhead light reflected off the metal of the blade.

I could grab it. I could pick it up and make him tell me what he did with her.

She felt the heavy impact of his steps through the floorboards as he returned to the kitchen. He was wearing jeans and work boots and a red flannel shirt with the sleeves rolled up to the middle of his forearms. He reminded her of a lumberjack, or the giant at the top of the beanstalk from the story her mother had read to her when Erin was younger. It had always frightened her, that story: the image of the giant climbing down the beanstalk as Jack chopped frantically at the base of it from below.

He opened the refrigerator, took out a pitcher of juice—*Kool-Aid,* she reminded herself—and poured some into two tall plastic cups that he placed on the table in front of her.

"We can eat in the TV room," he said. "It's better than the kitchen."

He opened a drawer and plucked out two forks, and he handed one to her before picking up one of the cups and heading back to the living room.

Erin stood there with the fork in her hand and the cup of red liquid in front of her on the table. The knife was still resting on the counter.

"We can watch cartoons while we eat," he said, and he clicked on the TV in the corner of the room.

Erin turned around as the man stepped over the train tracks and sat down on the couch. The plates of spaghetti and hot dogs were resting on the coffee table. He picked one up, speared a piece of hot dog with his fork, and popped it into his mouth. An episode of *Tom and Jerry* was playing on the television. Erin watched as the mouse stuck the cat's tail into an electric socket.

"Your dinner is ready," he said. "You should come and eat before it gets cold."

Erin stood in the kitchen doorway. There was enough room for her to sit on the couch, but she would be *right next to him,* too close to do anything if he tried to grab her. There were chairs at the kitchen table. She could get her plate and sit here, or carry a chair into the living room. It would be hard to find a spot where she could sit without knocking over some of the train equipment.

She looked around the floor again at the tiny plastic people. They seemed disconnected from one another, gazing at the station or in the direction of the television. Some of them were looking at plastic trees or across the room as they waited for a train that would take them to the other side of the couch and then right back to the place where they first started. They weren't going anywhere. Every ticket out of here was a ticket back to Wolf Point.

"What are you doing?" he asked, and Erin looked up to find him staring at her. He had turned sideways on the couch. His right forearm drooped over the backrest.

"Come over here and *sit down*," he said. "Stop standing there like a silly rabbit."

Erin's eyes flashed to the television. The episode of *Tom and Jerry* had ended. The Cartoon Network had gone to a commercial.

"I'm going to have to throw it out if your dinner gets any colder," he warned her. "You want me to go through all this work making you a nice home-cooked meal just to have to throw it in the garbage?" He looked past her, as if there was someone else standing at the kitchen counter. Then he turned back to the television, picked up his drink, and swallowed half the glass in four rapid gulps.

Erin approached the couch with her cup in one hand and her fork in the other. The side of her left tennis shoe brushed against one of the miniature people as she stepped over the track. The plastic figure teetered, but it did not topple over. She froze as the man shot her a tense sideways glance. "Be *careful*," he said.

"Sorry."

He finished the rest of his Kool-Aid and set the cup down on the coffee table with a bang.

Erin stood next to the couch with the large armrest between them. "I came to ask you . . . I want to know . . . what happened to my mother."

He was facing forward, his attention on the television.

"My mother," she continued. "I know that you took her. I want to know what you did with her."

"Nothing," he said. "There are no mothers here. I live by myself."

"But you *did* take her. I know that you did."

Erin went to the television and turned it off. She could've grabbed the remote sitting on the coffee table, but that was too close to him. It was important to keep her distance.

"*Hey,*" he said. "I was *watching* that."

Erin stood in front of the television. "You've watched enough TV," she said. "Now I want to talk to you about something."

"No," he said. "We can talk later, after the show."

"We can talk now."

He was still for a moment, his knees together and his shoulders hunched forward. He tried to look past her at the television.

"It was last October," she told him. "She was driving her car along Indian Highway. It's the place where I was riding my bike when you stopped to talk to me."

"Nope," he said, and he shook his head again. "I don't know nothing about that." He stood up and took both plates into the kitchen. "I'm going to have some dessert. You don't get none because you didn't eat your dinner."

Erin unslung the backpack from her shoulders, opened the zipper, and placed it at her feet. She could hear the sound of him scraping spaghetti off her plate.

She couldn't see him from where she was standing, but she heard the plates and forks go into the sink, the sound of running water as he rinsed them. Erin waited for him, and while she was waiting, she reached into the bag to pull out the things she had brought with her. She stepped forward and placed one of them on the coffee table.

"Oreo cookies and chocolate milk," he announced from the

kitchen. "That's what good boys get to eat when they've finished their—"

He stopped in the entryway to the living room. He was holding a plate of cookies and a glass of chocolate milk, but his eyes were on the thing that had been in her backpack a moment before.

The grip was big for her hands, but she held the revolver with confidence, the muzzle pointed in his direction. It was her father's .38. She'd watched him shoot with it and had practiced with the gun on several occasions since the day her mother went missing. He had taken the time to show her, and although Erin was not a great shot, she wasn't an awful one, either. At this range, she could hit the big man in front of her if she needed to.

"Come over here and sit down on the couch," she told him. "You can bring your milk and cookies with you."

"You're gonna . . . shoot me?"

"I want to talk to you."

"I don't know nothing about your mother."

"Sit down."

He took a step backward and turned his head to glance down the hallway that led to the back of the house.

"Mister," Erin said, "if you try to run, I *swear to God* I will kill you."

"I don't want you to shoot me."

Her hands were shaking, and her palms were damp with sweat. She took a step toward him, and this time she accidentally stepped on one of the plastic people. She felt it beneath her shoe, a little softer than a pebble.

"You shouldn't have done that," he told her. "You've got *no right* to step on other people's things."

"I'm sorry," she said. "It was an accident."

He shook his head. "You did it on purpose."

"I didn't. If you had sat down like I told you, it wouldn't have happened."

"It wasn't my fault."

"You're right," she said. "It was an accident. It was nobody's fault. Sometimes things happen and it's nobody's fault."

He took a step toward her.

"The couch," she said. "Sit down on the couch and eat a cookie."

"My stomach hurts. I don't want any now."

"Fine," she said. "Put them on the table. But sit. You make me nervous when you're standing."

He walked forward, took a seat on the couch, and put the plate of cookies and the glass of milk on the coffee table in front of him.

"Good," she said. "Now we can talk."

"I don't know nothing about your mother."

"You already said that." Erin took a breath and let it out. "Why did you stop to talk to me last week while I was riding my bike along Indian Highway?"

"It was hot outside. I thought you might like to come inside for a nice cold drink."

"You were going to kidnap me, just like you did to all the others."

"Nope."

"That's a picture of my mother on the coffee table. I know you've killed a lot of people, so . . . I brought it to help you remember what she looked like."

He looked down at the picture. "I don't kill people. I don't do any of that."

"Yes, you do."

"No," he said. "Sometimes they just . . ."

They were both silent for a moment.

"Sometimes they just what?"

"Nothing. I . . . didn't mean to say that."

Erin adjusted her grip on the revolver. "But you *did* say it. You didn't mean to, but it came out anyway. It was an accident. I understand that. I just . . . I just need to know what happened to her. You can tell me, can't you?"

He shook his head. "I can't. I'll get in trouble."

"I don't care about getting you in trouble. I just want to know. If it's possible . . . I want to take her home with me."

"You can't," he said. "I already buried her out there in the marsh."

Erin took a deep shuddering breath. She took two steps backward and leaned against the wall.

"I'm sorry," he said. "I didn't mean for it to happen. It was an accident, just like you said."

"Oh," she said, but it felt like all of the strength had left her body. The gun was heavy in her hand, and the muzzle was pointed at the floor now as her right arm hung limp from her shoulder. She tried to cover her face with her other hand, but it stopped halfway at the level of her chest. She left it there, covering the gaping wound in her heart.

"I put the tape over her mouth so she wouldn't scream. It's better that way. It keeps them calm."

"Yes," Erin said, not agreeing with him but needing to hear the rest of it. She was crying now, the room a jumble of broken images in front of her.

"She must've moved it somehow while she was lying in the van. Or maybe I put it over her nose, too, and I didn't notice. I've never done that before. It was a mistake. She couldn't breathe. I was sitting in the front seat and didn't notice. By the time we got to the house she was already dead. That was bad. I was so . . . stupid and clumsy."

He curled his hand into a fist and struck himself in the side of the head three times. Erin could hear the repeated smack of it, like a piece of steak when her mother struck it with the tenderizer.

"Stop it," she said. She used the heel of her hand to wipe the tears from her eyes.

He looked up at her, shamefaced and miserable. "I had to bring your mother here to take care of it. I gave her a proper burial. I said a prayer and everything."

"She's out behind the house, out there in the marsh? That's where you buried her body?"

He pressed his lips together and nodded. "I'm sorry," he said. "I didn't mean for it to happen. I didn't mean for her to die like that."

"What about the others? Are they out there, too? Did you bury them the way you buried my mother?"

"No," he said, and his eyes went wide. "No, I'd . . . I'd never . . ."

She brought her hands together and used her left thumb to cock the hammer. Erin stepped forward until her legs were up against the coffee table and the gun was pointed at his head.

"I'm going to kill you now," she told him. "I'm going to pull this trigger in the name of my mother."

He closed his eyes and nodded. "Okay," he said, and his lower lip was trembling. "We live and die and don't ask why."

"You understand why I'm killing you?"

He continued nodding, his head bobbing up and down like a puppet on a string. His fingers were laced together and resting on his lap. There was a sudden smell of ammonia, and Erin glanced down to see an expanding patch of darkness on the front of his jeans.

"Do you have anything else to say?"

He kept his eyes closed and shook his head. "No," he said. "I just thought that maybe . . . maybe we could be friends. I don't know how to make friends. I don't know how to do anything."

Friends, she thought, and she tightened her finger on the trigger.

"Goodbye," she said, and she was speaking not only to the man sitting in front of her, but to the small bit of hope she had kept locked away until now. Her mother wasn't just missing. Her mother was dead. She had suffocated in the back of a van, and maybe that was better than whatever horrible ending he'd had in store for her.

The gun went off in her hand, and the man's head exploded into a mass of flesh and bone. She could see the spray of blood and brains on the wall behind him, and his body rocked backward before falling to the left and coming to rest against the arm of the couch.

Erin eased up on the trigger and lowered the gun. The man was still sitting there, trembling, waiting for her to pull the trigger. She'd imagined it but not done it. She wasn't a murderer after all. Not even to this man who had killed her mother.

"Go ahead," he said. "I've never been good for nothing anyway."

She took a step back from the table and felt the crunch of more plastic figures beneath her feet. She stood there looking at him for a full minute, willing herself to raise the gun and fire the way she had intended.

He deserves to die, she told herself. *That's why you came here, isn't it? Not just to find out what happened to your mother, but to prevent him from doing it to anyone else.*

She looked down at the gun in her hand, and suddenly it was all she could do to keep from dropping it.

Erin put her thumb on the hammer and pressed lightly on the trigger to decock the revolver. Her fingers were slick with sweat, and the hammer almost slipped from her grasp. She lowered it to its resting place, flipped on the safety, stuffed the gun into her backpack, and walked quickly out of the room. By the time she reached the hallway she was running. She hit the screen door at a full sprint, the door flying open on its hinges and smacking against the exterior of the house.

"*Wait!*" he called after her. "*Don't go!*"

She was on the front porch now, and she looked back over her shoulder to see him following her down the hall. The screen door slapped shut, and Erin ran in the direction of her bike. She forgot about the two steps leading up to the porch, and she stumbled and fell forward into the grass.

He came through the door and stood over her, a gigantic man whose jeans were wet from his own urine. She could smell the biting stench of it mixed with dust and the taste of fear in her mouth.

He placed a hand on her upper arm and yanked her to her feet. "You forgot your picture," he said. "I have something to show you."

"No," she said. "Let go of me."

"I can show you the spot. I can show you where I buried her."

Erin tried to pull away from him, but he was strong. The more she struggled, the deeper his fingers sank into the flesh of her arm.

"We can still be friends," he said. "You don't have to run away."

He turned and walked toward the steps. His hand was still

locked around her, and when she made her legs go slack, he simply dragged her through the yard. Erin snatched at the crabgrass, but it pulled loose from the earth and did nothing to slow their progress. She slid along the dirt and grass as he dragged her. She could see the steps and the bottom of the screen door leading to the hallway.

If he gets me in there, I'm never coming out. He'll bury me in the marsh alongside of my mother.

She struggled harder, twisting her body and digging her heels into the earth. He placed his boot on the first step—*clump*—and again she thought of the giant descending from the beanstalk as the little boy chopped madly from below.

Something came around the corner of the house. Erin was turned away from it, but she heard a wild battle cry and a series of quick scampering steps across the wooden porch. It was a child's voice, thick with fury and determination, the way Erin had felt when she held the gun to the man's head and willed herself to pull the trigger. The sound of it built to a scream—something not quite human—and she looked up in time to see the arcing swing of wood and metal against the bloodred sky.

She felt the solid thud of the impact, a heavy shudder that moved through her body and was gone in the space of a second. The boy was still holding the weapon by its long wooden handle, but he let go of it as the man stumbled backward.

Erin covered her head with her free hand, but the shovel did not fall to the porch. Instead, the handle did a strange sideways dance, and she followed it up to see that the metal part was buried in the man's head.

He let go of her then, using both hands to try to pull it out. His eyes were wide and unblinking, and his mouth opened and closed as if a piece of bubble gum had gotten stuck in his throat.

At first there was very little blood, just a trickle of it down the side of his face. It tracked a jagged path between his eyes and over his right cheekbone. He staggered backward and away from them across the yard, and on the fourth step his feet became tangled and he fell sideways into the grass. Erin got to her feet and watched him. He curled his body in on itself, and then arched his neck and back as his hands continued to pull at the shovel. The right side of his face was in the grass, and the skin on that side was now coated with a mix of dirt and blood. She could see his left eye, though, about two inches from where the metal blade was buried in his skull. The man's eye locked in on her, a bewildered, lopsided gaze that was full of shock and unanswered questions.

She took several steps forward and bent down to touch the handle.

"Don't," Robbie told her, and Erin looked back, surprised to see him standing there.

"Got . . . something stuck . . . here," the man said, and Erin turned back around to see that he had let go of the handle and was reaching out to her.

She took a knee beside him in the dirt and placed her hand inside of his own massive palm.

"Can't . . . seem to . . . get it out."

"It's okay," she said. "It's nothing."

"Oh," he said. "That's . . . good."

He tried to smile at her, but it was only the left side of his face that moved. The right half was locked in place, the corner of his mouth on that side pulled back in a grimace.

"I put her in a real . . . good spot. Said a prayer for her and . . . everything."

"Thank you."

"Sure," he said. "You and me, we can be . . . friends."

"Okay," she told him. "I'm okay with that."

He exhaled slowly, and he let go of her hand. The next breath was harder. He ratcheted it into his chest, a series of broken gasps.

"Thanks," he said. "I don't make . . . too mannnn-yyy."

His gaze slipped away from her face, and his body went still. She could hear the air sliding out of his lungs, and when that breath was finished, he did not try to draw in another. Erin closed her eyes and knelt next to him for a bit, but there was someone else behind her, and she heard him now, a voice that was not quite certain.

"I had to stop him. He was going to kill you. Wasn't he?"

She stood up and turned around. Robbie was still standing there on the front porch, exactly where she had left him.

"Yes," she said. "I think that he was."

Robbie looked past her at the body of the man lying in the dirt. "I knew you would come here," he told her. "When you rode off on your bike like that . . . somehow, I just knew."

She nodded.

"I kept thinking, maybe she doesn't want me here. Maybe she wants to do this alone." He looked down at his shoes and back up at her. "But I had to come, right? I had to be certain that you didn't need me."

"Yes," she said, and she was sobbing now—they both were—their bodies shaking from the terror and adrenaline and thoughts of what had almost happened but didn't. The man lay motionless in the grass a few yards away, and that was somehow even more terrible than the rest of it, that a minute earlier he was breathing and talking and now he was not, and they were to blame for all of it, and there was nothing they could do to take it back.

She took a few steps forward and so did he. They met somewhere in the middle, stumbling into each other like two people lost in the dark.

"I needed you," she said. "Thank you for coming."

"Yeah," he said. "Yeah, okay." But he was still shaking, and it seemed that there was no end to it, as if he had stepped backward into a bottomless pit and would go right on falling for the rest of his life.

"You did the right thing," she told him. "He would've killed me, just like you said."

"Okay." He tried to smile, but it broke into pieces in front of her. He looked past her again at the body lying on the ground. "I didn't like it," he said, and he took a deep shuddering breath that reminded her of the one the man had taken as he lay on the grass with her hand in his palm. "I didn't like it at all."

She leaned in and hugged him, and Erin slowly pivoted Robbie's body until he was facing the empty street instead of the man in the dirt.

"I know," she said. "I didn't like it, either."

He held on to her until the worst of the shaking was over. When he let go, his face was pale and devoid of expression. "What do we do now?" he asked, and he looked to her, as if the answer was simple and right there in front of them.

"We get him inside," she said, "and then we go get my father."

"You're going to tell him?"

"Yes," she said, "we have to." Erin looked at the dead man and then back at Robbie. "I don't know what else to do."

38

IN HER MEMORY, THE PLACE ALWAYS LOOKED THE SAME, THE WAY IT
had looked on the day she first saw it. Now, sitting in the driver's seat of her pickup two decades later, Erin was aware that
there was part of her childhood still trapped here, the ghost of
a bike lying against the curb. She had not yet gotten out of the
truck, but she could feel the crunch of the crabgrass beneath
the soles of her sneakers, the weight of the straps of her backpack pressing down on her shoulders. She was thirteen again,
if only for the space of this moment. The place beckoned to her
with its sagging walls and screen-door hinges dense with rust.
There was something inside that was still waiting, some part of
herself that could still be saved.

She leaned over and grabbed the instrument from the passenger footwell, opened the door, and climbed out of the truck.
The bench seat was empty beside her. She had left Diesel with
her father and the people who'd come to listen to his statement.
By now it must be over. The police would be discussing the
case. If they arrested him, the lawyer would call her. She hadn't
wanted to witness that, her father being placed in handcuffs for
a crime he didn't commit.

The white van that had once been parked here had been

replaced by an aging Jeep Cherokee, but the windows were dark and there was no light or hint of activity from inside the house. The heavy front door was closed, but she remembered the hallway beyond and the sound of his singing in the kitchen. She had come here to find out what he had done to her mother. He had discovered her standing in the backyard and strangely enough had invited her in for dinner.

("Got . . . something stuck . . . here. Can't . . . seem to . . . get it out.")

She looked to the left, at the spot where the man had fallen. After he was dead, she and Robbie had to drag him into the house while the shovel was still lodged in his head. They hadn't been able to remove it. It was buried too deep. Her father had to place his boot on the man's chest to yank it out. It had made a squeaking noise as he worked it loose.

Erin watched him lean the shovel against the wall. "We should call the police," she said, "and tell them what happened."

Her father was sweating, although the sun was below the horizon and the evening air was cool against her skin. She watched as the swell of his Adam's apple slid up and down, as if he needed to retch but had decided to do it elsewhere when the eyes of his daughter were not upon him.

"You spoke with Chief Ward at the police station earlier today," he said. "You both did. Is that correct?"

They nodded.

"And you told him about your suspicions?"

Again, they nodded.

"What did he say?"

"He said we didn't have any evidence and that we should just stay away from him," Erin replied.

David closed his eyes and pressed the fingertips of his left hand against his temple. "And then you rode your bike home, took your mother's gun, and came here."

Your mother's gun, Erin thought, but her mother was dead. She felt the pain of this new reality rise to the surface, the way it would a thousand times in the months ahead.

Her father looked at Robbie. "Did you know that she was coming here?"

"No, sir. Not exactly."

"Then how did you find her? How did you know to come here?"

Robbie swallowed. "Erin was mad," he said. He stopped and glanced over at her. "She said she was going to take care of things herself. I figured she would come here. It was a guess. When she took off on her bike, I figured that's where she was heading."

David turned to his daughter. "So you went to the police chief, told him you thought Mr. Griffin was responsible for the disappearance of your mother, and when you didn't get the response you were hoping for, the two of you came out here and killed him."

Erin shook her head. "That's not how it happened."

"No," he said, "but the police will see it that way. Mr. Griffin didn't kidnap you. You rode out here on your bikes. You came with a gun."

"*Daddy,*" she pleaded, but she didn't know how to finish. Her intentions in coming here were all jumbled in her head.

He walked to the kitchen and looked at the dishes. "It's hard for a child—even one as strong as you, Robbie—to drive the blade of a shovel that deep into someone's skull."

"It was a lucky shot. I swung it as hard as I could."

David stood near the kitchen table. His eyes were on the

floor. "What's more believable," he said, "is that *I* swung the shovel."

They were silent, staring at him.

"You came home and told me your suspicions, and I drove out here to confront him. We argued, he attacked me, and I killed him with the shovel."

Erin was shaking her head. "That's not how it—"

"I know," he said, "but it's what the police will believe. Or . . . they'll think I attacked him first."

"They'll understand," she said. "If I explain it to them, the way it really happened . . ."

"And tell them what, that he invited you in for dinner?"

She looked around the room.

"Jesus," he said, and ran a hand through his short hair as he stood there, head down, trying to think things through. "Robbie's fingerprints are on the handle of the shovel, but so are yours and mine. My boot tracks are in the yard."

"If we find Mom," she said. "That'll prove that—"

"It doesn't prove anything," he said, and his words sounded harsh and angry in the confines of the house. "Maybe he buried her and maybe he didn't." He looked down at the body of Abel Griffin. "He covered her mouth and nose with duct tape? Is that what he told you?"

"Yes," Erin told him. "He said it was an accident the way she died. He didn't mean to stop her from breathing."

David stood with his back to the children, facing the kitchen. He made a noise that Erin couldn't quite decipher, followed by the question: "What did he mean to do to her instead?"

The room was quiet as they watched him. Her father stood there for a long time, his head down, his right hand covering his face while the other one hung limply at his side. The children looked at each other, and neither of them spoke. And

David was quiet himself, so quiet that Erin could hardly hear him sobbing.

Eventually he cleared his throat and lifted his head. "Once the police get involved," he said, "it's hard to predict what direction things will go. I could be found guilty of murder, or they could come after you. I've already been to prison once. It won't be hard for them to put me there again."

Erin winced as something dug into her right ankle, bringing her back to the present. She was alone and standing in the backyard now, looking toward the cluster of trees behind the house. Beyond that was the marsh where they'd found her mother's body. Abel Griffin had marked the site with a tiny cross made of two Popsicle sticks that he'd glued to a tree.

She was back here, Erin thought. *During all that time that we were searching for her, she was behind this house, waiting for us to find her.*

She reached down and removed the thistle from her ankle. One of the thorns pierced the flesh of her thumb, and she watched as a small bead of blood rose to the surface.

It doesn't matter now, she told herself. *What's done is done. All of those things happened a long time ago.*

She turned around to face the back of the house. Here was the solid wooden door, a bit flimsier than the one in front.

Erin looked down at the metal instrument in her hand, a small crowbar she had brought from the truck.

What do you hope to find in there? she asked herself. *It's over. Why can't you leave it well enough alone?*

"Because part of me is still in there," she said, "and maybe the evidence of all those others he brought to this place."

She reached into her back pocket and pulled out her cell phone. She'd called and left Robbie a message that she was coming here. It hadn't seemed right to do this without him.

Erin looked down at the phone. On her home screen was a picture of her father and Diesel returning to the house from one of their walks. She'd taken it from the front porch three days ago, during the golden hour just before dusk. They were in midstride, not looking at the camera. To their right, tan slender blades of knee-high grass were bending toward them in the breeze.

"You didn't have to take the blame for us," she said, and clicked off the phone and returned it to her pocket.

She stepped forward and placed her hand on the back door. The wood felt cold and hard against her skin. She tried the doorknob and was surprised to find that it turned in her hand. The door itself resisted her efforts, and she put her shoulder against it and gave it a shove.

The door popped open and swung in on its hinges.

The interior hallway was dark, just as she remembered. For a moment, she could hear him in the kitchen, boiling the spaghetti in a pot and chopping hot dogs into fingertip-size pieces on the cutting board.

("Hut-two-three-four. Come on in and close the door.")

Erin stepped inside but left the back door open. She took a few steps down the hallway toward the front of the house. The black-and-white-checked tile sagged beneath her feet. Vacant picture hooks hung from the walls. She found a light switch and flipped it, but nothing happened. To her right was a bathroom, but the light didn't work in there, either. Most likely the electricity had been shut off a long time ago.

She came to a closed door on her left. Erin tried to open it but found that it was locked.

The back door was open, but this one is locked. Why would that be? she asked herself.

She considered going through the drawers and cabinets in an

effort to find a key. Instead, she placed the tip of the crowbar between the door edge and its frame. It took about ten seconds for her to pop it open, and she stepped inside and gave her eyes time to adjust to the darkness.

Should've brought a flashlight, she thought, but it didn't make sense to go back for one now. She stood there until the contents of the room came into focus, a collection of ill-defined masses of different shades of gray. She moved around the room and touched some of them: a chair stacked high with books; a collection of rubber boots and coats; cans of paint and a Shop-Vac in the corner; metal shelving with boxes of games and puzzles. There was nothing in here worth locking up, and she was about to leave before she saw it resting against the far wall next to a mop.

Erin stepped forward and ran her fingers along the plastic rim. It seemed smaller than she remembered. She lifted it up and felt the insignificance of its weight. She could still remember their conversation on the bus that day, while the snow was piling up on the streets and yards all around them.

("Jacob's Field, right? You going?")

("Yeah. Who else will be there?")

("Me, Deirdre, Robbie, Emily . . .") She ticked off the names of their friends in her head.

("I have to shovel the driveway before I go.")

("Can't you do it tomorrow?")

("No, I have to do it today. Otherwise it turns to ice and my dad gets mad.")

Erin brushed away the cobwebs from where they clung to the plastic sled. "I'm sorry," she whispered. "I'm sorry I didn't help you."

She carried it into the hallway, stood it up against the wall, and placed the crowbar at its base to anchor it so it wouldn't fall. *How many other things are in there?* she wondered. *How many of those coats and boots belonged to the people who went missing?*

She stood there in the hallway for a while, looking at the sled. She would take it with her when she left. It had already spent too many years locked away in this sad and forgotten place.

Erin sighed and walked to the kitchen. This was where Abel Griffin had stood at the counter and prepared their dinner. He hadn't seemed like a horrible person. Instead, he had spoken and behaved like a child. How had he managed to commit all of those abductions and never get caught? What had he done with the other bodies? She and her father hadn't found any other crosses back there in the marsh.

She turned to the living room. It was dark like the rest of the house, but she could make out the train track encircling the couch, the shape of the transit station and the little plastic people waiting for their ride. On the day she first came here, she had stepped on some of them, knocking them over. Her father had instructed them to put things back in order while he carried the body to the truck. It was important, he said, to erase any signs of a struggle.

It was strange how the past and the present melted into each other. In the dim light of the room, Erin could still see him sitting there on the couch. The television was off and there was nothing for him to look at, but he sat upright, facing forward in the dark, as if he, too, was waiting for a train that would never come.

She turned away from him and looked at the heavy front door from the inside. It had been difficult for her and Robbie to drag him across the yard and into the house. Getting him up the two steps to the level of the porch had been the hardest of all. *Dead weight,* people called it, and Erin shuddered as she pictured the way the shovel handle had bobbed up and down in the air as they moved him.

She turned back to the living room. The man's head had swiveled to the right. He was staring at her from his spot on the couch.

"What are you *doing* here?" he asked.

"*Oh . . . oh Jesus,*" Erin whispered. She scrambled around the table and put her back against the kitchen counter.

The man remained where he was, his body facing forward with his face turned toward the kitchen. It was a hallucination, pure and simple, or the trace of a memory that had come back to haunt her. She had watched him die. She had knelt in the grass beside him and held his hand as he slipped away. He had asked her, inexplicably, if they could be friends. Erin had told him yes, and then watched as her father buried him on the farm.

The man rose from the couch and began to walk toward her. There was something wrong with the shape of him. His body was shorter and wider than she remembered.

"No," Erin said. "You're not real. You're nothing but bones now. They dug you out of the ground a month ago."

The apparition stopped in the entryway to the kitchen. There was only the table between them.

"Erin Reece," the thing said, but it was not the deep rough voice she remembered, but something older and more feminine. "I was hoping that I'd get a chance to see you again. You've grown up a bit, although not for the better. You're still sneaking around, I see. You're still trespassing on other people's property."

"I didn't . . . I wasn't trying to . . ."

"What are you *doing* here? Haven't you learned by now that you ought to leave well enough alone?"

The figure took a half step forward, into the dim light that filtered through the window. It was Connie Griffin, a couple of decades older than the last time she'd seen her but still tall and stocky, with wide shoulders that gave rise to thick arms that barely tapered until they got to the wrists. Her gray hair was pulled up into its usual bun, but it was lopsided and slanted to the right, like a mound of melting ice cream, and clusters of untethered hair hung like vines along the sides of her face. The flesh beneath her eyes was dark and puckered, and the creases around her lips had deepened. She was in her mid-fifties now, Erin guessed, but she looked stronger and more hardened than the woman who had looked down at them from behind the concession counter of Prairie Cinemas.

"I came . . . to pay my respects," Erin told her. "Your son was—"

"Oh no," she said. "You don't get to talk about my son." Connie smiled with a mouth that was too small for her face. A row of densely packed teeth glinted and then disappeared in the space of a second. "You don't know anything about my boy," she said. "You have no idea what you and your father took from me."

"He was disturbed," Erin said. "Abel was killing people. He made a mistake when he killed my mother."

"My Abel was a *good* boy."

Erin shook her head. She reached back and felt the edge of the counter. "There were things you didn't know about him, things a mother never *wants* to know. That sled in the hallway belonged to Angela Finley. He kept it as a souvenir after he disposed of her body."

Connie turned and looked to her right, at the plastic sled standing upright against the wall. "That was *his* sled," she said, and she swiveled her head around again to look at Erin.

"No," Erin told her. "It belonged to Angela. I recognize it. The room where I found it is full of things like that. He kept them after he killed those people and got rid of their bodies. Your son was . . . he had a sickness. I'm sorry to have to tell you that."

Connie stood there and looked at Erin, her shoulders rising and falling with the rhythm of her breathing. "The things in that room don't *belong* to those people," she said. "Those were *his* things. He earned them. I told him he could keep them."

Erin stared at the woman on the other side of the table. "You *told* him he could . . . ?"

"Do you even *know* how his brother died? You found him, so I reckon I should ask you."

"He drowned," she said. "Abel's brother died in the river. Robbie and I found him along the north bank, facedown in the reeds."

"That was four days *after* he disappeared. He didn't die in the river, and it wasn't the fire that killed him, either."

"What fire?"

"The barn that burned to the ground the day Miles went missing. They chased Abel inside, then lit the place on fire and watched it burn."

"Who?"

"Local kids," she said, "a whole bunch of them. Abel pointed them out to me, every last one. At first he was afraid to tell me about *any* of it. He said he didn't know about the fire. But he came to me eventually and told me what he did."

Erin shook her head. "I don't underst—"

"Miles went in there to try to save him. But Miles died and Abel lived. Afterward, Abel carried him down to the river."

"Why?"

Connie shrugged and placed her hand on the back of one of

the wooden chairs at the table. "He was trying to save him," she said. "The boys were baptized in the river three years before. Abel remembered how Pastor Kimble had talked about being 'born again.' He thought that maybe . . . if he carried his brother to the river and put him in . . ."

Erin nodded, but her mind kept returning to what the woman had said earlier.

("The things in that room don't *belong* to those people. Those were *his* things. He earned them. I told him he could keep them.")

"And then what?" Erin asked. "He started killing people?"

Connie shook her head. "He started *collecting* them, the ones who set that barn on fire or members of their families." She reached up and touched the side of her face with the palm of her hand. *Got . . . something stuck . . . here,* Erin heard in the back of her mind, and it wasn't the voice of the son or the mother but something in between.

"We began with Angela Finley," Connie said. "She chased my Abel in there and watched the place burn with the rest of them. But after that *first one* I got to thinking: there's more pain in losing someone you love than there is in being taken yourself. The loss of Miles helped me understand that. During the funeral, I sat at his graveside and asked God why he hadn't taken me instead. It's what I wanted. It's what a merciful God would've done."

She took a deep breath and let it out. Her face was cast in shadows, and her voice wavered as she spoke, the sound of someone who has been beaten into submission but doesn't understand the reason why.

"God has never been merciful to me or my family," she said. "On the other hand, he *has* taught me a few lessons about pain and loss. It's so much worse to be the one left behind. You understand that . . . don't you, dear?"

Erin swallowed. She felt a click in her throat.

"After Angela," Connie said, "I decided to take a member of each of their families and leave the children behind. It was better that way, more effective. They'd grow up as lost souls. They'd never stop paying for the things they took from me."

Erin placed a hand on the counter, her legs weak and unpredictable beneath her. "All of those people," she whispered, the weight of it pressing down upon her. It was not just the loss of *so many* lives, but the pain and horror left in their wake. "What did he do with them?" she asked. "Did he torture them and bury them in the marsh like my mother?"

"No," she said. "You haven't been listening. My Abel was a *good* boy. He collected them and brought them to me."

Erin was silent, staring back at her. The man who had killed her mother wasn't the monster she had once imagined him to be. The true monster was standing right in front of her.

"In a way," Connie said, "I'm thankful that they found him on your father's farm. I wasn't certain what had happened to him. I thought maybe he'd decided to run away. Children do that sometimes, you know. They head out on their own thinking things will be better, but their lives are almost always worse because of it." She glanced toward the window, and the flesh of her face looked pale and tired in the darkness. "No one will ever love them like their mother."

Erin scanned the counter, her eyes falling on the knife rack to the right of the sink.

"It's the pain," Connie continued. "There is no end to the amount of pain we are willing to endure for the sake of our children. And there is no end," she said, "to the amount of pain we are willing to inflict on those who take them away from us."

Erin lunged for the knife rack. She pulled out the one with

the largest handle, a chef knife with a broad blade that felt lethal in her hand. "Please," she said, "it can be over. We don't have to—"

"Oh, but I *want* to," she said. "I've been sitting here in the dark, missing my boys and thinking about how I'm going to get to you and your father. And then you just show up, like a gift from the heavens. Maybe I was wrong," she said. "Maybe God is finally paying me back for all the times that he did me wrong."

Erin pressed her back against the corner of the counter. There was a small wooden table between them. It didn't seem like very much at all.

Connie studied her for a moment. Then she turned and walked down the hallway. A moment later, the plastic sled clattered to the floor.

She reappeared in the entryway to the kitchen, holding the crowbar. Her arms hung loose and casual at her sides, but her head was flexed slightly at the neck, and her eyes were on the knife.

"It's going to get ugly after this," she said. "Do you want to take a moment to enjoy the way your body feels before I begin to take it apart?"

"*Please,*" Erin said. "It doesn't have to be like this. I don't want to have to kill y—"

Connie let out a cry that started deep in her throat and rose in pitch and volume until it filled the house. It reminded Erin of the sound that Robbie had made before he buried the blade of the shovel in Abel's head.

The crowbar flashed in the slanted light from the window as Connie raised it above her head. She was still screaming, and Erin caught a glimpse of the metal against the darkness of the hall. Connie threw it with both hands, the bar turning once in the air on its flight across the kitchen. It struck a glancing blow to the side of Erin's face, smashing into her cheekbone and slamming her head against the wooden cabinet behind her.

A moment later Erin was on the floor, the palms of her hands pressed against the tile. Her left eye had stopped working, and the vision through her right eye was teared and blurry. She could see blood on the floor, large drops that fell from her face and spattered on the black-and-white-checked tiles.

She put a hand to her head to search for the place where her skull had been split apart. Would she find the wound, she wondered, or part of her brain bulging out through the opening? She had seen the weapon coming and had flinched to the right, avoiding a direct hit. Maybe that was why she wasn't dead already.

Her fingers found a gash in the left side of her face. The flesh around her left eye had swollen shut. It was hard to know whether there was anything left of the eye itself.

The woman was still screaming. Erin looked up in time to see her raise the small wooden table like a battering ram before she ran across the kitchen with the table out in front of her.

Erin wrapped her arms around her head as the table slammed into her and she was shoved back against the lower cabinets. Something in her neck snapped, and she felt the crunch of ribs along the left side of her chest. She struggled to suck in a breath as the tabletop pressed down on her, the woman throwing her ample weight against it from the other side.

(*There's a knife. You dropped it when you got hit with the crowbar.*)

A knife, she thought, and she placed her right hand on the floor to search for it. It was just cold tile beneath her, that and the slick feel of blood and whatever else was leaking from her body.

(*Get the knife. Find it! It's important.*)

Above her, Connie was still pressing down on the table. She had stopped screaming at least, and in the silence Erin heard the *shink* of something being pulled from a sheath. Erin recognized that sound. She had heard it a few minutes ago, just before the attack.

(*She's pulled a knife from the rack above you. She's going to jab it into your head or the side of your neck!*)

Erin felt cold steel with the tips of her fingers: the knife, lying beneath her. She followed the blade until she found the handle, wrapped her palm around it, and pressed herself low against the tiles. There was an opening between the edge of the table and the floor. She stuck her foot into the space to keep it open, then reached through with her free hand and found the woman's ankle.

A two-pronged carving fork came plunging down at her from above. The tips of the prongs pierced the air where Erin's head had been a few seconds before.

(*Do something! Do something to defend yourself!*)

She cupped her free hand around the back of the woman's ankle and shoved the knife into her lower leg as hard as she could. There wasn't much room between the edge of the table and the floor, and she couldn't see where the blade was going. She could feel it, though, the knife stabilizing as it entered the flesh. There was a sickening density to it, a slowing of the blade as it sliced through muscle.

Connie howled and tried to jerk away. Erin let go of the handle, but kept her left hand cupped around the back of the woman's ankle. The heel pulled tight against her palm, and a moment later Connie toppled backward and the table slid away from her.

Erin got to her feet and lurched down the hall toward the

door at the rear of the house. She could hear the table moving, the sound of Connie struggling to get up again. Would she be able to walk with the knife in her leg? *It doesn't matter,* Erin thought. *Get the hell out! Leave this house and Wolf Point, too, if it lets you.* It had been a mistake to return here. The separation between life and death was too thin. Nothing rested, on this side or the other.

She reached the open door and tumbled out into the yard. Here she was again, and for a few seconds she actually saw him, standing in the grass at the corner of the house. He put his hand on the metal wheels of the toy locomotive and gave them a spin.

Erin blinked and the man was gone—not a man, really, but a child in a man's body. She could hear his mother in the house, lumbering down the hallway.

Erin got to her feet and backed away from the open door. The hallway was dark on the other side of it.

(*Go! Don't wait for her! She's got the carving fork and the crowbar, and a lot more in store for you if you give her the chance.*)

The door slammed shut with a bang. Erin screamed and stumbled backward.

(*Go! Go go go!*)

She raced through the yard, the weeds snatching at her ankles. The truck was parked against the curb. She ran to it, her right hand digging for the keys in her pocket.

(*You lost them in the house. They fell out when you were lying on the floor.*)

No, she realized. Here they were. Her fingers closed around them and she pulled them out. The teeth snagged on the lining of her pocket, and the keys almost fell from her hand.

(*Don't drop them. If you drop them, you keep right on running.*)

She closed her hand around them and kept running. She was

near the front corner now. The house would be behind her in a second.

There was sudden movement to her right. Connie came off the front porch at the corner, head down and legs pumping. She didn't so much tackle Erin as run into her full force, their bodies colliding like sumo wrestlers.

They crumpled to the ground, and Connie landed on top of her, forcing the air from Erin's lungs. She wrapped her pudgy hands around Erin's neck and squeezed, her fingers sinking into the flesh.

"Gonna show you pain," she said. She lifted Erin's head by the neck and slammed it against the earth.

Connie's mouth was stretched into a half grin, half grimace. Most of her hair had pulled free of the bun. What was left of the bun leaned so far to the right that it hovered over her ear, as if that part of her head was somehow melting. Her eyes were wild but triumphant. "Aaauuuuggghhh!" she screamed. "Now we'll see where your train is going."

"Go to hell," Erin told her, but her voice was barely more than a whisper. She reached up to push the woman away, but her arms felt distant and disconnected from her body.

Connie lifted her by the neck again so that their faces were almost touching. Her breath was old and stale, like the air in a forgotten closet. "Don't you worry, child," she said, and she squeezed tighter. "Hell ain't that far from here. I know the way. We'll be gettin' there soon enough."

39

THEY BURIED ABEL GRIFFIN AT THE REAR END OF THE PROPERTY, AS far from the house as possible. David used the tractor's backhoe to dig up the earth and to fill it back in again. He'd never been able to grow anything good at that spot, and it seemed like an appropriate place for a man with nothing good about him. It was the acidity of the soil, maybe, the way the land responded in some areas but not in others. People were like that, too, he imagined. There were a few—a small minority—who were unsalvageable.

There was nothing ceremonial in the burial of Abel Griffin. David dug a hole, kicked in the body, and filled in the dirt. He'd taken greater care with Helen, of course, exhuming her remains from the marsh and reburying his wife beneath the oak tree next to the home they'd shared for fifteen years. David wished it could've been longer, the time they'd spent together. He'd wanted to grow old with her, the decades passing as they moved through the varying struggles and goodness of their lives. He'd imagined them in their eighties, sitting next to each other on the porch swing, the sun low in the sky as lengthening shadows filled the yard. When night fell, they would go inside and fall asleep to the familiar sounds of a house that was still settling on its foundation. It wouldn't happen now. He would grow old without her. If he made it to his eighties, he would sit on the porch swing alone and sleep in a place that whispered her name.

David buried his wife with the help of the children. He'd called Robbie's mother and asked if her son could spend the night on the farm. "We're going to build a bonfire and roast marshmallows," he said. "The kids are looking forward to it." And true to his word, David put them to work doing just that while he carried what was left of Helen to the barn and built her a modest casket. It was a simple thing, constructed of wooden planks and nails. When it was done, he laid her inside and folded the skeletal remains of her hands across her middle. It was the position in which she usually slept, and David told himself that now that his wife was home, she could finally rest.

It was almost morning by the time they were finished. All three of them carried the casket from the barn to the oak tree and lowered it into the ground. He'd used the tractor to dig the hole, but they filled it in with shovels, sprinkling the dirt gently over the wooden box.

They worked in silence. When the hole was filled, they tamped it down with their feet and sat next to the remnants of the bonfire: a collection of charred wood with embers glowing in the ashes.

"She's . . . home," David said, but his throat tightened on the second word and he looked away from them, his rough and calloused hands clenched at his sides.

Robbie extended his leg and toed one of the remaining logs. It crumpled and mixed with the ashes.

"They'll find out I killed him," he said. "They'll call me a murderer. That man is dead because of me."

David took a moment to compose himself, then reached over and placed a hand on Robbie's shoulder. "You're not a murderer," he said. "You saved my daughter's life. If you hadn't gone there—if you hadn't done what you did—Erin would be buried in the marsh now alongside of her mother."

Robbie's eyes were still on the fire. He was fifteen—a year older than Erin—tall and well-muscled. Ten hours ago, he'd buried the blade of a shovel in a man's skull, so deep that it had taken all of David's strength to pry it loose. Still, he looked scared and vulnerable as he sat there staring at what was left of the fire. His legs were pulled tight against his chest, his arms crossed in front of his body. He rocked a bit as his eyes moved back and forth across the embers.

"I'll go to prison," the boy said. "I won't survive in a place like that."

"Son," David said, and he waited for the boy to look at him, "you will never go to prison. I'll take the blame myself if it comes to that."

"He was going to kill her," Robbie whispered. "He was dragging her back to the house."

"I know. You did the right thing. You have nothing to be ashamed of."

Robbie searched their faces. He appeared lost, as if he'd just stepped through a door with nothing on the other side of it but empty space. He was falling now, and it seemed to David that he might go right on falling, and maybe there was nothing they could do to catch him.

"I'm not a murderer," he said. "I never meant for him to die like that."

Erin scooted over and wrapped her arm around her friend's

shoulder. She rested her forehead against his temple and spoke to him in a volume that was too low for David to decipher.

David turned his head and studied the horizon as the sky lightened above them. They were quiet for a while, each of them lost in their own contemplations.

David stood up and stretched. "We should get some sleep," he said. "I'll wash your clothes while you take a shower." He looked at Robbie. "There's a spare bedroom where you can lie down for a few hours before I take you home. I've got some shorts and a T-shirt you can borrow in the meantime. They'll be too big for you, but it's only for sleeping."

"I'm not tired," Robbie said. "I don't think I can fall asleep."

"You should get cleaned up and try. We all should. Things will look better after we get some rest."

They went inside and washed away the evidence of the things they had done that night. There was blood on their clothes, and David did his best to get rid of the stains. There was blood beneath his fingernails, too, and he reminded himself to check the children's nails after they woke.

He'll talk, David thought. *Maybe they both will. It won't be long before I have to explain what I've done here.*

It didn't matter. Helen was home now, at least for a while. As for the children, he would do what he could to protect them.

He made a pot of coffee and sat on the porch swing as the sun crested the horizon. He could see the oak tree from here. Its limbs swayed in the shifting morning breeze.

"I'm sorry this happened to you," he said, and he closed his eyes and listened to see if Helen would say anything in return.

40

(October 1995)

ABEL GRIFFIN RAN FROM HOUSE TO HOUSE, COLLECTING HIS CANDY. He had dressed as a scarecrow this year, and his skin itched from the straw stuffed beneath his clothing. He wore a funny-looking hat with a wide brim, and a raggedy shirt and pants that his mother had bought for him from the clearance section of Bryan's department store off Main Street. "You're sixteen, man," his brother said, "too old for trick-or-treating." But Miles had driven him anyway, dropping him off in the neighborhood before heading off to see his friends.

"There's a party over on Granville," Miles said. "I'll be there for a while. Swing on by when you're done with this kiddie stuff."

Abel nodded. He held a plastic pumpkin bucket in his right hand and used the other hand to scratch at his shoulder. "I'll get you some candy," he said. "Maybe they'll have some Kit Kats. You still like those, don'tcha, Miles?"

His brother smiled. "Yeah, I guess. Bring me a Kit Kat and I'll get you a beer when you come to the party."

Abel made a face. "Beer tastes gross," he said. "They got any soda?"

Miles shrugged. "I don't know. You'll have to see when you get there. You got your watch?"

Abel looked down at his wrist and nodded.

"Good. It's seven-thirty. Meet me at Charlie Husker's place at nine. It's two blocks over. It'll be the house with all the people and music."

"Okay, Miles," he said, and ran off to get started.

This was a good neighborhood for Halloween. The first house Abel came to had a thick cobweb along its walkway and a black spider the size of a dog clinging to its threads. The spider came to life as he approached it, the body quivering and the eyes flashing red. Abel took a few steps backward, summoning up the courage to walk past it.

Two small kids raced by him on their way to the front door, but Abel stood there, looking at the spider.

"Out of the way, scarecrow," an older kid said, and he bumped Abel on purpose as he and his friends walked past him on the sidewalk.

"Hey, Vinny," one of them said, "this guy's, like . . . forty."

The boy in front turned and looked at Abel. "Hey, creeper," he said. "Don't be telling these youngsters to reach into your pants to get the lollipop."

The other boys screeched with laughter.

Abel felt his face redden, although it was dark out so no one else could see. *I'm not a creeper,* he thought, but he didn't understand what they meant by it anyway. He *liked* Halloween, that was all. He could dress up as anything he wanted and run around at night collecting goodies that would last him the *entire year* if he didn't eat too much all at once.

Abel walked to the front door of the house. There were

three small kids in front of him. He stood behind them and waited his turn.

A woman stood in the doorway, handing out the candy. "Are these your kids?" she asked, and Abel shook his head no. He didn't have any kids. He didn't even have a girlfriend.

"Trick or treat," he said, and he smiled, hoping for a Kit Kat.

She paused. "Wait a minute. Is that you, Abel?"

"Yes, ma'am."

"You look different this year. You've gotten even taller. Did your brother come with you?"

"He's getting beer," he said.

The woman laughed. "Okay, I'll bet he is."

"Do you have any Kit Kats?" Abel asked her. "Miles likes Kit Kats."

The woman looked down into her plastic bag. "I'm afraid not," she said. "I have raisins, gummy worms, and snack-size Heath bars."

Abel thought about it. "I don't know," he said. "He likes Kit Kats."

She reached into the bag and brought out a Heath bar. "Try this," she said, dropping it into his bucket. "Maybe your brother will appreciate something new."

"Thank you," Abel said, and he was off to the next house in search of more Halloween treasure.

It went that way for about an hour. During that time, Abel covered just about every house in the neighborhood. A few of the houses were dark, and some of the people told him he was *too old* for trick-or-treating and refused to give him any candy. He got something from most of the houses, though, and his pumpkin bucket was almost full. Abel looked down at his watch. It was a digital because the other type was too confusing to read. It glowed in the dark when he pushed a button on the side of it. The watch read 8:35 P.M. He had twenty-five minutes left before he had to go meet Miles at the party.

"Hey, creeper," someone said, and Abel turned to see the boy they'd called Vinny walking up to him. A small crowd of kids followed from behind.

Vinny stopped a foot in front of him, and the rest of them spread out in a half-circle around him.

Abel looked from one face to the next. He recognized most of them, and he wondered if they recognized him in his costume. He removed his hat to make it easier for them to see his face.

"What are you *doing here,* creeper?" Vinny asked. "You like hangin' around little kids in their tights and pajamas?"

Abel shrugged. He didn't mind little kids. They left him alone mostly.

"Yeah, I'll bet that's it," Vinny said. "You like hangin' around the little ones so you can show them your lollipop."

Abel looked down at his bucket. He had a few lollipops. He wondered if any of them were root beer, his favorite.

"You gonna show me your lollipop? Let's see it. Probably all shriveled up like a worm." Vinny looked back at the others, and they laughed. "Take it out, then," he said. "Show us what you got."

Abel looked at them again, hesitated, and reached into his pumpkin.

The boy reached out and knocked it from his hand. The plastic bucket fell to the pavement. Its contents spilled out onto the street and scattered in every direction.

"Oh, gross," Vinny said. "Did you see that? He was gonna *do it,* too. He was gonna reach in there and yank out good ol' Mr. Creepy."

Abel shook his head and stomped his feet. His candy was lying in the road. He bent over and tried to pick it up.

"Leave it," the kid said, and he kicked him in the seat of his pants.

Abel stood up and pushed the kid backward. He didn't like being kicked in the bottom, and the boy had already stepped on some of his candy. It wasn't a hard push, but it was harder than Abel had intended. Vinny was much smaller than Abel, maybe nine or ten, and the force of the shove was enough to send him stumbling backward. He tripped over his feet and went down in the road.

"*Hey. Hey, asshole,*" a larger boy called out to him from across the street. He was almost as tall as Abel, but not as wide in the shoulders. He crossed the street, and a few others joined him, drawn by the commotion. "That's my brother you just pushed. How'd you like me to smash your teeth in?"

A girl reached out and put her hand on the boy's arm. "Come on, Nick. He didn't mean nothin' by it. Let's get outta here, okay?"

"Shut up, Katey," he said. "This guy's been comin' here for years. He's big, but he's stupid. If he wants to push kids, he can push me." He put his hands on Abel's chest and gave him a shove. "What about it, huh? You wanna fight someone your own size for a change?"

Abel shook his head. He didn't want to fight anyone. His candy was all over the road. Most of it had already been trampled.

SNAP! Something went off close to his feet.

SNAP! SNAP!

Flashes of light. Like angry fireflies, biting at his ankles.

"*Bees!*" one of them yelled. "*Killer bees in the roadway!*"

Abel's eyes grew wide with terror. Another flash of light went off at his feet, and he turned and ran. He was allergic to bees. If one of their stingers poked through his skin, he'd swell up for sure. Miles too. Both of them had been to the emergency department when they were younger.

"*Here come the bees!*" they yelled, and they followed him down the street.

No, Abel thought. *I can't get stung. Mother said I could die if I did.* He ran along the street—a man-size scarecrow fleeing the swarm—and the rest of them ran after him, screaming in pain.

The road turned left at the end of the street, but Abel didn't follow it. He ran through the field, heading for the trees on the other side. The others were right behind him, howling from the bee stings. He looked back once. They were spread out along the horizon—ghosts and goblins and pirates and monsters—but under the costumes they were just kids, running for their lives, same as him.

He ran through the trees. Branches scratched at his face. He wove through the trunks like a football player returning a punt, and when he emerged on the other side, he saw a house in the distance. *If I can get to that,* he thought, and he ran as hard as he could, the cool night air turning to fire and burning in his chest.

He could still hear them behind him, but their voices were spread out and distant. *Maybe some of them are dead,* he thought, and he wondered if maybe he should go back to help them.

("Don't you get stung, Abel," his mother told him. "You do whatever it takes to stay away from them.")

The house was closer now, and Abel slowed but kept running. *Why are there so many bees?* he wondered. *Why have they come out at night when they usually wait for the sunshine?*

He was almost there, but as he drew nearer Abel realized his error. This was not a house at all, but a barn. Most likely, it would have no people inside, no one who could help him. *It doesn't matter,* he decided. *It'll have to do.* The muscles of his legs ached from the running. He would go inside and close the door. When the others arrived, they could do the same.

Abel reached the barn, grabbed the handle of the large sliding door, and opened it just enough to slip inside.

It was dark in here, and he couldn't find the light switch. He waited a minute or two for his eyes to adjust. There was a tractor, and bales of hay stacked one on top of the other. Above him was a loft, and a wooden ladder to climb up there if anyone wanted.

Something banged against the side of the barn, and Abel jumped.

"Hello?" he said, but no one answered. A few seconds later something else banged against the other side.

He stood there and listened. The banging noises were all around him now, a rumbling thunder from every side.

"Wooooo–woooooooo–wooooooo–wooooooooo . . ."

BANG-BANG-BANG-BANG . . .

Abel covered his ears. He could still hear them, hammering away at the side of the barn.

BANG-BANG-BANG-BANG . . .

"Wooooooo–wooooooooo–wooooooooo–woooooooo . . ."

"Go away. Leave me *alone!*" he yelled, but they kept right on drumming with their hands and feet. *BANG-BANG-BANG-BANG-BANG-BANG*. Abel lowered his head and moaned.

The door slid open on its track.

Oh no, he thought, and he ran for the ladder. He tripped over a stack of cans lying on the floor and almost fell. Two of the cans toppled over. Something oily that smelled like pine trees spilled out of one of them, getting on his shoes and the legs of his pants.

SNAP! SNAP! The bees were in the barn now, their bodies exploding in tiny flashes of light.

Someone flipped on the light, and Abel scampered up the ladder to the overhead loft. When he reached the platform, he looked down to find one of the older kids, Craig Raffey, climbing up behind him. Abel grabbed the top of the ladder and shook it. The kid jumped off, falling a few rungs to the floor below but landing on his feet.

"Hey, what's *wrong* with you? You trying to make me fall?"

"Leave me alone," Abel said, and he pushed the ladder away from him. It teetered for a moment, the top of it thirty feet in the air.

"*Watch out! It's gonna fall!*" someone yelled, and they scattered to the edges of the interior as the ladder tipped over and clattered to the floor.

"Hey, idiot," the kid named Nick called up to him. "Nice going. You almost hit Angela right in the head." He kicked one of the overturned cans. It skittered across the floorboards and banged against the far wall.

"Josh, give me some of them poppers."

"He's had enough, Vinny, leave him alone."

"Mind your business, Stacey. He almost smashed your friend's head in. Stupid kid needs to be taught a lesson."

SNAP! Flash of light on the support beam to Abel's right. He scooted away from the edge and hid behind a bale of hay at the back of the loft.

"Come on. Let's go."

"I'm not done with him yet."

"Yes, you are. He's stuck up there with no ladder. It could be *days* before old man Turner wanders out here and finds him."

"Maybe. But he should take a beating for shoving me. That's what I think."

"This is worse. Let him enjoy the stench of this place. What was that thing your brother kicked over?"

"I don't know. Smells like pine farts. Hey, Josh, you got a smoke?"

They stayed there for a while, talking and lobbing poppers into the loft. Abel cowered in the back, crouched low behind the bales of hay. He had to pee. If he didn't pee soon, he was going to wet his pants.

"I'm leaving," the girl named Angela said. "You can hang out here with the creeper if you want to."

"Is he still up there?" one of them asked. "Hey, creeper. What are you *doing* up there?"

Abel shook his head and didn't answer.

"Come on. Let's go, Vinny. You comin'?"

It took the mean boy a few seconds to answer. "Yeah, okay. Turn off the light and let him sit in the dark."

The light went off. Abel heard the barn door open and close again.

It's a trick, he thought. *They're still down there. They'll get me if I climb down the ladder.*

But no, that wasn't true, he realized. He couldn't *get* to the ladder. It was lying on the floor, thirty feet below.

(*Why did you push it away? Why did you do that? You can't get down now. You're stuck up here forever.*)

He hit himself in the head with the side of his fist. *Stupid,* he thought. *Why am I always so stupid?*

He stood up. It was dark in the barn, and scary. He had to pee. He couldn't hold it any longer.

Abel walked to the edge of the loft, feeling with his foot as he got closer. He would pee off the edge to the floor below. That way, he wouldn't be stuck up here with the smell of it.

He was wearing green sweatpants stuffed with straw. He undid the drawstring and lowered his pants to his knees. Clumps of straw fell to the floor. Some of it had worked its way under the waistband of his underwear.

Abel pulled down his underwear and peed off the edge of the loft. The stream disappeared into the darkness, but he could hear the spatter of it as it struck the floor below. It was a relief to empty his bladder. He closed his eyes and sighed. Now that it was done, he could concentrate on getting out of here.

(*Miles will be worried about you. You were supposed to meet him at the party at nine.*)

Abel pulled up his pants and tied the drawstring. He pressed the button on his watch that lit up the numbers. It was 9:35. He was late. Very late. His brother would be angry.

"I'm giving you this watch so you can be responsible," his mother had told him. "I want you to know when it's time to come home."

Abel had nodded. He loved his watch, and he was proud to wear it. It was a very special thing. He wanted to be responsible. He did not want to disappoint them.

He paced back and forth in the loft. *How am I going to get down?* he wondered. It was too high to jump. He would break his leg, especially in the darkness. If he could find a rope, then maybe he could lower himself to the—

SNAP!

Abel shrieked and jumped backward. He was lucky he wasn't closer to the edge.

I stepped on one of them. I stepped on one of the—he tried to remember what the boy had called it—*poppers.*

He bent down and picked it up. It was just a little bit of paper with something rolled inside of it. He got down on his hands and knees to look for more of them, the ones that hadn't popped when they landed.

Abel crawled around the loft. He found three of them, little balls of paper with one end twisted around itself like a tail. He threw one of them off the edge. It snapped when it hit the floor.

Abel smiled. *Poppers. Snappers.* He could think of all kinds of names to call them. They were fun when you knew what they were.

He threw another one. It hit the metal side of the tractor. *SNAP!*

These were the bees the kids had been yelling about, but they weren't bees at all. He threw another one off the edge and it snapped in the darkness.

Abel searched for more. Three wasn't that many. The kids had thrown a bunch at him, and not all of them had popped.

He found two more and crawled to the edge, but there was something else down there: a row of tiny dancing flames, creeping along the floorboards.

Fire, he thought, alarmed by the sight of it.

It spread quickly, moving across the floor and up the sides of the barn. *Oh no,* Abel thought. This was worse than bees. He was trapped up here in the loft. He could feel the heat from it already.

Smoke filled the space above him. When he looked up, he could no longer see the rafters.

"*Help!*" Abel yelled. "Someone, please. *The barn is on fire!*"

I'll have to jump. I can't stay up here much longer.

He looked down. The entire floor was ablaze beneath him. The inside of the barn was starting to feel a lot like an oven.

(*You'll be jumping right into the fire. You'll burn up if you touch it.*)

The flames crackled all around him as the place filled with smoke. *Oh no, oh no,* he thought. What was he supposed to do?

"Think, Abel. *Think!*" He hit himself in the side of the head with both hands—*whack, whack!*—and tried to come up with a plan.

The flames continued to spread around him. They were everywhere—on the floor and walls and even the ceiling. The barn was thick with smoke. He coughed but couldn't breathe. His eyes burned from the sting of it.

The barn door slid open and someone stood in the doorway. Abel could see the dark shape of him through the smoke.

"*Abel! Abel, are you in here?*"

"Miles," he yelled, relieved to hear the sound of his brother's voice. "I'm stuck up here and I can't get out."

"Where are you?"

"*Up here, in the loft.*"

"Is there a ladder?"

"On the floor," he said. "It fell and I can't get to it."

Miles ran into the barn, right through the flames. He was beneath him now, searching for the ladder.

"I see it," he said. He bent over and tried to pick it up, but withdrew his hand, cursing. "It's on fire. It's too hot. I can't pick it up."

"*Help me, Miles! Help me get out of here!*"

Miles looked up. Abel could see his face directly below him.

"I can't jump," he said. "It's too high."

Miles coughed. "You don't have a choice. You've *got* to jump. You jump or you'll die in here. Do you understand me?"

"Okay," he said. "You'll catch me, Miles? You'll catch me, you promise?"

The smoke was thicker now. He could no longer see his brother.

"Lower yourself over the edge as far as you can go. Let go and I'll catch you. *Do it now,*" Miles said. "Do it *right now* and I'll catch you."

Abel lay flat on his tummy and lowered himself over the

edge. His feet dangled in the air. Somewhere below him his brother was waiting.

"Let go, Abel. Let go and I'll catch—"

There was a loud crack and suddenly Abel was falling. He was still holding on to the wood, and it seemed like the entire loft was falling with him. He struck something and then struck the floor. Several pieces of wood tumbled on top of him.

Abel pushed the boards off and got to his feet. *He had made it!* He'd jumped and Miles had caught him, just like he'd promised.

"Let's get *out* of here," Abel said, and he reached down to help up his brother. His fingers touched wood, and he moved the boards to the side until he uncovered the shape of him.

"Miles," he said. "Miles, we have to go." Abel shook him, but his body was limp and silent. "Hey," Abel said, and he shook him again.

He grabbed Miles by the arm and dragged him to the doorway. There was a crack and an explosion of embers as another part of the loft gave way above them and crashed to the floor. Abel kept going, dragging his brother out of the barn and across the field until he could no longer feel the heat of the fire on his skin. "Miles," he said. He let go of his arm and got down on his knees beside him. He slapped him lightly on the cheek. "Wake up," he said. "Wake up, it's time to go."

Miles lay there without moving.

Abel wiped the soot from his brother's face. He shook him again. "Come on," he said. "We've got to get going."

Nothing. Abel looked back over his shoulder. The barn was engulfed in flames. They had gotten out just in time.

Those kids did this, he thought. *Those kids made this happen.*

"Miles, what's wrong with you?" He grabbed him by the

shoulders and turned him back and forth, back and forth. His brother's head rolled to one side. There was something pushing up from beneath the skin of his neck. Abel touched it with the tip of his finger. It felt hard, like the edge of a stone.

Abel heard a siren in the distance. The police were coming. He was going to get in trouble for burning down Bill Turner's barn.

He looked down at his brother. "Hey," he said, "you want me to carry you?"

Miles didn't answer, so Abel picked him up in his arms and carried him away from the barn and across the field. He wasn't sure where he was going, but he knew that he couldn't stay here. If the police found him sitting in the grass near the burning structure, they would blame him for sure. "They'll tell Mother," he said, and he shuddered at the thought of it.

He kept walking until they got to the river, where he lowered his brother's body to the bank. He couldn't go any farther. Miles was big like him and too heavy to carry for very long. Abel shook him a few more times and called his name, but he wouldn't wake up and it was hard to tell if Miles was even breathing.

Maybe he's dead, Abel thought, and a moan escaped the back of his throat.

"*You* did this," he told himself. "*You* landed on him when you fell."

I can make it better, he thought, but he didn't know how. He couldn't go to his mother or the police, and he didn't have any friends who could help him. Pastor Kimble had always told him that the best thing to do when you've done something wrong is to apologize and make it right. But how could he make *this* right? How could he undo this thing that had happened to his brother?

"Salvation is easier than you think," the pastor told them on the day Miles and Abel were baptized down here at the river. "Confess your sins and ask the Lord for forgiveness. God is always willing to give you a second chance. He's stronger than death. He's stronger than any problem you'll ever face."

Abel had liked the sound of that, a God that was always watching out for him.

"Today you are born again in the eyes of God," the pastor continued. "May the healing powers of these waters restore you."

Abel pulled off his boots and socks and waded into the water. It was freezing, like ice picks in his skin, but as he stood there beneath the night sky the cold began to soften. He remembered the way he'd felt that day, on the day of their baptism. He hadn't understood everything the pastor had said, but he *had* felt protected and cared for. It was nice to know that no matter how much he messed things up, God was willing to give him a second chance. God was stronger than death. He was stronger than any problem Abel would ever face.

He reached back and pulled his brother to the edge of the water.

"Do you remember, Miles?" he asked. "Do you remember what Pastor Kimble said that day?" Miles didn't answer, but Abel scooped up a handful of water and placed it on his forehead. "You'll be better," he said. "God will fix you."

He stood there in the water with his brother on the bank beside him, until Abel's feet were so cold that he could no longer feel them. He got out, fetched his socks and boots, and lay down on the bank next to Miles. The sky was vast above them. He looked up at the stars and tried to pray, but Abel was cold and tired and eventually he fell asleep.

He awoke two hours later, the river lapping at his shoulder.

Abel sat up to find himself alone along the water's edge, his brother gone, no matter how frantically he searched for him.

God has taken him and will bring him back, he told himself, and that was true, although Miles was no better when they found him along the riverbank a mile to the east four days later. Less than a week after that, his brother was buried, and his mother's sadness was like nothing he had ever seen. It would be a month before he told her what had happened, and everything that followed was an attempt to make it better.

41

ERIN OPENED HER EYES IN THE DARK, HER BODY PRESSED AGAINST the floor. She felt movement, then a sudden jolt from below. *Where am I?* she wondered, and the first realization that occurred to her was that she wasn't dead. Not yet anyway. She had been hit in the face with a crowbar, and something else had happened after that. Or maybe it was before. It was hard to remember the order of things. There had been an electric train on a track, and tiny plastic people waiting for a ride. *Thank you for visiting Wolf Point,* she thought. *All departures have been canceled for the day.*

Erin tried to swallow. Her neck felt thick and swollen, and the cartilage clicked as it moved. Someone had knocked her to the ground and then choked her into unconsciousness. She could picture the woman's face looming over her, her eyes bulging in their sockets.

("What are you *doing* here? Haven't you learned by now that you ought to leave well enough alone?")

The space around her wasn't completely dark. Her left eye was swollen shut, but she could see part of the floor and could feel fabric against her skin: a blanket maybe, thrown on top of her. Erin tried to push it off, but her arms were behind her back, bound at the wrists.

Squeak of hinges. The heavy *chunk* of a door as it swung shut.

Erin bent her knees and tried to get to her feet, but her ankles were bound together as well. She heard the soft crunch of footsteps on gravel. Then another door opened and the blanket was pulled off her, letting in faded sunlight through a rectangular window caked with dirt.

She could see the swell of a wheel well and felt a seat pressed against the top of her head. She was lying in the back of an SUV. Connie Griffin was standing beneath the open hatch.

Connie grabbed hold of the duct tape wrapped around Erin's ankles and jerked her out. Erin's body slid along the floor of the truck. As soon as her shoulder cleared the bumper, Connie let go of her feet, and Erin fell to the dirt driveway, landing on her side. The impact was like running full speed into a wall. She heard something snap—her collarbone, maybe—and a jolt of pain exploded in her right shoulder. She gritted her teeth against the agony, until it settled down and mixed with the rest of the things that were already broken.

Connie's shoes were directly in front of her, brown sneakers with tan laces. *Sensible shoes,* Erin's mother would've called them, although the pants—white capris with grass stains and a hole torn in one of the knees—were less appropriate for the weather. There was a deep gash in her left lower leg about two inches above the ankle. Blood had dried against the skin like the remains of a tattered red sock, and the edges of the wound puckered outward as she shifted her feet.

"You stay here for a moment," Connie said. "I'll be back in a jiffy."

The woman turned and walked away, leaving Erin lying in

the dust. She looked around as best she could. The driveway was flanked on both sides by flat land, although there was a long ditch that ran along one side of the front yard. When she used her feet to rotate the position of her body, she could see the corner of a house and part of the front porch. The place looked similar to the one they had just left. It was larger and less neglected, but for a moment Erin was struck with the disorienting notion that she was still back there, lying in the spot where Connie had choked her into unconsciousness.

She will drag me inside and there will be train tracks circling the couch, the smell of spaghetti and hot dogs coming from the kitchen.

There were no other houses that she could see. Erin opened her mouth and yelled for help. It came out as a whisper, a pathetic sound that fell away to nothing.

She heard the *clump-clump* of feet descending the front porch steps.

"You can scream all you want," Connie said as she returned to the truck. "I'll scream right along with you if you want me to. Not that it'll help. We're miles away from my closest neighbor." She dropped a metal chain in the dirt, then squatted down and used a pair of heavy-duty scissors to cut away the duct tape from around Erin's ankles.

"What do you want from me?"

"Shush-shush," she said, scooping up the chain with a beefy hand and holding it out for Erin to see. "These are ankle shackles. You'll be able to walk with these, but you can't run. If you try, you'll fall flat on your face and I'll be forced to drag you the rest of the way. If it comes to that, I can assure you that the rest of the trip will not be a pleasant one." She grabbed Erin by the chin and turned her face upward. "You think you can handle that, sweetie?"

Erin glanced at the shackles and nodded.

"Good," she said, snapping them around her ankles. "Let's get you up on your feet, shall we?"

She reached out and grabbed Erin by the hair, stabilizing her while Erin got to her knees and then to her feet. Erin's vision blanched as she stood up. She staggered and leaned back against the side of the Cherokee.

"Rest for a bit," Connie told her, letting go of her hair. "Slow and steady wins the race."

Erin stood there for a few seconds while her body adjusted to its new position. She could see more of the house now, a one-story bungalow with a deep front porch and a few low-lying bushes along the perimeter. There was no light coming through the windows, just the house itself, waiting to envelop her.

"That's enough resting," Connie said. She put her hand on Erin's shoulder and turned her in the direction of the porch. "Let's get you into the house where we can spend some time together."

Erin took a few shuffling strides toward the house. The porch steps were difficult to negotiate with the shackles around her ankles. She ascended them slowly, knowing that Connie would let her fall if she started to topple. It was best to avoid that if possible. With her hands bound behind her, she wouldn't be able to use them to lessen the impact. The two-foot drop out of the back of the Cherokee had been bad enough.

There was a screen door that swung outward, and Connie held it open for her as Erin crossed the threshold. They walked down a short hallway and entered the kitchen. It was a small and tidy room with a bump-out window above the sink. There was a table with two chairs, a closed door to the left, and an open entryway to what looked like the family room straight ahead.

"I'd offer you a drink of water, but I'm too excited to show you my collection. It's vain of me, I realize. But what good is having something if you can't share it with others?"

She opened a drawer next to the refrigerator and pulled out a key. "Keep everything valuable locked away, then share it with others when it's time to play." She smiled at Erin. "You are my special friend today. We are going to have *so much fun* together."

She talks like Abel, Erin thought, *or rather, Abel had picked up some of his sayings from his mother.* She watched as Connie walked to the door, placed the key in the lock, and gave it a turn. There was a click as the dead bolt retracted into its housing.

"I can tell you're excited," Connie said, "and you *should* be. Not too many people have seen the things that I'm about to show you."

She placed her hand on the knob, opened the door, and flicked on the light. On the other side were steps leading down to the basement.

"Please," Erin said. "You don't have to do this. You could let me go. I won't tell anyone. I won't even—"

"*Blabbity-blabbity.* You are *such* a talker." Connie scrunched up her nose and gave Erin a half-smile. "You and I have a lot in common. We've both had people taken from us, but we don't just sit around feeling sorry for ourselves. No, ma'am, and thank you, Sam. We know how to *hit back,* and we've got bodies in the basement to prove it." She stood there studying Erin for a moment. "This may sound strange from a woman whose son was found buried on your farm, but I respect you and your father for what you did. It's why I brought you here to show you. I know you'll appreciate it."

Erin looked down at the basement. She could see concrete flooring and a cinder-block wall. A naked light bulb protruded from the ceiling. The damp smell of mildew was mixed with something much older as it wafted up the staircase.

"Whatever happened here happened a long time ago," Erin told her. "I don't need to see it. It should be left in the past where it belongs."

Connie put a hand on her shoulder, and Erin flinched. "Nothing in the past stays there forever. Buried things *want* to be discovered. Even the darkness seeks the light."

She walked to the counter, retrieved a plastic cup from the cupboard, and filled it with water from the faucet. Erin turned around to face her, her back to the stairs.

"You know," Connie said, "*you* have a collection of your own, back there on your father's farm. Or at least you did until the police started digging it up. Maybe you think you're better than me. Maybe you think this one won't be anything special."

"No," she said. "That's not it."

Connie took a sip of water, looked at her, and then polished off the rest of it. Her throat moved up and down as she drank, the band of fat beneath her chin wobbling like a bow tie made of Crisco. "Ahhhh," she said when she was finished, "I was thirstier than I thought." She turned and placed the cup on the counter. "So what do you think? Are you ready?"

Erin shook her head.

Connie sighed. "Well, I don't know why you're being so *difficult*. You wouldn't have broken into Abel's house if you didn't want to see what we'd been up to."

She walked up to Erin and gave her a shove. It was enough to topple her backward, and Erin felt herself falling into open space. She bent at the waist and twisted her body as she tried to get her feet beneath her. Her broken ribs screamed in protest. She fell a quarter of the distance to the basement before she landed on the stairs, her right hip and ankle taking most of the impact. She bounced sideways, hit the rail, and tumbled the rest of the way until she came to a jolting stop at the bottom.

Sound of footsteps on the stairs above her.

She's going to kill me. Going to chop me up into little pieces down here in the dark.

Erin squeezed her eyes shut against the tide of rising panic. Her ankle was broken and her pants were soaked with urine. The acrid stench of it should've filled her nostrils, but it was trapped beneath the other odors, the rancid smells of decay and utter hopelessness that filled the basement.

Her mind flashed to an image of Abel sitting on his couch, his bladder letting go as she leveled the gun at his head and willed herself to pull the trigger. "You understand why I'm killing you?" she'd asked. His head had bobbed up and down like a puppet on a string.

"You will do what I tell you," Connie said as she got to the bottom of the stairs and stepped over her. "I have no tolerance for people who won't listen."

Erin opened her right eye, the one that wasn't already swollen shut. "You made him kidnap those people. You forced him to do it against his will."

"I was *teaching* him," Connie said, and she gave Erin a soft kick in the ribs. "I was trying to make him responsible. Discipline and obedience. Children learn that early or they don't learn it at all. Abel was slow, so in his case it took a little bit longer."

Erin tried to look up at her, but the woman's face was lost in the shadows. "You ruined him," she said. "Everything he did was because of you."

"I *saved* him," Connie replied. "I taught him to take a stand. *Your father* ruined him. He ended my child the way I'm going to end you."

The words hovered above them, like a hawk circling in the sky.

"They killed my father and one of my sons," she continued. "They raped me beneath the bleachers and terrorized my family from one generation to the next. We had a *right* to be here. *Do you understand that?* Sooner or later, there comes a reckoning. 'We have to *carve out* our survival.' That's what I told him. 'We either take our place among the living, or we surrender ourselves to the dead.'"

"You made him take innocent people. My mother. Six-year-old Jimmy Raffey. What did they ever do to you?"

Connie toed her again in the ribs. "Jimmy's older brother Craig was one of the kids who chased Abel into the barn that night. He almost burned alive, my boy, and when Miles came to rescue him, the place collapsed around them. So, innocent? No," she said. "We bear the weight of our families and all of the evil things they do in the darkness. You of all people should understand that."

"My mother. She was kind and good and never had a bad thing to say about anyone."

"Your mother's maiden name was Fisher. Her brother, Jason, was the boy who raped me when I was fourteen years old. He raped me and made a joke of it. I was too young to even know what was happening."

"No," she said. "That's a lie." Erin shook her head, the muscles of her neck tight and aching.

"*It isn't,*" Connie said, and she kicked her hard this time, her foot connecting with Erin's upper thigh. "*Fourteen,*" she repeated. "My mother sent me away to have the babies. I came back, though. I came back because I thought that maybe I could put it behind me. Instead, I lost *both* of my children. So you tell me about innocence. You stand aside while your father murders my boy and buries his body, and then you *lecture me* about this thing we call vengeance."

Connie turned and looked at the basement. "This room," she said, "I built it for Abel. I wanted him to have something to remember me by, a testament to the things we accomplished together."

Erin looked up. The place was heavy with dust. There was a water spigot with an attached hose, and a drain in the center of the concrete floor. An assortment of tools were hanging from nails on the far side of the wall. She could see a handsaw, a sledgehammer, and a flathead axe. She turned to look at the rest of it. Skeletal remains were propped against the wall. They were clothed in the way that Abel had found them, and each of them had a necklace with a name tag resting against their chest.

Erin searched the room with her one good eye until she found her, a child's skeleton with a name tag that read *Angela Finley*. Her stomach clenched as she choked on the taste of it, the memory of all the things she had tried so hard to forget.

"What have you done?" she whispered, but it was suddenly her mother standing over her, her arms folded across her chest.

"Angela was your friend," Helen told her. "You could've helped her shovel the driveway. You could've gone to the hill together."

"I'm sorry," Erin said, but she was back at the candlelight vigil and she could see faces in the darkness, shifting features that moved in and out of focus. They stared blankly back at her, mothers and sons, husbands and daughters . . .

"Angela Finley," a voice said, and Erin trained her gaze on the skeletal remains of the body in front of her.

"Rose Perry," she whispered, and she shifted her gaze to the left.

". . . Curt Hastings . . . Marian Montgomery . . ."

She focused on each of them in turn, just as they must have focused on the remains of the bodies before them. *Except Angela,* she thought, *the first one. How long did she survive down here on her own?*

She closed her eye until the images faded, until she could no longer hear the names of the people who had been taken from this town all those years ago. "You don't even *know* them," she told Connie.

"I know them better than you do, my dear. You'll get to know them, too, before we're finished."

"But you mixed up the clothes," she said. "Or maybe Abel did it by accident when he was helping you with the bodies."

"The clothes are correct," she said. "I washed their bodies and dressed them myself. These are my friends now. It wasn't like that when they first arrived. But people grow on you. They've kept me company over the years and remind me of Abel."

Erin rolled onto her side so she could see them better. "It's not correct, though. I saw Angela Finley on the day she went missing. That's not what she was wearing."

"It is," Connie told her. "You were too young to remember."

"She was wearing a red scarf, the one you have on the body over there. I remember because I talked to her on the bus on the way home from school. It was the last time I ever saw her."

Connie walked over to the body and looked down at the scarf.

"Abel must've switched it," Erin said, "because he thought it looked better. Or maybe he was playing a joke on you. Maybe he thought it was funny."

"He wouldn't switch things. He knew better than that."

Erin curled her body as she rolled onto her knees. The railing was attached to a wooden post at the bottom of the stairs, and she leaned against it as she got to her feet. It was difficult with her wrists bound behind her back. Her right ankle was swollen and throbbing, but she found that she could put some weight on it. She limped across the room and bent down over the remains of Marian Montgomery. "You see?" she said. "This shirt belongs to Rose Perry. It's got the name of the diner where she worked."

Connie stormed across the room to look at the body. "I'm afraid you're mistaken," she said. "Abel wouldn't do that. He knew how particular I was with the—"

Erin straightened herself quickly, throwing her head back as hard as she could. It connected with Connie's face. There was a loud crunch and the big woman stumbled backward and fell to the floor.

Erin took two lurching strides toward the stairs before the chain connecting her ankle shackles pulled tight.

"Where do you think *you're* going?" Connie asked as Erin fell forward onto her knees and then toppled the rest of the way to the floor. She looked down to see Connie's hand clutching the chain. The bridge of her nose was shifted to the left, and there was a gash in the center of her upper lip. Her eyes hadn't changed, though. They were still wild and devoid of reason.

Erin kicked out at her with her left leg. She caught Connie in the face with the heel of her boot. The woman grunted but kept coming, digging her hands into Erin's urine-soaked jeans as she clawed her way up her legs.

Erin cocked her leg back and kicked again, but Connie tucked her chin and ducked. The boot struck a glancing blow to the back of her head.

Erin scissored her legs and kept kicking until the chain went taut. It had gotten snagged on something. The more she pulled, the tighter it got.

Connie lifted her head. Her face was dark red. The chain was wrapped around her neck, the metal links burying themselves in the ample flesh beneath her chin.

"*Gaaaaggght. Thaaaaaaat.*" Connie's mouth opened and closed. A string of saliva hung from her lower lip and dangled above the concrete floor.

Erin slid her legs apart, tightening the chain. Connie's face was dusky now, the way the sky had looked on the day she'd caught them sneaking back into the theater, the same day that Erin's mother had gone missing.

Connie's thick fingers dug at the chain. In another minute, she would be unconscious. *I can get to a phone and call the police,* Erin thought. She would use the axe to cut through the duct tape. If she could find the key, she would hop in the Cherokee and drive as far away from here as possible.

She felt a wrenching pain in her right ankle. Erin screamed and looked down to see Connie's hands wrapped around her right foot, twisting it hard to the right. Something in her lower leg snapped, and the chain loosened. Erin pulled hard with her left leg, but it wasn't enough. Connie had gone back to working on the chain. She got her chin under it and pulled the links over her head.

The woman let out a shrieking noise as she began to breathe again. She dropped the chain and lay with the side of her face against the concrete.

Go, Erin told herself. *Go now or she'll kill you as soon as she recovers.*

(*Your ankle. You won't be able to walk on it.*)

Watch me, Erin thought, and she forced herself to her feet.

"Dirty girl," Connie whispered, but she was still facedown, still breathing with a loud whoop that sounded like a scream in reverse.

Erin's right foot was turned outward at a grotesque angle. She took a step forward and felt the grind of bone ends as her weight settled upon it. The pain was unbearable. It rippled up her leg and then down again. *No, I can't,* she told herself, but she did it anyway, taking first one step and then another.

She got to the bottom of the stairs and vomited without slowing. It was a thin yellow liquid that burned her throat and splashed down the front of her. Her mouth was filled with the metallic taste of fear and adrenaline. There was a slight tingle to it, like meat that had already begun to turn.

She moved up the steps as quickly as she could. The ankle had gone numb, which was good for the pain but bad for her footing. It was like trying to walk on a wooden stump, and twice she came close to falling.

(*Not so fast. Your feet will get tangled up in the chain.*)

Screw that, she thought, but something else was vying for her attention. The sound of Connie's shrieking breaths had subsided. Instead, she heard footsteps across the concrete floor, the creak of wood below her as Connie reached the bottom of the stairwell.

(*Don't look back. Get to the door and get it closed.*)

She reached the top of the stairs, entered the kitchen, and turned to close the door.

Connie was on the stairs, halfway up, only five or six steps from the kitchen.

(*Close the door. There's a key in the lock. You can use it on the dead bolt.*)

Erin swung the door shut with her foot and pressed her

shoulder against it. The key was in the lock, just as she remembered. She turned sideways and reached for it with hands that were still taped together behind her back.

Connie hit the door from the other side, forcing it open. It swung outward less than a foot before Erin threw her weight against it, forcing it closed again.

(*Wedge your foot against the bottom. Do it now and work the lock.*)

She turned to face the hinges, jammed her left boot against the bottom of the door, and tried to turn the key. It made a quarter turn and then got stuck, the dead bolt jamming against the metal strike plate.

Connie hit the door again, pressing against it with the force of her body. She was heavier than Erin, but the wedge technique was working. The door moved an inch or two at the top, but held tight at the bottom.

Erin waited for her to ease up and for the door to return to its fully closed position. As soon as it did, she turned the key, and this time there was a *thunk* as the dead bolt slid into the strike plate.

She stepped away, just as Connie hit it again from the other side. The wood crackled beneath the force of the impact.

(*It'll hold for now, but it won't hold forever. If she hits it enough times, she'll eventually get it open.*)

Erin looked around for a phone, but she didn't see one in the kitchen. There were keys hanging from a hook on the wall, though. If the keys to the truck weren't still in the ignition, chances were pretty good that one of these would get it started.

(*Get your hands free. You can't drive the truck with your hands bound behind your back.*)

Erin moved her wrists back and forth as she tried to work them free from the duct tape. Connie had wrapped it tight, but it had been only a temporary measure, enough to get her into the house.

WHAM! The door shuddered in its frame.

Erin moved around the kitchen, opening drawers until she found the utensils. She pulled out a steak knife with a serrated blade. She could use the sharp point to punch through the duct tape. The trick was not to slice open her wrists in the process.

She pulled out a chair with her foot, sat down sideways in the seat, and placed the handle of the knife under her right buttock with the blade sticking out. Erin brought her hands around to her right hip, spread her wrists as much as possible, and pressed the tape against the point of the knife. It sliced through the center. She slid her wrists back and forth as she sawed through the rest of it.

WHAAM! The blade of an axe smashed through the door to the basement.

Oh no. Oh my God.

Erin got to her feet and staggered across the kitchen as Connie yanked the axe back through the gaping hole it had left in the door.

The knife clattered to the floor. She'd forgotten about the shackles and the chain pulled tight as she attempted to run. She fell to the floor, getting her arms out in front of her this time to break the fall.

Erin looked back over her shoulder. The basement door exploded again as the axe crashed through it. Erin screamed. There wasn't much left of the door now. Connie would be through it in another couple of seconds.

She stood up and grabbed a handful of keys off the hook on the wall. There were too many of them, and no time to figure out which one would work on the Jeep.

Erin hit the screen door and stumbled out onto the porch. She descended the steps, but on the second step her right ankle cracked again. She couldn't feel it, but she could hear the sound of it, like a burning log snapping in the fire.

She missed the next two steps and pitched forward into the yard.

Inside, she could hear the wooden chair topple to the floor as Connie burst through the door and made it into the kitchen.

"*No!*" Erin screamed. There was something coming for her. It meant to chop her up right here in the dirt.

She dragged herself to the truck, got her left leg under her, reached through the open window, and pulled herself to a standing position.

The keys! Where are the goddamn keys?!

She looked back and saw them lying in the grass.

I'm dead. I'm dead if she didn't leave them in the ignition.

She yanked open the door and pulled herself inside. Erin reached down with her right hand and felt for the ignition.

Nothing. No key. Just empty space at the lock cylinder.

"*Shit!*" she screamed. She reached up and flipped down the sun visor. Nothing. She was going to die, either out here in the yard or back in the house, it didn't really matter.

The screen door smacked open and struck the siding as Connie erupted from the house. She had the axe in her hands, and her lips and chin were caked with blood. Gray strands of hair hung in listless clumps along the sides of her face. Her eyes were wide and full of murder.

Connie looked across the yard and saw Erin sitting in the truck. She shrieked with rage.

This is it. These are the final seconds of my life.

The open window was powered by an electric switch. There was no way to put it up, not that it mattered with the axe in

Connie's hands. Erin leaned away from it and placed her hand in the passenger seat to lift herself over the center console.

Connie was still shrieking as she ran down the porch steps. She was in the yard now, forty feet from the truck.

Something metal pressed against the flesh of Erin's palm. She lifted her hand and looked down at the seat.

(*It's a key. The key to the ignition is sitting on the seat next to you.*)

Too late, she thought. *I'll never get it started in time.*

She snatched up the key and jammed it into the ignition anyway. It turned when she twisted it, and the engine sprang to life.

The blade of the axe swung through the open window. Erin jerked away from it. The wooden handle struck the A-post with a loud *SMACK* and the axe ricocheted backward.

It almost got me. It almost embedded itself in the side of my head.

Erin grabbed the shifter and dropped the truck into Reverse. Her right foot and ankle were useless. She got them out of the way and stomped on the accelerator with her left foot. The truck lurched backward, away from the house.

The engine raced as Erin pushed the pedal to the floor. There was a limit to how fast the Cherokee would go in Reverse. Connie sprinted alongside of the vehicle. She brought the axe back again and swung it. The blade hit the metal A-post with a bang.

(*Run her over. Run her over before she kills you.*)

Erin jerked the steering wheel to the right. The front end of the Cherokee swerved to the left, striking Connie in the hip. She stumbled sideways and fell to the ground.

"*Take that! Take that, you bitch!*"

The tires bounced across the open yard, and Erin lost sight of her in the dust.

(*Doesn't matter. Put this thing in Drive and get the hell out of here.*)

She turned the wheel to the left and swung the front end of the truck around so it was pointing toward the driveway.

Erin let up on the accelerator. Her left foot was stuck between the two pedals and the Cherokee continued to drift backward. The front end of the vehicle tilted upward and there was a loud *thunk* as the truck came to an abrupt stop.

"*What the hell?*" She dropped the shifter into Drive and pressed down on the accelerator. She could hear the engine racing and the tires spinning on their axles. The truck nudged forward a few inches, slid sideways, and then settled back again.

No. Not now. Not when I was so close to getting out of here.

She hit the accelerator again and felt the same brief movement of the Cherokee before it returned to its resting position.

Erin put her head through the open window and looked down. She had backed herself into a ditch, a dried-out riverbed about six feet across. The rear end of the SUV was braced against the far side of it, and the wheels were only in partial contact with the ground. As for the front end, it was pointed skyward, the wheels touching nothing but air.

I'm stuck. I'll never get it out in time.

(*Then run. Climb out of the truck and run from here.*)

No. She couldn't run. She couldn't even walk.

(*Crawl, then. Crawl away and hide in the bushes.*)

Erin looked around her. A cloud of dust still hung in the yard. There were no bushes, just a smattering of weeds along the bottom of the ditch.

(*She's coming for you. She'll be here any second!*)

"I know," Erin whispered. She opened the driver's door. The vehicle was tilted backward, and the door swung shut again on its hinges.

(*Find something in the truck, a weapon you can use against her.*

Your mother kept a gun in the glove compartment. Maybe Connie does, too.)

Erin reached over and opened the glove compartment. There was a map of Northeast Montana, a tire pressure gauge roughly the size of a pen, and the vehicle registration.

The left rear passenger door opened and Connie climbed inside. Her face was a mess of blood and dust—*just like Abel's,* Erin remembered, *on the day that we killed him.* There was a deep purple bruise around the flesh of her neck where the chain from the shackles had dug into her skin. The mixed odor of mildew and human decay still clung to her clothing.

She grabbed Erin by the hair and shook her back and forth. "You wasted your chance, missy. You had a chance to escape and you ended up in a ditch, didn't you?"

Connie reached forward and released the lever to recline the seat back. She pulled Erin over the seat and out through the rear passenger door by the hair. When they were on the ground Connie latched her hand around Erin's left wrist. She dragged her through the weeds of the riverbed.

"You're a fighter, I'll give you that," she said as she stopped to catch her breath. "How many body parts do you think you can lose before you bleed to death, I wonder. I've got a belt. We can use that as a tourniquet."

Connie dragged her up and onto the bank of the riverbed. She let go of Erin's wrist and stood there with the dust settling around her. The Cherokee's engine idled in the background.

"There you are, my sweet," Connie said. She bent over and picked up the axe from where it lay in the yard. "It's not subtle, but it does the job. We all have parts that we can live without. That's the first lesson, my darling. You'll learn that right here in the yard."

She raised the instrument high over her head and brought

it down as hard as she could. Erin jerked her leg away from it. The blade struck the earth where her left ankle had been a moment before.

"*Don't do this!*" Erin screamed as she rolled away from her.

Connie took a step forward, raised the axe, and swung again.

Erin rolled to the right. The blade bit into the soil an inch from her left shoulder. She felt the *whump* of it, the impact of the axe head through the ground.

She heard an engine racing, and under that the rapid thudding of her own heart. It wanted to save itself. It wanted to go right on beating for as long as it could.

I can't get away from it. She'll keep swinging until I'm dead.

The sound of the engine in her ears. The open sky above her. And somewhere between this place and heaven was more pain than she could possibly imagine.

Erin pulled herself into a ball and got her left foot under her. She caught a glimpse of the axe rising again, a hint of smoldering sunlight reflecting off the grim metal surface.

Erin pushed off with her left leg and propelled herself upward into a standing position. The tire pressure gauge was in her right hand, its base nestled against her palm with the thin cylinder protruding between her fingers. She slammed it into the front of Connie's neck just to the right of midline.

The big woman staggered backward. Half of the thin metal rod was buried in her neck.

"*Gaaaaack,*" she said. "*Daaazzn't maikk uhh differanss.*" She laughed, but there was an odd sound to it, like the hiss of air leaking from a tire.

(*Run! For God's sake, run!*)

Connie took a step forward. A flow of dark red blood was spilling from her neck where the tire gauge was lodged. A few bubbles seeped out from under the skin.

The axe was still high above her head, poised for the next swing. She screamed, a sound that started low and then built to a crescendo. The sound of the engine screamed along with her. Erin looked to the right just as a massive shadow appeared in a haze of swirling dust from the driveway. It was something new coming fast in their direction. Not the Cherokee, but—

Erin threw herself backward and rolled down the embankment. She left Connie standing there with the axe held high. The woman turned in the direction of the vehicle, her mouth open and the scream still rising from her throat. The Wrangler struck her in mid-scream, launching her body backward.

Erin looked up as the woman and vehicle sailed across the open stretch of the embankment and struck the far wall of the riverbed, the weight of the Wrangler crushing Connie's body against the earth.

Everything settled. The axe was lying a short distance from Erin's feet. She left it there and dragged herself through the weeds until she could see the woman lying beneath the front end of the vehicle. Connie's face was turned sideways, her eyes wide and staring. She opened her mouth as if she intended to speak. "Gaaaaaaaaaaa," she said, and the tire gauge bobbed up and down in her neck.

She died right there in the riverbed, the awareness leaving her face like a mask she had decided to remove for the evening. Erin called to her, spoke her name, but the woman was gone, just another ruined soul checking out of Wolf Point.

Erin went to the Wrangler and opened the door. Robbie's head was tilted forward, but his body was still held in place by the seat belt. She reached in and touched the side of his face. "Are you hurt?" she asked. "Is anything broken?"

He opened his eyes. "I'm okay," he said. He started to move, then winced with the effort. "Should've gotten here sooner. I got your message, but . . . I wasn't sure. I didn't know if I could go back there again."

"It's okay," she said. "You got here in time." She turned her head and looked at the axe. It lay silent and motionless in the ditch, like a snake in the weeds. "How did you know where to find me?"

"Your truck was parked in the street, so I went inside," he said. "There were signs of a struggle. I figured if you ran into anyone in that house, it was probably her. It made sense, didn't it? It made sense for me to come here?"

He winced again and held his left hand against the lower part of his rib cage.

"Yes," she said. "I would be dead if you hadn't."

"Good," he said. "I wasn't sure. Part of me was worried that you might be . . . you know . . . back there in the marsh."

"Looking for something?"

"No," he said, "not looking." He swallowed and tried to move but winced again. His skin was pale and slick with sweat. Whatever saliva he'd been able to muster seemed to catch in his throat.

He stared at the instruments on the dashboard, then turned his gaze in Erin's direction. "I thought that maybe . . . you'd already be buried back there in the marsh . . . in the same spot where we found your mother."

"I'm not," she said. "I'm right here. You tracked me down and saved me . . . just like before."

He took a shallow breath. He was looking away from her again, his eyes focused on something only he could see. "I'm not a killer," he said. "I didn't want to have to hit him with the shovel."

Erin put a hand on the back of his neck and leaned into him, their foreheads touching. "They're gone," she said, "Abel and his mother. They can't hurt us any longer."

"Okay," he said. "It's just that . . . Erin . . . it still feels like they're with me."

"I know," she said. "It feels that way for me, too. But it's over. We can let them go if we want to."

He closed his eyes, a child succumbing to sleep at the end of the day.

"You're hurt," she said. "I should call an ambulance. Do you want me to unfasten your seat belt?"

"Yeah. Okay, Erin. Maybe you could do that."

She reached across him and released the clasp. He slid forward in his seat but she caught him, cradled him in her arms.

"Take it easy," she said. "Can you climb down? You can hang on to me if you need to."

"What's wrong with your foot?"

"Broken. I can't walk on it."

She leaned on him, and he leaned back. Together they made their way up the embankment.

"I didn't have any booze before coming here," he told her. "I wanted to, but I didn't. I told myself, 'You need to be sober for this. If you're not, and something happens to her because of it . . .'"

"Thank you."

They made it to the yard and dropped down onto the grass for a second to rest.

"How does it feel?" she asked. "Being sober, I mean."

"It feels like shit," he said. "I threw up on the way over here."

"Me too," she said. "I threw up in the basement."

He turned to look at the house.

"What happened in there?"

Erin opened her mouth to tell him, but then closed it again

without saying a word. It could wait, she decided. Robbie's head was filled with enough horrors already.

He reached into his front pants pocket and pulled out a cell phone. His hand was trembling, much worse than before.

He's going to be in trouble, she thought. *He's already in withdrawal.*

"Can I help you?"

He nodded and handed her the phone. "You could dial this for me. I don't think I can do it."

She took the phone. "Only one bar," she said. "I hope this'll make it out."

"We'll make it," he said, and he rested his head on the grass.

Erin dialed 911, gave them the information, and clicked off the phone.

"Don't let them run over me when they get here," he said. "One person is enough."

"Okay."

She scooted over and lay next to him in the yard. He was shaking, his hands clasped tightly over his abdomen. Erin turned on her side and placed an arm around him. "We're gonna make it," she told him. "We just have to hold on a little bit longer."

"Yeah," he said, and neither one of them said anything else until the sirens grew loud in the distance.

42

TIME PASSED, BUT SELDOM IN HER HEAD. IN THE MONTHS THAT FOL-
lowed, it was hard for Erin to shake the feeling that she was still
back there, lying on the concrete floor of the basement or rum-
maging through the room where she'd discovered the plastic
sled. She was laughing with Robbie on the hillside behind Jacob's Field or biking next to the BNSF Railway as the massive
steel cars trundled past her. Erin visited the places she remembered while she was awake and then again when she closed
her eyes to sleep. In her dreams, things sometimes turned out
differently. She dug her mother up from the marsh and found
that she was still breathing. The axe sliced through Erin's ankle
and lifted again to finish off the rest.

They met her at the hospital: her father, Matta, and Lieutenant Stutzman. There were so many questions to answer,
and Erin told them what she could that night and the rest of it
when she was able. There were two operating rooms at Trinity
Hospital but only one surgeon. Robbie's case took priority. His
spleen had been shattered in the crash that put an end to the life
of Connie Griffin, and Erin waited in the emergency department while the team worked to save him.

"We're gonna make it," she'd told him in the yard next to

the dried-out riverbed, but by the time the ambulance arrived, Robbie had closed his eyes and was no longer responding. The medics brought them both to the hospital, Erin riding shotgun in the front seat as the siren wailed and the paramedic worked frantically in the back to keep her friend alive.

"Come on now," he said as he started the IV and connected it to a bag of fluid hanging from a hook in the ceiling. "You stay with me, okay?"

Erin looked back through the open walkway. "What's the matter? What's wrong with him?"

"His abdomen's rock hard and his blood pressure's in the toilet. Step it up," the medic called to his partner. "He's got a heart rate of one-fifty and he's pale as a ghost."

"He crashed his Jeep," Erin told them. "He was wearing a seat belt."

"Any medical problems?"

"He's an alcoholic. He was showing signs of withdrawal before you got there."

"Anything else?"

"I don't know."

"How are you related exactly?"

Erin thought of the many ways she could answer. "We're friends," she said. "We've known each other since we were kids."

Erin looked down at Robbie from her seat in the cab of the ambulance. She could see the top of his head, the dark swath of hair against the stark white sheet pulled tight across the mattress.

The medic leaned across him and fished something out of the cabinet. "I've got two large bores going full tilt," he called out to his partner. "He's clenched down, so I can't intubate. Make sure they know we're coming in hot."

The man in the driver's seat picked up the radio and called it in to dispatch. "Tell them to get the OR ready. He's in class IV hemorrhagic shock. Blood pressure's next to nothing."

"If he needs a transfusion, I can donate," Erin told them. "Please don't let him die. He wouldn't have come if I hadn't called him."

The medic sitting next to her kept his eyes on the road. "Left-hand turn coming up," he called back to his partner, who grabbed a handrail as the rig swung around the corner.

They pulled into the hospital a few minutes later. "Stay here," the driver said. "You're injured as well."

Erin sat in the passenger seat as they pulled the stretcher out of the back and wheeled it through the open doors of the emergency department.

"Please," she whispered, "he's got to make it." She looked through the windshield, but the world beyond was blurred and foggy on the other side of the glass.

"—waking up now," he said, and Erin lifted a hand to her face to find a plastic oxygen tube with a prong inserted into each nostril. "She might be a bit sleepy for a while," a voice said, "but the sedation should wear off over the next thirty to forty minutes. I've straightened the bones in her ankle, although she'll still need to go to the OR to have it fixed. It can wait until morning, though." Dr. Houseman put a hand on her forearm. "We'll want to make sure your friend is stable before tying up the OR on an elective case."

Erin started to close her eyes, and then opened them again. "How is he doing?" she asked. "He scared me, the way he looked in the back of the ambulance."

"Dr. Jamison is a good surgeon," he said. "Robbie is getting the best care possible."

"He's going to make it? You can tell me that, can't you?"

"He's in critical condition. Things are going about as well as can be expected." He turned to Matta. "If I can get some additional information . . ."

"Of course," Matta replied, and the two of them left the room together.

Erin closed her eyes and drifted off. She was back in the basement, standing over the skeletal remains of Angela Finley. "She needed a friend," someone said, and when she turned around, it was Robbie the way she remembered him as a child. He stood at the foot of the stairs and wouldn't look at her. His eyes were on the cement floor as his dark hair hung limply in his face. "I've got to go now," he said, and Erin watched as he ascended the stairs, the sound of his footsteps hollow against the wooden boards.

She awoke with a start, her hands clutching the crumpled sheet beneath her. "Where is he?" she asked. "What's happened to him?"

Her father was sitting in a chair at the bedside. He stood up and hovered over her, taking her hand in his own. "Are you talking about Robbie? He's still in the operating room. There's no word yet from the surgeon."

She looked through the open doorway and saw Jeff Stutzman standing in the hallway, talking on his cell phone. He glanced up at her, hung up the phone, and entered the room. "How are you feeling?" he asked.

"Horrible. How's Robbie?"

"I don't know," he said, and shook his head. "I don't have any more information than you do."

Erin turned to her father. "When will we know? Why can't they tell us anything?"

"Let them work," he said. "Let them focus on Robbie. They'll answer our questions as soon as they're able."

"Okay," she said, and looked back at the lieutenant.

"You've been to Connie's house? You saw what was in the basement?"

"Briefly," he said. "It's a crime scene. I've called in the state forensics lab. They have people heading out there now."

"And the other house, too? There are some things in the closet that belong to the victims."

"Yes," he said. "We're on top of it. Right now you should rest. And I would really appreciate it if you and your father would stay in one place for a while and let us sort this out."

"Okay," she said. "I won't be going back to either of those houses."

"Good," he said, and glanced at her splint. "How's the ankle?"

"Hurts," she said, "but not as bad as before."

"Well, that's progress." He smiled. "Don't take this the wrong way, but . . . I'm kind of glad that you broke it. It limits your mobility. Maybe it'll be enough to keep you out of trouble while it heals."

"I doubt it," she said. "I've still got the other one."

"Right." He sighed. "Guess we'll have to keep an eye on you, then."

She looked at her father, then back at Jeff. "You want to hear about what happened?"

"You already told me," he said, "before the sedation."

"Oh."

"I'll listen again, though. I'll listen as many times as you want to tell it."

"I don't remember what I told you when I first got here."

"All the better," he said. "Of course, if you'd like to have an attorney present . . ."

"No," she said, "I can tell it myself."

David reached out and put a hand on her shoulder. "Erin—"

"It's okay," she said, and locked eyes with her father. "I just want to tell him about today."

Jeff pulled out a pen and a pocket-size notebook. "Go ahead," he said. "Tell me again what happened."

She recounted things as best she could, letting her father's lies about what had happened in the past stand for now. Perhaps later their story would need to be amended. She would talk to Robbie first. The decision belonged to all of them.

"What will happen to the remains of the bodies?" she asked.

Jeff closed his notebook and put it away. "They'll be sent to the state crime lab in Missoula," he said. "After they've finished examining them, I expect they'll be returned to Wolf Point to be cremated or buried . . . in a proper cemetery," he added, glancing at David.

They talked for a while longer, and then it was time for Erin to be moved to the inpatient unit of the hospital. David asked if he could stay with her overnight, and although it was against the rules, the hospital staff decided to allow it. The nurse brought in a reclining chair that she placed beside the bed, and Erin and her father spent the rest of the evening in quiet conversation as they continued the delicate task of repairing the parts that were still broken between them.

Matta came to the room to let them know that Robbie was out of surgery and doing well, although Dr. Houseman was concerned about the severity of his alcohol withdrawal. The news that he had stabilized came as a great relief to Erin, and an hour later she fell asleep. There were no dreams that she could recall the next morning, but only a sense of reassurance that her father was watching over her. If she awoke during the course of the night, reliving the horrors that had happened that day, David never mentioned it. Erin opened her eyes seven hours later as the light of early dawn sifted through the window. Something had changed, she realized, and for a moment she was six again, awakening in the barn after delivering Miss Pepper's calf the night before. Her mother would be fixing breakfast in the kitchen, only, Erin was older now, and Helen wasn't with them. She had been put to rest like all the others, and maybe now the families of Wolf Point could mourn them as a community—united instead of divided—as they surrendered the dead to make way for the living.

Her father was sitting next to her with his face turned toward the window. She reached out and took his hand, and they watched the daybreak together as the first hour of the new morning unfolded before them.

43

THEY SAT ON A GIRDER FACING WEST BENEATH THE LEWIS AND
Clark Bridge. They'd come here to search for her initials. Erin
had worried that maybe the letters would be gone by now,
painted over or faded from existence. She'd been ten years old
when she etched them into the support beam. It was the year
her father had returned from prison, but still three years before
her mother went missing. The letters were here, though, as
if she'd placed them only yesterday, and Robbie took the opportunity to scratch his own initials into the beam with the
same knife he'd used as a kid to etch his name into the base of
the tree behind his house. The blade was dull and rusty, but
he worked with a patient diligence as the low-hanging sun
reflected off the surface of the water and the hawks circled in
the air above them.

"Will you stay in Wolf Point," Robbie asked her, "or do you
need to get back to Colorado?"

"I don't know," she told him. "I've been thinking about sell-
ing my practice in Fort Collins, and maybe starting a new one
here on the outskirts of town."

"You've got the farm," he said. "I could help you with that
if you'd like me to."

She nodded. It was hard to see that far into the future. For now she intended to spend time with her father.

"How do you feel," she asked, "now that you're in recovery?"

"I feel like I have my life back," he told her. "The next step is knowing what to do with it."

"What've you decided?"

Robbie folded the pocketknife and held it in the palm of his hand. "I've decided not to take it for granted. I've decided to spend time with the people who are most important to me."

"Me too," she said, and she leaned over and bumped him with her shoulder.

They were quiet for a while. Erin looked toward the horizon and followed the twisting spine of the river as it coursed through the landscape.

"Your father was kind to me when I first got back," she said. "I was grateful to know that he was looking out for me."

Robbie nodded. "He became a nicer person when he stopped drinking. I guess I did, too."

"You were nice *before* you started drinking. I'm glad to have you back."

"Says the person who skipped town for a decade and a half." He reached out and poked her with his finger. Her ribs were still tender in the area where she'd broken them.

"Right," she said. "Sorry about that. I was trying to get my head together."

He tapped twice on the metal girder with the pocketknife. "*Well, golly gee, ma'am.* You can do that right here in Wolf Point."

"I noticed," she said. "Next time, I'd prefer to do it without being lit on fire and attacked with an axe."

"So you want to do it the *easy* way."

"If I can," she told him, "not that it wasn't fun the other way."

"How do they do it in Colorado?"

"I don't know," she said. "I think people usually go to an office and lie down on a couch or something."

"Hmm," he said. "Our way's better."

She smiled and looked down between her feet at the surface of the water. It was darker than she recalled from the days of her childhood.

"Do you remember what you told me," she asked, "after you saved my life for the second time?"

"That this was getting old and I was going to have to start charging you for it?"

"No," she said. "You said that sometimes it felt like they were still with you, Abel and his mother."

He nodded.

"Does it still feel that way? Do they still haunt you the way they used to?"

He took a moment to think about it. "I can still feel them," he said. "They're just quieter than they used to be."

"I feel them, too," she told him. "It'll get better, I hope. I need to get past them. I want to let them go."

Robbie sighed and put the folded knife back into his pocket. "It takes time, I guess. We're shaped by the past and the places we come from, but it's not everything. We get to decide what happens tomorrow and the day after that." He gave her a nudge, and Erin felt it in her ribs, but only a little. "It's the way we do things here in Wolf Point," he said. "We spend the rest of our lives living somewhere in between."

44

ERIN STOOD BENEATH THE OAK TREE AND RAN HER HAND ALONG the rope. It was frayed and weathered, but it still held the tire she had sat in as a child as her father pushed her from behind. *"Higher, Daddy!"* she had screamed, her body arcing toward the sky. She remembered the feel of it: the press of his hands on her shoulder blades, a little girl's certainty that they would always be together.

"I wouldn't trust it," David called out to her. "It's been a long time since you swung on that thing."

Erin turned and looked back at him. "You startled me. I didn't hear you coming."

"Sorry," he said, and smiled as he approached from the farmhouse. He stopped halfway to the oak tree and placed his hands on his hips, and Diesel—David's constant companion—stopped alongside of him.

"I made us some dinner if you're interested," he said. "You've been standing out here for a while now. It's almost seven."

"Thank you. I was just . . . enjoying the evening."

David nodded. "Late May is my favorite time of the year. All that warm weather is still ahead of us." His face brightened. He was thinner now and had a tendency to become winded when he walked. It had been six months since he'd been diagnosed with lung cancer. Robbie had insisted on telling the truth about what had happened to Abel Griffin. Once it became clear that the district attorney was not going to press charges, Erin had accompanied her father to the oncology center in Billings. He'd been pleasant and even jovial with the doctors as they discussed his options—chemotherapy, radiation, immunotherapy, and a few experimental trials that were under way at the time. David had listened carefully to the things they had to offer, but he had declined all of it.

"I'm sorry," he told Erin on the long drive back to Wolf Point. "You can be angry with me if you want."

"I'm not angry. I just . . . don't understand why you won't at least give it a try."

"Would you?"

"*Yes,*" she said. "I would keep fighting. I wouldn't give up on this."

"I'm not giving up," he said. "I just don't want the treatment. There's a difference, you know. They might be able to extend my life for a couple of months, but . . . we're not talking about a cure here. There are side effects. It's not how I want to spend the time I have left."

Erin wrapped her arm around the tire swing as a breeze kicked up from the east. The leaves rustled above her, and somewhere in the sway of the branches were the years they had shared together, the time never quite as long as she wanted it to be.

They lived on the outskirts of Wolf Point, Montana, a place where people sometimes went missing. A long time ago, they had buried her mother here, beneath this very tree. She was buried in Wolf Point Cemetery now, along with all the others.

A modest headstone bore her name: HELEN REECE. BELOVED WIFE. CHERISHED MOTHER. They went there often, not just to visit her mother but to visit all of them. Angela Finley, Rose Perry, Curt Hastings, Marian Montgomery . . .

At the other end of the cemetery were the headstones for Miles, Abel, and Connie Griffin. There had been a strong debate about whether to allow them to be buried in the same graveyard as the others. In the end, the city had held a vote, and the people of Wolf Point had decided to let them stay. The town had bulldozed the two houses but had paid for the burial of Abel and his mother. Erin visited those sites as well. Many of them did. It was the process of forgetting and remembering— making peace with the past as they looked toward the future.

She walked the short distance from the oak tree to where David stood in the yard. Her right ankle ached a bit. It was stiff in the mornings, and maybe it would be for a long time to come. It was okay, she decided. She was alive and finding her way again. The ankle was one more thing to help her remember.

"Will you stay in Wolf Point," Robbie had asked, "or do you need to get back to Colorado?" It was a question Erin had been contemplating since she'd first returned here.

She had blamed her father for *so much* of what had happened after the disappearance of her mother. Had he really given up on finding her, or had he been dealing with the loss of his wife in the only way he knew how? In the time that followed her disappearance, David had fallen deeper into himself and had pulled away from his daughter in every way that mattered. *You abandoned us,* Erin had thought as a child, and then she'd left him here for *fifteen years* while she struggled with her own loss and fury, telling herself that her hometown had nothing left for her.

Now that she was back, Erin was rediscovering her father and realizing that there were things here worth holding on to. She wanted the time back again, the years that she had squandered, but the best she could do was to take advantage of the days ahead.

Erin wrapped her hand around her father's arm and walked with him to the house. They mounted the front porch steps and turned for a moment to look out across the land and the sweeping expanse of the sky above them.

This is Wolf Point, Montana, she thought, *a place where people sometimes find their way home again.*

"It's beautiful," she said.

David looked at her and nodded. "It's been waiting for you," he told her, and he leaned over and kissed her on the temple. They stood there for a while surveying the landscape, and when he opened the screen door for her, the soft creak of its hinges was a sound from her childhood, exactly as she remembered. "Welcome home," he said, and the years since then and now seemed like nothing at all.

Acknowledgments

THIS IS A STORY ABOUT LOSS AND FORGIVENESS, THE STRENGTH OF family, and the unrelenting pull of home. This is my fourth novel, and I should know the landscape by now, and the cost of engagement. Then again, things are different in the trenches. Each effort requires more than I anticipated, gives back more than I deserve, and lays claim to a part of me I did not want to surrender. In order to move forward, the people of Wolf Point must find a way to heal, but the wounds run deep and must heal from the inside out. In medicine, there's a term for this kind of healing, where the body has no choice but to start at the base of the injury and work its way to the surface. It's called healing by secondary intention, and it's reserved for the big wounds, or the ones we've chosen to ignore.

There are lots of big wounds here. I grew up in Maryland but moved to California in 2007. As was true with Erin, there were people I left behind, the most important of which were my parents. I travel home to see them once or twice a year, but it's not nearly enough.

My sister, Kristin, does better. She moved to Colorado for veterinary school, but made her way back to the East Coast after that. Of the three siblings in our family, she lives the closest to what I still think of as home. She visits my parents often, helps them in ways that I cannot, and gently reminds my brother and me when too much time has passed since we came together as a family. She is a wife and the mother of two young boys. (And although one of them is only seven at the time of this writing, I've given him a cameo in this novel as the Montana State Crime Lab pathologist in chapter 21.) The choices my sister makes are grounded in her commitment to the people she cares about. Last year she made a six-thousand-mile round-trip journey to California just to watch my child perform in a school play. Who does that? Kristin does, without fanfare or hesitation. She understands her priorities and lives her life accordingly. It is with much love and admiration that I dedicate this book to her.

The character of David Reece is loosely based on my father, Dennis. There are differences, of course. Unlike David, my father is vibrant and healthy. He's in his mid-seventies now and can still beat me in a footrace. (Embarrassing, I know, but I want to give you an accurate picture.) He was an electrical engineer, not a dairy farmer, but he shares David's qualities of strength, kindness, and love for his family. My mother has fallen ill over the past decade. It's been a slow and insidious process with a persistent downward trajectory, and my father has cared for her through all of it with a calm inner fortitude. It's the most personal act of love I have ever witnessed, and I dedicate this novel to him as well, the most decent man I have ever known.

There are others to acknowledge. My agent, Paul Lucas, kicked my ass on this one, refusing to send the initial proposal for the story to my editor until we had something with a proper set of teeth. My editor, Jessica Williams, always pushes me to raise the story and its characters to the next level, and she did that here with her typical editorial letter that starts with,

"Once again, you have devised a fantastic framework for a taut and twisty novel," and then continues with, "I think this early draft will need a considerable amount of developmental work to realize its full potential." Thank you, Jessica. As always.

Julia Elliott coedited the novel. Her insights and suggestions were spot-on and raised the level of the story even further. This was my first time working with Julia, and I look forward to collaborating on future projects together.

Thank you to my copyeditor, Nancy Inglis, and production editor, Jeanie Lee, who made sure I had my facts straight and put some expert finishing touches on the manuscript. Thanks also to all the folks at HarperCollins for their continued support. It's so much fun to watch a project go from completed manuscript to completed novel sitting on the shelves of my local bookstore. I realize the tremendous amount of work that goes into that from the perspective of the publishing house, and I appreciate it immensely.

And finally, thanks to my family for continuing to tolerate this strange obsession. I'm coming out of the office now. You do remember me, don't you?

About the Author

JOHN BURLEY is the author of *The Absence of Mercy,* honored with the National Black Ribbon Award; *The Forgetting Place*; and *The Quiet Child.* He attended medical school in Chicago and completed his emergency medicine residency at the University of Maryland Medical Center and the R. Adams Cowley Shock Trauma Center in Baltimore. He continues to serve as an emergency medicine physician in Northern California.

MORE FROM JOHN BURLEY

A gripping and darkly psychological novel about family, suspicion, and the price we are willing to pay to protect those we love the most.

It's the summer of 1954, and the residents of Cottonwood, California, are dying. At the center of it all is six-year-old Danny McCray, a strange and silent child the townspeople regard with fear and superstition, and who appears to bring illness and ruin to those around him. Even his own mother is plagued by a disease that is slowly consuming her.

Sheriff Jim Kent, increasingly aware of the whispers and rumors surrounding the boy, has watched the people of his town suffer—and he worries someone might take drastic action to protect their loved ones. Then stranger arrives, and Danny and his ten-year-old brother, Sean, go missing. In the search that follows, everyone is a suspect, and the consequences of finding the two brothers may be worse than not finding them at all.

A female psychiatrist at a state mental hospital finds herself at the center of a shadowy conspiracy in this dark and twisting tale of psychological suspense.

When Dr. Lise Shields arrived at Menaker State Hospital five years ago, she was warned that many of its patients—committed by Maryland's judicial system for perpetrating heinous crimes—would never leave.

But what happens when a place like Menaker is corrupted, when it becomes a tool to silence the innocent, conceal an injustice, contain a secret? Why is it that the newest patient does not seem to belong there, that the hospital administrator has fallen silent, and that Lise is being watched y two men with seemingly lethal intent? The answers are closer than she realizes and could cost er everything she holds dear.

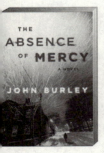

A harrowing tale of suspense involving a brutal murder and dark secrets that lie beneath the surface of a placid, tight-knit Midwestern town.

When a brutally murdered teenager is discovered in the woods surrounding a small Ohio town, Dr. Ben Stevenson—the town's medical examiner—must decide if he's willing to put his family's life in danger to uncover the truth. Finding himself pulled deeper into an investigation with devastating consequences, he discovers shocking information that will shatter his quiet community, and force him to confront a haunting truth.